PRAISE FOR *ONE SMALL SACRIFICE*

"Davidson's latest novel is her best work yet. *One Small Sacrifice* is a fast-paced winner. Highly recommended."
—Harlan Coben, #1 *New York Times* bestselling author of *Run Away*

"Davidson has crafted a tightly woven mystery. Each thread of the intricate plot draws you toward one surprising revelation after another."
—Sandra Brown, #1 *New York Times* bestselling author of *Tailspin*

"Hilary Davidson's *One Small Sacrifice* is both a heart-pounding procedural and a rich, mesmerizing tale of the weight of trauma and the elusive nature of memory. Twisty, absorbing, and deeply humane, it's a thriller you won't want to miss."
—Megan Abbott, *New York Times* bestselling author of *Give Me Your Hand*

"Packed with secrets, lies and surprises, *One Small Sacrifice* kept me guessing to the very end. A gritty kaleidoscope of a thriller."
—Riley Sager, *New York Times* bestselling author of *Final Girls*

"A taut, compelling narrative with a nerve-tingling climax. Davidson turns clichés of the contemporary novel on their heads to create a wholly believable cast of characters. I hope we'll see more of Detective Sheryn Sterling."
—Sara Paretsky, *New York Times* bestselling author of *Shell Game*

"*One Small Sacrifice* is a terrific thriller with a big heart. A smart, compelling examination of guilt, blame, and responsibility that will keep you turning the pages. Hilary Davidson is a rising star of suspense."
—Jeff Abbott, *New York Times* bestselling author of *The Three Beths*

"Hilary Davidson is one of the best crime writers on the planet. This novel is a dazzling work by a master operating at the height of her abilities. Dark, twisty, and psychologically complex, *One Small Sacrifice* kept me guessing and gasping until the final page. I couldn't put it down, even though I didn't want it to end."

—Chris Holm, Anthony Award–winning author of *The Killing Kind*

"*One Small Sacrifice* hooked me hard. Hilary Davidson has written a riveting and beautifully layered thriller that satisfies on every level. The characters surprise, the plot twists, and the pages turn themselves."

—Lou Berney, Edgar Award–winning author of *November Road*

"I tore through this book! Hilary Davidson is at the top of her game with this masterful and twisty new novel that's jam-packed with suspense. Filled with wonderfully diverse characters, breakneck pacing, and surprises at every turn, this modern mystery will thrill even the most old-school crime fiction lovers. This book satisfied me on so many levels."

—Jennifer Hillier, author of *Jar of Hearts*

PREVIOUS PRAISE FOR HILARY DAVIDSON

"Hilary Davidson is the master of plot twists!"

—Tess Gerritsen, *New York Times* bestselling author, on *Blood Always Tells*

"Hilary Davidson delivers the goods—an exotic, atmospheric setting, a rocket-paced plot, and . . . a top-notch mystery—exciting, harrowing, and smart."

—Lisa Unger, *New York Times* bestselling author, on *Evil in All Its Disguises*

"An atmospheric mystery with an ending that packs a punch. Lily Moore is a passionate and tenacious heroine."

—Meg Gardiner, *New York Times* bestselling author, on
The Next One to Fall

"The story is deliciously twisty, the characters engaging. I know I can't be the only reader looking forward to more Moore."

—Laura Lippman, *New York Times* bestselling author, on
The Next One to Fall

"With *The Next One to Fall*, Hilary Davidson knocks it out of the park . . . If this book doesn't get your motor running, have someone check you for a pulse."

—Reed Farrel Coleman, Shamus Award–winning author

"Sinking us into the noir New York of Sara Gran and Charlie Huston, Hilary Davidson's lush novel *The Damage Done* delivers on all counts, offering both slow-burn suspense and creeping pathos . . . A rich, haunting debut."

—Megan Abbott, *New York Times* bestselling author

ONE

SMALL

SACRIFICE

OTHER TITLES BY HILARY DAVIDSON

The Damage Done

The Next One to Fall

Evil in All Its Disguises

Blood Always Tells

Short Stories

The Black Widow Club:
Nine Tales of Obsession & Murder

ONE SMALL SACRIFICE

HILARY DAVIDSON

THOMAS & MERCER

Text copyright © 2019 by Hilary Davidson

Published by Thomas & Mercer, Seattle
www.apub.com

Amazon, the Amazon logo, and Thomas & Mercer are trademarks of Amazon.com, Inc., or its affiliates.

ISBN-13: 9781542042116 (hardcover)
ISBN-10: 1542042119 (hardcover)

ISBN-13: 9781542040266 (paperback)
ISBN-10: 1542040264 (paperback)

Cover design by Christopher Lin

Printed in the United States of America

First edition

For my beloved husband, Daniel
This time, you get to say I told you so.

SUNDAY

Too long a sacrifice can make a stone of the heart.

—William Butler Yeats

CHAPTER 1

ALEX

When he heard the gunshot, Alex Traynor threw himself face-first onto the pavement. He lay as flat as he could, his right leg throbbing from an old bullet wound. *Play dead*, he warned himself, even as his leg twisted from side to side, never quite obeying. Blood pounded in his ears. He couldn't get enough air into his lungs. While he struggled for breath, he strained to hear any noise around him: footsteps, voices, another shot. There was a black car parked by the curb next to him; it shielded his body, but it also made it impossible to see what the hell was going on.

Sixteen years of photographing war zones had left him with a fear of snipers. He'd witnessed a twelve-year-old boy murdered not twenty feet in front of him, the top of his head flying into the air from the force of the blast. That wasn't even the worst he'd seen; at least the boy had died instantly. There were others who'd screamed in agony as they bled out in the street; Alex had heard them as he crouched in the shadows, under an awning or inside a doorway, waiting out the shooter. He remembered every single one of the dead because he'd memorialized them in photographs. That work had brought him, several times, inches from his own death. *Not your turn today*, his best friend, Maclean, used to tell him. Not your turn today, until one day it was.

There was another shot. Then a third. Alex's arm felt like it was on fire. He lifted it slightly and saw blood. His first thought was that a bullet must've grazed him, and he turned his head to look for the shooter. He stared at the buildings on either side of the street, confused for a brief moment about why none of them had broken windows.

You're not in Aleppo anymore, he remembered. The realization should have been a relief to him, but instead it was a torment. He'd been betrayed by his own brain. Again.

He swallowed hard as shame coursed through him. He was home. New York. Eleventh Avenue. He could hear the traffic on the West Side Highway. He forced himself to sit up. There was dark-green glass sticking out of his arm. He'd hit the sidewalk where someone had broken a beer bottle. Some drunk's way of celebrating a warm October weekend in the city.

There was another shot. Alex flinched, but he turned around to look. That was when he saw them, the only other people on the block. Two middle-aged women and a boy who might've been ten. The kid tossed a little white sphere on the sidewalk, and there was the sound of a shot. It made Alex's stomach clench. He wasn't afraid anymore, just angry.

"You can't do that here," Alex called out. His voice was hoarse, as if it hadn't been used in days.

Three pairs of eyes zeroed in on him. "It's just a snap 'n pop," the boy answered coolly.

One woman put her hand on the boy's shoulder. "Don't talk to the homeless man, Mason. Those people are crazy."

Homeless man? Alex thought as they walked past him, the adults averting their eyes. The boy stared, fascinated by him. When they were ten feet down the block, the boy threw another little white sphere. He laughed when Alex flinched.

"Just a snap 'n pop," Alex muttered. That didn't make him feel any better. It had been months since he'd had a full-blown PTSD episode.

Life had been good, and he'd believed his brain had settled down, quieted by steady routine, exercises in mindfulness, and a domestic bliss he'd never expected to find. But the bottom had suddenly dropped out of his world, and he knew he was in free fall. Where he'd land was anyone's guess.

He got to his feet, dusting shards of glass off his jeans. He was almost at Hudson Yards. He'd been bound for the martial arts studio where he trained, but red stripes of blood were running out of three gashes in his left arm. Two still had glass poking out. The smart thing to do, Alex knew, would be to duck into a walk-in clinic for a doctor to clean up the cuts and put in a stitch or two. But when did he ever claim to be smart? It was late afternoon on a Sunday. He could take care of it himself.

On the walk home, he found himself edging along the sides of buildings. It was second nature in a war zone, a strategy for making yourself less of a ready target. Only he wasn't in a war zone anymore. The fact he had to keep reminding himself of that made Alex uneasy. If his brain could so easily slip back into that familiar groove, how else might it betray him?

As he got near his building, his imagination was still in overdrive. He spotted a broad-shouldered man with a tattoo of a spiky black dragon slithering up his left calf, and that brought Maclean to mind again. Alex reached into his pocket for his dead friend's silver lighter before remembering it had gone missing over the weekend. That was yet another way his brain let him down: his memory was flawed, and he had no one to blame for it but himself. *No more booze, no more weed, no more pills*, Alex reminded himself. He'd had a relapse on Friday night, and even though he hadn't dug himself into an opiate-filled hole, the pit he'd found himself in had been bad enough. He'd woken up on the platform of an abandoned subway station in the small hours of Saturday morning, unsure of how he'd gotten there. On his way home, he'd come close to being mugged at Times Square. *How am I going to help Emily if*

I can't keep it together? he thought. The last thing he needed was for the blackouts to start up again. How many hours—how many *days*—had he lost to them when he'd come back from Syria after that last trip?

Thinking about his fiancée made it easier for Alex to focus. As he turned onto his street, he caught sight of a man who reminded him of another friend, Will Sipher. That apparition seemed to be watching Alex's building from across the street, eyes disguised behind a pair of shades and his head tucked into a hoodie. *Get a grip. No one is spying on you.* Alex shook his head, determined to rein in his chaotic thoughts. The man's phone buzzed, and he turned away. Alex crossed the street without another glance at him.

His apartment was a fifth-floor walk-up in Hell's Kitchen, inside a redbrick building that used to be a warehouse. The super was loitering in the lobby, shining up the rusty metal of the mailboxes. Bobby was built like an old-fashioned icebox, low to the ground but bearing serious weight. He had dark curly hair and a sloping brow, which was usually beaded with sweat. His eyes were small in his round ball of a head, like raisins set on a snowman's face. They popped as he took in Alex's disheveled appearance, and he whistled. "You get into a bar fight or something?"

"Too early for that," Alex said.

"You got blood all over you, you know."

"Do I?" Alex didn't have much use for the super, even though he'd known him for the better part of a decade. The man had taken up the habit of hanging around his apartment since Emily had moved in. It took a lot to motivate Bobby to make his way up to the fifth floor, and the panting sounds announcing his arrival could be heard down the hallway.

"Blood's a bitch to clean up, man."

"I'll try not to get any on the floor, Bobby."

"What's Emily gonna say about this?" the super called after him.

Alex hiked up the stairs as fast as he could. As he unlocked the door to his apartment, he started to breathe easier. He dropped his keys into a ceramic bowl on the small wooden table next to the door. The light was fading toward sunset, but it streamed in through the south-facing window overlooking West Forty-Eighth Street. He expected to find his dog lying on the large wooden table in front of the window, lapping up the last of the rays, but Sid wasn't there. He wasn't on the plush red sofa in the center of the room, either, or on any of the chairs. The galley kitchen was to the left of the front door, but it was empty.

It took Alex a moment to realize what was wrong: the bedroom door was open. It was a hot day, and he'd left the air-conditioning on in the living room for Sid. He knew he'd shut the bedroom and bathroom doors to keep the place cool. He set his gym bag on the sofa and stood still, listening. Someone was moving around in the bedroom. He felt a sudden glimmer of hope. Emily had come back.

"I was getting worried," Alex called out. "I thought I had . . ."

There were only the sounds of a drawer slamming shut and then the window screeching in protest against being opened.

Alex rushed to the doorway. There was a woman he'd never seen before in his bedroom. Her platinum-blonde head was already halfway out the window to the fire escape.

CHAPTER 2

SHERYN

The way Sheryn Sterling was feeling, it might not have been the best idea to put a knife in her hand. Her family had a Sunday-dinner tradition of rotating host duties, and it was her turn; that was fine since her husband, Douglass, had a passion for cooking that, in another life, would've made him a Michelin-starred chef. Instead, his family, his friends, and occasionally his students were the main recipients of his gourmet adventures. Sheryn's role was sous chef, slicing and dicing vegetables and prepping a salad while Douglass fussed over the duck cassoulet. He was whispering sweet nothings to it when Sheryn accidentally slammed the knife into the countertop. It clattered to the floor, and she jumped back; the blade stuck a landing with a gymnast's grace an inch from her foot.

"Damn it," she hissed, bending to pick it up.

"You're lucky your mama isn't here yet," Douglass said. "Because you'd be filling the coffers of her swear jar."

"Oh, like that's the biggest problem we've got." Sheryn walked the knife over to the sink and turned on the water to wash it. "Never mind that tonight she'll be sitting across the table from a criminal."

"I had a feeling that was on your mind," he said. "You've been prickly since your sister called this morning."

"Who are *you* calling prickly?"

Douglass moved behind her and wrapped his arms around her waist. He was a lanky man, so fit that he still wore clothes he'd owned in college, when he was on the basketball team. To Sheryn, he looked like Billy Dee Williams in his Lando Calrissian days, minus the moustache. After twenty years together, eighteen of them married, he knew how to calm her down. "It's going to be okay," he said. "You need to stop stressing."

"I'm a cop, and my baby sister is dating a convicted car thief," Sheryn said. "There's no part of this scenario that is okay."

The call that morning was still running through her mind. *I need to tell you something*, Sandrine had said, *before you run Jeremy's name through your databases.* She'd been cagey for months about the man she'd been dating, refusing to give Sheryn his last name. Now Sheryn understood why.

"Convicted when he was eighteen," Douglass said. "He's what, thirtysomething now?"

"Thirty-three, same as Sandrine."

"Okay. Then he's had a lot of time to turn his life around."

Sheryn turned off the water and set the soapy sponge and clean knife down. She turned to face her husband. "You are not turning this into a Lifetime movie of the week. Sandrine's been hiding this from me for a long time, which means there's more to the story and it's all bad."

"Sandrine is scared of you—and rightly so," Douglass said. "She might be a grown-up in other ways, but she's more afraid of you than she is of your mama, and that's really saying something."

"How can you be so calm about all this?" In the background, Sheryn heard a phone ringing.

"Because I've got students who've been convicted of all kinds of shit," Douglass said. "And most of those things are also done by rich white kids who didn't get arrested. I'd like to think every fool thing a teenager does won't haunt him for the rest of his life."

Sheryn rolled her eyes, but at the same time she leaned in and kissed him. Douglass taught literature and history at a school for teenagers, mostly African Americans, who were categorized as "at risk." She knew that the color of their skin—so similar to her own—affected how the justice system treated them. But her compassion for kids from troubled homes didn't translate into sympathy for a man who could be described as a convict, especially one involved with her baby sister.

"Get a room, you two," said a voice from the doorway. Sheryn pulled back and stared at her fourteen-year-old son, Martin, tall and slender as a beanpole. He was holding the house phone in one hand. "It's for you, Mom. Someone from work. He asked for *Detective* Sterling."

"Thanks." She set the knife on the cutting board. "Why don't you make yourself useful?"

"But I'm studying, Mom."

That was his excuse any time there was a job he didn't want to do. "Do I look like I'm kidding?"

Martin slunk over to the counter, muttering. She took the phone from him. "Detective Sterling speaking."

"Sorry to bother you at home on a Sunday, Detective." She recognized the desk sergeant's voice immediately. "But you've got some names flagged in the system, and one of them came up. Note said to call you immediately."

"Which name?" Sheryn's pulse sped up.

"Alex Traynor."

Sheryn took a deep breath. He had her full attention. "What happened?"

"He was roughed up at Times Square station about four fifteen a.m. on Saturday."

She frowned at that. "You're saying *Traynor* was the victim here?"

Douglass froze at the sound of that name and glanced her way. Martin's head swiveled back and forth between them, like they were having a badminton match.

"One of the Elmos tried to roll him," the desk sergeant said. "You know how the Elmos are."

Sheryn sighed. Elmo had been her daughter's favorite *Sesame Street* character; it bothered her that so many of the troublemakers in Times Square chose to wear a costume with his distinctive red fur and innocent face to disguise their identities. "Yeah, we all know how the Elmos are. Is Traynor pressing charges?"

"Nope. Turned out the Elmo had a couple outstanding warrants. He's in jail now."

"So, if this happened early Saturday, how come I'm only hearing about it now?" Sheryn asked.

"Cop who collared the Elmo is with the Transit Police. Doesn't work out of this precinct."

"I appreciate your calling me," Sheryn said. "Can you give me the name of the cop who made the arrest?"

She made a note as the desk sergeant spelled it out. *Spencer Koch.* She thanked him politely and hung up, but she couldn't tamp down her frustration. "Damn it," she muttered.

"I can't wait till Grandma gets here," Martin stage whispered to his father.

Douglass raised an eyebrow at him. "You think your grandma is going to be impressed by your T-shirt? This is Sunday dinner, son. Go put on a collared shirt."

Martin slouched out of the room.

"You heard what that was about?" Sheryn asked.

Douglass nodded. "Crime never sleeps," he deadpanned. "Nor does it make time for Sunday dinner."

"I need to make a call."

"Your whole family is about to converge here, and you want to work?"

"You heard me on the phone, right?" Sheryn asked. "You know this is about Alex Traynor."

Douglass didn't try to argue with that. She took the phone into their bedroom, closing the door and ignoring the chiming of the doorbell.

She sat on the edge of the bed. It could be nothing, but what was Alex Traynor doing out at four in the morning on Saturday? She knew it shouldn't matter. He had every right to be in Times Square. But the Elmos preyed on confused, intoxicated tourists, so if one had tackled Traynor, what did that mean? It wasn't right to hope that the man was using heroin again, but after what he'd done, no one could blame her for taking advantage of any misstep on his part to bring him down.

She dialed Koch's number and got voice mail. She left a short message, emphasizing how urgent it was for him to call her back. Sending a uniform over to check on Traynor was a tantalizing possibility, but on such flimsy reasoning, it smacked of harassment. She had to be careful.

There was a soft knock on the door, and Douglass poked his head in. "Your mama is here, you know."

"I'll be there in a minute," Sheryn said. "I need to talk to this one guy."

"You're relentless," he said. "And that's normally a good thing. But it's Sunday, and you need to turn your cop brain off."

"There's no switch for that," Sheryn answered.

"There should be," Douglass muttered, closing the door.

Sheryn dialed Koch again. She couldn't let up. There was a dead girl she'd never managed to get justice for, and she'd be damned if she ever stopped trying.

CHAPTER 3

ALEX

Alex ran to the open window, grabbing the woman by the shoulders and roughly hauling her back into the room. She shrieked and flailed her arms wildly, accidentally scoring a bull's-eye when a couple of her fingernails raked across his cheekbone. She went for the fire escape again, but she wasn't fast enough. Alex pulled her back, spun her around, and shoved her against the wall. Finally, Sid was standing on the bed, barking his gentle heart out. He'd never been much of a guard dog.

"You're not going anywhere," Alex said. "I'm calling the cops."

The woman's eyes were scrunched tight, but tears rolled down her face. "I'm sorry—I just wanted . . ." The rest of her words were garbled by a sob.

"How did you break into my apartment?"

She shook her head. "I didn't."

"You're not much of a liar," Alex said. "You're going to stand there and pretend you're not a thief looking for drug money?"

She opened her eyes and gulped back a sob. "Emily gave me a key," she whispered.

That made Alex let go of her, as if she'd invoked a safe word. But it didn't make him any less suspicious. This woman could've picked up Emily's name from a piece of mail lying around. "And why would Emily do that?"

"She's trying to help me." The woman was shaking now, and she wrapped her arms around herself. "I'm sorry. I freaked out. I don't know what I was thinking. You're Alex, aren't you?"

"You know who I am?"

"Emily's boyfriend. She talks about you." She wiped her face, clearing away the tear tracks but making her mascara smear so that she looked bruised. She cleared her throat. "That's Sid Vicious on the bed. He likes Ziggy's Disco Fries. I brought him some."

She edged around him, picking up a bag of dog treats and rattling it. Alex glanced at Sid. His dog scared a lot of people when they first saw him. Sid was only twenty pounds, a mongrel mix with short brown, black, and white fur, but his most obvious attributes were his blind left eye, which was a milky white, and his stubby, broken tail. If people looked more closely, they saw that Sid was missing toes from a couple of his paws and that there was a long pink scar on his belly, where fur didn't grow. It took a little longer for some people to appreciate the dog's boundless friendliness. Alex used that as a litmus test for humans: if you didn't like his dog, you definitely wouldn't like him.

But Sid seemed to like the woman. He bounded off the bed, nuzzled against Alex's leg, and tilted his head toward the woman's knee for petting.

Alex took a step back. "If you know who I am, why'd you attack me?"

"I'm sorry." She wiped her eyes again. "I was expecting Emily. But I caught sight of you in that mirror." She pointed to the three-way mirror above Emily's dresser. "I was so scared. I should've remembered you live with Emily, but my mind went blank. I just wanted to run." She shook her head. "I was afraid."

Alex looked her over. The woman stared back with wide, frightened eyes. They were a startling shade of violet that Alex suspected wasn't any more natural than her platinum hair. The woman's features were a blend of Asian and Caucasian, but with her outlandish coloring, she could've been from Mars. She was about five foot six, with a pale, heart-shaped face painted like a fancy porcelain doll's. She wore a black sundress, which seemed appropriate for a hot day, with a lacy cardigan and tall, skinny heels. At the very least, Alex figured, she wasn't dressed for cat burglary.

"Emily said she'd help me when I was ready to leave my boyfriend," she added. "I've been calling her all weekend, but she doesn't answer. Will she be back soon?"

"What's your name?"

She stared at him suspiciously before answering. "Diana." He took it for a fake, but if the gist of her story was true, that wouldn't have mattered. Emily was a bighearted person who took care of strays; Alex could count himself in that category. This wasn't the first time that Emily had told a virtual stranger to come to the apartment either. Those undocumented people with sick kids used fake names too. But the timing of this woman's appearance—she'd materialized two days after Emily left—made Alex uneasy.

"Are you okay?" she asked.

"What?"

She pointed at his arm. "You're covered in blood. Do you need help?"

Alex had forgotten his injury when he'd set foot inside the apartment. As he held up his arm, he saw glass jutting out at odd angles. "Yeah, I should do something about that. Come with me."

He stopped at his desk in the living room, checking again for Maclean's silver lighter. It had vanished about the same time that costumed creep had tackled him in the empty hours of early Saturday at Times Square station, and Alex had the sinking feeling it was lying on a subway track. He didn't smoke anymore, but the lighter was his idea of a utility tool; at that moment, he wanted to cauterize the tweezers he was about to jab into his arm. Failing that, he went into the bathroom and laid out the antibiotic and gauze. The cuts in his arm burned, but that was nothing compared to the eye-watering pain that dug its claws in as he poured rubbing alcohol on them. He pulled the tweezers out of the medicine cabinet, drowned them with alcohol as well, and tackled the glass shards.

"I thought that Emily was the doctor in the family." Diana stood in the doorway, arms crossed, staring at him.

"You learn a lot when the only hospital in a hundred miles has been bombed into the Stone Age," Alex said, washing the wounds in his arm with soap and water. "Why don't you tell me what you're doing here."

"Emily really didn't say anything?"

"About what?"

"Me."

Alex racked his brain but drew a blank. In fairness, he didn't have the sharpest memory. Emily's mind was an information superhighway; his was a dirt road pockmarked with craters. "Not a word."

"Well, she told me about you. You wrote a book about being a war photographer." Diana's oddly light eyes were appraising. "You went to Syria and Iraq and Afghanistan, recording what was going on for the rest of the world to see."

"And you're quite the hustler," Alex said. He'd gotten the glass out, but he probed his skin, hoping to dislodge any splinters before they got infected. Finding none, he dosed his arm with rubbing alcohol for a second time. "Tell me why I shouldn't call the cops on you."

"I'm not trying to play you. Believe me, the last thing I want is any trouble. Please don't call them."

"How long have you known Emily?" He patted his arm dry with a fistful of tissue and applied the antibiotic.

"I met her a few months ago." Diana's voice was nervous, but the words didn't sound like a lie coming out of her mouth.

"Where?"

"Does it really matter where it was?"

"It's a hot day," Alex said. "And you're wearing a sweater that covers your wrists, which are bruised, by the way. That makes me think you're an addict looking for something to steal."

Something in Diana's face shifted, and she stood straighter. "I have *never* stolen anything from anyone," she said. "You're a fine one to be talking about drugs. You almost killed yourself with heroin."

Alex froze for a moment. Okay, maybe this woman really *did* know Emily. Because there were plenty of details about Alex's career you could find in the media or online, and the story of his kidnapping and rescue in Syria had made the evening news. He stared at the bandage he was holding. For a moment, it was like he was overseas again, standing in some makeshift hut while a medic pretended you could put humans back together with gauze and glue. "Emily told you about that?"

"I'm sorry. I shouldn't have said it." She gave her head a gentle shake. "It's just I really do need to talk to Emily. When will she be back?"

"She didn't say."

"If you called her, would she answer?" Diana asked. "Because she hasn't been answering me."

"She's gone away for a few days," Alex said. "I can't tell you anything more than that. By the way, where's the key?"

"What key?"

"The one you used to let yourself into my apartment," Alex said. "Hand it over."

Diana bit her lip, clearly annoyed yet too nervous to argue. Her fingers fished into the pocket of her dress and pulled out a brass key. "Here."

He took it from her and stared at it for a long moment. His front door had two locks, but they used the same key, and this looked like the right one. What if Emily really had told the girl to come by? Was he supposed to do something to help her? Before he could formulate his next question, there was a knock on the door. Alex hesitated at the thought of opening it; Emily wouldn't knock, and he didn't want to talk to anyone else at that moment. But Sid went skittering across the floor to the door, yipping excitedly. "That's my boy!" announced a loud voice in the hallway.

"Do you really need to get that?" Diana whispered as Alex headed to the door.

"She has a key too." Alex sighed. "She'll let herself in since Sid's here."

When he opened the door, his elderly neighbor from across the hall smiled up at him.

"Surprise," Mrs. DiGregorio said. "I'm here on behalf of your fan club."

"I don't have a fan club," Alex said. "Unless you started one."

Mrs. DiGregorio leaned down to scratch Sid behind the ears. "That's my sweetie," she cooed. She glanced up at Alex. "One of the ladies in my book club has a crush on you . . ." Her voice trailed off as her eyes caught movement in the apartment. "Oh, I didn't realize you had company. Who's this?"

Alex half turned and saw that Diana had retreated toward the bedroom but hadn't made it through the door.

"Hi." Diana gave an anxious little wave and a forced smile. "I'm Diana, a friend of Emily's."

"Nice to meet you. Where is Emily? I haven't seen her all weekend."

"She took off for a few days," Alex said.

"Not another marathon, I hope. She's always on the run. She needs some downtime." Mrs. DiGregorio thrust a copy of Alex's own book into his hands. "Lillian—your admirer—wants this signed."

"Sure thing," Alex said, feeling awkward. Of course his neighbor had to stop by while a strange woman was in his apartment. At least Sid would be a distraction, he thought, as he went to the far end of the apartment for a pen, but it didn't work out that way.

"How do you know Emily, dear?" Mrs. DiGregorio asked as she bent down to pet Sid.

"She volunteers at a clinic where I work," Diana answered. "I stopped by because I thought she'd be here, but I guess I should head out."

"Oh, no, don't leave on my account," Mrs. DiGregorio said. "I'm on my way out to supper with the girls. Are you a doctor too?"

"No, just an administrator."

Alex glanced at Diana. She seemed flustered now, ill prepared to deflect the nosiness of an elderly lady. He kept his mouth shut, curious now about what his neighbor would coax out of her.

"Where's this clinic?"

"Oh, you wouldn't know it," Diana said.

"Dear, at *my* age, you become an expert in medical clinics," Mrs. DiGregorio said. "Much more interesting than following celebrities. All the ones I cared about growing up are dead, anyway. Where's this clinic?"

"Out in nowheresville," Diana said.

"What does *that* mean? New Jersey? Connecticut?" Mrs. DiGregorio prompted.

"Um, yes." Diana gulped. "Sorry, I need to use the bathroom. I'll be right back." She dashed in and shut the door behind her. Alex heard the lock turn.

He shrugged. "She was here when I came home," he said. "I don't know where she came from." He handed his neighbor the signed book. "You are the best, by the way. For making people read this."

"I love it." She held it up and gazed at the cover. It was a photograph Alex had taken in Aleppo, the ruins of a series of bombed-out apartment buildings at sunset; if you looked closely, there was a group of very young, malnourished kids playing in the wreckage. "I look at that photo and think of all my cousins who died in the war." Her voice was soft. "I always wanted to think the world learned from that, but we've learned nothing."

"I used to think that if the public saw what was going on, wars would stop," Alex said. "But that's not what happens."

"History repeats itself," Mrs. DiGregorio said.

Alex took a deep breath. The book had been his attempt to communicate what life in a war zone was like. It had garnered a lot of media interest, but not for the reasons he'd hoped. It turned out that the public at large didn't want to know about the omnipresent fear and the stench of rotting things and the bodies you stepped over because you were alive and you had to carry on. It overwhelmed him when he dwelled on it for too long. Emily understood; she was one of the few people he knew who truly did. She'd lived it herself, and that knowledge was in her bones.

"Thanks again for sharing it," he said.

"Of course. Take care of yourself." Her eyes darted toward the bathroom door. "And maybe lock down the silverware." She gave Sid one last pat and headed out.

After the room was quiet for a couple of minutes, Diana opened the door. "Is she gone?"

"For now. So where was this clinic where you met Emily?"

Diana ducked her head. "Sorry, I just made that up. That lady was . . . I don't like being asked a lot of questions like that."

"Here's what we're going to do," Alex said. "I'm going to try calling Emily. I want to hear what she says about you."

"That would be great. Thank you." For the first time, Diana's anxiety appeared to abate. It was as if she wanted him to talk to Emily. While Alex's inclination was to be suspicious of her, it almost made him think that she was telling the truth about being there to see his fiancée.

"Don't thank me yet. If she's not there, I'm calling the cops."

Diana blanched at that. While he dialed, Diana examined the wall of bookcases. Neither Alex nor Emily had ever been interested in collecting possessions, so it hadn't been hard to merge what they owned into Alex's one-bedroom apartment. The one exception had been their books. They both liked to read on paper, and they found it hard to part with books even after they'd read them. One wall of the apartment was a mass of double-packed shelves, a haphazard blend of hardcovers and paperbacks; framed photos perched precariously at the outer edges, taking up every final inch of space. The most prominent shots were of a grade-school-age Alex hugging his mother, and a teenage Emily with her arms around her brother and their parents. But there were plenty of others, including a couple of Emily with her Doctors Without Borders colleagues and Alex's friend Maclean holding up Sid in front of a burned-out wreck of a building in the Syrian city of Homs.

Emily's phone went straight to voice mail, again. He hung up and tried a text instead. Then he opened up his email and wrote a short message. *I'd try carrier pigeon if I could*, Alex thought, feeling his own fear for Emily's safety rising again. *I have to trust her. That's all I can do.* But in that moment, it wasn't a reassuring thought.

Diana suddenly made a strange sound, as if she were choking. She stepped back and tried to cover it up with a cough, but Alex realized she was staring at a particular photo. It was taken the day his friend Cori had dragged him to the Bronx Equestrian Center. In the shot, Alex looked terrified, as if he knew the horse was about to throw him; Cori, who'd been riding since she was six, looked coolly confident.

Alex moved next to her. "You knew her?"

She gave him a furtive look. "Cori Stanton. How did *you* know her?"

"Before I had Sid, I had a dog named Lupo," Alex said. "He was a rescue, too, and he had a lot of health problems. I met Cori at her father's veterinary clinic."

"Cori was pushed off the roof of a building in Hell's Kitchen," Diana said softly. "It was *this* building, wasn't it?"

"She fell," Alex answered brusquely. "No one pushed her."

He waited for Diana's next question, but she didn't speak. She picked up a miniature brass dinosaur but immediately dropped it. He noticed that her hands were shaking when she picked it up again. In that moment, Alex realized Diana had figured out exactly who he was. A hard lump formed in Alex's throat, and he struggled to swallow it down.

Diana dropped the brass figure again. "Sorry," she muttered.

"No worries." Alex crouched to pick it up. The dinosaur was Emily's; she had told him it was from a set she'd had as a child, but only a couple had survived into her adulthood: a stegosaurus and this greenish T-rex. He held it in the palm of his hand for a moment, wondering where Emily was and what she would think if she came back while this odd woman was waiting in her home. He didn't notice that Diana had moved until he heard the front door open. As he turned his head, he caught a glimpse of Diana fleeing his apartment just before the door slammed shut behind her.

MONDAY

CHAPTER 4

SHERYN

Sheryn loved Monday mornings; from her perspective, the earlier they started, the better. At five thirty, she was up and heading into the shower. By six, Douglass had breakfast for four on the kitchen table, and she was dragging the kids out of bed. Come seven o'clock, Sheryn was in her car, driving south from Washington Heights, dropping off eight-year-old Mercy at her before-school program in Harlem and Martin at Hunter College High School on the Upper East Side. By the time she got to the Midtown North Precinct on West Fifty-Fourth Street, it wasn't quite eight yet. It should've felt like a good morning, but it didn't because thoughts of Alex Traynor were dogging her every step. She wasn't satisfied with the answers she'd dug up so far about his weekend misadventure; there had to be something more. It was too odd, too out of character. She couldn't let it slide.

"Morning, Detective," the desk sergeant greeted her as she walked in. "It's going to be one of those days."

"When isn't it?"

"This one's starting early. A woman called about her missing coworker, Emily Teare."

"Dr. Emily Teare?" Sheryn repeated. "As in, Alex Traynor's girlfriend?"

"You're quick." The sergeant handed her a folded note. "I took the call ten minutes ago. Lady who called is named Yasmeen Khan."

His words were like an electric shock jolting Sheryn's spine, snapping her to attention. This was shaping up to be serious, her first real break in almost a year on the Traynor case. Something had gone wrong over the weekend; she was sure of it. It wasn't a coincidence that the man was wandering around Times Square in the middle of the night while his girlfriend was suddenly missing.

"Thanks," she murmured, but she was already off and running. There was a catch in her chest when she got to her desk. It had been eleven months since she'd flagged Alex Traynor in the system, along with every close associate of his she could find. Any police contact those people had, no matter how insignificant—a noise complaint, a parking ticket—was routed to her desk. The call that had come in that morning was no small thing: a doctor named Yasmeen Khan who worked at NewYork-Presbyterian had called at seven forty-eight, asking how to file a missing persons report. She was worried about her friend and coworker Dr. Emily Teare.

Sheryn called her back and got voice mail. Her first instinct was to hustle over to Traynor's apartment, just a few blocks away on West Forty-Eighth Street. But she didn't have to be told that was a bad idea. Her new partner wasn't even at his desk yet, and showing up solo could open her up to a charge of misconduct or even harassment. Alex Traynor had had a smart, tough lawyer in his corner when she'd investigated Cori Stanton's death. There was no reason to think he wouldn't use the slightest miscalculation or misstep on her part to screw her over. She couldn't go after Traynor until she was damn good and ready.

But she was too impatient to sit on her hands while waiting for a return call. Instead, she reclaimed her car and headed for the hospital where Dr. Khan worked. That took her up to East Sixty-Eighth Street, where a massive series of buildings between York Avenue and the East River made up NewYork-Presbyterian's Weill Cornell Medical Center. In all her forty-three years, Sheryn had never set foot in the complex. She knew NewYork-Presbyterian's outpost on West 168th Street all too well, since that was where some of the gunshot victims she interviewed ended up. The complex on the East Side was another world altogether, calm and serene, at least at this early hour. There was noise from the cars on the FDR, but also a view of the East River.

Dr. Khan worked in the Brain and Spine Center. Sheryn found herself striding through a series of labyrinths to get there, which felt like a bad joke. *I'm trapped like a rat in a maze*, she thought. Sheryn had a fine sense of direction, if you left her outside. But malls and casinos and anywhere else devoid of natural light threw her off. The hospital, with its endless corridors lit with overly bright fluorescent light, made her disoriented. It was a relief to finally hit the right clinic.

"I can't believe you're here in person!" Yasmeen Khan said, shaking Sheryn's hand. "I got your message, and I . . . well, I was going to call you back, but I kept hoping Emily would call me first." She was a short, solidly built woman with long black hair woven into an elaborate topknot. Her skin was sepia brown, and her long-lashed eyes were so dark the irises looked black. Sheryn pegged her at close to forty, and in the initial eyeball sweep she'd mastered long ago, she noted that the doctor wore expensive gold earrings and a bangle at one wrist, but no jewelry on her hands.

"I take it that hasn't happened."

"No." The doctor shook her head. "I don't know what's wrong. Emily would never do this. I really think something's off."

"Let's start from the beginning, Dr. Khan."

"Please, call me Yasmeen. I hope I'm not wasting your time. Honestly, I'm worried that I'm overreacting. The main reason I called was because I wanted to find out *how* to file a missing persons report. For some reason, I thought you had to wait seventy-two hours."

"There's no set amount of time in New York," Sheryn said. "Tell me what's going on."

"I saw Emily at work on Friday," Yasmeen said. "We're good friends, but we didn't get to talk much that day. That isn't unusual. We both had busy mornings, and then I was out in the afternoon. But when I was leaving, I said, 'See you tomorrow?' and Emily said, 'Definitely.'"

"You had plans to meet Dr. Teare on the weekend?"

"We have a standing date at nine o'clock Saturday morning. Emily's my running partner. I'm training for my first half marathon." She gave Sheryn a shy look. "You didn't laugh."

"Why would I?"

"When I started running, my husband told me I looked like a dumpling with legs," Yasmeen said. "He's my ex-husband now. But I still expect everyone to laugh at me like he did."

"Sounds like you're well rid of him."

Yasmeen smiled. "Emily loves to run, but she wants to share that love of the sport too. She's been helping me train for months." Yasmeen's face clouded over. "But she didn't show up for our run on Saturday. I texted her but never heard back. I tried calling her a few times on Sunday, but the calls went straight to voice mail. Her phone didn't even ring."

"And this is out of character for Dr. Teare?"

"Definitely. She's the most responsible person I know. If she makes a commitment, she will meet it, come hell or high water." Yasmeen shook her head. "I actually checked to make sure she wasn't in a hospital. I don't know what I thought, maybe that she was hit by a car or something."

"You called really early. She might still come in today."

Yasmeen shook her head. "She should've been in at seven thirty this morning. Something is wrong."

"Has she missed work lately?"

"I've known her for four years. In that time, she missed work once, because of food poisoning. Even then, she called in." Yasmeen paused for a moment, frowning. "Before I called the police this morning, I tried her cell again. I also called her fiancé, but he didn't answer. It made me wonder if something happened to both of them."

"Her fiancé?" Sheryn cleared her throat. "I didn't realize Dr. Teare was engaged."

"Emily and Alex got engaged six weeks ago. She didn't make a fuss about it, but she has a ring."

"How well do you know Alex Traynor?" Sheryn asked.

"We've met several times. I really like him. They're a great couple." Yasmeen's gaze dropped to the floor, which made Sheryn suspicious. There was a *but* in there somewhere, a qualifier that meant she'd seen something off about the relationship.

"When did you first meet Mr. Traynor?"

"In February, just after they moved in together. They threw a house-warming party. It was lovely."

Sheryn filed that bit of intelligence away for future reference. There was something ghoulish about hosting a housewarming party in the very building where Alex Traynor had thrown a woman off the roof. She'd been stunned when Emily moved in with him. It was one thing to alibi him, quite another to put yourself in a vulnerable spot. Then again, Sheryn had never understood the ladies who'd lined up to marry Charles Manson either.

"Lovely," Sheryn repeated. Her tongue felt like it was tipped in acid as it tapped against the roof of her mouth. "Have you socialized with him beyond that?"

"We had dinner one night, the three of us," Yasmeen said. "When my divorce was finalized."

"I know this is a tough question, but did you ever see any evidence that your friend was afraid of her boyfriend?"

"Afraid of Alex? No, never." Yasmeen sounded incredulous at the thought. Yet her hands moved anxiously as she spoke, reflexively touching her ring finger as if a band of gold was supposed to be there.

"But?" Sheryn prompted her.

"But what?"

"I've been doing this job for fifteen years," Sheryn said. "In my experience, most people, when they tell me a story for the first time, tend to leave some details out. They think they're not important, or they're worried about getting someone in trouble. What is it you're not telling me? Everything was great, but . . ."

"It's not a big deal," Yasmeen said. "It's just . . . well, this one thing. Alex came here, to the office, on Friday."

"Why did he do that?"

"I don't know. He walked in at lunchtime, around noon. He wasn't here for long. They had a fight." Yasmeen's dark eyes were worried. "I don't know what it was about. I didn't hear details, just the shouting."

"They were shouting at each other?"

"No," Yasmeen said. "Alex raised his voice at Emily: 'How could you do this?'"

"*Yelled* it?"

Yasmeen nodded. "Yes, he yelled it. He was upset about something."

"That's why you called early this morning. That's why you're worried about your friend."

Yasmeen blinked at her. A shadow passed behind her eyes, and Sheryn leaned forward, ready to ask what *else* she was holding back. "I don't want to get him in trouble," Yasmeen said softly. "I know he's had problems with the police before . . ."

So that was it. Sheryn sat up straighter. "Don't worry about that. Don't even think about it. Just be straight with me. Does Alex Traynor come into the office often?"

"Not really, though sometimes he meets Emily after work. He doesn't come in during the day, though. The only other time I can think of was on the anniversary of her parents' death, in May."

Sheryn racked her brain, trying to pull up some detail about Emily's family. "Haven't her parents been dead for some time?"

"Yes. A drunk driver killed them when she was in college. It's always a hard day for Emily. She's not someone who talks a lot about personal things, but I know she still struggles with this. Alex came in with flowers and took her to lunch. It's so clear that he cares deeply for her."

"In other words, it's rare for Mr. Traynor to come here," Sheryn said, brushing aside any sentimentality. "His showing up on Friday was the exception, not the rule."

"That is true."

"So, Alex Traynor came by here on Friday and fought with Emily Teare. Then she disappeared by Saturday morning," Sheryn mused.

"I'm not saying their argument had anything to do with it." Yasmeen looked startled. "That's not what I meant. I truly doubt that it did."

"I'm a person of faith," Sheryn said, "but there's one thing I definitely don't believe in, and that's coincidence."

CHAPTER 5

ALEX

Alex slept badly that night, but when he finally started dreaming, it was of Emily. They were standing at the edge of a medieval monastery, looking out over a river. For a moment, while the scene came into focus, it felt as if they were in some romantic European village together. Then Alex looked beyond the river and saw New Jersey. He was dreaming of the Cloisters in New York's Fort Tryon Park, which sat above the Hudson River. Only it wasn't so much a dream as a memory: it was hot, and the sun was high in the sky, just as it had been on the August day they'd visited the museum. He looked at Emily beside him. Her dark-blonde hair was bleached by the intensity of the sunlight, like a halo. She was casually dressed in denim shorts and black sandals. Her white cotton T-shirt was knotted loosely at her waist. Even in the simplest clothes, Emily was dazzling to him. That had been true when he'd first met her in a makeshift medical unit in Syria; she'd been in blood-splattered scrubs. He could remember that, even in the dream. It was as if he were reliving the moment.

Love isn't about looking at each other but about looking in the same direction, Alex said.

Emily turned to him, smiling. *You stole that from Saint-Exupéry,* she teased him.

I can't believe you just accused me of stealing. Borrowing, sure. There's a difference.

Emily laughed. Alex felt joy and terror all at once. This was it.

The thing is we do look in the same direction, Alex said. *I've never met anyone so intent on helping people as you. You're fearless.*

Look who's talking, Emily answered. *The man who gets shot but keeps returning to war zones without armor.*

That just means I never learn, Alex said. *Without you, I'd be in some gutter somewhere. Or dead.*

That's not true.

He touched her face. *It is. You know it. There are so many reasons I love you.* His insides quivered like jelly as he got down on one knee. *And so many reasons I want to marry you.*

He'd caught her by surprise, he knew. Her face registered shock. *Marry me?* she echoed, as if the idea were astonishing.

Too traditional? he joked, but his heart was in his throat.

Can I wear jeans to the wedding?

For the first time, he'd realized she was going to say yes, and he was so happy he actually felt dizzy. *I was thinking barefoot on a beach.*

Barefoot sounds good, Emily agreed. *So that's a yes.*

That was the moment he woke up, and for a full thirty seconds, he was elated. He was engaged to the woman of his dreams; he couldn't have asked for anything more. Then reality closed in around him, and his heart went into free fall. He was alone in their apartment with no idea where Emily had gone, just a gnawing fear that she was in serious trouble.

He sat up suddenly, and Sid let out a yelp, tumbling off his chest. "Sorry, buddy," Alex said.

He sat for a minute, petting Sid's head and reminding himself to breathe. When he felt steady enough, he padded barefoot to the kitchen and found the small brown vial he hid in the back of a cabinet. He used its eyedropper to place a couple of drops under his tongue, then sealed the bottle tightly and replaced it. He pulled a light jacket over his T-shirt and pajama pants and took Sid out for a quick walk. They were at the corner of Forty-Eighth Street and Eleventh Avenue when the last dregs of his sunny memory turned cold and drained out of his body. There, on the other side of the block, he spotted a towering figure in a black suit. The man's bald head, partially covered by a fedora, was turned away from Alex, but he was sure he recognized Kevin Stanton.

Sid was sniffing happily at a fire hydrant and resisted when he tried to tug him along by the leash. The last thing Alex wanted was another confrontation with Cori's father. The man had made his life hell after Cori's death. Alex understood enough about grief to know that it could silently devour your mind and soul, leaving nothing but a hollow rage in its wake. Part of him felt sorry for Kevin, who was divorced and had lost his only child. Alex knew how brutal it was to be alone in the world. But he'd seen how controlling Kevin was with Cori, how angry he got when he wasn't obeyed. There was more to it than that, because Cori would hint at things and then deny them. The end result was that Alex wasn't sure what to believe, but he was left with a feeling of deep unease where Kevin was concerned. The man had turned up at Alex's building several times after Cori died, but that had stopped months ago. What did it mean if he was making another appearance?

While all of this ran through Alex's mind, the big man in the fedora continued down the avenue without a backward glance. He turned a corner and vanished from view.

Alex felt rooted to the spot. Had he mistaken a stranger for Kevin Stanton? Was this just another trick his unreliable brain was playing on him?

It's your own guilty conscience, Alex told himself. *Because you should've stopped Cori from jumping. Instead, you chose to get high and blank out everything else.*

That realization always hurt. Deep down, he knew he should've died that night, not Cori. But there was no way to change how events had played out, and nothing he could do except move forward and try to make something out of the life he hadn't even wanted a year ago.

When he and Sid got back to the apartment, Alex shoved those thoughts aside and headed for the shower. His brain was foggy, swimming in happy memories with Emily and painful ones about Cori. He turned the cold water on full blast to shake himself out of that funk. Most people he knew wouldn't choose a cold shower, but then again most people he knew had never lived anywhere without running water. After years in dusty camps and gutted buildings with blown-out windows, it wasn't something he'd ever take for granted.

He forgot about the gauze on his arm until it was hanging off him like a mummy's bandages. Seeing it brought Sunday's misadventures back in waves. He'd never even made it to the dojo, and there he was, a pulpy mess from a close encounter with the sidewalk. He wanted to make light of it, but the memory left him tasting shame. When he'd come home from Syria eighteen months earlier, he'd been in a black hole of PTSD-induced depression. It made him jump at shadows and fear crowds, so he'd kept his blinds down permanently and avoided going outside for days on end. The only thing that made him leave his apartment was Sid, who got used to being walked in the dead of night. He'd self-medicated with a variety of drugs, relying on them to the point where he'd almost killed himself. It was an ugly time in his life that he thought was behind him. But when Emily left, it felt like she'd taken the better part of his nature with her.

Why he'd dreamed so vividly about their engagement, Alex couldn't quite figure. Maybe it was just a yearning to get back to a better place and time, one that lived in recent memory, yet seemed completely out of reach. Funny, he thought, how he'd only dreamed about the most romantic part of their engagement. What came next—he'd dropped the diamond ring, and they'd had to search for it in the dirt—had been conveniently elided.

The thought of Emily tugged at his brain, and he found himself wondering why that woman who'd called herself Diana had been so desperate to find her. Was there a chance that her odd story had any truth in it? He'd wondered if she might be looking for something to steal, but aside from his camera equipment, old laptop, and some weed, there wasn't much in the apartment with street value. There *was* Emily's engagement ring, though. She'd left it behind on Friday night, along with a note. The folded sheet of white paper had been lying in wait to ambush him when he'd come home from teaching his photography workshop that evening. It had been on the coffee table with Emily's engagement ring perched on top of it. Her words were seared on his brain.

Thinking about them made his chest hurt, as if he'd swallowed a rock and could feel it sliding down, inch by inch. Emily was in trouble; that was the one thing he was certain of. He couldn't understand why she couldn't tell him about it, why she'd decided to take off as soon as he'd clued in to the fact that there was a problem. Maybe she was only trying to protect him, keep him clear of it, but there was a darker possibility that haunted him: maybe she didn't think he could handle it.

Sid followed him into the bedroom. Alex slid open the top drawer of the dresser. Right on top was the blue velvet box where his mother's engagement ring had lived for years, since cancer had pared her flesh down to the bone. She'd died when he was in high school. The ring had languished there until he'd gotten it resized for Emily's elegant but work-strong hands. He'd returned it to the box on Friday night, after he read her goodbye note.

He opened the box. The ring was right where he'd left it.

Swallowing hard, he pulled it out of its little bed of velvet. The diamond was small, but it winked at him conspiratorially. *She won't be gone for long*, it seemed to promise.

Okay, at least Diana hadn't broken in to steal Emily's jewelry, he reasoned. That was something. But, in that case, what had she been doing? When he thought about it, he was sure he'd heard the dresser drawer closing after he'd come into the apartment. Diana had been hunting for something. It obviously wasn't Emily's note, which he'd anxiously folded down a dozen times into the size of a sugar cube. Even though he knew it by heart, he picked it up, smoothed out the page, and read it again.

Alex, I can't live like this anymore. I'm going away for a few days. When I get back, I'll pack up my things. Please don't try to contact me. I don't want to talk to you. Emily

Was that a code? he wondered. It wasn't the first time he had that idea. Emily was careful, circumspect. He felt that he should be able to read between the lines and hear what she was really saying to him. It felt like a Keep Out sign, one that told him not to meddle with her problems. But she knew him better than that. No matter what she'd done—and he felt a little queasy, thinking of the small part he knew of—she had to know he'd do anything to help her.

He set the note on the dresser and topped it with the velvet box to hold it in place. What else would Diana have been looking for? Emily had a little jewelry, but nothing seemed to be missing except the diamond stud earrings she wore on a daily basis. The fact they were gone meant nothing; she'd been wearing them when he'd seen her on Friday.

There was another possibility that belatedly occurred to him. Was Diana looking for the very same papers he'd found on Emily's dresser on Friday morning? In that case, she'd definitely gone away empty handed. But did that put Emily in less danger, or more?

He shut the drawer and went back to the living room. The first thing to catch his eye was a framed photo from the bookcase. It was a close-up of him and Emily in Syria; she was volunteering there with

Doctors Without Borders, and he was still working as a photographer, still telling himself that he was making a difference in the world. They looked improbably happy, and their heads blocked out most—though not all—of the backdrop of ruined buildings behind them. He stepped closer and picked it up. Emily wore a white T-shirt and the heavy silver Saint Christopher medal that he knew had belonged to her mother. Alex couldn't see the inscription around the edge of the disk, but he knew it by heart: REGARDE ST. CHRISTOPHE ET VA-T-EN RASSURÉ.

"Behold Saint Christopher and go on in safety," Alex murmured. Emily had been wearing the medal the first time he'd seen her, standing over him in a rickety tent while bombers sounded in the not-too-far-off distance. He hadn't seen her wear it in New York, but it hit him suddenly that the medal wasn't in the drawer with the rest of Emily's jewelry. That alarmed him, not because he thought it was missing—Diana hadn't made a beeline for a silver necklace that wouldn't fetch a hundred bucks on the street—but because Emily must have taken it with her. A while back, he'd asked her about the necklace. *It's my talisman. I wear it in war zones*, she'd told him. If it was missing, that meant Emily had taken it into battle with her, alone.

He returned the photo to the shelf. Maybe Emily thought she had to deal with this herself, but he was determined to find a way to help her. He looked at his watch. He had a class to teach at NYU, but if he rushed, he'd be able to talk to someone who could help Emily, no matter how much trouble she was in.

CHAPTER 6

SHERYN

"I can't believe you already talked to this woman," Rafael Mendoza complained. "Why didn't you wait for me? We're supposed to be partners, right?"

"We *are* partners," Sheryn drawled, "which is why you need to get your butt in here earlier in the morning."

They were sitting together in the squad room at the precinct, Sheryn in her chair and Rafael perched on the edge of his desk. He wasn't tall, but he was built, and he wore his gray bespoke suit well. Sheryn had only worked with him for a month, and she didn't yet feel as if she knew him at all. He was a big change from her former partner, a white-haired Irishman who'd introduced her to poker and Laphroaig scotch. Rafael was more mysterious, with the dark half-moons under his eyes and the tattoos barely hidden on his wrists by french cuffs. If she'd passed him on the street, she'd have eyed him as a potential perp.

"I'm not an early bird," Rafael said. "You can have all the worms for yourself."

"I thought Californians kept early schedules. All that sun out there."

"Not when you work homicide at the LAPD. That's for nighthawks."

Sheryn smiled. "Well, Dr. Khan didn't have an awful lot to say. The crux of it is this: Emily Teare is nowhere to be found. She left work a little after five on Friday. At noon that day, she had a fight with her boyfriend. Excuse me, her *fiancé*."

"Fancy. That's this Alex Traynor character you mentioned?"

"Right. And if we're going to talk about him, we need to talk about Cori Stanton. How much do you know about the case?"

Rafael frowned. "You said something about it when I transferred here. The drugged-up girl who fell off a building and died?"

"I know that's how the papers reported it," Sheryn said sharply. Was she annoyed that he hadn't followed through on the reading homework she'd given him? More than a little. "But it was my case, so let me give you the inside scoop. At approximately one a.m. on Thanksgiving Day last fall, a thirty-year-old woman named Corinthia, or Cori, Stanton died in a fall from the roof of Alex Traynor's building. Her body landed in the street. She died on the scene, before paramedics arrived."

"She was an actress, right?" Rafael asked.

"Yes, and a close friend of Traynor's," Sheryn said.

"How close? Like fuck buddies?"

Sheryn grimaced. "According to Stanton's father, she was planning their wedding. He never heard her mention any guy but Traynor. It sounded like she was serious. In Traynor's version, she was his good pal and his drug dealer. Nothing romantic between them at all. But we found a burner phone smashed to pieces in Traynor's apartment. It had been used a bunch of times to call Stanton."

"Booty calls, drug buys, or both?"

"Traynor denied the phone was his," Sheryn said. "Unfortunately, it was wiped clean of prints, so there was no way to definitely prove the connection. Traynor's lawyer claimed Stanton must've brought the busted phone into the apartment with her, since it was stuffed in a Duane Reade bag under the table beside the door."

"Any reason Traynor would use a burner phone to call her?" Rafael asked.

Sheryn shrugged. "She *was* his drug dealer. There's that."

"Huh. What did the dead girl's friends say?"

"She'd dropped coy hints about ring shopping and getting engaged soon, but she referred to the guy as 'the Beau.'"

"That sounds . . . odd."

"Whatever it was, Stanton seemed to think it was serious. She made a comment to one friend about how hard it would be to give up angel dust if she got pregnant."

Rafael raised his eyebrows. "A real party girl."

"You know what? Forget I said that."

"Why?"

"Because now you're judging the victim." Sheryn sighed. "Look, I do the same thing without meaning to. I shouldn't have said that. It's not relevant to the case."

"I like it when you're human," Rafael said. "It doesn't happen that often. Go on."

Sheryn resisted the urge to snap back at him. There was a teasing quality about Rafael that might be amusing in another context, but it drove her nuts at work. "If I had to bet, I'd say there was a romantic triangle going on," she said. "Traynor was also involved with Emily Teare at that point. They'd been together for three years, off and on." Sheryn took a deep breath. "Here's where the story gets really dark: Traynor's girlfriend, Dr. Teare, was the person who came upon Cori Stanton's body on the street. She gave the dying woman CPR and called 911. Actually, she called twice. The first time, the call cut out before she said anything. Then she phoned back, and the operator stayed on the line with her until the ambulance arrived."

Rafael's face registered shock. "What was she even doing there?"

"She'd just gotten off a plane from Paris and was coming over to see the man she thought was *her* boyfriend." Sheryn shook her head.

"The timing was eerie. Her flight had gotten in late, and she'd gone to her apartment. Then she got a text from Traynor and went running over to his place."

"What the hell did he write?"

"I don't even have to look it up," Sheryn said. "It's tattooed on my brain. 'I love you with every last piece of my heart. Goodbye.'"

Rafael's dark eyes scanned her face. "That sounds like a really succinct suicide note."

"That's what it was supposed to be. Traynor admitted that when we brought him in. He wanted to die. But hold on, I'm getting ahead of myself." Her phone buzzed. She glanced at the screen and turned it over, not wanting to be interrupted.

"We were at the part where Girlfriend Number One meets Girlfriend Number Two on the street in front of Traynor's building . . . while she's internally bleeding to death?"

"Yeah. Teare was holding Stanton's hand when she died. She's a spine surgeon, a pretty damned talented one from what I hear. But nobody could do a thing for Cori Stanton at that point."

"Where was Traynor while his girlfriend was playing Florence Nightingale?"

Something in the flippancy of Rafael's tone needled her. Gallows humor was a given among police detectives, but his mocking tone was a mile off from her own dark sense of irony, and the discrepancy nagged at her. She reminded herself that, after working with the same partner for a decade, anyone new would rattle her cage, but that didn't make her less uneasy. "He was still on the roof, high on ketamine and heroin."

"Horse tranquilizer?" Rafael asked incredulously. "Good times. Like heroin isn't strong enough?"

"Stanton was high on ketamine, and there were traces of PCP and MDMA in her system."

"Damn, she must've had technicolor hallucinations," Rafael said. "No wonder she went off the roof."

"It's true that we've had cases where jumpers were just high and delusional," Sheryn answered, her voice steely. "But there's more to the story. Traynor confessed to her murder. We have it on video." Sheryn pressed a couple of buttons, and a video started to play on the screen. In it, Alex Traynor was slumped over a table in an interrogation room at the precinct. Sheryn wasn't visible, but it was her voice that came on first. "Tell us about the girl, Mr. Traynor."

"I never meant to hurt her." His voice was slurred and unusually slow, like he was operating at a different speed than the rest of the world. He clutched something in one hand; there was a glint of silver. "I never would've done it if I thought she was going to die. I killed her."

"What did you do to Cori?"

"Cori?" Traynor seemed confused, almost dazed. "What happened to Cori?"

"She died early this morning," Sheryn said. "Why don't you tell us what happened?"

"I . . ." His voice trailed off into something inaudible.

"Speak up, please, Mr. Traynor. What did you say?"

"We were going to kill ourselves."

"You were . . . planning to jump off the building, Mr. Traynor?"

On the video, the room was silent except for Traynor's labored breathing. He opened his fist and gazed at the silver lighter he was holding. "I told her I was going to kill myself. Overdose. She also wanted to die."

"Did you kill Cori Stanton?"

"It was like I infected her . . . ," he murmured.

"Did you push her off the roof?"

"Push her?" He seemed startled by the idea, but his head drooped, and he mumbled unintelligibly.

"Speak up, please."

"I . . . I don't know. She wanted to jump . . ."

"And what happened?"

Traynor convulsed suddenly, wrapping his arms around himself. "I don't remember."

Sheryn paused the video. "You can watch the rest of it, if you want, but he doesn't say much after that. Basically, he started retching and threw up. We had to send him over to Bellevue."

Rafael arched an eyebrow. "Everything you've shown me makes what I'd call a strong circumstantial case," he said slowly.

"Excuse me?"

"Drugs. No witnesses. A kinda-sorta confession he made while his brain was looping around another planet. No physical evidence."

Sheryn's eyes narrowed. "There *was* physical evidence. Scratches on Traynor's face with Stanton's DNA in them, and Traynor's skin under Stanton's nails. There was clearly a physical confrontation between them."

"How'd Traynor explain that?"

"He said she'd been enraged when he refused to have sex with her."

"A likely story."

"Unfortunately, it was backed up by one of Traynor's neighbors, a Mrs. DiGregorio," Sheryn said. "He came to her door at midnight and asked her to take care of his dog. She saw the scratches on his face then."

"So, there was a fight, but it didn't happen right before Stanton flew off the roof," Rafael mused.

"Then there was the way Stanton fell from the building," Sheryn added. "She landed in the street, some distance from the building."

"So, it wasn't just an accidental fall."

"More than that, she landed on her back."

That made Rafael lean in. "So, unless she flipped position in mid-air . . . how tall is this building?"

"About fifty-five feet."

"Wow. She either jumped backward, or she was pushed." He was quiet for a moment, his face frozen in contemplation. "Tell me why Traynor's not in jail."

"Two reasons," Sheryn said. "One: the video was thrown out. Traynor was at the station for questioning. He wasn't under arrest, and he hadn't been read his rights. He had a high-priced lawyer who got the confession quashed."

"Aha. Maybe Los Angeles and New York aren't that different after all."

"It didn't help that Traynor was flying high on powerful drugs. He'd calmed down by the time we brought him into the station, but before that he was raving. Sandy, my old partner, heard him say something about an angel."

"An angel?"

Sheryn shrugged. "The second reason Traynor's not locked up is worse: his girlfriend changed her story. The first uniforms on the scene swear Emily Teare told them she was on the corner and saw a woman fall into the street. She didn't make a formal statement until the next day. At that point, she claimed she saw Cori Stanton jump from the edge of the roof onto the street."

"She changed her story from a fall to a jump?"

Sheryn nodded.

"But wasn't there other physical evidence she was pushed?" Rafael asked. "There was a case I worked—a fall that was really a push—where the autopsy showed hematoma on the victim's upper arm. She'd been forcibly grabbed and shoved out a window."

"Nothing like that here," Sheryn said. "There was hematoma of the ventral neck muscles, but that was consistent with the fall and how her head hit the pavement. Stanton had a heavy persian lamb coat on, so if she *was* grabbed, that prevented any marks from showing." Sheryn paused for a moment. "She had one strange injury. There was a fresh cut in the palm of her right hand. The ME said she might've grabbed something to keep from being pushed off the roof, or that she tried to grab the fire escape on the way down. But there was nothing to grab.

The roof has a low parapet around it, no railing at all. We never found any of her blood on the fire escape."

"Were there any witnesses?"

"None. Traynor's neighbor who took the dog, Mrs. DiGregorio, is going on seventy-five and hard of hearing. Her apartment faces the wrong way, so she didn't see anything. Everyone else on the fifth floor—Traynor's floor—had cleared out. It was one a.m. Thanksgiving morning. Manhattan was a ghost town on account of the holiday. There's no security camera footage. There was one other big thing against us: Stanton had a history of suicide attempts. No jumps, but pills and razors. Between that history and the girlfriend's testimony, the ADA thought our case was too weak to go to trial."

"There's a real possibility Cori Stanton actually did off herself," Rafael said.

"This jump was nothing like the other attempts. Those were in front of other people, basically cries for help. They were part of a pattern for a troubled young woman. Leaping off a building wasn't part of her repertoire."

"You think Emily Teare was covering up for her boyfriend?"

"That's how it looked to me. Still does. She claimed she was too horrified and shaken up by the woman's death to think straight the night it happened."

"You sound dubious."

"This woman's a surgeon who's gone into war zones with a relief group," Sheryn said. "I don't believe she was so traumatized by Cori Stanton's death that she gave a false statement. I believe she decided to help her boyfriend out of a murder rap."

"You couldn't shake her?"

"Believe me, I tried," Sheryn said. "I told her that woman's death was a preview of what could happen to her down the road. She swore Alex Traynor wasn't dangerous. She wouldn't listen."

"And now she's missing," Rafael said.

"You got it," Sheryn said. "Maybe Emily Teare ran away. Maybe he hurt her. Either way, I can promise you one thing: this time, I'm nailing Alex Traynor's ass to the wall."

Rafael's cool expression didn't shift, but he crossed his arms. "That sounds personal."

"It's not. All I care about is justice."

"Sure," Rafael said. "But I have to be completely honest with you. With this evidence, I see why Traynor walked. It's not all circumstantial, but a good lawyer could spin alternate theories that fit." He was quiet for a moment. "There's something else to this story. You're holding something back."

"I've shown you all the evidence," Sheryn answered, forcing herself to keep her tone even. Because there *was* one more thing about this case, something that didn't fit in an evidence locker. But she'd be damned if she was going to share it with someone she didn't trust fully.

CHAPTER 7

BOBBY

Bobby Costa had a love-hate relationship with his job as a superintendent. On the plus side was free room and board, because there was no way he'd be living in Manhattan otherwise. He was responsible for the care and maintenance of two low-rise buildings owned by the same company, and he made some extra scratch doing chores for a couple of brownstones too. Sure, he had tenants complaining at him all the time, but taking care of different buildings let him do a round-robin with them, so nobody knew exactly where to find him at any given time. It wasn't that he was lazy; the buildings' public spaces might be old, yet he kept them gleaming, and he made sure the aging guts of the properties stayed in good working order. But tenants were like monkeys, always doing stupid shit in their apartments. That was the problem with rentals: no one cared what they broke.

Another downside: when he was at home, trying to get some rest after a long, anxious night wrestling with a diva of a water heater, people felt free to lean on his buzzer for hours. Worse, they'd come banging on his door. That Monday morning, he had both. He played possum as long as he could, but when he heard shouting in the hallway—"NYPD! Open up!"—he gave up and lurched to the door.

"Hello, Mr. Costa. I'm Detective Sterling," said a tall woman who flashed a gold shield. She had one of those faces that looked like it belonged on a statue: ebony skin, black hair pulled back in a strict bun, high forehead, full lips, and catlike eyes that cut right through him. "You'll remember me from last year."

Bobby's head was still swimming. "Huh?"

"I interviewed you last November when Cori Stanton died in a fall from this very building."

"Oh, riiiight." He remembered *her* all right. This lady cop was a hard-ass.

"Meet my new partner, Detective Mendoza," she added. "When's the last time you saw Emily Teare?"

"Who?" Bobby rubbed his eyes. *Don't give anything away too easily*, he reminded himself.

"Looks like *somebody* had a rough night," the guy said. "Maybe you should take an aspirin, pal."

The lady cop had as much sympathy as a brick. "She's one of your tenants. Lives up on the top floor."

"Oh, *Emily*," Bobby said. "Riiiight. I dunno. Last week, I guess."

"Last *week*?" Her tone shifted. "What does that mean? Last Monday?"

"Uh, no. More like . . . Thursday?" He pretended to think about it. "No, wait, it was Friday evening. She was going out for a run." He could've told them more than that, if he'd been so inclined. He could've revealed that Emily went running in Central Park every Tuesday and Friday night. On Sundays and Wednesdays, she had her karate class with her loser of a boyfriend. She was hard core, that Emily. He knew her schedule inside out.

"What about her boyfriend, Alex Traynor. When did you last see him?"

"Sunday." He didn't need to pretend to think about that. "Yeah, Sunday evening. He was, like, bleeding all over the place."

"Bleeding?" Her cold expression was faintly incredulous.

"His arm was cut up, dripping blood. I don't know what happened to him. He's antisocial. Doesn't talk much."

"Emily Teare has been reported missing," the lady cop said. "We need you to let us into her apartment."

"Is that legal?"

"She's *missing*." The lady cop glowered at him, dark eyes stormy and suspicious. "Step one is making sure she's not at home. She could be injured. You better believe that's legal."

"Okay, okay." He didn't like pushy broads. "Lemme get the keys."

He had nothing against cops, per se—he had a cousin on the force in Philly, after all—but he never liked dealing with them directly. He could feel their suspicious eyes on him while he grabbed the keys. He glanced back and saw the woman staring at him hard, and he realized how she was reading him. Like a sucker, he'd gone straight to his desk and grabbed the key for 5C, which made him look like a stalker who let himself into that apartment on the regular. He muttered, "No, that's not it," and tossed the key back, then fumbled around for a bit before grabbing the same key ring again.

The lady cop didn't look convinced by the performance. "Let's go."

Another thing Bobby hated about being a superintendent was the fact that he was stuck with walk-ups. A couple of floors were fine, but by the time he got to the fifth, he was winded. That day it was especially bad, what with the shadow of a hangover and the trickle of fear running down the back of his neck. That Alex Traynor was nothing but trouble.

He knocked on the door. "Hello? Alex? Emily? It's Bobby, the super."

No answer.

"Unlock it," the cop said, as he started to knock again.

"But maybe they're still sleeping. I mean, it's pretty early."

The look the lady cop gave him made it clear she was used to being obeyed. He turned the key in two locks.

"Same key for both locks?" the lady cop asked.

Bobby nodded.

"We'll take it from here," the male detective said. "Stand back."

Bobby shifted a little to the side, but when they entered the apartment, he followed them in. There was a sound of claws scuttling on linoleum, and suddenly that creepy hellhound bolted at him.

"Oh, is that Sid?" asked the lady cop. "C'mere, boy. Sweet boy. What a good boy you are." The dog went running to her, stubby tail wagging. The sight of it made Bobby wince. The dog looked like hamburger meat, all gnarly and defective. Why would anyone keep a mutt like that around? It snuggled up against the lady cop, and when she introduced the dog to her partner, it licked the man's hand. Then it stopped dead, stared at Bobby out of its one good eye, and growled.

"Any reason you don't like him, boy?" the lady cop asked the mutt, but her eyes were on Bobby.

"I don't like dogs," Bobby muttered.

"I find they tend to be good judges of character," she said. "If anything, they're too forgiving of people."

The male cop walked over to the bookcase and picked up a photograph. "This is Emily?"

"Yes." Bobby and the lady cop spoke at the same time. She gave him a side-eye glance that said, *What are you still doing here?*

"And who's this other woman?" her partner asked. He held another photo up.

"That's her," the lady cop breathed, as if not believing her eyes. "Cori Stanton. The woman he killed."

"Pretty girl."

"Interesting he has her photo front and center." She stared around the room. She was like a heat-seeking missile, the way she launched herself through the space and into the bedroom. A minute later, she called out, "Rafael? You gotta take a look at this."

Bobby quietly followed the man into the bedroom. It didn't look that interesting to him. The bed was unmade, and there was a pretty green silk robe lying on a chair. That was one of Emily's, he knew. She liked pretty, silky things. She wasn't an ostentatious lady, that Emily, but she always smelled good. He reached out one hand and ran a finger along the collar.

"'I can't live like this anymore,'" the male cop read aloud. "'I'm going away for a few days. When I get back . . .'"

Bobby yelped. He couldn't help it; he recognized those words. The sound got the attention he didn't want: two pairs of hostile cop eyes settled on him. "You said something, Mr. Costa?"

He needed to push their curiosity off him any way he could. "Sorry. I thought that might be one of the letters," he said.

"What letters?" the male detective asked.

"A while back, Emily got a letter that really upset her," Bobby said. "She came to see me about it."

"Why would she come to *you*?"

The contempt in the question dripped like rattlesnake venom, but he chose to ignore it. He was the superintendent; people came to him with all kinds of problems. "She wanted to know if I'd seen who delivered it."

That caught their interest. "Did you?"

"No. But I can tell you she seriously freaked out about it." Boy, had she ever. Emily was one of those girls who was friendly enough, but frantic like a hummingbird. She couldn't sit still. He knew she had a stressful job and worked out like a maniac. She was hot, but she needed to learn how to chill out. Some wine, some weed, and she could be a different person. A happier person. Of course, he wasn't going to say any of that to the cops. They'd want to know how he knew so much about Emily, and he couldn't tell them that.

"Did she show you the letter?"

"I don't think so. At least, I don't remember it."

"Can you remember, precisely, when you saw Emily Teare on Friday evening?"

Bobby considered that. He needed to be careful. The way that lady cop stared through him made Bobby feel like she had ESP.

"It was around eight," Bobby said. "She was coming back from her run."

"She told you she went running?"

"We didn't really talk—she just said hi," Bobby said. "She always goes running Friday evenings. And she was wearing her running gear."

"Can you describe it?"

"Black leggings, sneakers, a gray hoodie. Emily runs a lot." That was accurate; he'd seen her leave the building, and that was what she'd been wearing. Her ass was really cute in those leggings.

"Where did you see her?"

"On the stairs," he improvised. "She was coming up; I was heading down."

"Was Alex Traynor with her?"

"Nah. That guy just mopes around," Bobby said. "There's something wrong with his leg."

"I remember that," the lady cop said. "He was shot back when he was covering the war in Syria. Bullet left him with a slight limp."

"And a bad temper," Bobby added.

That got a raised eyebrow. Suddenly, the lady cop was intrigued. "Tell us about that."

"It's just how he is." Bobby shrugged. "Always angry about something."

"Did he and Emily fight?"

"Oh, yeah. Not all the time, I mean. Just sometimes."

"You hear anything specific?"

"Well . . ." Bobby gave it some thought. This was something he *should* come clean about. "There's been a couple times where there's been some crazy screaming and shouting from their apartment in the middle of the night. The guy in 4C, the apartment below, told me they woke him up in the middle of the night. Said it was like they dumped a tray of silverware on the bedroom floor."

"What's this neighbor's name? We should talk with him."

"Raj Patel," Bobby answered. "He's a programmer. He moved out, like, five months ago. I think maybe he's in Hong Kong now. That or Singapore."

"Did you talk to Traynor or Teare about what happened?"

"Hell, yeah. I told them they can't be waking up the neighbors with their fighting. Emily was all apologetic about it. She's always really nice. Alex kind of brushed me off. He didn't want to talk about it."

The lady cop made a bunch of notes, her hot eyes finally off his face. That gave Bobby a surge of relief. She wasn't a human lie detector, and she couldn't read his mind. She took everything he said at face value. And he *was* telling the honest truth about those weird middle-of-the-night incidents. But she had no way of knowing that he wasn't telling the whole story about seeing Emily return from her run on Friday night. It wasn't like he *could* tell that without incriminating himself. He was no dummy, after all. He'd come close to being put away in jail a couple times, but he'd always managed to wriggle off the hook at the last minute. *Sorry, Emily*, he thought. *But if this is about choosing between you and me, I'm choosing me.*

CHAPTER 8

ALEX

When the taxi pulled up on Second Avenue, in front of the stately building that housed the law offices of Leeward, Stein & Hoskins, Alex caught sight of a tall Chinese man heading for the building. There weren't many people he knew who could carry off a vintage serge-blue suit. This timing was too perfect. "CJ!" he called, rushing out of the cab.

CJ Leeward's sleek, pomaded head turned. "Alex? What are you doing here?"

"I'm sorry to crash in on your day like this, but I have to talk to you."

"Is everything all right?" CJ's dark eyes searched his face.

"No, it's not," Alex answered quietly.

"Okay." CJ instantly snapped into business mode. "Do you want to come up to my office?"

"This is . . . kind of delicate," Alex said. "Do you have time to walk down to Dag Hammarskjöld Plaza?"

"Barely, but now I'm completely intrigued and a little worried. What's happened?"

"I tried calling you a couple times over the weekend," Alex said.

"I saw that, but you didn't leave a message. I thought you might be butt dialing me." CJ smiled. "Jayson and I were away in Chicago with the kids for the weekend. Family wedding."

"I was wondering if you'd heard from Emily."

"No, why?"

"Because she's gone," Alex said.

CJ stared at him in alarm. "Gone where?"

Alex shook his head. "She didn't tell me. Look, there's something going on with her. I don't have a lot of details, but I think it's serious. How much can I tell you, without . . . ?"

"Without causing a problem? Let me stop you right there," CJ said. "Hypothetically speaking, if we're just talking about a . . . situation Emily's in, this conversation isn't privileged."

"Even though you're my lawyer?"

"I'm an immigration lawyer who has to deal with criminal law on a regular basis," CJ said. "That was why I was able to help you out last year. If Emily were speaking to me directly, I might be able to help her too. But you filling me in on Emily's problem . . . that's not covered by privilege."

Alex weighed his words. He didn't feel like talking to anyone about Emily, but CJ was Emily's oldest and dearest friend. More than that, Alex knew what a solid, steady presence he was. If anyone could help him figure out what to do, it was CJ.

"Okay, here's what I can tell you," Alex said. "I came home Friday night, and Emily was gone. She left me a note with her engagement ring. She said she was going away for a few days and not to contact her, that she'd be back to pack up her stuff."

"I don't understand. You two are engaged. What would make her leave?"

"It's not about us or our relationship." Alex stopped in his tracks suddenly. "Or maybe it is. All weekend, I've been telling myself that Emily went away because she had to deal with an issue. Now that I hear myself saying it out loud, I feel like an idiot. She left me. Maybe there *was* something wrong between us."

"No," CJ said confidently. "I know Emily. When the four of us went out to celebrate, she was ecstatic. She loves you, and she wants to marry you." CJ and his husband, Jayson, had taken Alex and Emily to a restaurant called One if by Land, Two if by Sea, a romantic spot located in an eighteenth-century carriage house once owned by Aaron Burr. The rooms were small, and the ambiance was quiet. Even Emily, who rarely drank, had champagne that night. It had been one of the best nights of Alex's life. Had that really been a month ago? It had.

"Did she say anything to you about wanting to go away?" Alex asked.

"Yes, but it was about wanting to go away *with* you." CJ seemed dazed. "Somewhere with a beach. She was thinking about Cuba."

"I'm positive that's *not* where she went," Alex muttered darkly.

They were standing in front of Dag Hammarskjöld Plaza. "Let's go this way," CJ said. "Remember the Katharine Hepburn Garden?"

They took a few steps east on Forty-Seventh Street. The garden itself was small, just a narrow flagstone path running most of the length of the block, lined with trees and shrubs, but there was something serene about it. It had four fountains flanking it, each one under a squared-off metal trellis, and the sound of the water made the city recede. Alex could breathe easier there.

"We had a fight on Friday," Alex said softly. "I went to Emily's office at noon, and . . . well, we argued. I can't give you any of the details if this isn't privileged. All I'll say is that's why I'm worried about her."

"Now I feel bad," CJ said. "Emily and I were supposed to go out for dinner last week, but I had to fly down to DC at the last minute. Then I had to turn around and fly to Chicago. It's been a hectic month."

"All weekend, I've been trying to figure out where Emily would go," Alex said. "No one seems to have heard from her. I don't think they're lying. She just vanished."

"Did she take her brother's car?" CJ asked.

"I wondered about that, because the keys weren't there when I came home Friday." There was a fleeting image in Alex's mind of himself in the Bronx lot where Emily parked the car, staring into a window. Had he gone all the way out there? He'd meant to. He raked one hand through his hair. Was that where he'd gone in the middle of the night on Friday? It drove him crazy that he couldn't remember. All he knew for sure was that he'd found himself on the platform of Old City Hall Station at three in the morning, completely in the dark about how he'd gotten there. He was too ashamed to tell CJ; that would be an admission that he'd completely lost his mind. "I don't really know. But I called Emily's aunt and uncle in High Falls on Saturday. She's not there."

"It's not like Emily to run away from something," CJ said. "She's tough as hell."

"So how do I help her?" Alex asked. "If I know she's in trouble but I don't know what's going on?"

"I wish I knew. She hasn't tried contacting you?"

"No. The only thing is . . ." Alex cleared his throat again. "There was a woman who came to the apartment last night. I mean, she had a key and let herself in. She was looking for something, I think."

"How did she get a key?"

"She said Emily gave it to her. Diana, she called herself. She said she knew Emily, told me some fake story about leaving her abusive boyfriend. I don't believe anything she said, but she had enough details that I believe she knows Emily."

"You think she's involved in whatever Emily's mixed up in?"

"The thought crossed my mind," Alex said. "But it doesn't add up. The other thing is Diana ran out of the apartment like a bat out of hell when she saw Cori's picture."

CJ was silent for a moment. "Cori had a key to your apartment, didn't she?" CJ asked. "Maybe that's how Diana got it. She could be an addict, looking for drugs or money."

"I don't think she took anything," Alex said. "It's not like we keep cash in the house, and Emily's diamond ring was still there."

"I just don't like the sound of anything you're telling me," CJ said. "I know Emily is smart and levelheaded, but I also know she's perfectly capable of getting herself into trouble to help someone else. Am I getting warm?"

"Maybe." Alex's voice was noncommittal. Before he could say another word, his phone rang. He glanced at the screen and saw a friend's name. Still, he didn't want to answer it.

"Do you need to take that?" CJ asked.

"No. It's just Will." Alex pressed a button, sending the call to voice mail. "I'll talk to him later."

"Will Sipher? How's he doing?"

"About the same, I guess."

"I was sorry I couldn't help with his situation," CJ added. "It's far from my realm of expertise."

"What do you mean?"

"Emily asked me about overturning his conviction," CJ said. "Will heard about some hedge funders who got their convictions for insider trading reversed on appeal. Apparently, he thought that could happen for him too. I don't want to call it a lost cause, but it's not likely."

"It's a tough situation," Alex said softly. "He believes everything can go back to the way it was. He won't acknowledge reality."

Will Sipher was a childhood friend of his, a man he shared some history with. Alex had gone to a state school for a year and then dropped out to buy a plane ticket to Islamabad and a bus ticket to Kabul. Will had cruised from Princeton to Wharton to Wall Street, minting money and dating showgirls all along the way. On the surface, they couldn't have had less in common. But Will's mother had been like a second mom to Alex after his own had died, and the fact that Alex always stayed in touch with her had kept Will firmly in his orbit. Or maybe it was the other way around, since Will had always been the one who seemed to hold the world by the tail. That had all changed in recent years: Will's fabulous life had cratered in a public scandal. His mother had passed away that January. *You're Will's only friend*, she had told Alex the last time he saw her. *Will only knows how to impress people, not how to be close to them.* Even at his lowest point, Alex felt an obligation to help Will, even if his friend wasn't the easiest person to deal with.

"It's hard when everything in your life is turned upside down. Believe me, I know that firsthand." CJ glanced at his watch. "This Diana person you met . . . is there any way you can track her down?"

"I can try. You think she's important?"

CJ shot him a curious, sidelong look. "Emily takes off, and a couple days later you've got a strange woman in your apartment who claims Emily gave her a key?" He shook his head. "I'm not going to pretend I know what's going on, but there's no way I'd write that off as a coincidence."

Alex opened his mouth to answer, but there was a screech of tires from Second Avenue and the sound of metal crunching against metal. A woman screamed. Every synapse in Alex's brain was suddenly on fire, all of them transmitting the same message: *run*. He grabbed CJ's arm and pulled him off the flagstone and behind a tree.

"What are you doing?" CJ asked, clearly confused.

Alex froze, suddenly remembering where he was: not a war zone, just noisy Midtown. "Are you okay?"

"Yes, except for you trying to dislocate my shoulder."

Alex let go immediately. "I'm sorry."

There was a siren in the distance. "That sounded like a car accident on Second Avenue," CJ said. "What did you think it was?"

"I don't know." Alex could feel his face flush red. What the hell was wrong with him? First the snap'n pops had thrown him into a fugue state; now the sound of a fender bender was shooting him straight into panic.

"Be honest with me," CJ said. "Are you having PTSD episodes again?"

"I'm okay," Alex said slowly. "But since Emily left, it's been creeping back." He thought of himself like the wreckage of a bombed-out building; Emily was the supporting beam, and with her gone, he was close to collapse.

"You need to get some help," CJ said. "Can you talk to your doctor?"

"I've got a photography class to teach right now," Alex said. "I'll be fine."

"If you don't call, I will."

"Fine, I'll call," Alex lied. "But I need to get going. You'll let me know if you hear from Emily, won't you?"

"I'm not kidding. PTSD led you to a really dark place before. You need to get help."

"I don't really care what happens to me," Alex said. "I'm worried about Emily."

"You can't help her if you're crashing," CJ said. "You know that, right? Tell me something—are you having blackouts again?"

That stopped Alex in his tracks, but only for a moment. "Blackouts?" He'd never told CJ about them, which meant Emily had. She was the only one who could have. "I don't know what you mean. Sorry, I can't be late for my class." He raced out of the garden and toward the street, aware CJ's eyes were on his back.

CHAPTER 9

SHERYN

"Emily's not at work. She's not at home. The only witness we have so far last saw her three days ago," Rafael said. "This doesn't look good."

"Nor does it smell good." Sheryn turned in a circle, taking in a 360-degree view of the living room. She'd banished the creepy superintendent from the apartment and locked the front door. She hadn't liked Bobby Costa back when she was investigating the Stanton case, and her opinion of him wasn't improving. More than that, she wanted the luxury of time to take in what Traynor and Teare's life together looked like.

"That's from the dog," Rafael said. "It's why I'm more of a cat person myself."

Sheryn knelt to stroke Sid's head. "Don't listen to him, boy. He's new, and I haven't broken him in yet."

"Ha ha. Where do *you* think Emily Teare is?"

"I've got a couple of possibilities in mind. Of course, maybe she ran off. She could be in Barbados right now."

"Her toothbrush is still in the bathroom."

"Doesn't mean a thing," Sheryn said. "I keep a second toothbrush in my travel case."

"Yeah, I do too. Okay, you think she just took off?"

"That's what the note would lead you to believe," Sheryn said, giving Sid a final pat and standing up. "It's straightforward, right? 'Alex, I can't live like this anymore. I'm going away for a few days. When I get back, I'll pack up my things. Please don't try to contact me. I don't want to talk to you.'" Sheryn gave her partner a long look. "What does that sound like to you?"

"She's had it with him."

"Okay, sure, on the surface. Nothing else?"

"You really like asking questions, don't you? Questions you already have the answer to. I'm going to call you Socrates from now on."

Sheryn knew he had a point. She and her old partner, Sandy, had had a rhythm in their conversations that was hard to replace. She realized it wasn't fair to expect it from anyone else, but she missed it.

"What I'm trying to say is this. Maybe it *is* a legit Dear John letter," Sheryn said. "But what strikes me as strange is that it's all typed up. There's not even a signature. I know plenty of people don't handwrite notes anymore, but is there something sketchy about this?"

Rafael came over to stand beside her. Sid made it difficult; the dog was sniffing at a section of the rug and wouldn't go away. "Now that you mention it, it seems kind of weird."

"If Alex Traynor wanted to write a note pretending Emily went away, it would look a lot like this."

"What's your theory?"

"Which would you like to hear first?" Sheryn asked. "The dark one, or the even darker one?"

"You haven't known me for long, but the even darker one, obviously."

"They have the same starting point, which is this: Emily Teare lied for her boyfriend. Her statement is literally the main thing that kept Alex Traynor from being charged with Cori Stanton's death.

So, for the past year, Dr. Teare has been living with a man she knows is a killer. Maybe she's been justifying things to herself. You know, that because Alex Traynor was high as a kite when he pushed Cori Stanton off the building, it was really the drugs that did it, not the man, if that makes sense. We see the excuses people make all the time. There's some kind of mental gymnastics she's doing to keep her with him."

"I like how you're so formal when you talk about perps and victims," Rafael said. "It's weird, but kind of nice."

"It's one of those things I learned from Sandy," Sheryn said. "It reminds you that they're people. Anyway, I was winding up to say that it sounds to me like there was a straw that broke the camel's back."

"The fight they had at her office?"

"The one that was loud enough for Dr. Khan to hear? Yeah." Sheryn set the page on the coffee table. "Maybe Emily Teare had doubts about Alex Traynor. Maybe she swallowed them because she thought she could help him. Maybe the guilt was too much for her."

"What makes you so sure she feels guilty?" Rafael asked.

"She's spent a lot of time providing free medical care in war zones," Sheryn said. "That's an amazing level of sacrifice, something the vast majority of people who *think* they're moral human beings would never even consider doing. She knows right from wrong. She wants to do good in the world."

She was quiet for a moment, lost in her own thoughts. Sheryn had the tendency to shrink people, and she blamed that on her mother, who was a therapist. Back when she'd interviewed Teare about Cori Stanton's death, the good doctor had let slip that she knew Alex Traynor was using a lot of drugs. *He has PTSD, and he's trying to self-medicate*, was how she'd put it. If Sheryn had to lay down odds, she'd swear that Teare was determined to rescue Alex Traynor. He was a lost cause she was going to sacrifice herself for.

"I've never met her, so I don't have much of an opinion, but I get what you're saying," Rafael said. "You think something scared her off?"

"Maybe it just took her a long time to see Alex Traynor for who he really is. For all we know, he's still abusing drugs, so maybe there's been some signs of danger. Anyway, maybe Emily Teare has taken some time off from her life, because she's trying to figure out what to do. Maybe she's decided she can't live like this anymore."

"That's a lot of maybes," Rafael said. "What do you really think?"

Sheryn turned in a slow circle, taking in the apartment. There were books on the shelf about war photography, some of them by Traynor himself, and others by the likes of Don McCullin and Lynsey Addario. There were the remains of a bullet inside solid plastic, a grim souvenir of the time Traynor had been shot in the leg; she remembered seeing it last fall and thinking that it might have seemed strange to some people, but she got it. There were pictures of Traynor and Teare in war zones, then pictures of parents and friends. There was even a framed shot of Sid with his original rescuer; Sheryn wished she could remember the soldier's name. Her eye snagged on the shot of Cori Stanton on horseback next to a terrified-looking Alex Traynor. It was funny how confident Stanton looked and how scared to death Traynor seemed; what a funny choice of a photo to keep up.

"How do you want to handle it?" Rafael asked. "You get a call back yet from Emily's brother in California?"

"No, but I already know what we need to do." Sheryn leaned down to pet Sid again. "I want to go over every inch of this apartment . . ." Her words trailed off suddenly as her eyes fixed on the carpet. Sid had been worrying at it, and she suddenly realized why.

Rafael didn't notice. "I don't think we have grounds to do that."

"Take a look at the carpet." The wool rug under the sofa, chairs, and coffee table was a mix of rich blues and pale ivory woven in a geometric pattern with dark bands of red and maroon.

Rafael gave it a once-over. "Okay."

Sheryn pointed at a rust-colored triangle. "That's blood."

"I'm pretty sure that's a pattern."

"No." She got to her feet. "Look at it. One ivory triangle, then another, then one that's soaked in blood. I'm calling in a crime-scene team."

CHAPTER 10

ALEX

While he hadn't wanted to teach his class, facing a room of eager students had helped Alex file his problems away at the back of his brain. But that didn't last long. When the class ended, he escaped quickly.

His conversation with CJ had left him unsettled. Emily was in some kind of trouble, and it seemed impossible that Diana wasn't connected to it. Who the hell was she? And how did she know Cori? That connection bothered him, but it also gave him a shadow of a lead: Cori had studied acting, and all of her friends were actors. It wasn't a stretch to think that Diana was part of that crew. However tenuous, it was a place to start.

He felt faintly ridiculous entering the red door of the Lee Strasberg Theatre and Film Institute on East Fifteenth Street, just off Union Square. Everyone else in the vicinity was maybe eighteen years old, artfully dressed for a social-media age where your latest selfie might make you a star. It was clear he didn't belong. The woman who stopped him at the door, with her rainbow hair extensions blown out in all directions like a lion's mane, clearly sensed it too.

"Can I help you?" Her sharp tone didn't sound helpful.

Alex pulled out his NYU identification—the Strasberg school had a loose but important relationship with the university's own Tisch School of the Arts—and introduced himself. "I was friends with one of your students, Cori Stanton. I'm looking for another friend of hers, Diana."

"I don't think we can help with that." The woman had the brusque manner of a functionary used to fending off requests, but the sight of his ID made her less standoffish.

"Cori died last Thanksgiving," Alex said. "Some of her friends are organizing a special service to remember her. I know Diana would want to be there."

The woman eyed him suspiciously but relented, allowing Alex to hunt through the database of head shots. He scanned them quickly, expecting Diana's face to pop up at any moment, but it never did.

He was still disappointed on his walk home. *What next?* he wondered, trying to come up with another angle. Cori had never really worked as an actor—auditions had made her panic, and she'd self-medicated to deal with the anxiety, and that had rarely ended well. He was going to have to figure out another connection.

He was still working on that as he approached his apartment, when the sight of four NYPD vehicles parked in front grabbed his attention. *What the hell happened?* His mind immediately went to Emily, but he pushed that image away. If there were questions about Emily, one police car would be there; four suggested an emergency. Instead, he wondered about Mrs. DiGregorio, his widowed neighbor down the hall who doted on Sid, frying up bacon for the dog as a regular treat. What if something had happened to her?

There was a uniformed cop outside the door, scrolling through her phone. "Was someone hurt?" Alex asked.

"A woman who lives upstairs."

There was a surge of pain inside Alex's chest. Emily's face floated in front of his vision again. He ran up the stairs, feeling a stab in his leg with each step. The bullet that had ripped through it three years before had left an injury that—he was told at the time—would leave him with a permanent limp. Instead, he'd worked through it to the point where his gait was normal, unless he ran. By the time he made it to the fourth floor, he was gasping in pain. One more flight to go. When he finally looked down the hall, he realized it was his apartment door that was open. There was another uniformed cop standing guard, giving him the evil eye.

"What's going on?" he asked, walking up to the man. The cop glanced inside the apartment and jerked his head.

A moment later, a voice he recognized floated to the hallway. "Speak of the devil, and he will appear." It was a woman speaking, her voice low and resonant. Her leather boots clicked across the wooden floor, and suddenly she was in the doorway. "Good afternoon, Mr. Traynor. Do you remember me?"

Of course Alex recognized her. Not all of his nightmares were about war zones. In some of them, this woman was standing over him, staring at him as if he'd just crawled out of a sewer. *You know you killed her*, she would say in that same husky voice. *Admit it.*

"Detective Sterling." Alex swallowed hard. "What's going on?"

"I'm here about your girlfriend."

"Something's happened to Emily?" Alex's voice rose in a panic.

There was a pause as they faced off. Then the detective said, "Why don't *you* tell me how she is."

Alex stood his ground. "Do you have a warrant?"

"Of course." She held it out to him; he took it without reading it.

"Why are *you* in my apartment?"

"I'm the one asking questions," the detective said. "Starting with, where is Emily Teare?"

"I don't see how that's any of your business."

"She's been reported missing, so that makes this very much my business." Her eyes narrowed as she spoke. Even though her voice was calm, Alex could feel her smoldering anger. It was like standing before a volcano that was about to erupt.

"Reported missing?"

"Her colleague Dr. Yasmeen Khan phoned it in this morning. But Dr. Teare has been missing since Friday night, as far as we can tell. So, you tell me, Mr. Traynor. Where, exactly, is she?"

"She left."

"Left?" the detective repeated, drawing the word out as if it had multiple syllables. "Left for what?"

"She told me she was going away on Friday night," Alex said. "She said she would be back in a few days to pick up her things."

"Yes, we found her note," the detective said, and Alex flinched. "So, she left you after you two met up on Friday afternoon?"

Alex didn't answer that. If there was one thing CJ had drilled into him, it was to keep his guard up around cops. If they knew about his visit to Emily's office, what else did they have? Or was this a fishing expedition, designed to trip him up? "If you want to know why she left, you'll have to ask her."

"But I can't ask her, Mr. Traynor. She's *missing*."

The two of them were in a stare down, and neither gave an inch. *Emily's not missing*, Alex thought. *She's . . .* that was where he faltered. Where had she gone, and how much trouble was she in? What if she actually needed the help of the police? Only that didn't sit right with him. When he'd gone to her office, he'd known she was involved in something illegal. Knowing Emily, she was only trying to help someone in need, but the end result could be disastrous for her and for the career she loved so much. Talking to the police was more likely to hurt her than to help her.

"Emily isn't missing," Alex said. "She's taking a few days away. I'll let you know when she comes back."

"What about that woman who was in your apartment last night?" the detective asked.

For the first time, she'd truly thrown Alex. "What?"

"We spoke to your neighbors, you know. Miriam DiGregorio distinctly remembered seeing a young woman in your home last night. Someone between twenty-five and thirty—'exotic looking,' to quote her—wearing a platinum wig. Ring a bell?"

"I don't know her," Alex said. "She was only here to see Emily. Claimed her name was Diana. That's all I know about her."

Detective Sterling stared at him silently for a moment, taking that in. "You know, Mr. Traynor, I'm surprised you still live here, in this building. After what happened with your former girlfriend, I mean."

"Cori was my friend, not my girlfriend."

"I remember you telling us that." Her voice was cool, oddly detached, like a scientist studying a creature she was about to cut open. "But if it were me, I don't think I could stay in a building where someone I cared about had died."

Alex considered that. Cori's death was a tragedy. There wasn't a day that went by that he didn't think of her and experience shame and guilt, as if it had just happened. "It's not as if moving away to another part of town would make Cori's death any less sad," he said. "I'll miss her, wherever I am. I can't run away from that."

He had the sense, for the first time, of truly surprising the detective. Whatever reaction she'd expected from him, it wasn't that.

"You never explained what you're doing in my apartment," he added. "I get that you came here looking for Emily, but what the hell are *those* guys doing?" Alex stared through the doorway. The carpet had been rolled back. Two techs with their backs to him seemed to be studying it.

"That's an interesting story, Mr. Traynor. Your super let us into the apartment, just in case Dr. Teare was sick or incapacitated. And we found blood on the carpet."

"If you did, it's mine. I cut myself yesterday."

"It was a lot of blood," the detective added quietly. "Just how badly did you cut yourself?"

He held up his bandaged arm. "There were three cuts from broken glass."

She looked at it and shook her head. "There's no way you bled this much." The detective's tone was certain.

"Show me."

"Come on inside."

The detective had to be lying, Alex thought as he followed her in. The police played tricks like this, mind games to crack you open like a clam. The bedroom door was closed, and he could hear Sid whining behind it, unhappy to be left alone when there was a ruckus in the main room. The sofa had been pulled off to one side, blocking the door to the bathroom, while the chairs were stuck in opposite corners of the room, separated like kids who'd been fighting. A couple of cops with plastic bags pulled over their shoes were extracting fibers from the rug.

"This is Traynor?" asked a slick-looking man in a gray suit. He had black hair and inky black eyes and reminded Alex of a couple of drug dealers he'd known.

"Yes. Mr. Traynor, this is my new partner, Detective Mendoza."

The man didn't offer a hand to shake; he looked Alex over like he was about to fit him for an orange jumpsuit.

"You want to explain how that much blood got on the carpet?" Sterling asked him. "It was hard to detect it all at first, on account of the pattern. But as you can see, there's a lot."

Alex's eyes roamed over the rug. It wasn't hard for him to make out; there was blood—or something equally, opaquely red—in large splotches on the rug. "That wasn't there this morning."

"Didn't you tell me your arm was bleeding?"

"It was, but I meant drops of blood," Alex answered. "It wasn't . . ." His voice trailed off as he surveyed the scene. It was as if someone with a massive head wound had been lying there, bleeding out. He'd watched that happen enough times overseas, in the aftermath of a car bomb or IED, when civilians with shrapnel carved into their skin lay helpless on the ground. He'd photographed them and the people who had tried to help them; there were too many of the former and never enough of the latter. For a moment, he felt as if he were falling backward, into a pit he'd never crawl out of.

"Mr. Traynor?"

Detective Sterling's voice pulled him back from the edge. "I don't understand what happened," Alex said. "That blood wasn't there when I left this morning."

"Where were you today?"

"Teaching," he murmured.

"Where?"

"NYU's Tisch School. A first-year class on analog photography. It ran from nine thirty until one."

"Those are some long hours for a class," the detective said. "Anything else?"

"I saw a friend before that. CJ Leeward."

She raised her eyebrows at that. "Your lawyer? I suggest you give him a call right now."

Alex could barely breathe.

"We need to ask you a long list of questions," she added. "You have the right to have counsel present."

"I'm not going."

"You can come along of your own free will, or I'll arrest you right now," Sterling answered. "The choice is yours."

CHAPTER 11

SHERYN

"What I don't get," Rafael said, when they were back at the precinct, "is why you didn't just arrest Traynor at his apartment. I know you were itching to."

"We have blood on a carpet," Sheryn responded. "No victim, no body, no real evidence of a crime. You have any idea how much the ADA hates it when we arrest someone and have to cut them loose? It's better this way."

"There was no reason to suggest that he bring in his lawyer," Rafael muttered. "That was a bad call."

Sheryn turned on her heel to face him. "I had evidence thrown out last time around because of a technical glitch in how it was collected. I'm not going to let that happen this time." There was heat in her voice. She headed for the interview room, pausing long enough to glance back. "If that's a problem for you, stay out of the room."

She didn't wait for his reaction. Instead, she headed down the hall, knocked on the door, and stepped inside.

Alex Traynor was slouched behind a metal table, his hands clasped in front of him like he was trying to arm wrestle himself. His dark hair was shaggy, and his face was pale and drawn. Beside him, his lawyer,

CJ Leeward, looked relaxed in his dapper suit, but Sterling recognized the pose. His composure was artful, not natural.

"Gentlemen," Sheryn said. "I've given you time to confer. Now I have some questions."

"Just to be clear, my client is here of his own free will," the lawyer said. "He's deeply concerned about the blood you found in his apartment and about his fiancée's whereabouts and wishes only to assist your investigation. However, he is free to leave the precinct at any time."

"Of course." Sheryn took a seat and spread her upturned hands. *Nothing to see here, nothing up my sleeve.* "Obviously, we're doing a DNA analysis on the blood. Right now, all I can tell you is type. There were traces of type O blood, but most of it is type A."

"I'm type O," Traynor said quickly. "Emily's type A."

His lawyer gave him a warning look.

Alex caught his gaze and shrugged slightly. "When you work in a war zone, you know what blood type you are. It goes with the territory."

"That's right," Sheryn said, watching Traynor carefully. "You both spent time in Syria. You talked about that the last time you were here. You told me about *another* girl who died."

"We're not here to talk about Syria or take any other trip down memory lane," the lawyer snapped. "If you have questions about today, I suggest you ask those before we leave."

Sheryn cleared her throat. "Do you have any idea how the blood got on the carpet?"

"No," Traynor said. "I swear it wasn't there this morning."

"You mentioned a woman named Diana coming to your apartment last night. Is there any chance she came back to your apartment?"

"I took the key from her last night, so I don't think so."

"Alex," the lawyer interrupted. "Let me tell you about the key-copying machine at my local Rite Aid. Not only does it copy keys, but it can keep them on file. You can go back any time and get a fresh key."

"Seriously?" Traynor frowned. "Then I don't know. When I came home, the police were already there. Furniture was moved around. I can't tell you if anyone else was in there."

"When Detective Mendoza and I went in with your superintendent, the apartment looked undisturbed. There were no signs of, say, a struggle. No broken furniture. Do you have any idea how Emily could have been injured?"

"There's no evidence *Emily* has been injured," the lawyer interjected. "Let's keep this factual."

"Let's," Sheryn agreed. "Starting with Mr. Traynor's whereabouts from Friday evening on."

"You want an alibi?" Traynor asked. "Fine. Friday, I was teaching a photography workshop until ten at night. When I came home, I found Emily's note and her ring."

"Did you go out again that night?"

"I . . . I walked Sid." Traynor's voice halted, as if he were turning an idea over in his head.

"What time was that?"

"I'm not sure."

"Okay, besides walking your dog, did you go out on Saturday?"

"I went out with Sid a few times."

"Sure, but did you go out without your dog?"

There was a long pause before he answered, as if he were conjuring up an excuse. But all he said was, "No."

That was a lie, Sheryn knew; he'd been at Times Square station at four in the morning. Her talk with the transit cop, Koch, hadn't netted her much; he'd described Alex as *not as far gone as most people I see in the subway at that time of night.* But it was the only ace she had in her pocket at that moment, and she wasn't about to flash it. Better to get his statement on the record and then prove he was a liar. "Sunday?" Sheryn persisted.

"In the late afternoon, I went out to our dojo," Traynor said. "Emily and I both work out there. But I didn't make it, and I headed home."

"What happened?"

"That's not relevant here," the lawyer said.

"I had a PTSD episode," Traynor blurted out.

Both Sheryn and the lawyer stared at him. "What?"

"There was a kid on the street popping these little gunpowder bombs," Traynor said. "I thought it was a shot, and I threw myself on the ground. I got glass in my arm, and I ended up going home."

Sheryn nodded. "Hence, the drops of blood. Can I take a look?"

"Don't be ridiculous . . . ," the lawyer said.

"It's okay." Traynor pulled at the bandage on his arm, unwrapping it. Sheryn gazed at the trifecta of puckered, red-rimmed wounds on his arm. Two of them were oozing pus. She saw no scratches or nail marks, nothing that looked like a defensive wound.

"Honestly, I would have a doctor look at that," Sheryn said. "I think a couple of those cuts need stitches."

"It's no big deal," Traynor said, wrapping the bandage again.

"Did you try to contact Emily Teare over the weekend?"

"I phoned her, texted her," Traynor said. "Never heard back."

"Tell me about the last time you saw her."

Traynor took a deep breath. "Friday, around noon. I went to her office."

"You had a lunch date?"

"No. I just stopped by." His voice was quiet.

"What happened?"

"We talked, and I left," Traynor said. "That's it."

"What about the fight you had?" Sheryn asked.

Traynor stared at her.

"You thought we didn't know about that?" Sheryn asked. "People at Dr. Teare's office, her coworkers, heard her. What were you fighting about?"

The lawyer got to his feet. "We're done here," he announced. "Alex has answered all of your relevant questions. He doesn't know where Emily is, and he doesn't know about the blood on that rug. If you've got any other questions, you can contact my office."

"Your superintendent told us about your fights with Emily," Sheryn added. "The ones that happened in the middle of the night. Those sounded pretty bad."

Leeward whispered in Traynor's ear and nudged him out of his chair. Then he put his hand on the man's back and guided him toward the door, as if he were a child in need of protection.

"One more thing, Mr. Traynor," Sheryn called out. "Are you worried about your fiancée?"

"Yes," Traynor said. Before she could ask anything else, the lawyer opened the door and whisked him through it.

CHAPTER 12

ALEX

"I'm going to be honest with you," CJ said, once they were on the sidewalk outside the precinct. "That didn't go so well."

"I wanted to be as honest as I could," Alex argued. "What else could I do?"

"That wasn't Sherlock Holmes back there. Sterling's not going to examine every clue and logically deduce the answer. She'd going to shoehorn every shred of evidence to fit her theory and incriminate you."

"I *am* worried about Emily," Alex said softly.

CJ stared straight ahead, as if he hadn't heard him.

"Aren't you concerned about her?" Alex asked.

"Emily's the toughest person I've ever met," CJ answered. "I learned a long time ago to let her do her own thing."

They walked on in silence. Without discussing it, they were heading in the direction of Alex's building.

"Did you see Emily's letter?" Alex asked.

"Her goodbye note? Yes." CJ's tone gave nothing of his thoughts away. To Alex, he sounded oddly clinical, as if they were discussing a book or a case study.

"What did you think of it?"

"Emily doesn't give much away," CJ answered. "Whatever it said or didn't say, I wouldn't read much into it."

Alex wanted to tell him that he'd figured Emily's goodbye letter was a way of telling him to steer clear, a warning to keep his distance until she'd done whatever she needed to do. She had her secrets, even if he'd picked up on a few, like the fact she provided medical care to undocumented immigrants.

"I should probably tell you why we had that fight," Alex said. "It was because I found—"

"Don't you dare," CJ warned. "I told you it wouldn't be privileged. You can tell me anything you did, but you can't tell me about a possible crime someone else committed. I'd be legally bound to report it. Don't open up a can of worms."

"But what if it's important?"

CJ shook his head. "The less you say, the better." His voice softened. "Believe me, I'm concerned about Emily too. But telling me something I'd only be obliged to reveal to the authorities . . . that's not the way to help her. We need to keep our heads."

But Alex was starting to panic. When he'd found a stack of prescriptions on Emily's dresser on Friday morning, he'd been surprised, because New York State had done away with all paper scripts, mandating that they had to be transferred electronically from doctor's office to pharmacy; it was a measure to reduce opiate abuse. Then he'd looked a little closer at the paper slips, and alarm bells had sounded in his head. He'd thumbed through them, one by one, and then he'd gone straight to Emily's office, surprising her.

How could you do this? he'd shouted at her.

Alex, have you lost your mind? What's going on?

This. He'd held up the prescriptions. *How the hell could you do this?*

Emily had stared at him calmly. *Give those to me.*

No. His voice was quiet then. *Tell me what's going on.*

I can't, she'd answered. *Not right now.*

Since when do you have an office on Hemlock Avenue? Is that supposed to be a joke?

It's no joke.

Are you in some kind of trouble?

Of course not, Emily had answered. She hadn't seemed perturbed. Then again, she was a hell of a poker player.

I think you are.

You'll just have to trust me.

Those were the last words Emily had said to him. *You'll just have to trust me.* But what did that mean, that he had to sit tight while Emily did . . . whatever she was doing? The more time that passed, the less possible that felt. More than anything, Alex wanted to help her. It wasn't just that he loved her, nor was it because she'd saved his life at least twice. This wasn't about a debt, but about Emily herself. She'd been through so much trauma and pain in her life, and still she devoted herself to helping other people. She wasn't perfect, but she was the most heroic spirit he'd ever encountered.

"Emily told me I'd have to trust her," Alex said. "And I do, more than anyone I've ever known. I believe she'll do the right thing. But that doesn't mean she hasn't gotten herself into trouble."

"You don't know that. I don't know that. You need to sit tight."

It bothered Alex that CJ didn't understand what was going on with Emily any more than he did. Those two were thick as proverbial thieves, and Alex believed him when he said he was in the dark. What did that leave? Emily didn't confide in many people. He would've checked in with Yasmeen Khan, but she'd been the one to report Emily missing. If neither CJ nor Yasmeen knew what was going on with Emily, that was a bad omen.

"I lied in there," Alex said quietly.

CJ stopped walking and turned to face him directly. "About what?"

"When she asked me if I'd been out without Sid . . . I remembered I had," Alex said. "I've had these images in my mind, but I was so out of it that I couldn't put them together. But I know I went up to the Bronx to see if Emily's car was still there."

"Was it?" CJ asked through gritted teeth.

"Yeah."

CJ turned away and started walking again. "Look, I'm going to continue to represent you, but I strongly suggest you hire a criminal lawyer."

"Why?"

"Because the NYPD is going to come at you with both barrels over this. I remember Detective Sterling from your last go-round with her. She wants to lock you up. I don't think the *why* matters. She doesn't give a damn about Emily. She's fixated on you."

"I haven't done anything wrong."

"That doesn't matter," CJ insisted. "Sterling was determined to put you in jail when your friend Cori died, and she failed. But that doesn't mean she's given up. I wouldn't put it past her to plant evidence. One way or another, she's going to nail this on you."

CHAPTER 13

SHERYN

"We need to talk," Rafael said when Sheryn returned to her desk.

She glanced around the room. It was mostly empty at this hour. None of the other detectives were at their desks. "Okay. Talk."

"I am not working a case with a partner who's holding back information from me."

"What makes you think I'm doing that?"

"I just listened to your whole interview," Rafael said. "Including the part where the lawyer cut you off."

They stared at each other for a moment. "The dead girl in Syria," Sheryn said quietly.

"You left that out of your summary of the case. Seems like a big omission to me."

"I wasn't sure if you were up for any fruit from the poisoned tree."

"Shit," Rafael breathed. "What did you do?"

Sheryn glanced around again. No one was paying them any mind, but what she had wasn't for other ears. "You got a pair of earphones?"

He did. She held up her phone. "Take a listen."

She watched his face as she played the audio for him. It was short, and she knew every word by heart. She knew she wasn't allowed to talk to Alex Traynor without his lawyer present, but she'd done it anyway.

I wanted to see how you were doing, she'd said. *You were really sick last night.*

I know, and I'm sorry, Alex had answered.

What happened to your friend Cori Stanton was a tragedy. You know that, don't you, Mr. Traynor? She deserves justice.

It's awful, he'd answered. *She deserved a much better life.*

That's why you killed her?

I didn't.

You confessed as soon as you came in last night. You said, "I killed her." You flat-out admitted it, Mr. Traynor.

That wasn't about Cori. That was a woman in Syria.

What? What are you talking about?

Ever since she died, things haven't been right. It was my fault. Nothing I can do will ever make up for it.

Let me get this straight: You killed *a woman in Syria?*

Yes.

But before Traynor had said another word, there was his lawyer, suddenly in the room and demanding to know what she was doing there. Sheryn shut the recording off at that point; there wasn't anything else her partner needed to hear.

Rafael removed the earphones. "Traynor admitted to you that he killed *another* girl?"

"He did. I've never been able to figure out who or exactly where. He was kidnapped while he was in Syria; it could be connected to that. There's no way to know. But he has more than one woman's blood on his hands."

"And you let him stroll out the front door with his swanky lawyer."

"I did. You have a problem with that?" Sheryn asked.

"Let me count the ways. His girlfriend is missing. There's blood in his apartment. He's had another woman over there since his girlfriend vanished. You ask him a question, and he rambles on about his bullshit PTSD. He's squirrelly and weird, and you know he looks good for it. I listened while you questioned him. There's something wrong with that guy."

"We agree on that last part," Sheryn said. "There's definitely something off about Alex Traynor. We just don't agree on what that is."

"I don't get what you mean."

"You have any relatives who served in the military?" Sheryn asked.

"Nope."

"Well, I have a few," she said. "It's something of a tradition in my family. My grandfather, my dad, a couple of my cousins. Some of them come back harder and stronger than ever, and some of them come back broken. Traynor's definitely someone who broke."

"I didn't realize he'd served in the military."

"He didn't, but he's been in more war zones than a lot of soldiers. I don't doubt that he has posttraumatic stress. It would be a miracle if he didn't. A lot of people who carry that burden self-medicate."

"What's this, sympathy for the devil?" Rafael asked. "When you talked about him this morning, I thought you had a hate-on for him."

"That's where you're wrong," Sheryn said. "I hate that Alex Traynor is walking around free, because I believe he's a ticking time bomb. All that wiring that went wrong overseas is still faulty. He's a danger to himself and to others." Her fingers drummed on her desk. "When he killed Cori Stanton, it wasn't premeditated. Hell, I don't believe he's even capable of that. But in the heat of the moment . . . yes, he could commit murder. That's what I think may have happened here. Whatever he did, it wasn't planned in advance. It happened in the moment."

"You think he went into some crazy fugue state?" Rafael wasn't even trying to disguise his skepticism.

"What, you don't think that's possible?" Sheryn's gaze was steely. "I'm glad for you, if you've never encountered that. But it's real. And it's why he should be under lock and key."

"You ever think about being a shrink?"

"No, that's my mother's territory," Sheryn said. "It would be like stepping on her toes."

A shadow of a smile crossed Rafael's face. "On the other side of this equation, I've seen perps claim they didn't know they killed the victim. Didn't remember it happening. It was like someone else was controlling them, they'd say. It's an ugly way to beat a murder rap. Not guilty by reason of insanity, and then after a little stint in the psych ward, they're cleared to be out in public."

"I know that happens," Sheryn said. "I believe this is the real deal. Alex Traynor's not pretending to be crazy."

"I noticed he blurts things out like a kid," Rafael said. "I got the feeling his lawyer wanted to strangle him. Traynor's got poor impulse control, at the least."

There was a ping from Sheryn's computer, and she looked at the screen. She'd been waiting for Emily Teare's cell phone records, and suddenly they were in front of her.

Rafael didn't notice how engrossed she was. "What bothers me most is the time frame," he said. "His girlfriend disappeared on Friday evening, right? And he doesn't care, because—he says—she left him. But he doesn't know where she went, and that fact doesn't alarm him."

Sheryn didn't answer. Her eyes were on the page in front of her. She clicked to the next.

"I'm just saying, if my significant other left me, and I didn't hear a peep all weekend, I'd be freaking out," Rafael said. "No contact whatsoever? Does that make any sense? That sounds guilty. Hey, am I just talking to myself here?"

"Want to see Dr. Teare's cell phone records?"

Rafael waited for a beat. "Anything useful?"

"Depends on how you feel about calls from an unregistered cell phone," Sheryn said. "Say, about a dozen of them last Friday night."

"You're kidding." Rafael got up and looked over her shoulder. "Could it be Traynor?"

"Not unless he spent his whole class at NYU calling his girlfriend. That's the one time slot he has a rock-solid alibi for. I called the registrar when we were on our way back from Traynor's place. He really was teaching from six until ten that night."

"Who would take a four-hour class on a Friday night?"

"Plenty of people, apparently," Sheryn said. "It filled up an hour after they announced it, and it had a wait list. It's an intensive course in field photography. Apparently the famous war photographer has die-hard fans."

"Ooo-kay." Rafael grimaced. "I know people think Los Angeles is la-la land, but New York is for weirdos."

"Remind me again why you transferred here?"

"I never said."

For a moment, it had seemed like they had some slight rapport, but suddenly it felt like having a door slammed in her face. That was another thing that bothered Sheryn about her new partner: she knew nothing about Rafael's personal life. He wore a wedding ring but never referred to his homelife. Wife? Kids? He was silent on the subject. She'd taken for granted the intimacy she'd had with her old partner, Sandy; she could've told you the birth dates of his kids, and she'd seen up close how his wife obsessively decorated their shoebox-sized Staten Island house for holidays large and small.

"Whatever. Take a look at Emily Teare's call log. I'm copying you on it." She pressed a few keys and sent him the file.

Rafael scanned his own screen. "We have no idea who was ringing her phone off the hook?"

"Nope."

"You're not supposed to be able to buy a burner phone without ID," Rafael groused.

"Yet criminals get around that requirement all the time."

"Whoever called really wanted to talk with Emily," Rafael said. "The first call was at six-oh-two p.m. It was two minutes long, so it looks like they had a conversation. After that, all the calls go to voice mail."

"But nobody left a message." Sheryn scanned the pages. "There's an interesting pattern to the calls. Look at this. There's a call from the burner cell every ten to fifteen minutes from six-oh-two until ten sixteen. After that, the calls stop cold turkey."

"And as far as we can tell, Friday night was the last time anyone saw Emily."

"What happened at ten seventeen that night—that's what I need to know," Sheryn said. She clicked through the pages on her screen again. "What do you know? That same burner cell called her on Friday night exactly a week earlier, six-oh-four p.m. And the week before that, Friday at six p.m."

"Someone's being lazy, not swapping out their burner phone," Rafael said. "Any smart criminal knows you need to ditch it and get a new one. Even a week is lame."

"What are the odds Emily Teare was talking to a criminal on the regular?" Sheryn asked. "Believe me, I looked into her background last year. Aside from a couple traffic infractions when she was in school, her record's clean."

"Figure of speech," Rafael said. "To me, it looks more like a booty call."

Sheryn did a double take. "I don't think so."

"What did the super say? Every Friday night, Emily left the building at the same time for a run. And, maybe not so coincidentally, that's the night her boyfriend is out teaching."

"And . . . ?"

Rafael gave her a disbelieving look. "Really now. Let's say the lady's coming home all hot and sweaty and disheveled. Who's going to question that if she's been out running around Central Park?"

Sheryn frowned. Rafael's theory had a straightforward logic to it. Maybe Emily Teare *was* involved with another man, and this drama was spun out of age-old human jealousy. Only Sheryn's gut wasn't buying it. Emily Teare had been involved with Alex Traynor for years; now that they were engaged, she was suddenly stepping out on him? Nope. Try again. "We need to look further back with the phone records. See if Dr. Teare's been getting a regular call after six o'clock on Friday evening."

"Find out how long this booty call has been going on."

"I told you I don't get the feeling that's the situation here."

Rafael shrugged. "Maybe it was more than just a hookup. Maybe Emily was kicking Alex to the curb for this new guy. Maybe he flipped his shit when he discovered Emily was leaving him."

Sheryn could feel her brow furrowing. Rafael's scenario didn't sit well with her, yet she couldn't write it off completely. It didn't contradict the facts of the case that they had; it only conflicted with her view of Emily. To Sheryn, the doctor seemed dutiful and loyal to a fault. If she'd lied to the police—and Sheryn knew she had—it had been out of misplaced devotion. How could she square that with the notion that this same woman was cheating on her lover?

"Hey, you're the one who said this guy was impulsive," Rafael went on. "Maybe he *did* go into a fugue state and kill her."

CHAPTER 14

ALEX

When Alex walked into his building, Detective Sterling's voice was echoing through his head. *You know, Mr. Traynor, I'm surprised you still live here, in this building. After what happened with your former girlfriend, I mean.*

He tried to shake it off, but he couldn't. Just like he couldn't shake off the guilt. *I'm still here because I deserve to be reminded of Cori every day*, he thought. *I'm still here because I don't deserve to move on. I never will.*

Instead of going to the wreckage of his own apartment, he knocked on the door labeled 5D. He heard a couple of barks from inside, just before Mrs. DiGregorio opened up.

"Thanks so much for taking care of Sid," Alex said. "You're the best."

"I love having him around," she answered. "He's like the grandson I never had."

Mrs. DiGregorio's face crinkled when she smiled. As far as Alex knew, she was somewhere between seventy and eighty, though she hadn't aged in all the years he'd lived in the building. Her Italian-born husband had died around the time Alex had moved in; Mrs. DiGregorio herself was a lifelong New Yorker who'd grown up in Williamsburg when it was still predominantly Jewish and who'd retained the distinctive accent of her home borough. She was one of the most outgoing, active people Alex knew. She was hard of hearing, but otherwise tremendously fit.

"I was going to take him for a walk," Alex said. "You know how he loves the dog run at DeWitt Clinton. Do you need anything while I'm out?"

"No, dear, I'm fine. Any word yet about Emily?"

He shook his head. Before he'd gone to the police station, he'd knocked on her door, asking her to babysit Sid, as he often did. He didn't want his neighbor asking too many questions, but he couldn't pretend there wasn't a problem.

"I'm sure she's fine," Mrs. DiGregorio said. "She takes care of everyone else, so she can definitely fend for herself. I hope I didn't put my hoof in my mouth, telling the police about that oddball girl from last night."

"You didn't," Alex said. "The bad thing was that I couldn't really tell them who that girl was. I don't know if they believe me."

"I believe you. You looked at her like she was an alien."

"She might be one. She beamed into my apartment and then vanished."

"She introduced herself as a friend of Emily's, but I don't buy it," Mrs. DiGregorio said.

"Why do you say that?"

"Emily's a serious person. Solid. Grounded. She likes other serious people. That woman didn't fit the bill."

She has a point, Alex thought as he grabbed Sid's red leash from his apartment and took the dog out to the park. But he didn't doubt that Diana knew Emily, even if they weren't friends. There was only one other thing he was certain of: Diana didn't know where Emily was any more than he did himself.

On his way back, his mind was still dwelling on his neighbor's words. Emily was great at taking care of other people, but he didn't think there was any correlation with how she took care of herself. In his mind, it was actually the opposite: people who were truly gifted at taking care of themselves rarely invested that effort in others. He put himself in that category: he'd done a solid job of watching his own back whenever he'd gone into a war zone, but he'd never tried to watch anyone else's. It was only now, as he looked back, that he saw how selfish he'd been. If he ever needed more evidence of that, all he had to do was think of Maclean. Reflexively he put his hand in his pocket, reaching for the lighter, before remembering it was gone.

When he got upstairs, he found he'd left his door unlocked. Cold fingers of dread ran down the back of his neck. Who was waiting inside now? Before Emily had moved in, Alex's place had been a crash pad for his friends. He used to come home and find a despondent yet droll Will leafing through his books. Sometimes Cori would be there, making herself tea in his kitchen while she smoked a joint. That had all ended after Cori died and Will moved out of the building.

There was no one inside the apartment, unless Cori's ghost counted as an occupant. Alex bent down to remove Sid's red leash. The dog nuzzled against his hand, then took off for the couch, leaping a little awkwardly but landing solidly in his spot. Part of Alex felt envious. If only he could let go of everything and relax. There was a tickle at the back of his skull, reminding him that there *was* an easy solution for what ailed him. Well, easy in a short-term way; if you factored the long-term cycle of addiction and rehab and relapse, the cost was sky high. More than that, he didn't want to let go. What the police said about Emily tugged at his conscience. They could be wrong, of course, misguided or even malicious, trying to trip him up. It wouldn't be the first time. But what if Emily really was missing?

At the dog run, Alex had texted Emily's brother. Matthew lived in San Francisco, and he claimed he hadn't heard from his sister in a couple of weeks. Sure, Matthew could've been lying, but why would he? Alex had met him only twice, once in New York and the other time in San Francisco. He was tall and athletic, like Emily, but his face was sunny and open. He had none of his sister's frantic energy or moody intensity. So what did that leave? Emily could've holed up at a hotel, but she wasn't a woman who wasted money like that. He knew she felt guilty if she bought herself anything more extravagant than a pair of new running shoes.

What could he do for her now? The police would check Emily's bank account and credit cards. Her laptop wasn't in the apartment, but even if it had been, Alex didn't know what passwords she used. Their money was in separate accounts, so there was no way to check up on her. Or was there? He could call the credit card companies; surely he knew enough about Emily to gain some kind of access, some hint of what she was up to?

He was lost in thought as Sid bumped up against his leg, wagging his stubby tail. "After all that exercise, I bet you're hungry, aren't you?" he asked the dog. Sid just smiled and wagged. How charming did you have to be to convince a cadre of US Special Forces to take you in on a battlefield? Sid had charisma to burn.

"You ever think about the soldier who adopted you?" Alex asked the dog. "His name was Elias Maclean. Do you remember him at all?"

Sid gave him a gentle head butt in response, followed by an endearing smile and tilt of his head.

"He rescued you," Alex said. "You're alive because of him. That's something we have in common. I'm only alive because of him too."

Sid barked and wagged his stub of a tail. What it meant wasn't clear, but Alex took it as agreement. He went into the kitchen, filled one bowl with kibble, and refreshed the water bowl. Sid went straight for the kibble and chowed down. Then, as if remembering his manners, he looked up, gave Alex a contented little yip of approval, and went back to eating.

Alex opened the kitchen cabinet where he kept the brown vial and was relieved to find it there. That meant the police hadn't completely taken the place apart, at least not yet. He put the bottle in his pocket and sorted through the rest of his stash. Most of it was legal, and while the cops might raise an eyebrow at velvet bean or reishi mushrooms or kava kava, those substances wouldn't get him arrested. He worried about the kratom, which was illegal in some states and seemed to be on the thin edge of legal in New York. It had to go, along with his stash of weed. He gave Sid a gentle pat and headed out again. Now that the cops were back at his door, he had to be ready for anything.

CHAPTER 15

SHERYN

The fact that some functionary had confirmed that Alex Traynor taught a course at NYU on Friday nights didn't carry much weight with Sheryn. She'd mocked her partner when he'd said it was crazy, a class that night from six until ten. It was New York, anything was possible at any time of day or night, and she was going to stand by that. Privately, though, she had doubts. When she left the precinct, she said good night, but she wasn't off the job. She took the West Side Highway south, grateful not to be fighting her way out of the city at rush hour. It took her longer to find a parking spot than it did to get there. Plenty of cops she knew would've double-parked, but that had never been her style.

Sheryn operated on the theory she got more out of a source by meeting in person than over the phone, but there were exceptions. "I don't understand the problem," the registrar told her. "We discussed this information over the phone. Alex Traynor is teaching a special workshop in advanced field photography every Friday night. He started in September."

"I need a list of the students who take it," Sheryn said.

The registrar was a tall, slender column of a woman with heavily powdered white skin that made her look like she was channeling an eighteenth-century aristocrat. She gazed at Sheryn through her reading glasses. "Do you have a warrant for that?"

"I don't, but I can get one."

"Well, why don't you do that, then?"

Sheryn sighed. "Where does the class meet each week?"

"There's no assigned classroom. Alex didn't want one."

"That sounds a little sketchy."

"It's a workshop in field photography, run by a superstar photographer," the registrar pointed out. "Alex runs that class so that each week they meet, um, in the wild, let's say. It's supposed to be very exciting."

"How nice," Sheryn drawled sarcastically. "Look, do you see my problem here? Mr. Traynor told me about the class as his alibi, but if the class consists of him out roaming around at large . . . well, that's not much of an alibi. You get that, right?"

The registrar frowned. "But why does he need an alibi?"

"His girlfriend is missing."

"Emily?" The registrar's face creased in concern.

"You know her?"

"Oh, no, I've never met her. I just . . . I know Alex often talks about her. In class, I mean."

Sheryn raised her eyebrows. "You know someone who's taking the class?"

There was a hot flush under the registrar's alabaster skin. She was a little too accustomed to dealing with students; she liked being the authority figure.

"How about this," Sheryn continued. "Let me talk to your friend. If what I hear checks out, that'll really help Mr. Traynor's alibi."

The registrar nodded and left to make a phone call. Sheryn wondered if she should feel bad. The way she was playing it, she was the good cop who was trying to help Alex Traynor out. If she'd told the registrar the truth, she'd have gotten nowhere. It was a deception for a good cause, and she was okay with that. Still, something needled her under her skin. Her kids were at an age where they had her pretty well figured out. Her son was already a teenager, and he was an easy kid who seemed to pick up that the world was largely made up of shades of gray. Her daughter was the opposite, a fierce, openhearted girl who saw the world in stark black and white. She knew her daughter wouldn't be impressed if she could see her at that moment. *A lie is a lie, Mama.* Her baby girl was an absolutist, and Sheryn wasn't sure how to feel about that.

When the registrar came back, she directed Sheryn to the Institute of French Studies, just north of Washington Square Park on an alley-like side street that bisected only that block. When she asked for Agathe Ngeze at the desk, the receptionist stood and shook her hand. "I am Agathe," she said, her French-accented voice smooth as old scotch. "My friend told me you would come."

Sheryn stared at her. Whatever she'd been expecting, this woman wasn't it. She was in her fifties, which made her about thirty years older than the average NYU student, Sheryn figured. Her close-cropped afro was graying, and while her movements were graceful, they were slow, as if she were performing a water ballet.

"You're taking Alex Traynor's field photography class?" Sheryn didn't mean to sound skeptical, but that's how she sounded, even to her own ears.

Agathe Ngeze didn't seem fazed. "Yes, it was an honor to be accepted. Alex has a rigorous application process. Shall we sit down?" She led Sheryn to a small, empty room across the hall. Her steps didn't appear to be easy. When she offered her coffee or tea, Sheryn turned her down.

"You're a photographer on the side?" Sheryn asked.

"No, but I always dreamed of being one." She smiled. "Alex says that, to be a good photographer, one must be a faithful witness. I have always been that."

Sheryn wasn't often stuck for words, but this tall, elegant woman—who spoke with a reverence of Alex Traynor—left her nonplussed. "The registrar told me it was an advanced class, so I just assumed . . . I figured you had to have been taking pictures for a while."

"Oh, I have, but not good pictures. Not framed well, not artistic. But I took them so that I would never forget what I saw. I took them so that I could share what I have lived, especially with those who do not want to believe."

"I know Alex Traynor made a name for himself as a war photographer . . ."

"And I am from a war zone," Agathe said. "I grew up in Rwanda."

Sheryn could only nod at the weight of her words; they were heavy, loaded with significance. She could remember news about Rwanda from when she was in college, the atrocities that were committed there. *I'm sorry* wasn't an appropriate response when a person told you where she's from, Sheryn knew; she had to choke back the words. "Can you tell me about Mr. Traynor's class?" she asked instead. "I heard that you go out into the field. Is he with you while you do that?"

"Part of the time," Agathe said. "We meet and talk, and he answers our questions. Then we go out and take pictures. In the last hour, we meet again. Sometimes I will see him between those times, sometimes not."

"Where did class take place last Friday night?"

"Old City Hall Station."

"You had a class in a subway station?" Sheryn asked.

"Not just any subway station," Agathe clarified. "It used to be the jewel of the New York system before they closed it. Too small a platform for the trains."

"Hold on. Your class met at the abandoned subway stop under City Hall?"

Agathe nodded enthusiastically. "It was spectacular."

"Alex Traynor made arrangements for you to go there?"

"Arrangements?" Agathe's face lit up in an amused smile. "No. That is part of the challenge. Alex says that, to be a good witness, you cannot worry about the rules. If a door tells you to stay out, you go through it. You cannot be a good witness if you only take pictures of the things society wants you to see."

Sheryn was incredulous. "I'm sorry, but you seem to have some trouble walking. How could you possibly get to a shut-down station? What did you do, walk along the track? That's dangerous, not to mention illegal."

Agathe surprised her by reaching forward and patting her hand. "I understand you are a police officer," she said. "And I believe, from the way you think, that you are a mother. You are a natural worrier."

"Yes, but—"

"Years ago, I was raped by men who told me they would break every bone in my body when they were done with me," Agathe said. "They tried. I think they came very close. There are two hundred and six bones in the human body—even more in children. Most of mine were snapped or crushed. And still, I survived. There are pins and wires holding me together." She smiled again. "But I survived. And I will be a witness as long as I live."

"But . . ."

"There is no sense worrying about me now. Alex is a good teacher. For the record, I did not walk along any subway tracks. There's more than one way into that station. Alex says he cannot teach anyone how to take a picture; he can only teach us how to think about taking it. For a man of thirty-seven, he is very wise."

"All right, you met at the station, and he . . . lectured? For how long?"

"Close to an hour. It was prolonged to give the stragglers a chance to get there."

"How many people are in this workshop?"

"There are twenty of us. Not typical NYU students. Few of us are that young."

"What happened after his talk?" Sheryn asked.

"We left together. After that, it was up to us to find our own subjects. I had my meeting with Alex at eight."

"Meeting?"

"He meets individually with each student during the workshop," Agathe said. "He talks with us about our ideas, any issues we are having."

"He does this every class?" Sheryn asked. If Traynor lectured, spoke individually with each student, and then spoke with the group again at the end of the night, that would be his time accounted for. He really did have a solid alibi.

"Always. He is a thoughtful man. He wants to help."

"Does he talk about his girlfriend in class?"

"Emily? Yes, sometimes. She is his fiancée."

"What does he say about her?"

"She comes into his stories because she was in the field with him—that was how they met. He was shot in Syria, and she dug the bullet out of his leg."

Sheryn considered herself an expert in Alex Traynor 101, but that piece of intelligence caught her short. "I knew they met overseas but not that she'd operated on him." She tried to think back to her interviews with them. Emily Teare had been so circumspect. Alex Traynor had been a disaster. "Anything else?"

"He has talked about her work with Doctors Without Borders. Alex has said too many photographers go looking for glory, when it is their job to document. To be witnesses. Like Catherine Leroy. Do you know her?"

Sheryn's ears perked up. "Is she a friend of Mr. Traynor's?"

For the first time, Agathe laughed. "No, no. She was one of the all-time great war photographers. She was French, and she went to Vietnam in the 1960s. You would recognize her pictures if you saw them. She said she wanted to give war a human face, and she did. Alex is a great cynic. He says too many photographers want fame. They do not want to be the fly on the wall." She cocked her head. "May I ask, why do you ask so many questions about Alex? My friend said you needed to know where he was last Friday."

"Emily has gone missing," Sheryn said. "We're investigating her disappearance."

"I am so sorry." Agathe pressed one hand to her chest. "Alex must be devastated."

For a split second, Sheryn thought about setting her straight. But Agathe kept speaking.

"Perhaps that was why Alex was so upset last Friday," she said.

"Wait, he was upset? You didn't mention that before."

"I didn't think it relevant." Agathe shrugged. "Alex tried to call Emily before I met with him. He seemed . . . concerned is the best way I can describe it. I remember he said, 'I don't think she wants to talk with me.'"

"Did he say why?"

"No, but it all makes sense now," Agathe said. "Because Alex was definitely not himself last Friday night."

"How do you mean?"

"He was distracted," she answered. "He kept pulling this sheaf of papers out of his pocket and looking through them. It was unlike him."

"Papers. Like a folded-up note?" Sheryn's mind immediately went to Emily's unsigned goodbye letter.

"No, no. Like a stack this thick." Agathe held up her fingers to indicate a half inch. "Small pages."

"Did you see what was on them?"

"There was some printed text and some handwriting on the top page. That was all I saw," Agathe said. "I have no idea what was on the rest."

CHAPTER 16

ALEX

Sorry, I can't meet tonight, Will texted. Maybe tomorrow? I'll take you out for drinks.

Alex didn't bother to respond. He was already on Will's block. He'd been ready to slip through the foyer—Will's building was more upscale than his, though it didn't have a doorman either—but there was Will, hurrying out the door and onto the street, typing frantically on his phone. Alex stood still, and his friend almost crashed into him.

"What a coincidence," Alex said. "Just the man I was looking for."

"Alex? Is that you?" Will peered closely at him, as if he suspected Alex of being a ghost.

"Are you okay?"

"I may have taken one too many Vicodin," Will said. "Also, I may have mixed it with alcohol. At the moment, I am a walking, talking chemistry experiment." He was unshaven, and his dark wavy hair stood on end. He was wearing a suit—Will only ever wore suits—but it looked as if he'd slept in it, worked out in it, and, possibly, showered in it.

"Were you heading out?" Alex said. "Because you probably shouldn't right now. Also, I really need to talk to you."

"I always have time for my friends." Will lurched a little to the right, as if he were attempting a mambo side-step. "Shall we go upstairs?"

Alex followed him inside and into the elevator.

"You never called me back on the weekend." Will spoke softly, but there was a sharp edge under his words. "Did something happen?"

"Kind of," Alex said. "It's been hectic."

Will's small apartment was on the fourth floor. The lighting was dim, but Alex could make out the oversized leather sofa facing a massive television mounted to the wall. There was an assortment of bottles on the coffee table—some lay flat, like drunks who'd passed out—and a tower of unopened mail tilting against a leather club chair. It smelled to Alex as if his friend had started a collection of used sweat socks.

"When's the last time you opened a window?" Alex asked.

"This from the man who used to kick pizza boxes under his bed." Will sniffed. "Did you come up here to critique my housekeeping?"

"No. I'm here because of Emily." The air changed as he said the words, as if storm clouds had gathered and turned the pressure up. "The police came to my apartment today."

"The police?" Will's eyes searched Alex's face. "Did I blank out for a minute? I feel like I missed something. What do the *police* have to do with *Emily*?"

"A friend of Emily's reported her missing this morning," Alex said. "I don't think anyone's seen her since Friday."

Will squinted at him. "I think you're burying the lede. Are you saying *you* haven't seen Emily since Friday?"

Alex nodded. "That's right."

"What happened between the two of you?"

"She left," Alex muttered.

"Left? Left for where?"

"I'm not sure," Alex admitted. "Her note didn't say."

"Emily dumped you?" Will blinked. "I am sorry to hear that."

"She *hasn't* dumped me." Alex's voice was louder than he meant for it to be. "She just needed some time for herself."

"Ah, it's not you—it's me. She just needs to find herself." Will sighed. "Speaking as a man who was unceremoniously dumped by his own wife immediately after being publicly humiliated in court, let me say that I've been there, Alex. I know it hurts like hell."

The way Will spoke was distant and emotionless, as if the wreckage of his personal life were a faraway country he'd once visited on a now-expired passport. Alex knew better: three years ago, Will had been printing money at a hedge fund, living in an apartment on the edge of Central Park, and married to a model named Hadley Everheart. When his life exploded, it was with supernova intensity. Job, home, and wife vanished in short order, but the thing that most shocked Alex was that when he'd half jokingly suggested that Will move into an empty apartment in his building to get his life together, Will had actually done it.

"It's not the same thing," Alex said. "Emily wouldn't do that." He didn't add that Will's ex had been the kind of woman who insisted on wearing a diamond tiara to brunch the day before her wedding. Emily was nothing like that.

"You sad, innocent fool," Will said. "If it could happen to me, it could happen to you. Hadley wanted the good life, and when I couldn't give her exactly what she wanted anymore, she ditched me. I didn't want to believe it either. But time is harsh that way. It rushes on while your head is still spinning. Whether or not you accept it, it's what happened."

Alex gritted his teeth. He'd known Will all his life, ever since their mothers put them in the same Bronx sandbox to play together. They hadn't always liked each other, but the fact that their mothers were close friends had kept them in each other's lives. And then, when Alex's mother had passed away, it was Will's mother who'd taken him in while he finished his last year of high school. He and Will hadn't become best friends that year, but Alex felt like he'd gained something akin to a brother. That didn't mean Will couldn't drive him nuts: back when

Will was flush with cash, he'd been an insufferable show-off; since he'd lost the things he cared about, Will had discovered an inexhaustible well of self-pity. Alex had known Will's wife was a gold digger the first time he'd met her; nothing that happened between them had been a surprise—though, to be fair to Hadley, Will's epic drug binges would've pushed most women away. But Alex also knew that Will never betrayed a confidence. He could tell him anything and be sure that his words wouldn't boomerang back at him.

"I need to ask you for a favor," Alex said. "Because the police are back at my door. Detective Sterling is looking for any reason to lock me up."

"Sterling? That shark who went all Inspector Javert on you last year?"

"That's her. She's back, so I can't keep this around." He held out the plastic shopping bag.

"What have we here?" Will asked, taking it into his hands. He started to pull it open as if it were a Christmas present but stopped suddenly. "There aren't any needles in here, are there?"

"No. I'm not using heroin again, if that's what you're asking."

"You know I'm not one to judge," Will said.

That was true, Alex thought. It was Will's other virtue.

"And what might *this* be?" Will asked, grabbing a tissue and doubling it over to lift out a bottle made of opaque mud-colored glass. Even stoned on Vicodin, he was sharp enough not to leave a fingerprint on it.

"LSD. I've been microdosing," Alex said.

"Would you believe that I've never tried LSD? What's it like?"

"This tincture won't make you trip," Alex explained. "I take a couple of drops every day. It doesn't fix anything, but with it, my head is clearer. I feel less depressed. Not undepressed, exactly. It's not playing with my mind. It makes me feel human again."

"You're not much of a salesman," Will commented. "You just made LSD sound as boring as a due diligence questionnaire." He gazed at the bottle. "Do you need to come over each day to take it? Because I'm at my mother's place most of the time now. I'm still clearing it out. Mother was such a pack rat."

"No, I'll just do without." The mention of the house brought a lump to Alex's throat. Mrs. Sipher had passed away in January, and he missed her deeply. Will, as her only child, had inherited the massive house in Riverdale; he'd talked about selling it, but Alex sensed that his friend was having trouble parting with it.

"Does Emily know you take LSD?"

Alex shook his head. "We've never talked about it."

Will gingerly set it back into the bag. "Your secret is safe with me. I'll keep it here as long as you need. But tell me more about Emily. I still don't understand why the police showed up at your door. That doesn't strike me as normal."

"Sterling claimed they came over to check on Emily. Then they just happened to find blood on the carpet while they were in the apartment. I don't know how it got there. It wasn't there this morning."

"Alex, either you are paranoid and high," Will said, "or else someone is setting you up. Have you had any strange visitors lately?"

"A woman came by last night. Diana. Claimed she was a friend of Emily's. She had a key to the apartment."

Will shook his head sadly. "You know what I don't miss about your building? How dangerous it was to live there. Anyone can get in. The owners won't invest a penny because they want it off their hands, but no one wants to buy it because they sold the air rights."

"It's not that bad," Alex said, knowing full well it was.

"Maybe the police put the blood on the carpet," Will said. "There's nothing I wouldn't put past them."

Alex considered that. He had no doubt Sterling would bust his ass for jaywalking if she could. But it was still hard to imagine her carrying evidence to plant on him. He might not like her, but the way she tried to squeeze the truth out of him made him believe she genuinely cared about it. "I went over to the precinct to answer their questions," he admitted.

Will slammed his fist into his own leg. "What the hell were you thinking, Alex? You don't talk to the cops. You don't answer their questions. Not ever. That's like playing Russian roulette."

"CJ was with me."

"CJ fucking *Leeward*?" Will's eyes bored into Alex's. "Please tell me that was a joke. I don't trust lawyers, and that goes double for frauds who use fake names."

"He combined his surname with his husband's when they got married. That's not fake."

"It's as made up as his diploma," Will insisted. "Because even an incompetent shyster would keep you away from the police. He should know better. He would let you walk into the lion's den with a fig leaf to cover yourself."

"He didn't like it either," Alex muttered. "But I wanted them to know I have nothing to hide."

"I can't believe I'm listening to this," Will said. "Did you learn nothing from what happened last year? Because the police were ready to lock you up for Cori's murder. The justice system screwed me over, and it is going to screw you over too. You don't need to be guilty. All you have to do is stand still long enough to let the authorities paint a target on you."

"You just called Cori's death a murder," Alex said slowly. "Is that what you think, that I killed her?"

Will looked startled. "Of course not. Alex, you know me better than that. I was just thinking of it from the cops' point of view. They tried to charge you with murder. If it hadn't been for Emily, you would've gone to jail."

"Maybe they were right," Alex said softly. "Maybe I should've gone to jail."

"Don't talk like that."

"It's not like I remember what happened," Alex said.

"None of it has ever come back to you?" Will's voice was gentle.

"Not one sliver of it."

"Maybe that's for the best," Will said.

"Why would you say that?"

"Because otherwise you would be tortured by the memory," Will answered. "You would replay it in your mind and wonder what you could've done differently to save her. But Cori didn't want to be saved."

Alex understood what Will meant, but the sentiment felt backward to him. He was haunted by Cori's memory precisely because he couldn't remember. It wasn't that he didn't have glimmers of recollection: he knew Cori had come over and they'd gotten high and they'd had a fight; but there were long blank stretches, like static on an old record.

"It's worse not being able to remember," Alex said. "Losing time like that makes me feel like I'm losing my mind."

Will's head lifted suddenly. "But those blackouts are a thing of the past, aren't they? You haven't had one in months."

"When I got home Friday night, I found Emily's note saying she was leaving." Alex took a deep breath. "I lost it. I got drunk and took some pills and got some crazy idea to go up to the Bronx to see if she'd taken her brother's car."

"Why do that?"

"I don't know. It made sense at the time." Alex shrugged. "Emily only ever uses the car to go up to her aunt and uncle's place. I was thinking if the car was gone, that would mean she was in High Falls with them. I . . . I wouldn't be worried about her if that's where she was."

"Was the car there?"

"I think so." Alex rubbed his forehead. "It's hard to picture, exactly . . ." He closed his eyes and tried to visualize the parking lot, but he couldn't. Instead, he saw a square sheet of paper with *Hemlock Avenue* printed at the top. Emily's handwriting was on it too. One more word—*fentanyl*—flashed through his mind.

"It's not so strange to forget things like that. That happens to me sometimes when I get drunk," Will said confidently. "At least it's not one of your stress blackouts."

"Posttraumatic stress disorder," Alex said quietly. "And I think I had one that night. I blanked out after I went up to the Bronx. When I came to, I was lying in a subway station."

"Which one?"

"Old City Hall. What used to be the end of the 6 line." Alex was quiet for a moment. "The strange thing was, I had just brought my workshop students there, earlier that night. I have no idea why I went back."

"Like a drunken homing pigeon," Will said. "Please tell me that you didn't admit any of this to the police, Alex."

"I didn't."

"Good. Don't. Because if you do, they'll think *you* did something to Emily." Will was quiet for a moment. "What did she say in the letter?"

Alex only shook his head.

"Of course you don't want to talk about it," Will said. "I understand that. But perhaps I could help."

"No one can help right now."

"Maybe if you told me what happened. I know Emily wouldn't leave without a reason." He paused, waiting for Alex to fill the silence; when that didn't happen, he went on. "Alex, why do you think Emily ran off?"

"She told me I had to trust her."

"Trust her to do what?"

"I have no idea," Alex said. "But that's what trust is, right? I don't need to know. I just need to believe in her."

CHAPTER 17

ALEX

Alex spotted Diana the minute he stepped into the Jane Hotel Ballroom. She was wearing a different black dress this time, tight as a tourniquet but with strategic cutouts on the back; he figured they were there to let her breathe. But the platinum hair was the same, and he watched her toss her head back carelessly as she served drinks to a group of women seated on a burgundy velvet sofa. The light was low, but the decaying disco ball hanging from the ceiling gleamed.

He'd figured out the connection between Cori and Diana after leaving Will's place. Cori had worked as a bartender at the Ballroom; it was the only steady job he'd known her to hold, besides working for her father at the veterinary clinic. Before Diana spotted him, he sidled up to her. "Excuse me."

Without turning her platinum head, she said, "No, you can't ask me out."

"Diana?"

She turned her head, and he realized he'd been mistaken. This woman was about the same age as Diana, but with huge blue eyes that made her look like an anime character and a rosebud mouth stuck in perma pout. "Guess again," she challenged.

"I'm looking for someone," Alex said, but she was already walking away from him. He didn't do any better with the rest of the staff. No one admitted to knowing Diana—or Cori, for that matter. It had been a long shot, and he'd struck out. Again.

When he got home, he took a shower and got into bed. Sid snored gently on the pillow beside him. Alex fell asleep quickly, but the dreams came on just as fast. There was a siren screaming near his head. He was in Syria again, taking pictures, shooting a building that had just been bombed into rubble. There were small fires everywhere, pieces of wood and people that continued to burn. Two men in white helmets were desperately digging through the broken concrete.

Help us! one of the men had cried out, half turning to look at Alex. He spoke the Mesopotamian Arabic Alex heard so often in Aleppo.

In the dream, Alex only saw the men through the lens of the camera. They were digging with their bare hands, casting broken hunks of wall aside. There was something white underneath that was slowly being revealed.

Help us!

And then another bomb went off. It sent a shockwave through Alex's system, yet it didn't wake him. Instead, he found himself chained to the wall in a basement cell. A man with a long black beard was explaining to him how he was going to die. Then a voice beside him whispered, *Not your turn today.* He looked around and saw Maclean sitting beside him sipping beer out of a glass bottle. For a moment, Alex felt relief; US Special Forces were there, and he wasn't going to die after all. But that comfort was short lived: there was the crack of a shot, and the glass exploded and there was blood everywhere.

Caught in that thin membrane between sleep and consciousness, Alex screamed. He jolted upright in bed. His body was coated in sweat. He couldn't breathe.

Beside him, Sid whimpered and reached out to touch his chest with one paw. Alex looked at his dog and caught his breath. He remembered where he was again. "Sorry, Sid," he said, patting the dog's head. "I didn't mean to scare you."

Alex was used to bad dreams. For years, they'd invaded his sleeping hours, whittling them down and turning them into a kind of torture. It had been better lately, but they never let go completely. Sometimes they crept into his mind only a couple of nights a week, and he'd wake in a panic but be able to shrug it off quickly. But there were periods when they would return night after night, unwelcome guests who never knew when to leave.

It was almost five, but he got up and dressed while Sid snored on the bed. He let himself out quietly. It was tough for him to navigate the subway during rush hour, when the swarm of crowds and frenetic pace pushed his PTSD triggers. But overnight was a different story. He got on the downtown A train and took it as far as Chambers Street. Then he walked through City Hall Park and headed down into that station. The board told him he had an eight-minute wait for the next 6 train, which meant he had more than enough time. At the far southern end of the platform, he disappeared down a metal staircase meant for MTA employees and hurried along, beside the empty subway track, to a dimly lit station a few hundred yards away.

Of all the abandoned subway stations in New York, Old City Hall was the easiest to sneak into but the hardest to enjoy. No trains stopped there, but the Lexington 6 line used it to turn from downtown to uptown. It was one of Alex's favorite spots in the city, but he knew its pitfalls. Every time a train trundled through on the sharp curve of the track, he had to run up a staircase to stay out of view. But the top of that staircase was, for once, his real destination. It was where he'd woken up early Saturday morning, still drunk and light headed.

When he lifted himself onto the platform, he felt his familiar awe of the place. Once again, he was standing under that great vaulted ceiling, covered in elaborate Gustavino tile work. It was studded with brass chandeliers and milky skylights, which allowed glimmers of lamplight from City Hall Plaza to trickle in. The station was designed to be a showstopper. Even if Alex hadn't known the history, one look at the grandeur would have spelled out its ambitions. Built at the turn of the twentieth century, Old City Hall was designed to show the world that New York had arrived. Alex knew that if he'd seen the station back in 1904, filled with walrus-mustached men puffing cigars and clapping each other on the back, he would have hated it. No, his affection for the station lay in the fact it had been shut down in 1945, too small to accommodate the ever-longer trains and too dangerous thanks to its sharp semicircle design, which left massive gaps between train and platform. Union Square had a similar problem, but it had been worth fixing. Old City Hall had been unceremoniously dumped.

Naturally, that was why Alex liked it.

In the low light, it was hard to see all of the decay and deterioration, but he could smell it. Years of water damage blended with layers of steel dust and dirt. It was a wreck, a beautiful ruin. Unlike other abandoned stations, it couldn't be used as shelter by the homeless—the combination of train traffic and transit museum tour groups made for enough prying eyes to scrap any would-be settlement. The station's loneliness and emptiness were palpable to him.

As he headed up the staircase, he heard a train coming in. That made him quicken his pace. But at the top, he froze. Against the wall was a mound of black ash. The sight of it hit him like an anvil. He knew what that was.

He crouched in front of it and reached out to touch the cinders. That was why he had come back to this place in the witching hours before dawn on Saturday. He'd needed to start a bonfire. New York was tough that way: there were people everywhere, and if you retreated to your own apartment to set a fire, you risked burning the building down. He'd needed total privacy, and so he'd come to this abandoned place.

Hilary Davidson

Earlier, he'd only vaguely remembered going up to the parking lot in the Bronx; more accurately, he recalled his intention to do so but couldn't quite picture the scene. He'd started to remember more details under Detective Sterling's questioning at the police station. But even though he'd recalled enough to tell parts of it to CJ and then to Will, the details were hazy, and they only began to come together now as he touched that mound of ash. Suddenly, he was certain he knew what had happened: he remembered taking the 4 train uptown and making his way to the lot. The car was in place, right where they'd left it after the last time they went up to High Falls.

He took a deep breath. The picture in his mind cleared. He could see himself peering through the car windows, looking for anything Emily might have left behind. She couldn't just leave; her passport was in the apartment, so she hadn't flown out of the country. He remembered staring at the car, trying to will a clue into existence. But it told him nothing; it was as spotlessly clean as always, without so much as a shred of paper out of place.

Alex fanned the ash out, curious whether anything had survived the flames. Nothing had; he'd been surprisingly thorough in his drunken, drugged fugue state. Instead, his fingers touched metal, and he fished a small silver cylinder out of the pile. It was Maclean's lighter, and the sight of it lifted his heart for a moment. He hadn't lost it after all.

Not your turn today, Maclean whispered in the back of his head.

Holding the lighter, Alex remembered the sheaf of papers he'd carried around all day on Friday. The ones he'd found on Emily's dresser, the ones he'd fought with Emily about at her office. The scene played out in his mind again.

How could you do this? That was how it had started. He'd been startled and angry.

Alex, have you lost your mind? What's going on?

114

This. How the hell could you do this? He'd held up the prescriptions, and he remembered Emily shrinking back as if repulsed, even though her voice remained calm.

Give those to me.

No. Tell me what's going on.

I can't. Not right now.

Since when do you have an office on Hemlock Avenue? Is that supposed to be a joke?

It's no joke.

Are you in some kind of trouble?

Of course not.

I think you are.

You'll just have to trust me.

That was the tough part: he trusted Emily completely. It wasn't that he believed he knew her innermost secrets; there were parts of her—like any other person—that were unknowable, and he accepted that. But he trusted Emily's judgment, her desire to do good in the world, her empathetic nature; those were elemental, and they made up the core of who she was. He couldn't reconcile those with the prescriptions he was holding in his hand, with drugs like fentanyl and Seconal and Sublimaze. It wasn't shocking that she might prescribe opioids or barbiturates, but those would go through her office. Instead, these scripts were tied to a fake office Alex was certain didn't exist. It was the kind of thing a doctor with a drug problem might do, only that wasn't the case with Emily—he was sure of it. What did that leave?

He held the lighter tightly in his palm, unwilling to let go of it again. He remembered using it to burn those papers, lighting page after page ablaze. He'd been lucid enough to complete the only task that mattered—destroying those papers—but drunk and drugged enough to sweep Maclean's lighter aside under the cinders.

Alex rose to his feet slowly. He'd needed privacy for his bonfire, and that was what that abandoned station had afforded him. He still had no idea what Emily had been up to, writing those prescriptions. All of the possibilities running through his mind—selling them, helping an addicted friend—were dark, and any of them would result in Emily losing her medical license and likely going to jail. The stakes were that high. All Alex could do to help her was burn the incriminating evidence. That, and pray Emily had meant it when she told him she wasn't in trouble.

CHAPTER 18

EMILY

The first time Emily Teare came to, it was only for a few seconds. She was lying on a cold surface with a bright light above her head shining in her eyes. How had she ended up there? Had there been some kind of accident? She tried to wiggle her fingers and toes, and they obliged grudgingly. Out of the corner of one eye, she spotted a gloved hand. When she opened her mouth to speak, all that came out was a sharp cry, like a hatchling chick's. Something jabbed her shoulder, and she gasped. It felt like molten lead was pouring into her body, deadening every nerve and synapse. Her brain couldn't resist. She went under again.

The second time Emily started to wake, the light was gone, and everything was pitch black. She blinked rapidly, but there was nothing to see. The absence of light was startling. *Am I blind?* she wondered, feeling the first shivers of panic. She was moving, but she didn't know how, because her feet weren't on the ground. In her mind, she was running. She was in the park again. She could hear footfalls over her own panting breath. But that sensation lasted only for a split second before Alex's face floated through her mind. She wasn't running. Strong arms were carrying her along. The heavy breathing wasn't her own, but his.

"Alex?" she whispered.

Something shifted in the darkness. Dizziness swelled over her as they came to a jerky stop. He dropped her legs, and she felt the softness of grass under her feet, even though her legs were too weak to support her weight. Then he pressed a cloth against her face, and she was overcome with the chemical stench of chloroform. It plunged her into unconsciousness again.

The third time Emily came to, the first sensation that hit her was that she was very cold. She moved her head from side to side, feeling stiffness in her neck. She was lying on a dirt floor. The room was dark, but it wasn't the stygian blackness she'd experienced last time, one that admitted no light at all. But what was the last time she'd been conscious: an hour ago, or a day? How long had she been knocked out?

There was a light bulb at one end of the room, maybe all of twenty-five watts, dangling from a wire in the ceiling. Emily blinked at it, grateful for any proof she hadn't lost her sight. She tried to lift her head, but it was too heavy, so she lay there for a minute, trying to focus her eyes. The bulb swayed back and forth gently, but there were dark vertical lines obscuring it. *What's happened to me?* she thought, feeling bile crawl up her throat. As her eyes started to focus, she realized the problem wasn't with her vision.

The dark vertical lines were bars.

She reached out one arm to touch them, unsure whether she was dreaming. This felt more like a nightmare than reality. Her arm unfurled slowly, as if she were underwater. But when her fingertips brushed against cold metal, it jolted her.

Even though her head throbbed like someone was hitting it with a mallet, she forced herself to sit up. The dirt floor was cold under her legs. She remembered that she had been running in Central Park. That was the last clear memory she had. She'd gotten home from work on Friday, changed into leggings and a T-shirt and a light jacket, and went for a run. It was part of her routine. That was what she always did on Friday evenings. What she struggled with was what had happened in the park. She knew it was bad, even if she couldn't figure it out. She squeezed her eyes shut and put every ounce of mental energy she had toward remembering. She'd followed her usual route. It had been a quiet night. At some point, everything went blank. If someone had attacked her, she'd blocked it out.

Moving slowly, she rose to her feet. The bars were freezing to the touch.

"Hello?" she called out, her voice cracking. Her throat was so dry. There was no answer.

She took in as much as she could of her surroundings. The ceiling wasn't high, and it was unfinished, with wood beams visible. If the dirt floor hadn't been enough of a hint, the rough ceiling told her she was in a cellar. *In a cage in a cellar*, she thought. *Behind bars in a basement*. Her body was stiff. Her leggings were torn at the knees. Her T-shirt was black, so she couldn't see any blood on it, but she could smell it. Her hands looked red and pulpy in the low light. She couldn't see the cuts, but she could feel them. Her arms were covered in dark bruises. When she touched her scalp, she moved her fingers gingerly until she found the bump. *Concussion*, she thought immediately. You didn't get a lump like that on your head without damage. Her medical specialty wasn't the brain, but she knew hers was in bad shape. Her area of expertise was the spine, and as she fought to stand straight, hers cracked and popped. Not a good sign.

Breathe deeply, she reminded herself. It was the same thing she would've said to a patient, and she wanted to kick herself, because it wasn't that helpful. There wasn't much to see in the room, besides the faint bulb and a set of wooden steps that only led into the darkness. Emily turned her attention to what was behind the bars with her. Her jacket was gone, but there was a mangy blanket near the bars. She picked it up, inhaled the fragrance of wet dog, and wrapped it around herself anyway. There was a plastic sports bottle filled with water. The only other item in her tiny cell was a bucket. She cringed, looking at it.

"Hello?" she repeated, quieter this time.

There was no answer.

She slid to the ground, pulling the blanket around her. She couldn't remember what had happened in the park, but she knew what had happened before she'd gone out. He was so angry. She'd never known him to lose control like that. *If he's capable of this, he'll do anything*, she thought. At that moment, she wondered how long she had left to live.

TUESDAY

CHAPTER 19

ALEX

Alex had only visited Emily's office a couple of times. She was busy, and he respected her work, but there was more to his avoidance than that. As a rule, he steered clear of anything that reminded him of the medical centers he'd encountered in the field. That wasn't to say that a posh hospital on the Upper East Side had much in common with the rough medical encampments he'd seen in Iraq and Syria, places that were located in basements to minimize the effect of mortar shelling, in tents when no buildings could be found, or—in one memorable circumstance—in a cave. By comparison, the hospital complex where Emily worked was a white-walled palace with state-of-the-art equipment. But that didn't make the balance between life and death any less frail. Alex could feel it as he stepped inside the automatic doors.

He navigated the labyrinth within, retracing the steps he'd taken on Friday. He hurried past the receptionist with a cautious wave, just as he had when he'd seen Emily the week before. She gave him an uncertain look, and if she hadn't been on the phone, he was sure she would've told him that Emily wasn't there. That didn't matter; it wasn't Emily he was there to see.

He found Yasmeen Khan's office quickly; it was just up the hall from Emily's, and the door was slightly ajar. No one was inside, so he stepped in and shut the door behind him. Yasmeen's office was a lot like Emily's: there was a metal desk and metal filing cabinets and off-white metal blinds over the windows. The one organic component was an anemic-looking snake plant that bent to one side, as if determined to eavesdrop on the doctor's conversations. The pictures on Yasmeen's desk were of her nieces and nephews. Alex remembered that she had divorced a year ago; he'd never met her husband.

"Alex? What are you doing here?" Yasmeen asked from the doorway. He could smell the cinnamon chai she was carrying from his metal chair in front of her desk.

"Sorry to bother you, but I really need your help," Alex said.

"Is there any word about Emily?" Yasmeen stepped inside and closed the door.

"Nothing yet."

She took a deep breath and walked around the desk, taking a seat in the ergonomic chair behind it. "Something's wrong," she said. "There's no way Emily would just take off like this."

"I know."

"The police asked me about you, you know," Yasmeen said. "They were wondering if Emily ever felt threatened by you."

"I'm not surprised. The police don't like me much. At least, Detective Sterling doesn't."

"I told them no, because Emily never said or did anything that made her seem afraid of you. But I can't help but wonder . . ." Her voice trailed off. She shook her head, and her cascading gold earrings made a soft rattle.

"Please don't think I'd ever hurt her, because I wouldn't," Alex said.

"It's not that." Yasmeen squinted at him, her black eyes piercing. "Why didn't you call the police yourself?"

"Me?"

"You live with Emily. You obviously knew she was gone, maybe as early as Friday night. Why didn't *you* call them?"

Alex studied her face. He had no doubt that her concern for Emily was real. *So much for pride*, he thought. "Emily broke up with me."

"What are you talking about?"

"When I came home on Friday night, I found a note from her," Alex said. "She said she was going away for a few days, and she didn't want me to contact her. She said she'd be back to pack her stuff."

Yasmeen frowned. "She never said anything about leaving you."

"The note was on the coffee table, along with Emily's engagement ring."

"I don't believe it." Yasmeen shook her head. "She was upset after you came in. But not . . ." Her voice trailed off for a moment, as if she were replaying the scene in her head. "She wouldn't tell me what had happened, but she made it clear she was upset with herself, not you."

"Did she talk about leaving?"

"Sure, but not like this. She said she thought it was time for her to go back into the field. I told her it might be too soon. On a practical level, the hospital is good about allowing doctors to take time for work like that, but when you come back, they expect you to be here awhile." Yasmeen gave him a long look. "I don't think she's stopped feeling guilty about cutting her last tour short."

"Because of me."

"After she came home last November, she never went back because she thought you were going to kill yourself with drugs," Yasmeen said.

"She was right," Alex answered. "I came close enough."

"I know she loves you, and she wanted to save you. Save you from yourself, as she put it. But since she's come home, she's . . . I don't know exactly how to put it into words, but Emily's different. Burdened."

Maybe that was from the stress of living with him, Alex thought. *Living with a recovering addict who can't sleep and hallucinates about dead people will do that to you.* "Because of me." It wasn't a question, the way he said it. Just a statement of fact.

"No, Alex. I'm not blaming you," Yasmeen said. "Emily's the toughest person I know. Also the most determined. She made the choice to come home early. You didn't force her to do a thing. Anyway, this isn't about blame, it's about . . . Emily. Haven't you felt that she's been different lately?"

"She's been stressed, but I thought that was my fault," Alex said. "She wakes up when I have nightmares. My problems have become her problems." He knew Emily loved him, but sometimes he wondered why. He cleared his throat. "Is there any chance she just re-upped and is already off in a war zone with some group?" Even as he voiced the words, he saw what a stupid idea that was; Emily would've told him flat out. Her secrecy was what made this situation so strange.

Yasmeen shook her head, and her earrings chimed again. "You don't just show up on a whim."

"Not like being a photographer, where any idiot can walk into a war zone. Okay, can you think of anywhere she would go?"

"The police asked me the same thing," Yasmeen said. "I can't think of a single place. I know she wouldn't just leave her patients in the lurch either. Something's happened to her."

"Emily doesn't let anything just happen to her."

"That's true." Yasmeen smiled. "It's what makes her such an incredible battlefield surgeon. She's completely prepared and has a course of action, but she can change in a heartbeat if she needs to. And she'll have steady hands all the while."

Alex ran one hand through his hair. "That's what makes me feel crazy asking this question, but . . . there's no way Emily has a drug problem, right?"

Yasmeen's face registered shock. "Emily? No." Her earrings clattered as she shook her head. "Definitely not."

"Look, I know you're Emily's friend. I know you're loyal to her. But something's been bothering me."

"What are you talking about?"

"I've been questioning my judgment," Alex said. "You know I came to see Emily here last Friday."

Yasmeen nodded.

"The reason I came into the office last week was because I found a batch of prescriptions Emily had written."

Yasmeen frowned. "New York State doesn't allow written prescriptions anymore. Everything has to be submitted electronically. Maybe she was making notes on old prescription pads?"

"No." The word came out louder than he intended. He lowered his voice to a whisper. "They were scripts for fentanyl and tramadol and a bunch of other drugs."

"Fentanyl?" Yasmeen looked incredulous. "No. She wouldn't do that. Tramadol and some sedatives, maybe . . ."

"You know something, don't you?"

"Emily isn't using drugs. There's no way."

"Tell me. What happened?"

"I don't want to make a big deal out of this," Yasmeen said slowly. "A few months ago, we got a call from a pharmacy in Yonkers about a prescription. There've been a few calls like that. Nothing problematic. Just . . . we don't have much call for certain drugs here. Certainly not methadone."

"Methadone?" That caught Alex by surprise. He couldn't remember seeing a script for that. "Did you ask Emily about it?"

"I did. She told me she was helping out a clinic. Which made a certain amount of sense, but . . ."

"But what?"

"She wouldn't tell me anything about this clinic, so I dropped it. But then I did a search. You know the pharmacies all scan prescriptions they fill, right? It's all on record for two years. Anyway . . ." She gulped.

"There were quite a few prescriptions. Nothing dramatic, some Vicodin and Seconal. Methadone too. All to different people in different places. And if it was all connected to a clinic . . . well, why are some of the prescriptions being filled upstate and in Connecticut and New Jersey? It doesn't track."

"What did you do?"

"I talked to Emily about it, mostly because I thought a con artist had hacked our system and was forging prescriptions in her name. But she didn't deny it." Yasmeen sank back in her chair. "She told me not to worry, that it wouldn't happen again. And it didn't. I know, because I've checked. But it all bothers me. Emily must've had a good reason. It's not like she was working for an online pharmacy, supplying drug addicts with easy prescriptions."

"She wouldn't do that," Alex affirmed.

"Definitely not," Yasmeen agreed. But that didn't make Alex feel any better. Something had happened to Emily. Maybe the stress she was under had nothing to do with him, but that idea only made him more afraid. Emily had vanished, and he had no idea where to find her.

CHAPTER 20

SHERYN

Sheryn arrived at work early as usual on Tuesday. She gave Rafael's empty chair the hairy eyeball and went about her business. It wasn't like she didn't have plenty to do. Emily Teare's financial records were far less interesting than her phone ones; there just wasn't much to go on. Dr. Teare wasn't extravagant; she lived well within her means. Her student debt was paid off, and she had no credit card debt. Boring and responsible was a good way to live, Sheryn figured, but it was a lousy way to lay out bread crumbs for the cops who might be following your trail. The one useful thing was that the good doctor liked to use her credit cards for everything: drugstores, groceries, even lunch. From that, Sheryn deduced that she really liked salads. She'd bought one on Friday, and that had been the last time she'd used the card.

Dr. Teare's bank account was a little more revealing. Sheryn tracked back a year, looking at the pattern of deposits and debits. The doctor's paycheck was deposited automatically. She paid her credit balances out of the same account. She normally withdrew a hundred dollars at a time, pocket money for whatever she couldn't pay for with a credit card, Sheryn figured. Six months earlier, there had been a withdrawal for a thousand dollars. That had happened again a month later, and again three weeks after that. Some fifteen thousand dollars had vanished from the account in a short space of time.

Sheryn made a note. It proved nothing, but it was suggestive. No one had hinted that the doctor had a drug problem, but that was one possibility. Another was that she'd been squirreling away money, maybe to leave her boyfriend. Sheryn wasn't buying that, since the account was only in the doctor's name. Something tugged at her memory, and she returned to the credit card files. That was it, she realized. Dr. Teare made regular, large contributions to certain aid groups. She hadn't done that in the past four months. Her money had been going elsewhere.

But where?

Sheryn wanted to kick this around with her partner, but Rafael was nowhere to be found. At nine, she shot him a curt text. She didn't hear from him for almost half an hour, when he finally called her.

"Guess what I found?" Rafael's voice was triumphant.

"I hope for your sake it's a time machine, because your sorry ass is late yet again."

"You're going to have to be nice if you want me to tell you where Emily Teare's car is."

"Her car?" Sheryn was nonplussed. "What are you talking about? She doesn't have a car. We ran her name through the system."

"Her name, sure. Not her brother's." Rafael's voice was laconic. He was obviously pleased with himself.

"Her brother lives in San Francisco."

"And his ex-wife lived in New York until she moved to Singapore," Rafael said. "She sold the car to her ex. He uses it when he comes to town."

"And he lets Emily borrow it." Sheryn chewed on that. "Good work, partner."

"Shucks. I do it all for the head pats. Prepare to be even more impressed: I found the car this morning."

"The suspense is killing me," Sheryn said drily.

"It's parked near Woodlawn Cemetery in the Bronx."

Sheryn inhaled sharply. "You find anything inside?"

"We haven't opened it up yet. Thought maybe I should wait for you, even though you're making me late."

"Hilarious," Sheryn said. "You've been waiting to say that to me since you transferred here."

"Guilty as charged. Meet me in the Bronx at East Two Hundred and Thirty-Ninth Street and Martha Avenue?"

It took Sheryn a solid forty minutes to drive to the far northeast side of Woodlawn Cemetery. When she thought of the Bronx, she pictured the crumbling buildings of the South Bronx. The northern part of the borough was nothing like that. Woodlawn Heights, in particular, was a beauty, filled with large houses that ran the gamut from romantic Victorian to redbrick federalist. The lawns were well kept, and the blocks were leafy. Sure, it was in the shadow of a cemetery, but even that was a scenic spot.

Rafael was leaning on a black Mercedes. He waved to her when she got out. "I figured you for a faster driver than that, Detective."

"You're a bundle of laughs today," Sheryn said. "Is this where Dr. Teare usually parks the car?"

"Nope. It's paid for by the month at a lot near a train station out here. Her brother has no idea why it would be left here."

"Too bad," Sheryn said. "I was hoping we'd catch the driver crossing a bridge or tunnel. If the car's normally out in the Bronx, we don't have that."

"Sorry it didn't come wrapped in a big bow," Rafael said. "Let's start with what we've got."

The uniform popped the driver's side door open for them. Sheryn got in and sat in the driver's seat, reaching over to unlock the passenger door for her partner. He got in. The two of them sat quietly, not moving for a minute, as if they were bound for a road trip but couldn't figure out where the hell they were going.

"So, is it just me, or is this the cleanest car you've ever seen?" Sheryn asked. "Aside from those handprints on the window, I mean?"

They both stared at the driver's window. There were two human paw prints, as if someone had braced themselves against the car.

"It's been around the block a few times, but it's in good shape." Rafael looked around. "Someone keyed it on the passenger side. Wonder when that happened?"

"No, I mean . . ." Sheryn paused for a second. "Everything about Emily Teare is so organized, isn't it? It's like her color-coded closet. Everything's in its own box. Nothing out of place."

Rafael opened the compartment in front of him. "Let's see, registration, map book . . . everything that should be there is there. Nothing more." He flipped through the map book. "Looks like she went up to High Falls on a regular basis."

"That's, what, ninety minutes north of here?" Sheryn asked. "I don't think she went there this time."

"Something to check out, though."

There was nothing at all in the back seat when they looked. Sheryn pulled up the floor mats, but there was nothing hiding underneath.

"Well, it was worth a shot," Rafael said. "Let's check the trunk."

Sheryn popped it open. As she walked around the car, the breeze caught her face. There was a hint of something metallic in it, and it made the back of her throat burn. Rafael stood in front of the open trunk, frozen. When Sheryn looked in, she understood why. There were bloodstains on the gray carpet inside.

CHAPTER 21

ALEX

"I guess the police already went through Emily's office?" Alex asked.

Yasmeen shook her head. "Detective Sterling wanted to, but our administrator told her no. She said the police would have to come back with a warrant."

"You've got to be kidding. I can't believe Sterling was shot down. She couldn't have taken that well."

"She didn't have a choice," Yasmeen said. "You've never met our administrator. The only thing she's afraid of is running afoul of HIPAA regulations."

"I don't know what that means."

"Patient confidentiality," Yasmeen explained. "Searching Emily's office means seeing her files. But the police haven't come back yet."

"Let's have a look."

"Number one, our administrator would kneecap you. Number two, I don't have a key for Emily's office," Yasmeen told him apologetically.

"I've already been shot by people who wanted to keep me out of their territory," Alex said. "I don't care if your administrator is a fire-breathing dragon. And I have yet to meet a lock I couldn't crack."

"I thought you were a photographer. Emily never told me you were secretly a cat burglar."

"Believe it or not, those skills go hand in hand," Alex said. "I got my start in photography going into places I wasn't supposed to be. Let's go."

They headed into the hallway; Emily's office was next to Yasmeen's. In ten seconds flat, Alex unlocked the door with a paper clip.

For all his bravado, he wasn't eager to step inside Emily's office. From the doorway, looking in, it was immaculate, as anyone who knew Emily would expect it to be. Her diplomas from Stanford and Cornell hung on the wall behind her desk, along with photographs taken during trips abroad for Doctors Without Borders. There wasn't a lot of personality on show otherwise. The furniture was metallic standard-issue stuff. Emily's blinds were closed. There was a twin of the snake plant in Yasmeen's office, but this one was smaller and spindlier; it looked shy and reclusive.

Breaking into the office was only the first step, Alex knew. If there was anything important, it wouldn't be lying out in plain view. Emily's computer was password protected, and her desk was locked.

"I sometimes tease Emily about keeping everything under lock and key," Yasmeen said. "She doesn't do that at home, does she?"

"Not exactly. But she does like her privacy." It occurred to Alex suddenly how odd it was that Emily had left that pile of prescriptions on her dresser. It was almost as if she had *wanted* him to see them. "I'm not a hacker, so the odds of my breaking into her computer are nil. But the desk drawers . . ." Alex held up the paper clip. "They won't take long."

He wasn't exaggerating. In less than a minute, all four drawers were unlocked.

"You're really good," Yasmeen said. "Also, really bad."

Alex smiled at that. "Let's see what we have here."

It wasn't much. There was Emily's Day-Timer, filled with appointments and running times. Unless it was written in code, it offered nothing useful. Alex didn't hit pay dirt until he dug into the large drawer at the bottom right. It was filled with manila folders, most of which contained patient files. He couldn't explain what he was looking for exactly, only that there had to be something that didn't fit. It was like he told the students in his workshop: it's not your job to see what everyone else sees; your work is showing them what they don't want to see.

Nothing seemed suspect until he hit an unlabeled folder containing a series of plain white envelopes. Emily's name and home address were computer printed in black ink. Each had a typed note inside.

"What do we have here?" Alex asked as he opened the first one. He froze as he read it.

The words hit him hard: Alex Traynor is a murderer. You need to get yourself away from him.

Alex stared at it for a few seconds, then passed it to Yasmeen. "Have you ever seen this before?"

She stared at it and exhaled a shuddering breath. "No."

"Wait, there's more," Alex told her. He pulled out a second typed note: Alex Traynor murdered Cori Stanton. He will kill you next.

He passed that one to Yasmeen as well.

"This is crazy," Yasmeen said.

The third one Alex picked up said, Alex Traynor got away with murder. He is a sociopath who will kill again.

The fourth, Alex Traynor has killed before. He is sick and he will murder again.

And a fifth: Alex Traynor is a monster. If you value your safety and your life you will leave him now.

There were six notes in total. The last one read: Alex Traynor destroys women. Save yourself before he makes you disappear.

Alex felt nauseous and dizzy. For a moment, it felt as if he were locked in a tight space again with no air and no light; the walls were closing in on him. Why had Emily never told him about these letters? From the look of it, she'd been receiving them for months. They'd arrived at their home address, but she'd hidden them away in her office. He cleared his throat. "You're sure Emily never mentioned getting any letters?"

"Positive." Yasmeen picked up the envelopes and paged through them. "These have stamps on them, but they haven't been canceled. There are no post office markings on the outside of the envelopes."

Anger was starting to crystallize in Alex's veins.

"This is absolutely insane," Yasmeen said. "Who would send this garbage to Emily?"

"That's not a mystery at all," Alex said. "I know exactly who wrote these notes."

CHAPTER 22

SHERYN

"That's a lot of blood," Sheryn said.

"Head wound?" Rafael speculated. "That would be a heavy bleed."

"It doesn't look right," Sheryn said. "You stuff a human body in a trunk, and there's not much wriggle room. There sure as hell is no room to flip over and have your head land where your feet were."

"True, that. Maybe she was bleeding from several wounds." Rafael shook his head. "If this is actually her blood, I don't know what the odds are that we find her alive."

Sheryn shoved that thought aside while she called in the CSU. "They're on their way," she told Rafael.

"A couple more uniforms are heading over too," he answered, hanging up his own phone. "We're gonna need a lot of warm bodies for the canvass."

"You want me to block off the area?" the uniformed cop who'd let them into the car asked. He looked fresh out of the academy, with brush-cut hair, bright-green eyes, and reddish-brown skin that was covered in freckles.

"Roll out the crime scene tape," Sheryn said. "We're going to need it."

As she was speaking, the front door of one Victorian house opened, and an elderly woman called out, "Excuse me!" She had short, frizzy gray hair, and her petite body was swallowed up by a magenta kimono. She peered at them through thick bifocals, which made her brown eyes seem enormous. "Did 311 send you?" the woman asked. "This is the first time they ever listened to me."

"No, ma'am. We haven't been in touch with the 311 folks," Sheryn answered. The 311 line had been installed in New York years earlier to allow residents to complain about everything in the city that *wasn't* actually a crime. Like most cops, Sheryn joked about it as a mental health hotline.

"But you're here about that car, aren't you?" The woman crept forward. She was hunched over, and her arms were crossed in front of her chest as if she thought someone was leering at her.

"Did you call about the car?" Sheryn asked.

"I did. It's extremely aggravating. My son couldn't park in front of my house when he visited Sunday. That stupid car was there."

"How long has it been here?" Rafael asked. "Did you see who parked it?"

"I watch everything on this street," the woman said. "And I wake up early. Five thirty, it was parked there. Some entitled bitch thinks she can park in my spot . . ."

"You saw the driver?" Sheryn nudged her.

"Yeah, sure," the woman answered.

"Can you describe her?"

"She was tall."

"Okay, what else?" Rafael prompted.

The woman thought about that. "She was wearing a coat. It's hard to say how big she was."

"What color was her hair?"

That brought on a deep squint. "I'm pretty sure she was wearing a hat."

"What about her clothing?"

"Black. She was all in black." The woman sounded jubilant, as if she'd presented a key piece of evidence.

"Could this be her?" Sheryn held up her phone. There was a picture of Emily Teare on the screen.

"Maybe," the woman answered. "I never saw her face. I only got a look at her from the back."

"Are you *sure* it was a woman?" Rafael asked.

"Of course I'm sure!" The elderly woman looked outraged.

"Because the way you described her, it's hard to know," Rafael said. "This person was tall and wearing black. Those seem to be the only details."

"Young man, it was *definitely* a woman." She drew herself up to her full, though still diminutive, height, like an aggressive meerkat. "She was wearing earrings. They were so big I saw them in the lamplight. *And* she had a purse."

"This is all helpful, ma'am," Sheryn said, glaring at Rafael. "Because you never know what detail might help. What's your name?"

"Orla West."

"Okay, Ms. West, what I want you to think about is what made you get up and look out your window," Sheryn said.

"I heard a car door close," the woman answered. "It wasn't loud, but I don't sleep well. I was lying awake, and I heard it. It was five thirty because I looked at my clock."

"And that made you get up?"

"No. A minute later, there was a big slam, like a jerk flung a car door closed. That was when I got up and looked outside."

"So, was there more than one person on the street?"

"No, just that woman. She was alone."

"But you heard two doors close, one quiet and one loud, correct?"

Orla West nodded. "I did. But the street was empty except for her."

"Was it you who keyed the side of the car?" Rafael asked.

The woman's mouth opened and shut quickly. "I need to get back inside. Excuse me." She hurried through her door and slammed it behind her.

Rafael whistled. "I guess we solved one mystery."

"What the hell did you do that for?" Sheryn demanded. "We need her to make a statement. You better not scare her off."

"Her statement isn't going to be worth much. She saw a tall person in black on the street."

"Emily Teare is what, five nine or five ten? We can't rule out the possibility she drove the car over here."

"Orla West is all of four foot ten," Rafael answered. "She probably thinks a tall person is five four."

Sheryn sighed. "Let's look at this rationally. A woman who may or may not have been Emily Teare dumped the car here in the middle of the night."

"Looks like it."

"But how does that make sense?" she asked. "If she dropped it off and walked away, where did all the blood come from?"

"Maybe she came back, and someone attacked her . . ." Rafael's voice trailed off. "Nah, that doesn't work. How could her blood be all over the rug in her apartment and all over the trunk?"

"Especially if there's a chance she walked away from the car. That doesn't add up." Sheryn considered the problem. "Maybe she was attacked in her apartment, rolled up in the rug, then put in the trunk. Only, how did she escape like Houdini?"

"Maybe we're looking at this the wrong way," Rafael said. "Maybe she left Traynor, and then she was attacked. He could've followed her."

"You think he brought her back to the apartment and got blood on the carpet?" Sheryn asked. "Say what you will about a fifth-story walk-up, but it definitely inhibits people from carrying a bleeding body home. All those stairs . . ."

"How do you make sense of it, then?"

"We don't know this is Dr. Teare's blood. We don't even know if it's human blood."

They both stared into the angry red void of the trunk.

"It's a *lot* of blood," Rafael said. "If that came out of one person, she didn't break out and walk away from the car. She would've been carried off in a stretcher, weak as a kitten."

"There was a woman in Alex Traynor's apartment on Sunday night. She was dressed in black, according to his neighbor."

"You think she's Alex Traynor's accomplice?"

"I'm just thinking out loud," Sheryn said. "Let's say Emily Teare was attacked at home. That's how her blood ended up on the carpet there. And then Alex Traynor put her in the trunk of this car . . ." She was quiet for a moment. "Only, if that's true, this vehicle would be on traffic cams on a bridge or tunnel. We'll have to check that."

"You think Orla West spotted Traynor on her street?"

Sheryn shook her head. "The way he's built? I bet no one ever mistook him for a woman."

"Then he's got an accomplice. *Cherchez la femme.*"

They were at an impasse. All that was clear was that the trunk had just complicated the case.

"We need a fresh angle," Sheryn said.

"Okay, let's go back to basics," Rafael said. "Why is the car parked here?"

"The only prominent landmark nearby is the cemetery."

"You told me Emily's parents died in a car crash. Are they buried in Woodlawn?"

"No. That accident happened in San Francisco. They were cremated on the other side of the country." Sheryn turned around slowly. "You know who *is* buried in Woodlawn? Cori Stanton."

"You think that's the connection?" Rafael asked. "It doesn't make a lot of sense."

"It doesn't. But you know how I feel about coincidences." She beckoned at Rafael. "Let's go for a walk."

"You're not dragging me into the cemetery, are you?"

"Aw, don't be scared now. Let's play this out." She headed toward Woodlawn, and Rafael followed reluctantly. "Okay, just for the sake of argument, let's say that Emily Teare came up to the Bronx to get her car. Why would she park it here?"

"Maybe she was seeing someone she knew in the neighborhood," Rafael suggested.

"But why would she go to the trouble of getting the car if that's all she was doing? It doesn't track." Sheryn shook her head. "It doesn't smell right."

"Well, another possibility is that Alex Traynor beat her to a pulp and stuffed her in the trunk. Maybe he was driving around looking for a place to dump her body."

"Yeah, right. What did he do, bring her bloody body on the train to the Bronx with him?" Sheryn asked. "No."

"Then enlighten me. What's your theory?"

There was a dim memory floating in the back of Sheryn's head. Alex Traynor had grown up in the north Bronx. There was another connection she couldn't quite make. She needed to look over her notes from the Stanton case again.

"It's possible that they came up here together," Sheryn said slowly. "Maybe they wanted to see a grave. Maybe it was to see a friend. What if something went wrong?"

"A lot of maybes in there," Rafael grumbled.

"Well, how about this: maybe Dr. Teare came up to get the car, and someone attacked her? Wouldn't be the first time someone was harmed over a nice car."

"That theory lets Traynor off the hook," Rafael said. "Don't you think he's good for this?"

"You know I want to lock him up. But I'm not going to lie. This feels off."

"Off, how?"

"Why is there so much blood in the trunk?"

Rafael shrugged. "I'm leaving that to the experts. I just want to get the guy." They were at the cemetery's entrance now, and he gave an exaggerated shudder. "We really have to go in here?"

"Don't tell me you're afraid of a graveyard."

"Afraid, no. Creeped out by, yes. It's not the same thing."

Sheryn's phone rang. "Hey," she said to the sergeant on the desk. "What's up?"

"Sterling, you got some kind of standing order for news on Alex Traynor, right?"

"Right."

"Then you'll want to know about this," the sergeant said. "He was just arrested downtown."

"What the hell happened?"

"I don't have details, just the name," he said. "But I heard the scene is a real mess."

CHAPTER 23

ALEX

There was a tightness in Alex's chest when he got out of the cab at Sara Roosevelt Park on the Lower East Side. There were too many people around, day or night, in this part of New York. One of the symptoms he'd struggled with after his kidnapping in Syria was an aversion to crowds. It made no sense, logically; most of his time in captivity had been in solitary, in a tiny cell with a ceiling so low he couldn't even stand up. But the feeling that his heart was being squeezed in a vise had nothing to do with his PTSD. It was all about the letters.

Alex Traynor murdered Cori Stanton. He will kill you next.

He tried to take some shallow breaths while his eyes swam, but it was hard for him to breathe. *It's a panic attack*, he told himself. *That's all it is.* But knowing that fact and somehow separating himself from the tentacles of fear and dread were different things. It took some time to pull himself together.

He headed for Stanton Street and followed it east, flinching each time he spotted a street sign. *Stanton, like the street downtown*, Cori had liked to say. *That's my street.* He knew that he was on a bad path, and he still had time to turn away from it. But he couldn't. He moved forward, mentally steeling himself.

He wished he could forget these little moments that popped into his head at the worst possible times. He couldn't think about Cori just then; he'd had ugly confrontations with her father after she'd died, and he knew he would never change that man's bile and hatred. That was how the drugs used to help him, albeit temporarily; they could lift Alex out of the skin he was trapped in and transport him into a fresh body, one with eyes that hadn't looked upon so many of the dead. They erased all of the things he didn't want to remember.

He passed a storefront clinic and caught sight of a tall blonde woman who reminded him of Emily. *You need to do this for her*, he reminded himself. Focusing on Emily calmed him. The first time he'd seen her was in a makeshift operating room. He was the patient, and he had wanted to shout and curse thanks to the pain he was in. He'd had to crawl to the clinic, leaving a trail of blood behind him like a snail dripped slime. He'd been convinced he was going to die, but that had changed the moment he'd seen Emily. It wasn't that she was beautiful, though she was; even with purple crescents under her eyes from a lack of sleep and a sheen of sweat clinging to her in the heat, she was stunning. But what got to him was her preternatural calm. There wasn't an ounce of doubt in her. *You're going to be fine*, she'd told him.

When she'd said it, he'd believed her. After the surgery, when he'd woken up on a cot with crying children nearby, he'd wondered if he'd dreamed her up, like an angel of mercy who'd appeared out of nowhere and vanished again. When she had come through to check on him, he had wanted to tell her that. Instead, he'd asked about the silver medallion hanging around her neck.

Behold Saint Christopher, and go on in safety, she'd told him. *It was my mother's.*

Alex snapped out of the reverie suddenly as he found himself standing in front of the Stanton Veterinary Clinic. It was housed on the ground floor of an old redbrick tenement building. The *S* in the sign was designed to resemble a snake, shiny black with red bands and amber eyes, a hint that the clinic specialized in exotic animals. But all Alex saw at that moment was a warning, a blinking red beacon screaming at him not to go inside.

"Abandon all hope, ye who enter," he murmured. Of course, he pulled the door open and walked right in.

The pale-blue walls hadn't changed since the last time he'd visited the clinic. At one point, he'd spent a lot of time there. The first dog he'd owned, Lupo, had been a rescue from Syria; he'd emigrated with a host of health problems that Kevin Stanton had mostly cured. Then Sid Vicious had come along, with just as many issues. Maclean had found the dog in Iraq, and he'd been the one to import Sid and bring the dog to New Jersey. But after Maclean died a hero's death in Syria, Alex had adopted the pup. While Alex gave Kevin Stanton full credit for the good work he'd done taking care of his dogs, he could only think of him with a cold fury.

Alex hadn't brought Sid back to the clinic since a couple of months before Cori died. But he had seen Kevin.

The last time was at Cori's funeral, when Alex had been standing at the edge of the gravesite, unsure of whether he should be there. Emily had insisted that they go, but when they'd arrived at Woodlawn Cemetery, her determination had given way, and she'd retreated into silence. Still, she'd had no difficulty slipping into a chapel pew and sitting quietly during the service, her head bowed as if it were too heavy to lift. Alex had been too shaky to sit still. He'd sat down and got up again. Then he'd made a jittery circuit around the chapel. Finally, he'd stepped outside for air, and Kevin Stanton had clocked him. Alex had ended up lying in the gravel, his one good suit torn and covered in grit, and he'd held his hands up, deflecting Kevin Stanton's frenzied punches. It had gone on and on, until Alex couldn't take it anymore and fought back. He hadn't meant to. On some level, he'd felt like he deserved what he got, because Cori had died and that was his fault. He also knew Cori had had her own demons, and her father had been largely responsible for those.

But that didn't mean he'd tolerate any harassment of Emily.

Alex didn't recognize the receptionist at the front desk. She was in her forties, with the pointy cheekbones of a runway model and cat-like blue eyes. She was dressed casually, in jeans and a green shirt, but with an elaborate silver necklace cascading from her throat down to her breastbone. Her shoulder-length blonde hair had streaks of silver woven in; it never failed to impress him how age only made some women more beautiful.

"Are you picking someone up?" she asked brightly as he approached her. Everything in the office was so cheerful, from the bright primary colors of the room to the perky staff. It only made Alex feel darker, as if the color had been drained out of him long ago. But the wattage of her smile dimmed as she regarded him closely. "Have you been here before?" she added uncertainly. "You look familiar."

"I'm here to talk to Kevin Stanton," he said. "My name is Alex Traynor."

The reaction in her face suggested that he'd announced he had bubonic plague and was there to infect the office. "Alex Traynor . . ."

"Kevin won't want to see me, but I need to see him," Alex said. He could feel the eyes of the people in the waiting area checking him out.

"I've heard all about you," the receptionist said. "You have some nerve, showing your face here, after what you did to his daughter. You should go before I call the police."

"You can call them," Alex said, striding to the red inner door. "I have some letters your boss wrote that the police should see."

When he went through the red door, Kevin Stanton was standing at the end of the hallway. He was a big bear of a man, tall and broad shouldered, though he'd lost weight since Alex had seen him last. He stared at Alex in astonishment. "What the hell . . ."

"We need to talk," Alex said.

"I have nothing to say to you. Get out of my sight."

"Not before you tell me what you were doing, writing letters to Emily." Alex strode down the hallway, passing glass cabinets filled with butterflies and lizards and other small animals.

Kevin crossed his arms. Up close, he looked old and tired. There were dark bags puffed out under his eyes, and the deep blue of his irises had somehow faded. "Letters? What letters?"

Alex held up the bundle of white envelopes he'd found locked in Emily's office. "You're denying that you wrote these to her?" He pulled one out. "'Alex Traynor got away with murder. He is a sociopath who will kill again.' That's literally a quote you gave the police. You wrote that to other people."

"Let me see that," Kevin growled, grabbing the letter out of Alex's hand, tearing the page so that the bottom flapped loose. He scanned it in a heartbeat. "It *does* sound like me. You've got a collection like this?"

"Six of them."

"Were any of them signed?"

"No," Alex admitted.

"I think you know by now I'll tell anyone and everyone exactly what I think of you. It's not a secret I'm keeping. You're the monster who murdered my daughter."

"I didn't murder Cori," Alex said. "I would never have hurt her."

"The fact you were drugged out of your mind when you killed her doesn't absolve you of responsibility," Kevin said. "You chose to get high. You gave her drugs."

"There's a lot I can't remember, but here's one thing I know for sure," Alex said. "*You're* the one who hurt Cori."

Kevin lunged at him, knocking him back and into a display cabinet mounted on the wall. The glass shattered, and Alex felt a million tiny shards digging into him. He'd been cut by flying glass so many times overseas. Windows blew out of buildings as bombs rained down on them and bullets raged through them. He'd always kept his head in a war zone. But in that hallway, he heard the echo of a thousand windows shattering, and it shook him to his core.

"Liar!" Kevin was shouting at him, his voice hoarse. He kicked Alex, then stomped his foot, holding him in place against the wall while he punched him. "Get out of here!" he shouted, hitting Alex again and again.

Alex grabbed the man by the shoulders and shoved him back against the wall, hard.

"I called the police, Kevin," the receptionist shouted from the far end of the hallway. "They'll be here soon."

Kevin backed away then. "How dare you come in here and attack me," he hissed.

"I didn't touch you," Alex said. "You went after me."

"More of your bullshit."

"Why were you harassing Emily?" Alex demanded.

"I did no such thing."

"You also denied writing to editors who hired me. But I know that was you."

Alex could feel the heat coming off Kevin's skin, see the fury in his eyes. The question was why he'd suddenly stopped pounding him. When he turned his head, the mystery cleared: there was a teenage girl next to the receptionist, holding up her phone and clearly recording everything.

Alex stooped to pick up the letters. There was glass everywhere, but no sign of the white envelopes. "Where are the letters?"

"The sight of you makes me sick." Kevin's voice was just a harsh rasp now. "You destroyed Cori. You're the reason she's dead."

His words didn't shock Alex—he'd heard all this before—but they made his heart pound in anger. If there was anyone to blame for Cori's bottomless sadness, it was her own father.

"Cori was my friend," Alex said. "She told me what you did to her."

That was when Kevin Stanton lost control. His fist shot out and struck Alex on the side of his temple, a hard blow that whipped Alex's head to the side. Alex reeled, but he didn't go down, and he threw a punch that connected with Kevin's jaw.

"Kevin!" the receptionist called. "Don't! You're being recorded."

The big man didn't seem to care, but he staggered back and slumped against the wall. Alex was ready to bring him down, but when Kevin didn't punch back, he dropped his fists. As he headed down the hallway, his shoes crunched on shattered glass. The receptionist stepped back to allow him by, but her face was a mask of pure hatred. Alex opened the front door just as the cops pulled up outside.

CHAPTER 24

EMILY

There were only a few things Emily was sure of, semiconscious in the low light of her prison. She was certain that she was in an unfinished basement or a cellar. There were no windows, no source of natural light. Just that dim bulb on a wire that swayed gently, as if it were enjoying the breeze.

She was positive that she wasn't in the city anymore. There was no noise from traffic; the absence of honking horns was deafening. She'd always lived in cities, and she'd worked in places where air raid sirens and mortar fire counted as background noise. The flat monotony of the silence baffled her. Occasionally there were footsteps overhead, but otherwise, all was quiet. She strained her ears to pick up any sound, keeping so silent that she could hear the little click her eyelids made when she blinked. The one time she heard a car, she realized it must've belonged to her captor, because there was no other traffic. The purr of the engine vanished into the distance, and everything went back to being still.

Once, she thought she heard a dog bark. She wasn't sure whether her ears were playing nervous tricks on her. She'd thought it was Sid for a moment as she came out of the trancelike slumber that devoured so many hours in that cell. But it wasn't her dog; for all Emily could tell, it was just part of a dream. She was having nightmares again, just as she'd had for years after her parents were killed. Only somehow, in the time since, her visions had shifted. In college, just after the accident, Emily would dream about her parents as they died, their car in a head-on collision with a drunk driver who'd swerved onto their side of the road. Now, in her subterranean trap, it had shifted so that Emily dreamed that she was on the road itself, just before the accident. She couldn't see her parents, but she recognized their car. And the other one, madly careening over the road, was clearly the drunk driver. Emily was filled with a desperate desire to stop the crash, but she had no idea how. Over and over, the drunk driver plowed through her and into her parents. There was no way to save them.

She woke up sobbing when it happened. The nightmare disoriented her, filled her with a queasy sense of injustice that she couldn't quell. Even before she remembered that she was in confinement, she would remember that the drunk driver had survived the crash. That would make her ball her hands into fists, digging her nails into her palms. The injustice of that almost drove her mad. It took her time to come back to herself. She wasn't the type to cry, but she would feel tears in her eyes. *This is what Alex lives with*, she reminded herself. *These dreams, these nightmares, they haunt him all the time.*

The thought of Alex left a hollow feeling in her chest, as if her heart had been surgically removed. It hurt to think about him. She remembered how he'd stormed into her office on Friday. He'd never looked at her like that before. His anger was brimming over. *How could you?* he'd demanded.

She'd had no answer for him, except to ask for his trust. Why should he give it to her, she wondered. At this point, she was certain she didn't deserve it.

As she drifted in and out of consciousness, Emily imagined that she was back in Syria. After the abandoned hotel outside Aleppo that she had stayed in was bombed, she'd slept on dirt floors for several nights, the dank smell of the earth oddly comforting. In her reverie, she remembered one of her worst days from that time. There had been a chemical gas attack, and civilians had surged toward them, arms outstretched like zombies. The chemical burns hardened their skin until it was like tree bark. The victims were still moving, but the flesh inside and outside their bodies was slowly petrifying. Emily was dreaming of one little boy in particular, maybe eight years old, who came in alone. He had blinked at her helplessly, and his small, bony shoulders had shuddered with the terrible effort it took to breathe.

"Help me," he had whispered at her in Arabic.

She had stared at him helplessly, fully aware of the truth. That little boy was going to die of suffocation. There was nothing she could do to stop that. She had knelt in front of him and touched his face.

"You'll be all right," Emily had told him. "I'll help you."

She had taken him to a cot and dosed him heavily with opiates. There was no way to stop his death; all she could do was make it painless.

She woke up crying, thinking of that boy, of all the people she'd wanted to help and who'd died anyway. For a minute, she was disoriented, because her first impulse was to get up and back into the makeshift hospital and try her damnedest to help people. It didn't take long for her to remember that she was trapped in a subterranean prison and that she wasn't going to be allowed out of it any time soon.

Stop calling me. I'm telling you it's over.

Emily sat up, shocked by the echo of her own voice inside her head. Everything around her swirled. She had been captured and roughed up and starved, but she knew something else was wrong. She'd been in similarly dire straits in the field, but she'd never felt nauseated every time she lifted her head.

The more Emily thought about it, the more certain she was: she was being poisoned in that little cell.

There was no doubt in her mind that she'd been doped up with tranquilizers. When she forced her brain back into Central Park, picturing her last run, she remembered something hitting her in the back. Not hard, not like a punch. It was more like a swift, expert jab with a needle, but it had unleashed a torrent of heat throughout her body, electrifying every nerve ending. Within seconds, everything had gone dark. Her brain hadn't been right since.

There was no tranquilizer that could keep a person down for days without being readministered on a regular basis. Even knockout sedatives like Propofol didn't last long on one dose; too much at one time left you dead, not dizzy for days. When her eyes started to focus, she saw plastic bottles of water left for her just in front of the bars of her cage.

That's it, she thought. *He's poisoning me through the water.*

She hadn't seen anyone enter or exit, but obviously he was checking on her and leaving her something to drink and the occasional protein bar. She had no sense of time, or whether it was day or night, so it was impossible to detect a routine. Her watch was gone, so there was no way to even guess at how long she'd been there. Emily had the sense that time was passing her by, that she was in a trance most of the day, lost on that cool dirt floor.

She reached a hand out and found a protein bar. The wrapper crinkled as she pulled it apart. She devoured it in seconds, ravenous like the kids she'd seen in refugee camps. It was a kind of hunger hard to imagine in some parts of the world, where food was always close at hand. It was an all-consuming sensation, a companion in every waking moment. It seemed as if it could never be filled up.

"Hey," she called out, but her voice was just a hollow croak.

She took a sip of water, knowing it was poison. She was dying of thirst, so what else could she do?

"Hello," she called out again, her voice stronger.

There was no response. There never was. The only rejoinder was the voice in her own head.

Stop calling me. I'm telling you it's over.

She knew he was angry, but she'd never imagined it would turn out like this. It was eerie, this ongoing silence. No demands, no ultimatums. Just the purgatory of solitary confinement. She put her hand on her chest, expecting to feel the weight of her Saint Christopher medal, like she always did when she was afraid in the field. But it was gone, and she remembered she'd stored it away.

There was a brief flash of red that caught her eye. Was she imagining it? It was like a laser tracker on a sniper's rifle. For a moment, she felt like Alex, trapped by waking nightmares. Only this wasn't a phantom. She stared and stared and stared at the spot where she thought she'd seen it. Finally, there was another little flash of light.

She couldn't see what was behind it, but she knew: there was a camera stationed on the ceiling of her jail. He was watching her every move.

CHAPTER 25

SHERYN

Sheryn had been excited when the desk sergeant told her about Alex Traynor's arrest. That feeling shifted on the drive downtown, as more details had filtered in. She was dreading her conversation with Kevin Stanton.

It was hard for Sheryn to think of Cori Stanton without feeling a squeeze under her breastbone. Murder victims got to her, though she tried not to show it. No matter the age of the victim, one thought always coursed through her brain: *This is somebody's child.* She could never suppress that notion, though she tried to set it aside. Cori Stanton had been thirty years old when she'd plunged to her death. She hadn't been a child, but she was still starting out in life: unmarried, no kids, no real job, no fixed address. For whatever reason, in spite of her well-off father—or maybe *because* of her well-off father—she'd never pulled her life together, and then her chance was over. Sheryn's own children were so full of hope and promise, and the idea that someone might snuff out a life in an instant twisted her guts. It was what fed her craving for justice: no parent should ever lose a child like that.

When Sheryn pulled up in front of the Stanton Veterinary Clinic, her heart lightened for a minute. Standing outside, wearing a burgundy pantsuit, was a fortyish woman with a close-cropped afro. She was talking on the phone, and her head was partially turned away, but Sheryn recognized the detective from the Guardians Association, the fraternal organization that represented the NYPD's black detectives. As often as the NYPD promised change, progress was glacial, but the Guardians never tired of pushing that boulder up a hill.

"Aren't you a sight for sore eyes, Norah Renfrew," Sheryn said as she stepped out of her car.

A broad smile crossed the other detective's face. "Weren't we supposed to make a date to go slumming on Park Avenue?"

Sheryn laughed at the reference to the Ella Fitzgerald song and gave her a quick hug.

"I've got two stories to tell you, and I'll let you guess which one is true," Norah said. "First up: a drugged-out psycho came into the clinic, threatened the receptionist, the patients, even the dogs. Then he beat up the vet who owns the clinic."

"I'm going with what's behind Door Number Two," Sheryn said.

"Good choice," Norah answered. "In that case, a photographer who discovered his girlfriend was being harassed by the vet who owns this clinic came here to confront the man. Things went sideways, and it got physical. We actually have some video."

Norah held up her phone, and Sheryn watched it play out. It was a little shaky, but she could clearly make out Alex Traynor and Kevin Stanton at the end of a hallway. Stanton was punching him and shouting. Traynor grabbed Stanton's shoulders and shoved him back against the opposite wall. That didn't stop Stanton, who came at him again. Then a woman's voice screamed, "I called the police, Kevin. They'll be here soon." Sheryn watched Stanton back off, saying, "How dare you come in here and attack me." Traynor's voice was muffled when he responded, but she heard Stanton clearly. "More of your bullshit."

"You were harassing Emily," Traynor accused him. Stanton denied it. After an exchange that wasn't clear because the phone wobbled to the side, it focused in time for Sheryn to witness Stanton punch a crouching Traynor in the head.

"Ouch," Sheryn said.

"The first cops on the scene made the mistake of arresting Alex Traynor, because the veterinarian and his employee were telling the same story," Norah said. "We're voiding that arrest because it was clearly a mistake."

"Where's Mr. Traynor now?"

"At the precinct with my partner. You want to talk with him?"

"Hell, yes."

"No problem," Norah said. "The question now is, what do we do with this pair of clowns."

"Kevin Stanton has had a rough time in the last year. He lost his only child. I believe Alex Traynor killed her, but I couldn't prove it."

"Murder?"

"Manslaughter."

Norah raised an eyebrow. "I'm going to remain agnostic on that subject. But Kevin Stanton has been a problem around here. He had a dispute last year with a nightclub on the same block. Suddenly, that club had glue poured into its locks and dead animals on its doorstep. We know it was him, but knowing it and making a case out of it are two different things."

"There's a lot of that going around."

"It's not the first dispute he's had with a neighbor," Norah added. "Brux and I like to say that there's a reason Stanton chose to work with animals instead of people."

"Thanks for the heads-up," Sheryn said. "I'll talk with Mr. Stanton now."

"Good luck talking sense into that man," Norah said. "Hope it doesn't turn into a conversation with the flying plates."

Sheryn took a deep breath and ducked inside. She'd been to the clinic multiple times, and to Kevin Stanton's home on Long Island, and even to his second clinic there. He used to visit her at the precinct, too, but it had been some time since he'd stopped by, at least three months. Sheryn had figured that meant he'd given up on getting justice for his daughter. She realized she'd been wrong.

"Detective Sterling."

She recognized the deep, resonant voice immediately. "Mr. Stanton. How are you?"

"Surviving, but just barely," he answered. He was a tall, broad-shouldered man who looked older than his sixty years. His head was shaved smooth, and his bright-blue eyes had faded since she'd seen him last. Cori had only been a little wisp of a thing, but her father looked like a retired linebacker.

"You've lost weight. Are you doing okay?"

"It's been a tough time. I've had more than my share of health issues."

"Are you still going to your grief group?"

Stanton shook his head. "After a while, I got tired of telling my story. Talking about Cori is still so hard."

"Maybe it's time to go back. A lot of people find it helpful."

He gave her a hard look. "Have you ever been to a support group, Detective? I bet you haven't. If you had, you'd know people say the most awful things. One woman told me I should consider myself lucky my daughter died quickly. It's like they think your grief is nothing next to theirs." He quickly wiped his eyes. "It's competitive grieving, and it's sick. People pretend to care, but they don't give a damn."

"I'm sorry to hear that."

"Do you have news about Cori's case?" His tanned face brightened for a moment.

"You know that's not why I'm here," Sheryn said. "This is about your . . . let's call it your altercation with Alex Traynor. What happened?"

"What do you think? He came over here like a madman looking for trouble."

"I saw the video, Mr. Stanton."

"Well, it doesn't show how it all started," Stanton said. "You've only got a partial idea, enough to screw me over. You don't have the truth."

"Mr. Traynor accused you of harassing Emily Teare. Did you?"

"How dare you ask me that after what I've been through."

"It's important. You probably haven't heard, but Emily Teare is missing."

"And you think I did something to her?" Stanton towered over her. His face flushed red. "I can't believe you'd even think of asking me that! She was involved with a killer. He destroyed my Cori. If something's happened to his girlfriend, it's because Traynor hurt her."

"Calm yourself down, Mr. Stanton. You know those other detectives want to arrest you for lying to them. They're standing down because I asked them to."

"Don't do me any favors, Detective." He spat the last word out.

"Look, you can get as angry as you want with me, but I've been in your corner from the start."

"What's going to happen to him now?"

"To Alex Traynor? He's going to be released, obviously. They're voiding his arrest right now."

"How can they do that?" Stanton's voice was strangled, almost pleading. "It's not right. He punched me right in the face."

"Unless someone faked the video, that was right after you slugged one to his head," Sheryn said. "The detectives from your local precinct looked at the evidence. This is their call. I don't disagree with them."

"You know what he did to my daughter, Detective," Stanton said softly. "Or have you forgotten that?"

"I swear to you, I have not," Sheryn said. "But I can't pretend he's guilty of another crime if he isn't."

"Of course you can. Look at OJ Simpson. He got off scot free for murdering his wife, but then the cops arrested him for some stupid sports-memorabilia fraud case. It was all made up to get him for the murder."

"I have been keeping close track of Alex Traynor," Sheryn said. "If he had so much as a noise violation or a jaywalking ticket, I'd know about it. And believe me, I'd come down on him hard. You have to trust me."

"I used to," Stanton said. "You told me you were going to get my Cori's killer, and I believed you. I don't anymore. All anyone at the NYPD cares about is clearing cases, and as far as they're concerned, Cori's is shut because some medical examiner ruled her death an accident."

"Death by misadventure," Sheryn corrected him gently. "Because she was so intoxicated, and because there were no marks of violence on her body that weren't from the fall."

"A distinction without a difference," Stanton said. "I thought you were on my side, Detective. You always swore you were."

"I am, because I care about justice. I thought Alex Traynor was guilty because of things he said, things that weren't admissible in court."

"He lied to you. He told you he wasn't sleeping with Cori, but when you looked at the GPS data on her phone, you found she spent nights at his apartment."

Sheryn blinked, realizing she'd forgotten about that detail. "Yes, but that wasn't conclusive. She could've been in the building next door, or on the next block."

"Stop making excuses. I'm all out of faith, Detective."

"Don't be," Sheryn said. "I haven't stopped looking for answers."

"I've made it easy for you," Stanton said. "You can arrest Traynor for what he did to me."

"That's not going to happen, sir."

Stanton stared at her, and she felt the full weight of his fury. "I trusted you," he hissed. "That was my mistake." He stormed out of the room, slamming the door behind him.

When Sheryn left the clinic, she didn't look back, but her heart felt like a stone in her chest.

CHAPTER 26

ALEX

"You know, you're pretty damned lucky," Detective Bruxton said. "If you stop to think about it."

"Depends how you define *lucky*," Alex said. "Because my version doesn't include hanging out in a police station after a guy kicks my ass."

They were sitting in an interview room in the NYPD precinct at 19½ Pitt Street. The table and chairs were metal, like the ones in Emily's office, but less fancy and with a lot more graffiti. There was a tiny window that refused to admit any natural light.

"A *sixty*-year-old guy busted your chops," Bruxton said. "That's my favorite part."

"His daughter was a friend of mine. He blames me for her death."

Bruxton stared at him appraisingly. The man had a rough-hewn face marked with scars and a blond brush cut that made him look like he'd just gotten out of the military. Another time, another place, and Alex would've wanted to shoot his portrait.

"It sounds like you blame yourself for his daughter's death," he said.

Alex thought about that. "I guess I do."

"How come?"

"Cori was my friend," Alex said. "We hung out together a lot. I bought drugs from her. When she came over that night, she was acting strange."

"She was high?"

"Yeah, but that wasn't it," Alex said. "Our relationship was platonic, always had been. But she started coming on to me. Aggressively." Alex could still picture Cori, her pretty, heart-shaped face flushed with some hybrid of excitement and fury. "She was talking about another guy. How she was going to . . . show him?"

"That sounds like soap-opera dialogue, my friend."

"Screw him," Alex corrected. "She said she was going to screw him over. I don't know who she was talking about. Some jerk she was dating. She said he owed her a ring. He'd promised her."

"And you slept with her?" Bruxton asked.

"Hell, no. I didn't want anything from Cori except heroin." He gave the detective a searching look. "You can't arrest me for that after the fact, right?"

"Nah. But if you're still using . . ."

"I'm not. I've been clean for almost a year." Alex stared at the table. Someone who'd sat in that chair had etched **GAN** into the metal table. Gangster? Gangbanger? They hadn't gotten very far. "I was the one who said let's go to the roof. She agreed, and we went up. Then she vanished."

"Vanished . . . off the side of the building?"

"No. She went down the stairs, I guess. I don't know. I only cared about getting high. But Cori gave me ketamine in addition to the heroin. I didn't realize that until it was too late. I was so strung out. I don't know what happened next."

"You were on ketamine *and* heroin? I doubt you were walking around, pal," Bruxton said.

"There was shouting," Alex said. "Cori was shouting. That's it. That's all I remember."

"Did the detectives who worked the case ever find the dude she was dating?"

"No. Her father told them we were engaged. Either he lied to the police, or Cori lied to him. He despised anyone she dated."

There was a knock on the door. "Come on in," Bruxton called. The door opened, and Alex recognized—with a sinking heart—Detective Sterling's stern face.

"I don't think we've met," she said to the other detective, "but I'm a friend of your partner's. Sheryn Sterling."

He stood and shook her hand. "Bruxton."

"One name, like Oprah," she said. "Norah told me. Thanks for keeping Mr. Traynor on ice. I need to ask him a few questions."

"You up for that?" Bruxton asked Alex. He nodded. "Okay then. Don't take this the wrong way, but I hope not to see you again, Alex." He left the room and pulled the door shut behind him.

Sterling came closer and sat down. "You want your lawyer here?"

The last think Alex wanted was to bother CJ again. He'd taken over most of his day on Monday. "No. Go for it."

"Tell me why you would go begging for trouble," she said.

"I found some letters Kevin wrote to Emily. They were at her office. I had to confront him."

"No, you didn't," she said. "If you found evidence, you should've turned it over to us." She put her hand out. "I really do want to see them."

"Don't you have them?" Alex asked.

"Mr. Stanton never mentioned any letters."

"I showed them to him. They ended up on the floor when he attacked me. I went to pick the letters up, and he punched me in the head."

"Do you want to press charges?"

"No."

"The thing that gets me is that you walked into the lion's den in the first place," Sterling said. "Obviously you know how Mr. Stanton feels about you?"

"Yes." Alex was quiet for a moment. "He hates me. That's why he wrote those letters to Emily. He was telling her I was evil, saying I was a sociopath who killed Cori. Claiming I'd kill again."

"He signed these letters?"

"He didn't have to." Alex raised his head and looked Sterling in the eye. "After Cori died, he wrote to all the papers and magazines I've worked for, telling them I was a murderer and that they were monsters if they ever hired me again. I didn't know he'd ever written to Emily. She never said a word about it to me."

"You never saw any letters come in?"

"No. They were at Emily's office. Her friend Yasmeen and I found them in a file folder in her desk."

That earned an arched eyebrow. For possibly the first time, he'd said something that intrigued her. "How did you convince the fire-breathing administrator to let you embark on this digging operation?"

"I didn't." He let that hang in the air. Sterling gave him a barely discernable nod, even though her stern expression didn't shift. It wasn't approval, exactly, more like she wished she'd jimmied open the lock.

"How long have you known about these letters?"

"We found them this morning." Alex blushed. "I went straight to Kevin's office afterward."

"But Dr. Khan didn't feel compelled to come with you?"

Alex dropped his head. "I didn't tell her where I was going."

"Okay, let's assume you're telling me the truth," the detective said. "Which, in the absence of the letters, is a leap. What did you think you were going to accomplish?"

"I didn't think it through—I know. But he was harassing Emily. He needed to answer for that."

Sterling was silent for a moment. "We found Emily's car this morning. It was parked in the Bronx."

"Sure." Alex shrugged. "That's where she parks her brother's car. The lot's near Belmont."

"No, not there. Want to guess where we found it?"

"Last time I saw it was in the lot. Where could it go?"

"Right by Woodlawn Cemetery. When's the last time you used the car?"

"About a month ago. We took Sid up to High Falls."

"That's the last time you were in the car?"

"*In* the car, yes."

"That sounds like a hedge," Sterling said.

"I haven't been inside the car since then," Alex admitted. "But I took the subway up to the Bronx late Friday night. I noticed the keys were gone, so I wondered if Emily had taken the car. But it was parked right where we left it."

"First time I'm hearing this story," the detective said. "I believe it should've come up when I interviewed you at the precinct and asked you for your whereabouts on Friday night."

"Talking to you that evening was what made me start to remember going to the Bronx," Alex said. "I was drunk, and I popped some pills. I know I wasn't thinking straight when I went up there. Later, I had trouble remembering it. It was like a hazy dream. I know I stared into the car windows. I have a flashlight on my key chain, and I used it to look inside."

"Did you pop open the trunk?"

"No. There's only one set of keys, and Emily took them with her. Her brother keeps the other set. I couldn't open the doors or the trunk."

"Would it surprise you to learn we found blood in the trunk of her car?"

"Blood?" Alex repeated.

"Yes."

"Emily's blood?" Panic flooded through him.

"We're waiting on DNA analysis. It is type A positive."

"You think she's hurt?" Alex's voice was tight. "Have you checked the hospitals?"

"We're taking care of that, Mr. Traynor. I want to know what *you* think. How did that blood get into your girlfriend's car?"

"Maybe someone attacked her," Alex said. "On her way out of town. Maybe . . ." His voice trailed off. "I don't know what to think. But this means she's in trouble. We've got to find her."

"Let's go over your alibi again. You last saw Emily when?"

"Friday, around noon, when I went to her office."

"And you had a fight. What was that about?"

"Work," Alex said softly.

"You want me to arrest you right here and now?"

"Emily works with some groups that help refugees and immigrants." He searched the detective's eyes for understanding. "Undocumented immigrants. I found some stuff that must've been related to that, and . . . I lost it."

"Why?"

"Because it was illegal." He shook his head. "I can't say more than that. I was worried about what she'd gotten herself into."

Sterling was silent for a bit. "Who would Emily know in the Bronx?"

"I can't think of anyone. She grew up in California. I'm the one who grew up in Riverdale."

"Well, then, who do *you* still know in the Bronx?"

"Aside from my friend Will, no one."

The detective sat up ramrod straight, as if she'd been jolted by electricity. "Will Sipher," she repeated. "Your friend who lived a couple of floors down from you, the one who was going through an ugly divorce?"

"You remember him."

"Let's just say he left an impression on me. He moved out of your building?"

"Last January. He went to a better building in Hell's Kitchen, closer to Central Park."

"He doesn't have a place up in the Bronx anymore?"

"His mother died in January," Alex said. "Will inherited her house in Riverdale. She never left the area where Will and I grew up."

"What's your fiancée's relationship with Will like?" the detective asked.

"She tolerates him, but she's not a fan of his." Alex paused. "Though she asked CJ for a favor on his behalf."

"What favor?"

"You know Will was convicted of insider trading, right?"

"Wasn't that part of the reason his wife left him?"

Alex nodded. "Will wants to get the conviction overturned. Emily asked CJ for help with that, but he said no."

"Why would Emily want to help Will?"

Alex turned that over in his mind. When CJ first mentioned the favor, Alex had brushed it off. After all, Emily was always helping people, so how was this any different? But the truth was that it wasn't the same, because Emily had never liked Will. *Your friend is a thoroughgoing creep*, she'd announced after Alex first introduced them.

Will's an acquired taste, like Campari, Alex had joked. *He takes some getting used to.*

He makes these nasty little digs at you. They're like poison darts, Emily had insisted. *He's jealous of you. He doesn't like the fact that your work is known around the world.*

I doubt he cares. He has more money than I'll see in my lifetime.

Emily had been right about the undercurrent between them, but brothers often competed with each other. Alex let Will's negativity slide off him. It had gotten worse when Will lost his job, his money, and his marriage, but how could Alex hold that against him?

"Cat got your tongue?" the detective prompted Alex, bringing him back into the present. He was still inside that airless cell, even if his mind was traveling through space and time.

"Sorry, I was just thinking about something Emily said. I don't know why she'd help him, except that Emily liked to say you should never give up on a lost cause. Maybe she figured Will for one."

"Do you think Emily and Will had contact over the past few weeks?"

"No," Alex answered immediately. "I saw Will last night. He didn't know Emily had left. It's not like she would confide in him."

"What did you talk about?"

"Emily, mostly. I told him about our conversation. I was still remembering pieces of my trip up to the Bronx to look for the car, so I mentioned that."

Her stern face shifted. "You mentioned the car to Mr. Sipher?"

Alex nodded, wondering suddenly if that had been a stupid thing to do. It had been on his mind, and so it had come out of his mouth. Yet again, he'd acted on instinct instead of thinking things through.

"Tell me about your relationship with your fiancée," Sterling said. "You met her in a war zone, didn't you?"

"Yes, in Syria."

"Seems to me like you're both attracted to danger."

"That's probably true about me," Alex said. "I wandered into my first war zone in Afghanistan thinking I was going to be a hero and become famous. But that's not Emily. The only thing she cares about is helping other people. She's the most dedicated, fearless person I've ever known."

"Does Emily know about the woman you killed in Syria?"

Alex stared at the detective. He knew if CJ were there, he'd order him to keep his mouth shut and beat a hasty retreat. Telling the truth wasn't smart; it could bind him up in seven hells' worth of legal trouble. But at that moment, Alex understood something he hadn't before:

Sterling saw him as a stone-cold killer. If he didn't make her understand, she'd continue wasting her time tailing him instead of finding Emily.

"Yes." He took a deep breath. "I tried to explain it to her. She thinks I shouldn't feel responsible, but I know I am. If I'd acted differently, that woman would be alive."

"What was her name?"

"I never knew," Alex said. "I wanted photos. That was all that mattered to me then. Pictures."

Shame coursed through him, heating up his blood and making him sweat. He didn't want to add another word, but Sterling was frowning at him, intrigued in spite of her loathing.

"I'd been in Aleppo for weeks," Alex said. "The government was bombing the rebels holding the city, day and night. Everything was already in ruins. Every block, the buildings were busted wide open. They had snipers they'd send in. More than once, I was walking down a street, and I saw someone shot dead ten feet in front of me. The whole city reeked of death."

"Why did you stay?"

"I told myself it was to be a witness," Alex said. "That was a good reason, a pure reason, to be there. To show the world the horrors going on. People wouldn't believe how bad it was without evidence. But later, when I had a lot of time to think, I realized it was arrogance. I'd had so many close calls, but I always came out unscathed. I was famous for being this brave, intrepid war photographer, and I made a lot of money in the process."

"You got yourself shot," Sterling pointed out. "If you had nine lives, you're down at least one."

Alex didn't laugh at that, but he smiled inwardly. The cop didn't like him, but he admired her. Sterling's toughness and grit and gallows humor reminded him of Maclean. *Not your turn today*, his friend had liked to say. It wasn't flippancy, but a grim acknowledgment that one day your number would come up. Not many people got it, but he knew instinctively that Sterling would understand.

"True," Alex said. "But at least I'm still above ground."

"Winning," Sterling answered drily. "Tell me about the woman."

"People still took shelter in the remains of the buildings. They had nowhere else to go." He took a breath. The scene was playing out in front of his eyes, as if he'd been transported back to Syria. "When the next bomb hit, the building would crumble. People would be buried alive. That's what happened. I was talking with some guys I knew, and a bomb landed down the block and turned a building into rubble. We all ran to it. They started pulling bricks and beams and shoving them aside. I stood there and took photos."

He was dizzy as he spoke. His throat was dry, lowering his voice to a croak. But he didn't stop.

"The guys kept yelling at me to help them," Alex said. "I didn't. I stayed back, behind my camera. I got every second of the rescue. Every detail. Their hands were cut and bleeding, but that never slowed them down. They found a young woman under all that rubble, alive and crying for her mother. She looked like she was wearing a white dress, because she was covered in ash. I remember thinking how a photo of her rescue would be in every newscast and on the front page of every paper. Then another bomb came down and ripped them all to pieces."

Sterling gasped audibly, but she didn't say a word.

"They called it a double tap," Alex said. "The planes would come back and drop another bomb on the same site, so they could kill the rescue workers there."

"You *told* me you killed a woman," Sterling said. "Those were your words."

"I did," Alex said. "If I'd helped dig her out, she would have lived. Literally one minute would've made all the difference in the world. Thirty seconds, even. She died because of me."

"What about the men who tried to rescue her? Don't you feel responsible for them too?"

"It's not the same," Alex said. "She could've been saved. But those guys were going to search the rubble for other survivors. They had friends who'd died like that. Nothing I did changed what happened to them."

Sterling stared at him for an uncomfortably long time. He couldn't read her dark eyes or stern expression, but it filled him with dread. It was like watching a storm on the horizon, one that you prayed would shift direction.

"Am I under arrest?" Alex asked finally.

Sterling didn't answer that. "When did your PTSD episodes start?"

"After that last trip to Syria," he answered.

"You think that was because of this woman's death?"

"I was kidnapped immediately after that," Alex said. "They held me for months. Tortured me. My mind wasn't the same after that."

"The night your friend Cori died, did you have a PTSD episode?"

"No," Alex said softly. "I was planning to kill myself. I asked Cori to bring the heroin over. At first, she thought I was crazy, but then she started talking about how much she hated her life. I told her how stupid that was, but she was angry and upset that nothing was working out for her. I should've listened to her. Instead, I shot up and checked out. I just wanted out."

"What's the last thing you remember from that night?" Sterling asked.

Alex closed his eyes for a moment. "The stars," he said. "The night was cold and clear, and I thought . . ." His voice trailed off.

"You thought what?"

Alex opened his eyes. "That I was joining them." He took a deep breath. In that warm, dark pocket of his mind, there was a faint echo, a memory about that night he'd cast off like a bottle hurled into the ocean, and yet the waves were ferrying it back to him whether he wanted it or not.

"You're free to go, Mr. Traynor," she said. "Just don't go too far. We'll need to talk again. Soon."

CHAPTER 27

SHERYN

When Sheryn finally returned to the Manhattan North Precinct, she found Rafael literally spinning in his desk chair. "What are you doing?" she asked.

"You're going to drive me crazy—you know that?" he said, whirling around again.

"When I went downtown, I thought you were coming back here to work," Sheryn said. "Didn't you tell me you had a lead to follow up?"

"I did, and you missed it. It was pretty damn exciting for a while. I had a suspect . . . nah, I'm going to make you wait for it," Rafael said. "Also, I need you to explain to me why you kicked Traynor to the curb."

"I didn't, the detectives at the Seventh Precinct did," Sheryn answered. "But it was the right call. The assault claim was bogus, and there was video."

"Okay, maybe he was pure as the driven snow this time. But what does that matter when you've got the guy you want in custody?"

"Are we going to have one of those ends-justify-the-means arguments? Because I'm down for that," Sheryn said. "And I'm not going to have a clean collar muddied up with false claims. I know Mr. Stanton lost his daughter, and that breaks my heart. I'm going to give him a pass on whatever went down because of that. But I'm not going to pretend black is white. Alex Traynor only punched back in self-defense."

"Correct me if I'm wrong, but you *hate* this guy," Rafael said. "The detective who laid this case out for me wanted to put a stake in his heart."

"Yep, you're wrong." Her tone was firm. "For the past year, I wanted him punished, but more than that, I wanted to make sure he didn't hurt anyone else. But I just spent the last hour talking with him. He's not a sociopath. He's a borderline case with drug issues and PTSD. He's basically a walking wound. That woman he told me he killed in Syria? He blames himself for taking pictures of her rescue instead of actually rescuing her."

"That doesn't make sense."

"She died because she wasn't saved fast enough. Alex Traynor has the guilt from that weighing him down."

"It sounds like the man made a convincing case for himself," Rafael observed. "Clever. How much of his new story do you think is true?"

"I don't doubt what he told me. He's never been a master planner. When he opens his mouth, he usually incriminates himself. I think this story has the ring of truth." She exhaled loudly. "Which is kind of pissing me off, truth be told. For the past year, I've been rock-solid certain that Alex Traynor is capable of violence, at least in his fugue state. Everything fit together with a kind of heartless logic. But now . . . it feels like I missed part of the big picture. The more I poke at this case, the more I feel something isn't right."

"A woman is missing," Rafael pointed out. "That's obviously not right."

"It's more than that. When we were up in the Bronx this morning, there was something tugging at the back of my memory, something I couldn't quite grasp. I realized what it was when I was talking with Traynor."

"What?"

Sheryn made a dismissive noise in the back of her throat. "Nope. Your turn to writhe around in suspense, partner. Who's this new suspect you found?"

Rafael sighed. "Fine, I guess I deserved that. Please note that I expect applause."

Sheryn rolled her eyes. "Get to it."

"You're going to be impressed. Wait for it. It's . . . Emily Teare's ex-husband."

Sheryn leaned so far forward in her chair that she nearly fell off. "What did you just say?"

"You had no idea she'd been married, did you?" Rafael grinned at her. "Sorry, Grasshopper."

"You need to explain this, like, *right now*."

"Emily Teare got married when she was twenty-one," Rafael said. "To a fellow Stanford student named Christopher Lee."

"Like the British actor?" Sheryn asked.

"No relation, I presume, but yes. She was premed, he was prelaw. If you want to hazard a guess, I'd say her parents' deaths played a part in it, on account of the timing. Anyway, the marriage only lasted a few months, but they stayed friends. He's married and has two kids. Lives east of Gramercy Park."

"Does he have an alibi for the weekend?"

"I dunno," Rafael said. "I figured we could have a word with him together. Unlike some detectives, I keep *my* partner looped in."

"But you do it so passive-aggressively," Sheryn said. "Okay, we'll add that to our to-do list. We also need to talk to a friend of Traynor's named Will Sipher."

"The name doesn't ring a bell."

"He's a shady character," Sheryn said. "He and Traynor grew up together in Riverdale."

"That's a real town? Not just from the Archie comics?"

175

"Riverdale is part of the Bronx. A very ritzy section of the borough these days. Some of the houses up there sell for millions. There was lots of land in the north Bronx, and some people built castles up there. It's a trip. You should go look sometime."

"Traynor and Sipher grew up in the lap of luxury?"

"Traynor didn't," Sheryn said. "His mother passed away from cancer when he was in high school. I don't know what happened to his father, but he floated out of the picture. Traynor moved into his friend's house and finished high school while he lived there."

"These two are tight?"

"Not exactly," Sheryn said. "They followed different paths. Traynor dropped out of college and went overseas to work. Sipher graduated from Wharton and worked on Wall Street. I don't know how close they were for years. But then the bottom fell out of Sipher's life. He was charged with insider trading."

"Wall Street leeches never serve time."

"True, but he lost his job and was banned from his industry," Sheryn said. "I know it's not enough, but the point is he reconnected with Traynor around then. Even moved into an apartment in Traynor's building. He was living there when Cori Stanton fell to her death. We got a statement from him that night."

"Was he involved?"

"My partner and I didn't think so. Sipher fractured his ankle the week before Thanksgiving and was having a seriously tough time getting around on crutches. He lived on the second floor of the building, and it just didn't seem likely that he went up the stairs to the roof. On top of that, there was a commotion in his hallway. A neighbor heard a girl crying in front of his door, begging him to open it. He wouldn't. That neighbor said Sipher never opened the door to her."

"By any chance, was that girl Cori Stanton?"

"Believe me, we thought of that. Sipher denied it. He was a dirtball about it. I remember him saying, 'You don't think I'd go near white trash like that, do you?'"

"A real prince." Rafael's eyebrows shot up. "There was no way you could prove a connection?"

Sheryn shook her head. "I remember Sipher telling us that he'd warned Traynor not to get involved with her. He dropped some hints that backed up Kevin Stanton's version, that Traynor and the dead girl had been sleeping together. He wouldn't state it outright, though. Overall, he said nothing to condemn Traynor, but nothing to help him either. I remember thinking he didn't seem like much of a friend."

"How does he fit into the Emily Teare picture?"

"Will Sipher inherited his mother's house in the Bronx," Sheryn said. "Remember where we found the car this morning? It's walking distance from Riverdale."

"Sure. From the Bronx Zoo as well," Rafael pointed out.

"I know it's a tenuous connection. It's all I've got right now."

"What's our next move? Check up on Will Sipher or Christopher Lee? Your call."

Sheryn froze in place. "My call?"

"Flip a coin. Sipher or Lee?"

"No, no, no," Sheryn said, typing furiously at her computer. "You're a freaking genius, partner. The calls. There we go."

"What the hell are you talking about?"

"These are Cori Stanton's phone records," Sheryn said. "She had bundles of calls from burner phones. We figured that was because she was dealing drugs. Maybe it was. But Emily Teare was getting an awful lot of calls from burner phones too. They follow the same pattern."

CHAPTER 28

EMILY

Stop calling me. I'm telling you it's over.

If there were ever any words that haunted Emily, it was the last words she'd spoken on the phone.

In her subterranean prison, she floated in and out of consciousness. There was no way to tell how much time had passed, or even how much time there was between her short intervals of waking and sleeping.

She tried to retrace every moment of Friday evening in her mind.

She'd come home from work. She'd been on edge. Who was she kidding, she thought. She was always on edge. The past year she'd been balancing on the blade of a knife. One false move, and it was over.

But that voice in her head mocked her. *Only for the past year?* It knew her too well. Even as a child, Emily had tried to run faster and jump higher and do whatever necessary to push herself ahead. She was like a rat in a wheel, only that wheel was her entire life. There was no way to slow down.

Stop calling me. I'm telling you it's over.

He wouldn't stop calling. She knew what he wanted, but her answer was going to be the same no matter what. A flat, solid no, a refusal that she should have made months earlier, when he'd first approached her.

No. How hard would that have been? Only she couldn't do it. Now she was paying the price. She'd thought she was being careful, recording their last few conversations. It felt like an insurance policy stored on her phone, uploaded into the digital cloud. But he likely had her phone, and even if he didn't, none of the people looking for her would be able to guess the long, random string of characters she used as a pass code.

"I'm no good to you dead," she said, startling herself, because she hadn't planned to speak aloud. Was she losing her mind? Whatever he was drugging her with made her feel like she was clawing through ether even when she was awake. It was in her water, or in her food, or both, because she woke up thirsty and hungry, her mouth dry like desert sand, and as soon as she quenched those desires, she went under again.

There was no way to win, she told herself. Except not to play.

She was hungry. She was thirsty. If she denied both those urges, maybe she could wake up, shake the cobwebs off her brain, figure a way out.

She lay there for what felt like a long time. She had discipline—there was no doubt about that. And that was one advantage she had over him: he had no idea how fierce she could be. He had thought he'd gotten the better of her. He had thought he was the one in charge. And now that he wasn't, he'd lost his mind and done this. Even though her throat was burning with thirst and her stomach twisted in hunger, she was determined.

Stop calling me. I'm telling you it's over.

As she lay there, pain only fueled her anger and cleared her head. There was nothing in that cell she could use as a weapon. Whatever she did, the element of surprise was going to be her only advantage. She was going to use it. Because she wasn't waiting for anyone to rescue her. He was careful, and he would cover his tracks. But he was about her height and far less fit. There was no doubt in her mind that, in a fight, she could take him down. She just needed to stay alert.

CHAPTER 29

ALEX

Alex tended to be early for meetings, but Yasmeen Khan was even earlier. She was waiting for him at the foot of Central Park. She'd even changed into running gear. Inwardly, Alex groaned.

"Thanks so much for meeting me," he said. "I know it's a huge thing to ask. I really appreciate it."

"Honestly, it's fine. If I can do anything to help Emily, I want to do it," Yasmeen said, bending down to greet Sid, who was on his red leash and obviously delighted at the prospect of walking in the park. "Hey there, you good-looking boy. Wish I'd brought some Ziggy's Disco Fries for you."

That made Alex think of Diana; she'd brought that very treat over for Sid. "How did you know he likes those?"

"Emily mentioned it. She's had them delivered to the office because she thinks Sid smells them even through a box."

Alex's heart skipped a beat. "Who handles boxes like that? Personal deliveries for doctors, I mean."

"The support staff."

"Is there a woman named Diana? That's probably not her name, actually. She'd be in her twenties, Asian, about five foot six, maybe dyes her hair different colors? She wears long sleeves to cover up track marks."

"There's literally no one on our staff who fits that description," Yasmeen said. "Who is this woman?"

"She showed up at the apartment with treats for Sid. Claimed she knows Emily."

"Not from the hospital," Yasmeen said. "She didn't explain the connection?"

"No. She left pretty fast," Alex said, feeling relieved. He was snapping at everything and suspicious of everyone. Paranoia was clearly setting in. "Sid gets a lot of treats. He's a charmer."

"He's so upbeat about everything. No matter what happens." Yasmeen gave his head a couple more pats and stood up.

"Is this where you and Emily usually meet to run?"

Yasmeen nodded. "Emily hates the Columbus Circle entrance because it's so crowded. The Seventh Avenue one's quieter. I usually get here a little early to do some stretches. Emily, as you probably know, never bothers to stretch and is fine anyway." She sighed. "Let's head in."

It was a warm day, and the Seventh Avenue entrance was packed with people, from Alex's point of view. When he went to a park, it was usually DeWitt Clinton for the dog run. Central Park looked like a special circle of Dante's hell designed for tourists.

"Sorry I gave you the wrong impression," Alex said. "About going for a run, I mean. I wanted to retrace Emily's steps."

"That made sense to me. And no worries about running. I should've known that running wasn't your thing."

"It used to be," Alex said. "Before I got a bullet in my leg. It's not great for running, but it's pretty accurate about predicting rain."

"That's a sweet superpower," Yasmeen said. "Did that happen before you met Emily?"

"Immediately before. I ended up on her operating table. That's how we met."

"Are you serious? Damn, Emily is cagey. She told me you met overseas, but I always thought it was glamorous—you know, a doctor on a mission to heal the world meeting a war photographer in a dark bar."

"I think you got a war-zone hospital mixed up with Rick's Café in *Casablanca*," Alex said. "But I like your way better."

"Do you remember her operating on you?"

"Not really. It hurt like hell. She put my leg back together. It was like a jigsaw puzzle, from what she told me. It's only thanks to Emily that I can walk at all."

Yasmeen shook her head. "She never said a word about that. Typical."

They were following Park Drive as it angled east, toward the Dairy. Alex was struggling to stay calm, but he was overwhelmed. It wasn't just the sheer mass of people; it was the realization that—with these crowds sweeping through every day like locusts—nothing stayed in place for long before being trampled or taken. What were the odds that he'd find any trace of Emily?

"I should tell you . . . ," Yasmeen said. "Detective Sterling called me just before I headed out."

"I was going to warn you about that." Alex shook his head ruefully. Of course the detective had. "Did she tell you what happened?"

"Not really, except that you had a confrontation with the man you accused of writing the letters. I didn't want to say anything, but I figured that's where that bruise on your face came from. It's not like it was there this morning."

"I've had quite the day since then."

"Who's the guy?" Yasmeen asked.

Alex paused before answering. "He's the father of a friend of mine, Cori Stanton. She died in a fall from the roof of my building last year."

"I remember that. Emily told me. Her father blames you?"

"He's convinced I'm a murderer."

"I thought her death was ruled . . . an accident, I think?"

"Death by misadventure," Alex said. "Because she was high. We both were. Her father wrote a bunch of angry letters to everyone who knows me. The ones we found were shorter, and they weren't signed, but they sounded just like him."

"Is there anyone else who would write them?"

"I don't think so. Cori's mother married some rich guy in Argentina and moved there when she was little. Cori was an only child. Unless a friend of hers . . ." Alex's voice trailed off. He had the oddest sensation at that moment. *Like someone's walking on your grave*, his mother would've said. It shook him to his core. Diana, or whatever her name was, had appeared just after Emily had vanished. Diana, who knew Cori. Alex didn't put much stock in anything she'd said, but her reaction when she'd spotted Cori's photo? That hadn't been faked. Was there a chance he'd been wrong about Kevin Stanton?

"What is it?" Yasmeen asked.

They were heading through the Mall, and even though the crowds had barely thinned, Alex was impressed by the statues lining the walk and the rows of tall trees on either side; they bent toward each other, forming a peaked ceiling that reminded him of a cathedral.

"Nothing. It just occurred to me that a friend of Cori's could've written those letters. She might even know Cori's father." Fat chance of getting that out of Kevin Stanton, he realized. That man wouldn't give an inch.

"But why would anyone do that?" Yasmeen asked.

"I don't know," Alex said. "Cori's father could just be flat-out lying to me. But he signed the other letters. If he wrote these, why not sign them too?"

They followed the Mall to its northern end, where it opened up to Bethesda Terrace. The plaza was packed with people. When he looked over the side, he felt sick. Below was the fountain, and there were kids running around it and playing. He remembered children playing around a fountain in modern Palmyra, the city adjacent to the famous ruins. He'd been there when ISIS attacked, and he remembered children screaming in panic when the shelling started. Alex doubled over, bracing himself against the side of the terrace.

"What's wrong?" Yasmeen put her hand on his shoulder.

Alex tried to answer, but he couldn't. He could feel his entire body shaking. He knew he was in Central Park and not a war zone, and still his body was betraying him. It was as if there were poison secreted inside his body, and every so often it flooded his system with toxins just to remind him it was there.

It was Sid who brought him out of it, leaping to the ledge and nuzzling Alex's ear. Alex gulped a few breaths and patted the dog's head. "I'm sorry," he said. "Maybe this wasn't the smartest idea."

"Take your time," Yasmeen said.

He rested there for another minute, until he was certain his legs wouldn't give out under him.

"You want to talk about it?" Yasmeen asked.

"Honestly? No."

"Don't worry about it," she said. "I was just thinking about how crowded everything seems when you walk through it. When you run, everything's a blur. All these people don't register the same way."

"I thought we could follow the path Emily runs, just in case . . ." He took a couple of breaths. "I don't know. I guess I thought some part of it was secluded."

"From here, we run up the east side, past the Great Lawn and around the reservoir," Yasmeen said. "I wouldn't call any part of the route secluded, except for the path through the Ramble."

"The Ramble? Isn't that where people go to score drugs and find anonymous hookups?"

"That used to be its reputation," Yasmeen said. "Now it's full of bird-watchers. Emily loves Belvedere Castle, so we jog past it, down

Tupelo Meadow, across the rustic bridge, and past Azalea Pond and Balanced Boulder. Here, I'll show you on the map." She held up her phone and pointed out the paths. Unlike the other ones Emily ran, they were small and narrow.

"Can we go around that way?" Alex asked. "Because I'm not dragging you up to the reservoir, but I'm pretty sure I'll never find my way out of the Ramble if I go in alone."

"It's just on the other side of the lake." Yasmeen pointed at a small bridge. "It's going to be a lot less crowded on the other side."

She wasn't exaggerating. Across the bridge and a few yards along the path into the Ramble and Alex forgot there were other people around. His breathing got easier.

"This is beautiful," he said. "Is there a way to get here where you don't have to cut through crowds?"

"We're really close to the Upper West Side. You could come in a taxi along the Seventy-Ninth Street Transverse and have it drop you off where it intersects with West Drive. It's about two feet away from that."

Sid gave an excited yip and startled Alex by darting ahead. The leash flew out of his hand, and it trailed along behind Sid, looking like nothing so much as a trail of blood.

"Sid! Get back here!" he called.

The dog turned and barked, then dove into the foliage. When he reappeared, he was holding a plastic turquoise cord with earbuds dangling.

"What have you got there, Sid?" Yasmeen asked.

Alex stood still, watching the dog trot toward them. "Emily has earbuds like that," he said.

CHAPTER 30

SHERYN

"Preliminary results are in," Sheryn told Rafael. They were outside, and the sun was shining, but the call she'd just taken had turned her mood dark. "That blood on the carpet? It's Emily Teare's. The blood in the trunk? That's looking like a match."

"You having second thoughts about turning Alex Traynor loose?" Rafael asked.

"I know where to find him if I need to," she answered. "It's the puzzle pieces I don't know how to locate that are bugging me."

They continued up Tenth Avenue in silence, until Rafael said, "Be honest. Do you actually have a plan?"

"Sure. We're going to shake Will Sipher's tree. *That's* the plan."

"And if he doesn't fall like a leaf, then what?"

"I want to see how he reacts," Sheryn answered. "That's going to tell us a lot."

Sipher's building was a little nicer than Traynor's, a little newer. There was no doorman, but from the foyer, Sheryn could see an elevator.

"You want to buzz his apartment?" Rafael asked.

"Nope. I like that element of surprise."

It didn't take long for a woman who was coming in from work to let them in. They took the elevator up to the fourth floor. When they knocked on Sipher's door, no one answered, but Sheryn heard footfalls inside the apartment. They came toward the door, and then there was the distinctive scratch of metal sliding against metal; he was staring through the peephole.

"It's the NYPD, Mr. Sipher," Sheryn said. "I'm Detective Sterling. We met last year."

Sipher's muffled voice came through the closed door. "Hold up your badge."

"All right." Sheryn lifted it up to the peephole.

"Your partner's too."

Rafael gave Sheryn a withering look, but he complied. "We'd like to ask you a few questions, sir."

The peephole slid shut. "I don't feel like answering any questions," Sipher said. "Goodbye, Detectives. Good luck."

Sheryn and Rafael exchanged a startled look; in her experience, there weren't many people who refused to answer their door to the police. Civil-liberties types liked to remind people that they didn't have to, unless the police had a warrant, but even they tended to open the door out of politeness.

"Are you not feeling well, Mr. Sipher?" Rafael called out. "Do we need to perform a wellness check?"

"I'm under no obligation to open my door," Sipher answered. "Go away."

"We can just ask you our questions from the hallway, Mr. Sipher," Sheryn said, loud enough so that the neighbors in the surrounding apartments could hear. "We want to talk to you about a missing woman named Emily Teare. We don't need to ask if you know her. We're aware that you do."

If she thought shame was going to motivate him, she was mistaken. "This is harassment," Sipher shouted back. "I've been harassed by the police before. I know exactly how to report you. Thanks for your badge numbers. That makes it easier."

"I'm going to strangle this asshole when he opens the door," Rafael whispered.

"You'll have to beat me to it," Sheryn whispered back. Then she raised her voice. "Look, Mr. Sipher, we know Alex Traynor's a friend of yours. We're sure you care that his girlfriend is missing. We just need your help to find Emily."

There was stony silence on the other side of the door. Sheryn waited.

"Don't you want Emily to be found?" she added, after several moments of quiet. "Don't you care what happens to her?"

Sipher didn't answer. She could feel his oily presence on the other side of the door. He was laughing at them, she was sure.

"We could knock on his neighbors' doors," Rafael muttered, sotto voce. "Find out if they've seen anything."

"Whatever we do now will just be fuel for his harassment claim," Sheryn said. "Let's go."

Rafael swore a blue streak on the elevator ride down.

"That's not going to help," Sheryn told him.

"Let's come back with a drug-sniffing dog," Rafael suggested. "I could smell drugs outside that door, so a dog could. We'd get him."

"You ever hear of Florida versus the Jardines?"

"Nah."

"Some Miami cops tried that," Sheryn said. "It was thrown out by the Supreme Court. Violation of the Fourth Amendment."

"What do you want to do? Stand here with our thumbs up our butts?"

"Now that's a mental image I need to erase," Sheryn said. "I'll call the ADA and see if I can get a warrant."

"It won't happen," Rafael predicted gloomily.

He was right. Sheryn hung up her phone, her ears ringing with the ADA's *You gotta be kidding me*, followed by laughter. "I'm not giving up," she said.

"What do you want to do?"

"Get your car," Sheryn said. "I'm going to wait in front of the building, because I'll recognize this creep on sight. Anywhere he goes tonight, we go."

Sheryn stood like a sentinel until her partner returned, then she got into the passenger seat of Rafael's black Mercedes. "I meant to tell you this morning, but I forgot in the heat of the moment. This is a sweet ride."

"Thanks."

"You don't see many detectives tooling around in a Mercedes," she added.

Rafael gave her a sidelong look. "This is your slick interrogation style?"

"Oh, no. Somebody outed my old nickname?"

"Slick Sheryn." Rafael smiled. "All it cost me was a coffee too."

"Just wait till I work my LAPD contacts. You know I've got some. I'll do a little digging of my own."

There was nothing more boring than a stakeout, yet nothing more effective at forcing bonding on you, even with someone you didn't much like, Sheryn thought. After the sun slunk down to the horizon, Will Sipher emerged from his building. It was twilight by then, but the man was wearing dark glasses and had a scarf pulled around the lower part of his face. Did he think *that* was a disguise? She had no trouble recognizing him—if anything, that getup only made him more conspicuous.

"Who does he think he is, Aldrich Ames?" Rafael asked when she pointed Will out.

"It's going to be fun taking that entitled creep on a perp walk," Sheryn said.

They watched Sipher get into a hired SUV.

"Follow that car," Sheryn said. Rafael actually cracked a smile at that.

It was a long drive up to Riverdale, and they pulled up in front of Sipher's place just in time to see him hurry inside. The house he'd inherited from his mother looked like it had been sitting on that plot of land since colonial times: it was a two-story federalist brick building, imposing and much too large for any modern family. There was a wrought iron fence around the property. There were other grand houses down the block, but this one—lying at the end of the cul-de-sac—appeared particularly forbidding.

"How much do you think it's worth?" Rafael asked, rapidly scrolling through his phone.

"A couple million. Why?"

"He's trying to unload it for five." Rafael held up his phone, and Sheryn scanned the listing. Five bedrooms, five baths, two fireplaces, and a sauna and hot tub.

"A lot of places you could stash a missing girl," she said.

"You're thinking this creep has Emily here against her will," Rafael pointed out. "What if my booty-call theory is right? Maybe she left Traynor to shack up with his friend."

Sheryn shuddered. "Let's try knocking. Maybe we'll get a warmer reception out here."

"You just want to peer in the windows," Rafael lamented. "And I would, too, if it weren't for that big wrought iron fence around the property."

Sheryn tried the gate, but it was locked. "Where's your sense of adventure?" she asked. "Give me a boost."

"You are kidding, right?"

"This isn't my joking face," she said. "Come on, that fence isn't even six feet tall. No barbed wire, no broken glass on top."

"I like the cut of your jib," Rafael said. "Last one over is a rotten egg."

The fence around Will's property was riddled with iron curlicues, which proved to be decent footholds. Sheryn climbed up and dropped down on the lawn. Rafael was just a couple of seconds behind.

They approached the house confidently. "Let's walk the perimeter," Sheryn said. "See what looks like probable cause."

That was easier said than done. Thick draperies covered the first-floor windows. There were two tiny basement windows—about the size a child could crawl through—that were covered with iron bars.

"Perfect for holding a prisoner," Rafael whispered.

"The man has his own dungeon," Sheryn answered. "Never a good sign."

They walked around the entire house, but there was no noise at all coming from inside. Sheryn had been praying for a chance to use an exigent circumstances exception, allowing them to break in to save a life that might be in danger, but the silence mocked her. Breaking a window without even a flimsy pretext was too much of a reach even for her.

"What do you want to do now?" Rafael asked.

"Let's ring the doorbell. What can it hurt?"

She pressed it, expecting to hear a chime inside, but there was nothing. "You think the house is soundproofed?" she asked.

"That's going kind of far," Rafael said. "But it does look like a fortress. Wish we knew if Sipher made the changes himself or inherited the weirdest house on the block."

They rang the bell again and waited. While they were talking about their next move, Sheryn's phone rang.

"One Police Plaza? What do they want?" she mused, just before she picked up.

"Sheryn Sterling? Larry Adler. I heard an ugly rumor that you and your partner just jumped over the fence of a private home in Riverdale."

"We are at that house, sir," Sheryn answered, trying to placate the deputy commissioner without admitting to any wrongdoing. It seemed impossible that they had been called onto the mat so quickly; Sipher must've phoned his lawyer immediately.

"Did you jump the fence?"

"We heard some strange noises, sir. We had to investigate."

"Did you find anything?"

"No, sir."

"Well, then get your asses out of there, pronto. This Sipher character's got a shark of a lawyer, and he's already threatening a harassment suit against the NYPD."

"But we didn't do anyth—"

"I don't want to hear an argument," Adler said. "I want to hear the screech of rubber as you burn out of there. Got it?"

CHAPTER 31

ALEX

Alex was no stranger to cemeteries, but the last time he'd set foot inside Woodlawn was for Cori's funeral. He entered from Jerome Avenue, at the southern end. Within moments, he was surrounded by grand stone mausoleums. Guardian angels with sightless eyes watched him. *Judged* him, he suspected. They stood beside Corinthian columns and windows made of Tiffany glass. He knew the angels weren't real, but it was getting dark out, and the distinction between reality and imagination was thinner. It was also getting cold; subtract the bright sun from the sky, and twilight felt like a different part of the planet. That was the wonder of desert lands to him: scorching hot during the day, freezing cold at night. He'd never acclimated to that. Even New York's vastly milder version of the switch made goosebumps rise on his neck.

He touched the turquoise cord in his pocket. Earbuds, of all the objects in the world to suddenly get sentimental about. Against every instinct, he'd walked into the police station to hand them over to Detective Sterling, only to be told that she'd left for the day. He'd kept them, superstitiously fearful that they would be lost if they were entrusted to anyone else.

After the chaos of Central Park, the serenity of Woodlawn at dusk was a relief. Cori's final resting place wasn't near the grander mausoleums and statues. She was tucked into a modest corner on the eastern side of the cemetery, with a flat headstone that lay atop the cold ground.

"Cori," he breathed aloud when he found it. What was there to say? He didn't have any firm ideas about what came after death, though the words of his high school science teacher sometimes bounced around his head. Energy does not die, old Mr. Speed had taught him. It merely changes form. Alex could be literal about that, ashes to ashes and dust to dust, an endless cycle of birth and destruction in the material world that he'd spent his adult life witnessing. But what about the part of Cori that made her who she was: her warm personality, her easy laugh, her adoration of horses, and her fondness for practical jokes. What of *that* part of Cori wasn't reduced to dust?

He'd brought a bouquet of white lilies from a corner bodega, and he knelt in front of her grave to set them down. Someone else had left a single red rose. It seemed like a strange choice for Cori's father, but who else would have been there?

"I'm so sorry," he said.

It was almost as if he heard Cori laughing at him. *Miss me much?*

He often felt her absence, like an old wound that never healed properly. It wasn't unlike his bullet-shattered leg; he could forget, for a time, but never for long. In some ways, Cori had understood him better than people he was closer to. She didn't wonder how he could carry such dark, destructive impulses inside him; she shared them.

One time, when they were smoking a particularly strong substance, she had asked him, *Do you think you were born fucked up, or did you get that way later?*

Without having to think about it, Alex had said, *Later.*

Why?

Because my mom was great, Alex had told her. *She was always there for me.*

But your dad left when you were little. Didn't that screw you up?

I was so young when he left I don't think I cared, Alex had answered. *What about you?*

A shadow had settled on Cori's face. *I can tell you what made me a mess: my father. After my mother ditched him, he made me into his little wife. In every way.*

Cori wasn't much for confidences, and she'd never wanted to talk about it again. When Alex had later asked her, point-blank, *Did your father abuse you?* she'd denied it with a desultory *Of course not.* When he advised her to go into therapy, she'd laughed at the idea. Then, when Alex had refused to take Sid back to Kevin's veterinary clinic, Cori had been baffled.

I don't want to see your father again, Alex had explained flatly. *He abused you.*

Plenty of things happen when you're growing up. You get over them, Cori had argued back. Alex hadn't pressed the issue, and he regretted that, but he'd been in a downward spiral himself at the time; not even three months after she'd first alluded to the abuse, Cori was dead.

Alex stood over her grave, his thoughts shifting from Cori to all of the friends he'd lost. There were other war photographers who'd been killed on the job, and one who'd killed himself. That colleague had taken some of the most haunting images Alex had ever seen, starving children in a refugee camp. *How did you live with yourself after you've walked away from a scene like that?* Alex had wondered. Maybe the answer was that you couldn't. But most of all, Alex thought about his friend Elias Maclean, and he instinctively reached for the silver lighter, now safely tucked in his pocket. He would've been dead but for Maclean. Even now, months after he'd shaken off the urge to end his own life, Alex didn't feel that he deserved to be there. Not at the expense of Maclean's life.

He had told Detective Sterling about the buried woman that afternoon, but he hadn't told her the full story. Emily knew it, of course.

Everyone knew a part of it, because it had made the evening news. Alex Traynor, hotshot photographer, kidnapped in Aleppo. Everyone wanted that story; he had no doubt it was part of the reason NYU had hired him to teach, and why they put up with his unconventional ideas and workshops. But it was impossible to convey the truth with words: the three months in various subterranean bunkers or caves, the way his captors would randomly put a gun to his head and pretend to shoot him, the beatings and sleep deprivation and Torture 101 classes that the men taught with Alex's body as a prop to be sliced and burned. He could talk about that; he knew those parts weren't his fault. It was how he'd gotten out of hell that he couldn't get over. The truth loomed over him like a shadow, blocking out any light. Deep down, he knew he didn't deserve to live. That was why he'd decided to kill himself. What sense did the world make when innocents and heroes perished while screw-ups survived? He hadn't been planning to tell anyone—except Emily, and by the time she got the message, it would have been too late to stop him—but Cori had wrangled the truth out of him. When she'd shown up the night before Thanksgiving with his heroin, she'd been in one of her moods.

What do you want with this much? she'd demanded. *You better not be selling it.*

I'm not. It's all for me.

This shit is pure, she'd warned him. *You could kill yourself with it.*

He'd opened his big mouth without thinking twice. *That's the idea.*

Really? She hadn't seemed startled so much as intrigued. *Why would you kill yourself?*

Alex hadn't wanted to talk about it, but he was in such a deep depression that he lacked the energy to put her off. *There are so many reasons, but the main one is that other people suffer because of me. They die.*

Did you kill someone? Cori had wanted to know.

Yes.

How did it happen?

The story had poured out of Alex like blood, hot and furious. His guilt over the young Syrian woman's death was palpable. *If only I'd put down the camera and helped,* he told Cori, more than once. That was the dividing moment in his mind: had he done the right thing, that woman would have lived. The second bomb wouldn't have killed her and her rescuers. That second bomb was the one that blew up in front of Alex's eyes, knocking him unconscious. When Alex had come to, he'd found himself in darkness. His hair was singed, and his hands were burned. When he tried to move, he found he was chained to a wall.

You blame yourself for getting kidnapped? Cori had been incredulous. *That still doesn't make any sense. You can't blame yourself for everything.*

Alex had struggled to explain. *After three months, Special Forces staged a raid to free the hostages. Maclean shouldn't even have been there; he was supposed to be on his way home. He only came on the raid because of me. My closest friend died because of me.*

Cori had given him a long, hard look. *You know what your problem is, Alex? You think you're at the center of every story.*

This isn't about my ego.

Actually, it is. You think you caused your friend to die. But you know the story of Death in Samarra?

Sure. Famous ancient Mesopotamian fable.

Then you know the point of it, Cori had said. *If it's your time to die, death will find you.*

If I hadn't been taken hostage, Maclean would still be alive, he'd insisted.

You're the linchpin that the world turns on, or so you think. My problem's the opposite: I know I'm expendable to everyone.

That's a crazy thing to say.

It's the truth. I'm thirty years old, and my father is still running my life. I'm dating a man who won't be seen in public with me. It's been two years since I had an acting job. I'd be better off dead.

Stop being ridiculous. Things will get better. He'd felt obligated to say the words, but they rang hollow.

If you think it's time to check out, it's definitely time for me to, Cori had said. *But hold that thought. I need to do something first. Don't kill yourself while I'm out. I don't want to come back to a mess.*

She'd disappeared for what felt like forever, but in reality was probably ten minutes.

Well, fuck that, she'd said after she returned. Her face was red and blotchy, as if she'd been crying. *Let's go out in a blaze of glory.*

You're not going to kill yourself, Alex had said.

If at first you don't succeed, try, try again. Cori had held out her wrists. *How does that Dorothy Parker poem go: Razors cut you, acids . . . something you? Well, I've tried razors and pills and gas. I'm sick of failing at everything.*

You're not going to kill yourself, Alex had insisted.

Yes, I am. But there's something else I want first.

That was the moment when Cori had shocked him. She had rested one hand on the side of his neck and leaned forward quickly to kiss him.

Alex had reflexively jolted away. *What are you doing?*

You know you want to. Don't pretend you've never thought about it. About us.

Alex had been shocked. Cori was a flirt, but she'd never propositioned him. *You've got to be kidding. Absolutely not.*

Why not?

You're my friend. And I'm in love with Emily.

The way Cori had stared daggers at him still made the hairs on the back of his neck stand up. *You're going to kill yourself, but you're still going to be faithful to your girlfriend?* She'd flown at him in a rage, slapping and clawing at his face. Finally, she'd stormed out of the apartment again. Alex had taken Sid—who'd been unusually quiet while all of this was going on—over to Mrs. DiGregorio's. Then he'd thought about what to say to Emily. He hadn't wanted to kill himself without a word, but he knew he'd lose his nerve if she responded. In the end, all he could come up with was this: *I love you with every last piece of my heart. Goodbye.* When Cori had returned a few minutes later, Alex had insisted that they go up to the roof.

I want to see the stars when I die, he'd said. Cori hadn't argued with that.

He squeezed his eyes shut, not wanting to remember anything else from that terrible night. He knew he'd taken an insane quantity of drugs. He was lucky to have survived. The last image he could recall was of the stars in the night sky. In New York, they were hard to see, but that night, the heavens had seemed alive. He'd wanted to be alone to die, but Cori had been ranting about something. He'd stared at the stars, and the world had slipped away. In his memory, Cori's words had been lost, but something had come back to him under the weight of Detective Sterling's baleful glare that afternoon.

Jump, he heard Cori say. *Jump. Jump. Jump.*

He couldn't tell if she'd repeated the word, or if it was simply stuck in his head like a broken record. *Jump.* He'd never considered diving off the building; maybe it was cowardly, but exiting the world on a cloud that deadened all pain was his fantasy. *Jump.* That was Cori's idea; she wanted to make a literal splash on her way out.

Jump.

"Stop it," he said aloud to the empty graveyard. He pushed the memory away. It was unnerving, having flat, dark patches of cold silence in his memory, but it was preferable to the alternative. He didn't want to think about Cori telling him to jump; if she hadn't spiked his heroin with ketamine, he wouldn't have been able to stand in the first place. If there was a moment he wanted to hold on to, it was emerging from the darkness to see Emily's face hovering above his. He'd caught glimpses of her that long night: while an EMT brought him out of his opioid coma with naloxone, at the police station, at the hospital. He'd never expected to see Emily again; at first, he'd thought she was an angel.

When he'd finally woken up fully at the hospital, it had been a shock to discover that his mind and body were still tethered together. More than that, he was alive, but Cori was dead. He didn't understand it. He didn't think he ever would.

The ringing of his phone brought him back to where he was. He almost didn't answer, because Will was about the last person he wanted to speak with just then.

"Did you send your cop buddies after me?" Will demanded.

"What are you talking about?"

"Don't worry; I got rid of them," Will said. "I just want to know how you're involved."

"I didn't send anyone after you," Alex said.

There was a long silence on the other end of the line. "We've known each other a long time, so I think you know when I'm telling the unvarnished truth," Will said. "Do not sic the cops on me. I can promise you that won't be good for Emily."

"What are you talking about? Do you know where she is?"

"No," Will said. "But I know her better than you think. Whatever you say to the police, leave me out of it."

CHAPTER 32

SHERYN

Rafael insisted on driving Sheryn back to the precinct, where her car was parked. They were mostly quiet on the drive in, except when Rafael cursed out the traffic. "You want to go for plan B?" he asked her as they inched along the West Side Highway.

"Remind me what that is?"

"Let's give Christopher Lee a shout."

"Why not?" Sheryn said. "What else can go wrong tonight?"

Rafael parked on East Twenty-Second Street, and they walked the rest of the way. Christopher Lee lived in a high-rise building that Sheryn was sure could be safely described as brutalist, a utilitarian concrete slab grudgingly dotted with windows. Inside, though, was oddly pleasing, with soft light and antique furniture and fresh flowers. Sheryn showed the doorman her badge, and they headed up.

When the door to apartment 18C opened, Sheryn stared at the man, struggling to keep her face neutral instead of revealing her surprise. She recognized his face, but that only made her wonder if she'd turned up at the wrong door. "CJ Leeward?" she said finally.

"Detective Sterling," Leeward answered. "I hope there's a good reason you're on my doorstep at this hour."

"We're looking for Christopher Lee," Rafael stated flatly.

"You didn't meet Mr. Leeward yesterday," Sheryn said, "but you heard his voice. We were in an interview room together yesterday. This is Alex Traynor's lawyer. A.k.a. Christopher Lee, I guess."

"Wait. What?" For the first time, she saw Rafael's composure slip. His mouth opened in surprise, then closed again. The whites of his eyes stood out against his olive skin. But what was much more curious to her was the lawyer's reaction: he shrank back, eyeing them warily.

"You know what you say about not believing in coincidences?" Rafael asked her. "I don't believe in them either." He smiled at the lawyer. "Which do you prefer, Christopher or CJ?"

"What is it you want, Detectives?" Leeward asked, but his attitude had deflated. "Because we're in the middle of a family dinner."

"We didn't mean to barge in on you, Mr. Lee, but . . ."

"I changed my name when I got married eight years ago. It's Leeward now."

There were footsteps in the background, coming closer. "Is everything okay?" The man asking the question was in his late thirties, roughly the same age as the lawyer, but with blond hair a little on the long side and sun-kissed golden skin. He was casually dressed in a T-shirt and yoga pants, and he was barefoot.

"It's fine, Jayson," CJ said. "I'll handle this. Give me a few minutes."

Jayson nodded politely at the detectives and moved out of view. Sheryn could hear giggling in the background; that had to be the couple's kids.

"I'll walk outside with you," CJ said. "No questions until then."

The ride down in the elevator was a silent one. "There's a small park on Second Avenue at Twenty-First. It's practically across the street," CJ said. "Let's head over there."

"Are your neighbors aware that you changed your name?" Sheryn asked.

"I've been public about that. There was a piece in the *Times* about men who change their names when they marry, and I was quoted in it."

"Did they also mention that you were married before?" Rafael asked.

They were at the park now. Aside from a couple of elderly people, it was empty.

"That was something Emily and I decided to keep between us," CJ said. "We were married for a very short time, just a few months, while we were in school. We've been best friends since we were nineteen years old, but anything romantic between us . . ." He paused and stared into the distance. "Well, that ended a long time ago."

"Your partner doesn't know?" Sheryn asked.

"My husband," CJ corrected her. "No, Jayson has no idea."

"What about Alex Traynor?" Rafael asked.

"I don't believe Emily has told him either. If she has, neither of them said anything to me." CJ watched each of them in turn. "A lot of people feel threatened by a friendship with an ex. And our circumstances are somewhat different than most."

"The circumstances are none of our business," Sheryn said. "Except as far as they pertain to Emily Teare's disappearance. When's the last time you spoke to her?"

"It's been a couple of weeks," CJ admitted. "We send each other links to articles all the time. But we had lunch a couple of weeks ago. That's the last time we talked."

"Did she say anything about heading out of town?" Rafael asked.

"Nothing."

"What about Alex Traynor. Did she talk about him?"

"Yes. She was starting to think about their honeymoon," CJ said. "Emily is a very informal person in many ways. I don't think she was prepared to stress about a wedding, but she and Alex both love to travel, and she wanted the honeymoon to be special. She was thinking of Madagascar, because neither of them had been there."

"We found Emily's passport in her apartment, so she definitely didn't leave the country," Rafael said.

"Alex told me Emily's involved in helping people who may not be in the US legally," Sheryn said. "What do you know about that?"

"Emily doesn't ask to see someone's visa before she treats them. There's nothing illegal in what she's doing."

"Mr. Leeward, the last thing I'm looking to do is build a case against Dr. Teare for helping folks," Sheryn said. "I only care about what she's involved in insofar as it relates to her disappearance."

"Sorry. It's a reflex," CJ said. "I don't know a lot of details. There used to be a storefront clinic in Corona, Queens, that she worked out of, but it's gone now. I think now there's been a place in New Jersey."

"She told you that?"

"No, I only found out because she was on a PATH train in the middle of that crazy shutdown in August. Remember that day the power was off for hours? She texted me because we were supposed to meet. I asked what she was doing out there, and she said it was work. Later, she didn't want to speak about it at all."

"Did that seem odd to you?" Rafael asked.

"Not really. Emily never boasted about her charity work."

"Was there anything unusual going on with Emily?"

"Not that I know of."

"Can you describe her relationship with Will Sipher?"

The taciturn CJ was suddenly animated. "Alex's friend? Is he involved in Emily's disappearance somehow?"

"We're still gathering information. But it's interesting that you'd ask that question. You have a reason to be suspicious of him?"

"It bothered me that Emily suddenly seemed interested in Will Sipher's welfare," CJ admitted. "She'd never liked him, but she tolerated him because of Alex's connection to his family."

"How was Emily involved?"

"She asked me about the prospects of overturning Will's conviction. I told her that was a dead duck with a lead tail. There were some hedge-fund portfolio managers who had their cases overturned on a technicality, but the ruling wouldn't have applied in Will's case." CJ paused. "The odd thing was that Emily brought it up several times. I assumed she'd taken pity on the man. I can't explain it otherwise."

"Is there any chance Emily could be romantically involved with Will Sipher?"

CJ laughed. "Absolutely not," he said. "She is very much in love with Alex. And whenever Sipher comes up . . . well, there might be some pity, but there's definitely dislike. Not love, that's for sure. From what she's said, that guy's a drugged-up mess."

"But a year ago, couldn't you have said roughly the same thing about Alex Traynor?" Sheryn's voice was soft.

CJ regarded her uneasily. "I suppose you could have. But Alex blames himself when things go wrong. Will Sipher blames everyone else." He cleared his throat. "I wish I could be more of a help, but I should get back to my family."

Sheryn regarded him thoughtfully. "You're holding something back. What is it?"

CJ's face was expressionless, as if he were in a championship round of poker. "I'm sorry, Detective, but you're mistaken. Good night."

The detectives watched him as he walked away.

"What do you think?" Rafael asked.

"He's lying," Sheryn answered.

"Really? Because I think he was being as truthful as a lawyer can manage. Which isn't saying much."

"He was just a little too controlled at the end," Sheryn mused. "There's definitely something he doesn't want to tell us."

CHAPTER 33

BOBBY

It had been a hell of a day. There was no upside to having cops in the building—that was for sure. Bobby had learned to always be cautious about when he let himself into Emily Teare's apartment—that loser Alex was always hanging around like a bad smell, and there was also his stupid dog to contend with. Friday evenings were the best, because Emily always went running, Alex taught a class downtown, and they left the dog with a neighbor. Bobby could unlock the door, step inside what felt like another world, and go through Emily's things for a solid hour, at least. That soft, soft silk that smelled so good it was almost like skin.

Over the years, Bobby had been obsessed with a few different ladies in his buildings. Before Emily, there had been a tenant named Michelle Turlock whom he'd fallen for. Michelle was a brunette with delicate features who smelled better than any lady he'd ever encountered. She traveled a lot, too, so she was like a dream tenant. She also had the sexiest lingerie, and there were mounds of it. He always wondered if that chick had a secret silkworm farm spinning thread just for her. He used to pocket a lacy underthing or two, but Michelle had eventually noticed that and contacted the police because she believed she had a stalker.

That whole episode still haunted Bobby, because he'd come within a hair's breadth of being found out and arrested.

It had made him so much more careful with Emily. He never took anything from her place, never dared.

But having cops in the building *was* a big problem. It wasn't like Bobby was into anything seriously illegal, but there were a few things cops could bust him for. He didn't need the hassle. While they were doing their thing upstairs—which took frigging *hours*, for crying out loud—Bobby had been relegated to his cave. One of the perks of being the superintendent was having access to parts of buildings nobody else could set foot in. Best of all were the ones tenants didn't even *know* about. Bobby had his own little den set up in the basement, in a room behind the boiler. He was smoking his second blunt of the day and fiddling with his phone when a hand dropped on his shoulder. Bobby jumped out of his chair, shouting.

"Sorry," Alex Traynor said. "I guess you weren't expecting anyone."

"What the fuck, man?" Bobby wailed. "You almost gave me a heart attack."

"I couldn't find you upstairs. I need to ask you a couple questions."

Alex was a big guy with one of those stone-cold faces that never betrayed what he was thinking. Sometimes he made hairs stand up at the base of Bobby's neck. It wasn't anything the guy had done, exactly. There was just something dark in the air around him, like a fog swirling around a grim reaper.

"You shouldn't even be down here. It's against the rules," Bobby said.

"This building has rules?" Alex asked. "That's a new one to me. What's this, the reefer room?"

There it was again, Bobby thought, feeling the heebie-jeebies from this guy. Something wasn't right inside his head. He held out the blunt. "You want?" Trust pot to soothe the savage beast.

But Alex shook his head. "I need to talk to you about Emily."

"What about her?"

"The cops told me you were the last person to see her."

"I don't know about that, man. But I saw her Friday night."

"Tell me about it."

Bobby racked his brain, recalling the details he'd given to the cops. "It was on the stairs. She was coming back from her run. We said hi. That was it."

"What time was it?"

"Maybe a little after eight." Bobby gave a shrug. "Could've been five, ten after, maybe."

"Did she seem . . . ?" Alex let the question trail off, as if he realized how hopeless it would be to ask about Emily's mood or demeanor. "What was she wearing?"

"Running gear. Black leggings, black hoodie. She had it pulled up."

Alex frowned. "She had a hoodie on?"

Bobby nodded. "Yeah. It was pulled up. I remember thinking she looked kind of like a turtle in it."

"But Emily's always overheated," Alex said. "She takes her jacket off even when she runs in winter. And it was warm on Friday."

That was true, Bobby realized. It *had* been unusually balmy on Friday. And he usually saw Emily come back after exercising with her hoodie tied around her waist. "That's weird," Bobby muttered.

"Are you one hundred percent sure it was Emily?"

"Definitely," Bobby said, but he was turning it over in his mind. The truth was he hadn't passed Emily on the stairs; that was something he'd made up for the police. He'd been inside Emily's apartment, treating himself to a luxurious date with her underthings. He'd had a stressful week, after all. When Emily had come back to the apartment that night, he'd thought he was busted. She never returned from a run that early. Bobby had been in her bedroom when the front door opened, and he'd frozen in shock behind the closet door. He could see Emily in the edge of a mirror, leaving a piece of paper on the coffee table and grabbing a laptop. Clad in black, she moved like a ninja. He heard the clatter of keys in the bowl by the front door. The funny thing, now that he considered it, was that she had her hood up the whole time. He'd never really gotten a look at her face.

"I mean, it all happened so fast," Bobby backpedaled.

"Did she actually speak to you?"

"I thought she said hi," Bobby said. "She definitely waved at me." He thought about it some more. "You know, it's weird."

"What is?"

"She was wearing gloves," Bobby said. "Black gloves."

"If it were winter, sure," Alex said. "But it's still like summer."

"I really think she had gloves. It's not like I studied what she was wearing. I saw her for, like, a nanosecond, man. Maybe it was a shadow. But it looked like gloves."

"This is important, Bobby," Alex said, his voice pleading. "Emily's life might hang in the balance. Are you one hundred percent absolutely, completely sure you saw her on the stairs? Could it have been someone else?"

Bobby thought about that. He liked Emily. It wasn't as if he'd ever want to see something happen to her. And while he didn't like Alex, a part of him felt bad for the man, who was clearly worried out of his mind about his girlfriend. But Bobby had to look out for himself. If he admitted any doubt, next thing the cops would be back at his door, and they would pull the truth out of him, and he'd be in deep shit. Michelle Turlock wasn't the only lady who'd called the cops about him, and once the NYPD put it together, he was done. He wasn't one of those stand-up guys who could withstand torture. He couldn't miss lunch and stay upright.

"There's no doubt in my mind," he said. "It was Emily, all right."

"There's one other thing," Alex said. "Why'd you tell the police we were fighting?"

Bobby considered him carefully. This was why he hated dealing with Alex. Sometimes, you could have a conversation with the guy, and then, without warning, it could all turn on a dime, and Alex would be eyeballing you like he was calculating the force it would take to snap your neck. Bobby gulped. "You guys . . . you fought. I mean, Raj complained to me."

"Raj complained about everything." Alex sounded disgusted. "Emily and I weren't fighting."

"Well, then . . ." Bobby would've made a joke about noisy sex if Alex hadn't been staring at him so intently. "What happened?"

But Alex didn't answer him. He turned on his heel and headed out. Bobby exhaled for the first time in what felt like a minute. Being completely honest, he was afraid of Alex. And he was starting to be afraid for Emily.

CHAPTER 34

SHERYN

When Sheryn finally got home that night, there was a storm cloud hanging over her head. Her husband spotted it the moment she came through the door of their apartment.

"You want to talk about it?" Douglass asked. In eighteen years of marriage, he'd seen her like this often enough to be wary.

"Not really. I might explode."

"Dinner's in the microwave," Douglass said. "Martin's studying for a math exam. Mercy's getting ready for bed. I'm in the middle of grading papers. When you want company, let me know. Oh, this has been calling your name." He handed her a glass of red wine.

She took a sip. "Malbec? You might just have ESP."

"I'd better, by now." He kissed her on the lips. "Last thing I want is you exploding. Don't mess up my kitchen."

He left her alone, and she sank into a kitchen chair. She was exhausted after a long day, but that wasn't the cause of her mood. The storm cloud had a name, and it was Will Sipher.

She sipped more wine and forced herself to get up. All she had to do was heat the lasagna that was waiting for her, but it felt like a lot of effort, and every muscle in her body ached. In spite of adroitly hopping a six-foot fence that evening, she felt ancient, as if she'd seen everything play out too many times already and couldn't deal with another rerun.

Will Sipher. Thoughts of the man were coiling around her brain like a serpent. She still didn't buy the idea he was behind Cori Stanton's death—he hadn't faked that fractured ankle, after all—but she was looking at his connection to Emily Teare in a new light. Everyone involved in this case had a shady side they were covering up, and that included the victim. CJ Leeward was holding something back, and she was willing to bet it was on that very subject. Bobby Costa, the superintendent, was bugging her; that guy was all flavors of weird, and he seemed to have an unhealthy interest in the missing woman. Most of all, it was Kevin Stanton who upset her. He'd been furious when she wouldn't arrest Alex Traynor on his say-so.

She took a bite of her lasagna and could barely taste it, she was so preoccupied. Because there wouldn't be any warrant to search Will Sipher's house now. They wouldn't be able to follow him or come within a hundred feet of him. Kicking the rock Sipher hid under had brought a boulder down on her head.

"What's wrong, Mommy?"

"Wrong?" Sheryn's head swiveled at the sound of her daughter's voice. "Nothing's wrong, baby. Mommy was just thinking things over. Why are you wearing a tutu? Daddy told me you were getting ready for bed."

"I am. I have to practice before bed," her daughter answered reasonably. "I know you were thinking about work."

"You're pretty smart," Sheryn said. "How'd you figure that out?"

"When you worry about work, you get a line there." Mercy's soft little index finger landed on Sheryn's face, in the furrow between her brows. "When you worry about other things, you pray."

"You're way too smart for an eight-year-old."

"You can tell me about it." Mercy pulled out a chair from the table and plunked herself down. "I'm a good listener."

"Yes, you are, baby. I know that." Sheryn couldn't suppress a smile. She was picturing a Charlie Brown cartoon, only with Mercy taking Lucy's place next to the sign that said THE DOCTOR IS IN. Mercy would also be drawn with a tutu and ballet slippers, given how obsessed she was with dance.

"What happened?"

"How about you tell me about your day?" Sheryn said. "I'd like to hear that."

Mercy shook her head. "It was bad."

Sheryn's heart fluttered into her throat. "Did somebody hurt you?"

"No, Mommy. One of the cats died."

"The cats?" With a start, Sheryn remembered the feral cat colony near Mercy's school. She worried about cat-scratch fever and other ills and always told her daughter to stay away from the cats, no matter how cute.

"It got run over," Mercy said. "Teacher said not to touch it, even though we wanted to give it a funeral. Everyone was sad."

"I'm so sorry, baby."

"You don't even *like* the cats," Mercy pointed out.

"That's true, but I also don't want them to come to harm."

"Okay, your turn. What about your day?"

Sheryn felt her resolve failing. She wasn't sure how healthy it was to tell a child about her cases, even a sanitized version. "Right now, my partner and I are looking for a missing woman."

Mercy's own brow furrowed. "Was it her husband? Because it's usually the husband."

"Where'd you get that from?"

"TV."

Sheryn contemplated that. "Well, it's sometimes the husband, or the boyfriend. I thought it was the boyfriend. Now I'm not so sure."

"Maybe somebody kidnapped her?"

"Why would they do that, baby?"

"To hurt the boyfriend," Mercy answered confidently. "Or maybe it's a stalker."

"Are all these ideas coming from TV? Because I'm going to check up on what you're watching." Sheryn tried to keep her tone light, but she was alarmed at the idea of the spot of sunshine that was her daughter speaking so nonchalantly about crime. Had Sheryn herself been like that at eight? She was certain she had not; her jaded facade was armor she had earned a little later in life. But she was struck by the fact that Mercy had essentially articulated her feelings. Because if Alex Traynor wasn't responsible, who was? Everyone she talked to sang Emily Teare's praises; they had yet to find an enemy. At the same time, the strange pattern of calls and meandering money trail suggested that Dr. Teare had a double life. What was still hiding in the shadows, eluding her?

After putting Mercy to bed, she went into her bedroom, shrugged off her blazer, and stood in front of the dresser, trying to calm her mind. When her husband appeared in the doorway, she hadn't budged.

"Hey," Douglass said softly. "Is there something you want to talk about?"

"Not really. I'm just tired." Embarrassed, she took off her watch and set it on the silver tray on top of the dresser.

"You are a terrible liar." He stepped inside. "Not that I'm doubting you need some rest. But there's something else going on."

"No, there isn't."

"You're obsessed with this case," Douglass said. "More accurately, you're obsessed with Alex Traynor. You ever stop for a moment to think about why?"

Sheryn didn't answer that.

"You've told me enough about Traynor that I feel like I know him, and I've never met the man," Douglass continued. "I know he has PTSD, and he can be violent. He's responsible for killing two women. He's a ticking time bomb, and he reminds you of your father."

There was an audible gasp. Sheryn belatedly realized it had come out of her mouth. She wanted to deny the truth of what he was saying, but she couldn't. Her father's ghost always lurked in the back of her mind, even when she examined Alex Traynor's apartment.

Douglass moved toward her. "I'm sorry. You never want to talk about your father. But I believe he's the reason you're taking this case so personally."

"You never met him," Sheryn said softly. "He wasn't a bad man. He came back from war with demons, and they ended up devouring him. It's why he killed himself. It's why he killed . . ."

Douglass wrapped his arms around her. Sheryn laid her head on his shoulder so that her forehead rested against his neck so tightly that she could feel his pulse. They stayed like that for a long time.

When Sheryn finally pulled away, she said, "This case has me questioning everything. I told you Traynor killed two women. Now . . . I don't think that's true. He's not a murderer. But he's still dangerous. Any man with PTSD is like a ticking time bomb."

"You're still talking about your father," Douglass said. "I'm not telling you your business, but I think you need to set all those feelings aside and start fresh."

"You're telling me to ignore my instincts?"

"No, just treat your gut with suspicion. People talk about their instincts like they're foolproof, but they're not. Think of all the black folks who've died because somebody had a *bad feeling* about them."

"That's not the same thing," Sheryn objected.

"It's a close cousin," Douglass said. "Instinct's not a superpower. It's made of experience and memory and belief. Prejudice is part of that. Believe me—I see it with my students all the time. In this case, I think the pain and hurt you feel about your father's death have been transferred over."

"I should've seen it coming. With my father, I mean." Sheryn swallowed hard. "And you have a point. With Alex, I've got that same feeling

I had before . . . only this time, I can do something about it. I couldn't with my father."

"Babe, you are brilliant at what you do. You are fearless and relentless. I know you give yourself over to the job completely. But in this case . . ." Douglass leaned in so close that she could feel his warm breath on her face. "You need some distance. Whenever your gut tries to tell you something, argue back. Put it in its place."

Sheryn leaned forward a millimeter and kissed him. "Right now, my gut's telling me to tear off your clothes," she murmured. "You want to fight with that?"

CHAPTER 35

EMILY

Time had no meaning in that bleak cellar. She was dying of thirst, but she wouldn't give in. *Think about something else, anything else,* Emily ordered herself. The last day she remembered was Friday, but who could tell how many had passed since? As she lay in her cell, pretending to be unconscious, she tried to reason how much time had passed. It felt like an eternity to her, but it could only have been a few days. The police had to be looking for her. Alex would be out of his mind with worry. The thought of him made her panic. What if he started using heroin again? She'd brought him back from the brink once before, but she knew he'd go off the rails worrying about her.

Would anyone figure out what had happened?

The police would, in the end, but that might be too late for her. There was evidence, nothing that would ever draw notice in day-to-day life, but enough that would damn her if the police took her life apart. They would find the prescriptions she'd written, and her career would be ruined. She would probably go to jail . . . if she ever got out of that cellar, which seemed like an ever-unlikelier prospect.

The question was, would they find the man who'd ruined her life? She was sure he'd never talk to the police. He'd been in enough legal trouble already. But she also knew he would sell her out in a heartbeat.

She thought of all the times she'd gone to his disgusting little apartment over the past few months, the stench of sweat making her gag. She didn't know how she'd gone through with it. No, that wasn't true. She'd done it for Alex. She had to protect him.

Stop calling me. I'm telling you it's over.

Emily would be the first to admit her sense of timing was off. But she'd panicked when Alex had shown up at her office, brandishing the prescriptions she'd written as if they were scarlet letters. How could she deny what was in black and white? It had to stop. She had to cut it off, go cold turkey.

She had no idea how impossible that would be.

As she lay there, eyes closed but facing the light bulb and the camera, she forced herself to stop thinking about it. If she got out of there—*when* she got out of there—she would fix things. Alex never needed to know. No one did. Instead, she focused on how she would take her captor down. Her one fear was that he'd enlisted a helper, some drug-addled wreck who'd kill for a fentanyl patch. That would be a problem, because in her weakened state she wouldn't be able to take two men on. Emily wasn't even certain she could take on one weaselly one who probably weighed less than she did, but she had to try.

She didn't know how long she'd been lying there when she heard a door creak open. The one thing she didn't understand was how little noise seeped into her prison. She occasionally heard a car faintly in the distance. Was the building that well insulated? She lay there, playing possum, while he came down the stairs, his steps hitting like thunder. Or was she so far removed from the world that the slightest noise reverberated inside her head?

She opened her eyes just the tiniest of cracks to see him, but all she could make out was a huge shadow coming toward her, blocking out light like an eclipse. She could feel his heavy breathing as he crouched to stare at her. There was a crinkling sound and a soft thud as he set a protein bar and a bottle of water in front of the bars. Emily opened her eyes and sat up, her arm shooting through the bars. She grabbed him by the collar and tried to yank him forward. In her reverie, she'd convinced herself she could smash his face against the bars. But he pulled free, and her hand grabbed at air, then dropped to the ground.

Before she could recover, he thrust a stick at her arm, and her body jolted back from the voltage he shot into her system. She cried out, but what emerged from her lips was a caw like a crow would make.

"Bitch," he muttered as she slid into unconsciousness. The pent-up hatred in that word would've sent her reeling if the fire under her skin wasn't burning through her synapses. Her body went limp as she passed out.

WEDNESDAY

CHAPTER 36

ALEX

When Alex woke up the next morning, he reached for the turquoise earbuds on his nightstand. He'd gone to sleep the night before threading the cord between his fingers, holding it with a reverence he'd seen others accord prayer beads. Were they Emily's, he wondered, or was he being a fool, tending lovingly to a pair of earbuds some random person had dropped or thrown away as garbage? His hand touched the top of the table and found it . . . empty. Alex sat up as if a gunshot had rung out. There was Sid, on the floor, tangled up in the cord and biting it playfully.

He had to wait for a minute for his heartbeat to slow down. "You're tampering with evidence, you know," he told the dog. Evidence? Even to his own ears, that struck him as a strange choice of words. If Emily had gone running on Friday night and didn't come home, what did that mean?

Sid barked at him, and Alex forced himself to get up. Having a dog wasn't a cure for depression, he knew, but it created a situation in which staying in bed for hours, struggling to get up, wasn't an option. He pulled on his jacket and took Sid out for a quick walk. When they returned, he went straight for the kitchen cupboard, remembering belatedly that Will was now in possession of his cache of pharmaceuticals. He was left with a variety of herbal ingredients—mushrooms and ginseng and the rest—which he was certain helped, but there was nothing to give his brain that firm but gentle nudge that two drops of LSD did. The thought that he was on his own without it, for the first time in months, left him on edge. He took a shower, hoping to clear his head, but thoughts nagged at him. The truth was he felt guilty about the fact he'd never mentioned his microdosing regimen to Emily. He knew she'd never approve. She stayed away from his shelf of herbal remedies, often telling him that if he thought they helped, that was the important thing. She clearly regarded them as placebos, even though she never came out and said so.

That made the thought of Emily writing prescriptions for opiates and sedatives even stranger. Emily generally avoided alcohol because of what had happened to her parents; she never used illegal drugs, to Alex's knowledge. What the hell had Emily been doing?

Back in the bedroom, he picked up the turquoise cord and threaded it through his hands. What kind of evidence was it, really? The police would laugh at him if he walked in with that. Alex saw only two possibilities about Friday night: either Emily had gone out for a run and never come home, or she'd come home from that run and had gone out again. At that point, the trail ran cold. He'd tried to follow her, but there were no other steps of Emily's to retrace. As far as he could gauge, she'd kept her usual routine on Friday. All of it was standard, except for the fact she'd disappeared from his life.

She left me a note. She left me her ring. If she hadn't done that, I would've been worried out of my mind.

Belatedly, he thought, *Maybe I should've been worried out of my mind all along.*

There was only one thing he could think of to do, and it felt like such a long shot it verged on the ridiculous. Besides the names of the drugs on the prescriptions, there was one other detail he remembered:

Emily had an address listed on the prescription pad, one he'd never heard of before. *Hemlock Avenue.* That was the only part his brain had snagged on. Hemlock, the poison of choice for ancient philosophers condemned to death. Of all the names that could've been on that page, it had to be one that made him think of suicide.

The actual street number was a blur, as was the name of the town. It hadn't been in New York, but in New Jersey. He went to his laptop, figuring it wouldn't be hard to figure out. How many Hemlock Avenues could one small state have?

Quite a few, it turned out.

Alex blinked at the screen. In one page of search results, there were Hemlock Streets in Newton, Sea Girt, Andover Township, Farmingdale, Laurel Springs, and Egg Harbor. Clicking through, he found others: Paterson, Cranford, Fair Lawn, Garwood, Roselle Park . . .

He was on a fool's errand, he realized. The pixels on the screen blurred and swam before his eyes for a moment. *You're not going to cruise every Hemlock Avenue in New Jersey*, he told himself. There was a possibility that Emily had faked an address, but he didn't see that as likely; she was cautious, and she thought things through. If she was using a New Jersey address, it stood to reason that there was some kind of medical center to stake it to. He added that to his search and struck out.

Physical rehab? No.

Walk-in clinic? Another strikeout.

It wasn't until he tried *nursing home* that he got a hit. There was such a place on Hemlock Avenue in Garwood, a small town southwest of Newark. He mapped the location; it would only take forty-five minutes to make the drive. Calling the place would be a waste of time; no one was going to cough up answers on the phone. He needed to talk to the staff face to face. It was the only way to find out the truth.

On his way out of the apartment, he knocked on Mrs. DiGregorio's door.

"Good morning, dear," she greeted him. "Any news?"

"Not yet, but I think I have a lead," Alex said. "I know I'm imposing, but is there any way you could babysit this little monster today?"

Sid barked in protest at being labeled a monster.

"I was just thinking of frying up some bacon," Mrs. DiGregorio answered. "Come on in, Sid."

The dog trotted in and turned to give Alex a long, accusing look over his shoulder, followed by a happy yip.

"Thank you," Alex said.

"Good luck."

Reserving a vehicle through a car-sharing service took no time at all. Fifteen minutes after he dropped Sid off, Alex was stuck in traffic in the Lincoln Tunnel. He took deep breaths as he inched along, aiming to keep his claustrophobia at bay. *Focus on Emily*, he ordered his brain. His own mind often wouldn't obey him, but today it did. Assuming he wasn't about to make a gigantic ass of himself—which seemed like a huge leap—he wondered how Emily would have connected with a nursing home. There had been several clinics in and around New York where she'd helped out; it wasn't impossible that a doctor she knew had pulled up stakes and moved. But the connection still felt tenuous.

It was a relief when he finally got to the turnpike. Traffic moved fast, and the rest of the trip flew by. Garwood was a tiny place, with a main drag defined by train tracks—North Street on one side of the rails, South Street on the other—and not much else beyond that besides residential streets stacked with homes that tended to be big boned and beautiful. This was what people meant when they talked about a bedroom community, Alex figured: close enough to the city for work, but far removed from the hustle at the end of the day. It had never occurred to him to live in such a place, but he found himself wondering if the bucolic calm would smooth out the rough edges of his nerves.

The Green Meadows Nursing and Rehabilitation Center wasn't anywhere near a meadow, but it was a stone's throw from Unami Park. Close enough for advertising purposes, Alex figured. He parked the car in the half-empty lot beside the two-story brick building. There was so much ivy covering its front and side that it seemed likely nature was in the process of repossessing the structure.

Alex had been working on his cover story on the turnpike. It wouldn't be hard to pretend that he had a parent in need of assisted care. It would allow him to talk to the home's staff, and he'd be able to casually drop Emily's name into conversation as the person who'd referred him. But when he walked through the front door, he realized immediately that his ruse would be useless. Sitting at the reception desk with a phone in her hand and a bored expression was Diana.

CHAPTER 37

SHERYN

"The lieutenant wants to see you, Detective." That was how the desk sergeant greeted Sheryn on Wednesday morning. His face looked hang-dog serious, like something unpleasant had transpired. And it had, Sheryn reasoned, as she walked to her lieutenant's office. Her visit to Will Sipher's house was boomeranging on her. Sheryn liked her lieutenant, even though he was stiff and formal and sometimes acted like he thought he was her white grandpa. He had a paternalistic air that could grate on her, but overall, the man was fair minded. She braced herself as she knocked on his door. "You wanted to see me, sir."

"Come in, Sheryn." He was a tall man with a white handlebar mustache that made him look like he'd served in the British Army at the turn of the last century. "I'm just about to go into a meeting, so let me get straight to the point. We've received a complaint about you."

Her shoulders slumped; she was expecting this. Will Sipher was a creep, but she'd jumped his fence. That was trespassing, no way around it. "I can explain. Rafael and I decided to—"

"Rafael Mendoza? What does your partner have to do with this?" The lieutenant stared at her, puzzlement making his mustache twitch.

"Isn't there a complaint against him too?" Now she was the one who was puzzled.

"No. He made no mention of your partner," the lieutenant said.

"Really?" Sheryn wasn't looking to pull Rafael into the quicksand with her, but something was off. Why would Sipher only complain about her?

"Listen, I would duck my head into Interview One and smooth things over if I were you. Your partner is in there now." He looked at his watch. "I know you can handle this. Sorry, but I must head out."

"Yes, sir. Thank you." Sheryn was baffled. There was no way Will Sipher was pissed off at her but not Rafael—he'd seen both their badges. Intrigued, she headed down the hallway. When she arrived at Interview One, she rapped on the door and immediately opened it.

That was when she got her first shock of the day.

There was Kevin Stanton sitting at the table. He looked pretty much as he had the day before, only the bruise on his jaw where Alex had slugged him was purpler. He had two new accessories: one was a neck brace, as if he'd been in an automobile accident; the other was an attractive woman with tanned white skin and artfully arranged blonde hair. She was standing, as if to show off her well-cut suit, which was the color of a fire engine.

"Hey," Rafael said. He was wearing a dark-charcoal suit today, sitting back in his chair with an elegant ease. The exaggerated eye roll he made in Sheryn's direction spoke volumes.

"Mr. Stanton?" Sheryn stepped inside the room. "What are you doing here?"

"Good morning, Detective," he said. "This is my lawyer, Miss Wiethop."

The blonde nodded at her. "Judy Wiethop," she clarified.

"Why are you wearing a neck brace?" Sheryn asked Stanton.

"I was so unwell yesterday after Alex Traynor attacked me that I had to seek medical attention," he answered. "My doctor informed me that my illness was gravely impacted by that maniac's attack on me."

"You mentioned yesterday that you'd had some medical problems," Sheryn said. "But nothing about a specific illness."

"I have pancreatic cancer."

"I am truly sorry to hear that," Sheryn said. "But I don't see what that has to do with the neck brace."

"I am in extremely frail health," he answered, raising his voice in a way that belied his words. "Traynor punched me in the face and snapped my head around. My neck has suffered an injury because of him. I want Traynor arrested for assault."

"You punched him in the head first," Sheryn said. "That's on video. If we arrest Alex Traynor, we have to arrest you too."

"I also want you punished for failing to do your duty."

Sheryn raised herself to her full height. "You want to come for me? Good luck with that. The detectives at the Seventh know you've been harassing neighbors you have a beef with. Maybe you didn't realize they'd trace the dead animals you left on their doorsteps back to you, but you were wrong."

"There's no need to make wild accusations, Detective," the lawyer announced. "I'm sure that Mr. Stanton will be satisfied when you arrest Mr. Traynor."

"That's why you're here? Because you think you can bully me into making an arrest?" Sheryn was incredulous. "Okay, let's do this. On your feet, Mr. Stanton."

"What? Why?"

"Because *you* are under arrest for assaulting Alex Traynor." Sheryn pulled out her handcuffs. "Hands behind your back."

Kevin Stanton turned to his lawyer. "She can't do this, can she?"

"Oh, she definitely can," Rafael informed him.

"This is all getting out of control," the lawyer interjected. "There's no need to arrest Mr. Stanton. He came here as a concerned citizen and as the victim of a crime."

"I take it you haven't seen the video," Sheryn said. "Because it clearly shows Mr. Stanton as the aggressor."

"But Mr. Traynor attacked a seriously ill man," Wiethop said. "That must be factored in."

"People don't get to throw free punches because they're sick," Rafael said. "The law applies just the same. This can go one of two ways. Either both men get arrested, or they can walk away from this and not end up at the Tombs."

"We're just here to have a conversation," the lawyer said, straightening her suit jacket. "That's all." She stared at her client, trying to catch his eye.

Stanton ignored her. "Traynor broke into my business and attacked me."

"He walked in the front door like any customer would," Sheryn answered.

"Whose side are you on, Detective?" Stanton's voice was a low growl.

"I can't arrest him when there hasn't been a crime. That's not how any of this works."

"Magda, my receptionist, will testify that she heard that bastard threaten my life. Will that help you make an arrest?"

"I'm going to pretend you didn't say that, Mr. Stanton. Because I do not want to arrest you for witness tampering. Maybe Ms. Wiethop can explain that law to you," Sheryn said.

"He murdered my daughter." There were tears in Stanton's eyes. "Why is he still on the street? Why isn't he behind bars?"

"Mr. Stanton, we've been over this territory before. This was a complicated case. The medical examiner—"

"Damn the medical examiner and the rest of them. They don't know what they're talking about. I could tell you all about Alex Traynor, how he cast aside my Cori for that doctor. The one who lied for him, who gave him an alibi. How convenient."

Sheryn studied him closely. "When you gave your statement, you told us that your daughter was planning to marry Mr. Traynor."

"She was. It's just . . . all her plans went out the window because of that woman." He wiped his eyes with the back of his hand. "Cori didn't tell me everything, of course. I've had to figure a lot of it out for myself. But I finally realized why he killed Cori that night. He wanted to get rid of her. She was in the way of his new relationship."

"You have proof of this?"

"Just look at what happened!" He was clearly exasperated. "And look at what's going on now!"

"What are you talking about?"

"That doctor-fiancée of his has gone missing. You told me so yourself. Do you think that's an accident?" He shook his head. "He's gotten smarter—I'll give him that. It was clever of him to come to my office and blame me. But that only makes him guiltier in my eyes."

Sheryn studied him closely, well aware that grief was as corrosive to the body and soul as any poison. Kevin Stanton didn't look well; there was something frantic about the man, as if a gun were being pointed at his head. He'd always been anxious, but that had been ratcheted up so far she could smell it. When you stare into the void, the void stares back into you. And Kevin Stanton had been staring into a bleak abyss for a very long time.

"Mr. Stanton, you have to trust us to do our jobs. I know justice isn't swift. But it is tenacious and unrelenting. I have not given up. I am working on this. I promise you that I will get to the truth."

"Just how long am I supposed to wait? My cancer is advancing. I don't have a long time to wait."

"I wish I could answer that," Sheryn said. "Did you write the letters Alex Traynor accused you of writing?"

"No."

"Mr. Stanton, where were you on Friday night?" Sheryn asked.

"What did you just ask me?"

"You're not actually asking my gravely ill client for an alibi, are you?" the lawyer added.

"I am indeed. I want to know your alibi for the whole weekend, starting with Friday night."

Stanton blinked at her. He didn't seem angry so much as astonished. "I was with Magda all weekend."

"Magda who?"

"Zimmermann. My receptionist. From the clinic downtown." He cleared his throat. "We've been seeing each other for a while."

"That's nice," Sheryn said, but inwardly, she was queasy. Not five minutes ago, Stanton had told her the receptionist would say Alex Traynor had threatened his life. Now he was using her for his alibi for the entire weekend. None of this felt right.

"I should go. I have appointments. Four-legged patients are waiting for me downtown." Stanton rose from his chair. That was the first time Sheryn noticed he was using a cane. He was milking his infirmity for all it was worth, even if he still looked like he could punch through a brick wall. "I shouldn't have complained about you, Detective. Obviously, I'll withdraw that. I apologize."

After Stanton and his lawyer departed, Rafael turned to face his partner, one eyebrow raised quizzically. "What just happened in here? I should've brought popcorn."

"That man is at the end of his rope," Sheryn said. "Desperation is leading him into bad places. He's got a vindictive side."

"You think we should kick this rock over? You really do have a thing for worms—you know that?"

Sheryn thought about what her husband had told her the night before. *Treat your gut with suspicion.* Her instincts told her Kevin Stanton was a grieving father grasping at straws; he had her sympathy. But she'd just heard the man in a frothing rage, calling Emily Teare a liar. "Let's be quiet about checking Mr. Stanton out. Can you start on that, please?"

"What are you going to do?"

"There's someone I need to talk to," Sheryn said. "I might be gone for a while."

CHAPTER 38

ALEX

Diana looked different than she had on the weekend. Her hair was still an unnatural shade of platinum, but it was rolled into an elegant chignon. She wore a long-sleeved pink cotton shirt blooming with roses. There was a small silver cross hanging from a thin chain around her neck. She was seated, so Alex couldn't make out the rest of the ensemble, but she looked ready to teach Sunday school.

Alex didn't hesitate. He strode up to the desk. "Nice to see you again, Diana."

She flinched when she looked at him. There were no colored contacts in her eyes today. Her irises were a soft, velvety brown, and they looked scared.

"I'm sorry, but you have the wrong person," she answered in a quiet voice.

"No, I don't. You broke into my apartment on Sunday."

"Lower your voice!" she hissed. There was an elderly woman in a yellow housedress slowly making her way toward the desk. Diana gave her a big smile. "How are you today, Mrs. Werner?"

"Fine, thank you, Susie," the woman answered. "I thought the chair yoga class was this afternoon, but Linda says it's tomorrow morning."

"Tai chi is this afternoon at three. Tomorrow at ten is chair yoga."

"Well, my brain is certainly going," Mrs. Werner answered. "Linda will be thrilled she was right again."

As the older woman headed away, Alex raised his eyebrows. "Susie?"

"Don't call me that," she murmured. "I hate that name."

"Fine. You can be Diana as long as you want. But you're going to answer my questions."

She crossed her arms in front of her chest, looking for all the world like a sullen child. "How on earth did you find me?"

Alex smiled. "Like I'm giving that up. Is there a place we can go to talk?"

"I have to stay at the desk," Diana said. "But it's going to be quiet for a while, because lunch is starting. No one in here misses lunch. But . . ." She looked around furtively. "If my mother comes along, you're just a guy in my support group."

"Your . . . mother?"

"My parents own this place."

"And . . . your support group?"

"Narcotics Anonymous." She was whispering now. "I kind of flamed out last year and went into rehab. That's how I ended up living in my parents' house and working here. This is life on the straight and narrow."

"But you've been veering off that course. What were you looking for in my apartment?"

"A place to hang out."

"It's like you're not even *trying* to come up with a good excuse," Alex said. "You were looking for the prescriptions Emily had written."

She squinted at him. "You found them? I hope you got good value for them. Those scripts are worth a lot."

"Who gave you the key to my apartment?"

She was defiant. "Emily."

There was only a tiny pause, but it was clear to him that she was lying. Alex leaned forward. "In that case, the police definitely want to talk with you. Emily's missing."

"Missing?" She stared at him. "Like face-on-a-milk-carton missing?"

"You can put it that way. You'll need to have a chat with them."

"No-o-o. Definitely not. Look, it wasn't Emily who gave me the key, okay? I only met her twice."

"How did you meet her?"

"I don't know the backstory, but she came out here to make sure everything was set up properly," Diana said. "She didn't want any blowback. That's why she was writing scripts for beta-blockers and other heart meds. It all looked legit."

Alex's heart sank. It was awful, having to acknowledge that Emily was knowingly mixed up in some scheme. Why would she do it?

"Who introduced you to Emily?"

"Cori's boyfriend."

Alex blinked. "Cori was dating a guy who treated her like shit. How the hell would Emily know him?"

"I thought Will was a friend of yours."

"Will?" Alex stared at her. It didn't make sense. A chill ran through him, and he realized he didn't *want* it to make sense. It was as if he'd put together a puzzle only to discover it was an image stolen from his nightmares. "Will Sipher set this up?"

Diana's expression was plaintive. "Please don't tell him you found me. He'll make trouble for me if he thinks I screwed up. If my parents find out I haven't exactly been following my program, I'll be homeless."

Alex couldn't process what she was saying. He was reeling. "I don't believe you."

"I'm serious. My parents—"

"No. About Will. He's . . ." Alex was about to say *He's my friend*, but stopped, realizing how ridiculous that sounded. "He wouldn't do this," Alex said, knowing that wasn't true but wishing it were.

Diana stared at him, eyes wide in disbelief. "Will would stab you in the back and ask why you're bleeding."

"I've known him all my life." It was a stupid thing to say, Alex realized, but it encapsulated how he felt. He knew Will had a manipulative, cunning streak, and he was aware of Will's ongoing issues with drugs. But that wasn't the same as discovering that Will had outright lied to him. Worse, Will had somehow snared Emily in one of his schemes.

"I don't know what he was like back then," Diana said. "But I know what he's like now."

Alex swallowed hard. "You pretended to know Emily. You had details about her. About me."

"Will coached me in case the worst-case scenario happened. He was supposed to stand guard outside your building and text me if you came in, but he screwed up."

Alex swallowed hard. "How did you know Cori?"

"I used to buy stuff from her."

"Stuff . . . like drugs?"

"Keep your voice down!" she hissed. "You're going to ruin everything for me! Will told me you were a psycho."

"Excuse me?"

She shrank back a little. "He told me . . . he told me you'd been known to hurt women."

"That's not true." Alex could feel his face growing red with shame at being accused of such a thing. It was not just a lie, but a particularly ugly one designed to go for his jugular. "I've got plenty of faults, but I've never abused anyone."

"What about Cori?" Diana's voice was barely a whisper.

"She was my friend, one of the few people I ever felt I could confide in." For all of Cori's complexities and rages, that was true. She was one of the rare people in the world who Alex felt never judged him.

"I mean . . . how she died," Diana clarified.

"What does Will think I did to her?" Alex asked. It was one thing to have the police be suspicious of him; that was their job. But discovering his friend believed the worst of him was devastating. "He wasn't even there."

"He warned me to be careful around you," Diana said. "He told me flat out that you killed Cori."

CHAPTER 39

SHERYN

"I knew you wouldn't be able to do without me for long," Sandy Reilly crowed when Sheryn showed up at his door. Since he'd retired from the NYPD three months earlier, she'd only seen him once. But as he pulled her into a hug, it felt like old times.

"You know I'm coming back out here soon with a bottle of scotch and my best poker face," Sheryn said. "Because I'm going to clean you out."

"Big talk, sure," Sandy said, leading her inside the house. He was Staten Island born and proud of it, and his tiny bungalow was barely a mile from where he'd grown up. "Hasn't that been your plan for the last decade? You're like Wile E. Coyote."

"Maybe I'll start ordering from Acme." Sheryn looked around. "Where's Maureen?"

Sandy shook his head. "Since I retired, she's threatened to kill me at least once a day. My wife likes the house the way she likes it. I'm messing it all up. I bought her a membership at the botanical garden over at Snug Harbor so she can go there with her friends and complain about me."

"Sounds like my in-laws," Sheryn said. "They both worked, but the house was still my mother-in-law's domain."

"Sexist, if you ask me," Sandy said. "How's Douglass and the kiddos?"

"Everyone's fine. Fingers crossed, a certain pint-sized ballerina is aiming to be in *The Nutcracker* this Christmas. Consider yourself warned."

"I wouldn't miss it for the world," Sandy said. "Do sit down. Coffee?"

"No, thanks, I'm jumpy enough." Sheryn sat at the kitchen table. "I told you I need to ask about the Cori Stanton case."

"I remember it well," Sandy said. "One of the only regrets of my career was that I never put the killer behind bars."

"Alex Traynor. Here's the thing. Looking back, we were certain that he did it. Why?"

"Well, him babbling out his confession on video at the station really helped," Sandy pointed out. "And what he said to you about killing a woman in Syria . . ."

"In our illicit little sting operation. Right. But if he hadn't *said* those things, would we have been so certain he was guilty?"

"I'm not sure I follow."

"What I mean is we didn't have any real physical evidence against Traynor," Sheryn said. "The scratches on his face happened earlier that night. There weren't any other wounds on him. No signs of a struggle on the roof."

"He was as high as an elephant's eye," Sandy said. "He could've done anything that night. Remember, we had him at the station and had to send him over to Bellevue. He was in rough shape."

"But Cori Stanton was just as high."

"She had that blood on her hand, remember? Her right palm was cut."

"But we never figured out how she got that wound," Sheryn said. "We had theories, but nothing proved out."

"Traynor lied to us about her being his girlfriend," Sandy said.

"Did he? We knew Emily was his girlfriend . . ."

"Fine, then Cori was his sidepiece."

"Cori's father insisted Alex Traynor and his daughter were a couple," Sheryn said. "He swore up and down that was true. Traynor said they were just friends. I'm worried that we took the word of a distraught father at face value, and that it influenced us too much."

"No, there was other evidence," Sandy said. "Cori had a key to his apartment. When TARU looked at her phone data, we found she was practically living with Traynor."

"Or with someone else down the block. That's not conclusive."

"She called her father, just before she died, remember? She told him she was bringing her boyfriend over to meet him the next day. Not the words of a girl who was about to kill herself."

"If you trust Stanton's version of the call. I don't know that I do anymore. He's been spinning some crazy stories the past couple of days, trying to get Traynor arrested."

"Like what?" Sandy asked.

"He punched Traynor and tried to get Traynor locked up for assault," Sheryn said. "When I wouldn't play ball, he lodged a complaint about me with the lieutenant. Even showed up with a lawyer this morning."

"Poor man has lost his mind," Sandy said. "Traynor also had that sneaky, snaky lawyer. You know who I mean. That Chinese fellow."

Sheryn rolled her eyes and sighed. "How many times do I have to tell you . . ."

"I'm just being descriptive," Sandy said defensively. "It's not like being Chinese is a negative thing. Leeward, that's his name. Thought he was a big shot. He just came in and took over."

"That's what convinced you of Traynor's guilt? You didn't like his lawyer?"

"Why is this important all of a sudden?" Sandy asked.

"Because Emily Teare is missing."

"Emily?" Sandy sat back in his chair. "That wonderful woman."

"I figured you for being a bit sweet on her."

"Who wouldn't be?" Sandy asked. "Beauty and brains *and* devoted to saving the world. The wonder of it was that she had anything to do with that Traynor character. No accounting for taste." He shook his head. "How long has she been missing?"

"Since Friday night. That's the last time anyone saw her."

"That's terrible. You think Traynor did something to her?"

"That's what I started out thinking," Sheryn admitted. "Now, I'm not so sure. Do you remember Will Sipher? Traynor's friend who also lived in the building. You know, the Caucasian investment banker."

"Ha ha." Sandy didn't sound amused.

"What? I'm just being descriptive," Sheryn said. "Anyway, he gave us a statement that night, which was basically that he saw no evil, heard no evil, et cetera. But it was pretty clear that guy likes his drugs. Why did we accept his statement at face value? How likely is it that he was home that night, sleeping soundly, and not part of the drug extravaganza?"

"No one ever put him on the roof. His ankle was busted up, remember? Traynor himself said Sipher wasn't there. Emily Teare said she didn't see him."

"Right, but Dr. Teare was on the street," Sheryn said. "I never believed she could see much of anything that happened on the roof."

"You think Sipher was involved in Cori's death?"

"I don't know," Sheryn said. "I can tell you he's been an asshole to deal with. My new partner and I went to his building last night, and he wouldn't even open his door."

"Sounds like you feel about him the way I felt about Leeward," Sandy observed. "Just because someone's a bastard, it doesn't mean they're guilty."

"I know. But it feels wrong. He should care about finding his friend's girlfriend, right? But he clearly doesn't."

"He may have been smoking or snorting a substance he knew he'd get arrested for," Sandy said. "There are other reasons he might not answer the door."

"There's someone else I wanted to talk to you about: Kevin Stanton."

"What about him?"

"Do you think he's all there, mentally speaking?"

"I only met the man after his daughter died," Sandy said. "Of course he seemed mad as a hatter. How could he not be? Her death broke his heart. I'm sure he's not the same man he once was."

"I know. But I think there's something off about him."

"If anyone harmed one of my kids, I'd hurt them too."

"That's exactly what I'm thinking," Sheryn said. "He hates Alex Traynor. What if he did something to Emily Teare as revenge?"

Sandy pondered that and shook his head. "Stanton's not a killer. I'm sure of that."

"How do you know?"

"Because he told me he thought of a thousand ways to kill Alex Traynor, and he couldn't follow through. He said it wouldn't be true justice."

Sheryn shook her head. "What if he's gotten tired of waiting for justice?"

CHAPTER 40

ALEX

Will wouldn't answer his phone, no matter how many times Alex called. He wasn't in his apartment, and he wasn't in any of his usual watering holes. There was one other place Alex could think of to look, and that was Mrs. Sipher's house in Riverdale. Alex hailed a cab and headed north. It was a long drive in rush hour traffic. When he finally arrived at his destination, twilight was settling into dusk.

He stood in front of Will's house for a minute. He had a lot of warm memories there. After his own mother had died, he remembered Mrs. Sipher saying, *You know, I always wanted to have more children. Come live with us. It will be good for Will to have a brother.*

That idea had always stuck with him. He'd put up with Will's grandiosity and superiority and everything else because he believed in that bond. His sense of betrayal was overwhelming. *If we're brothers, he's Cain and I'm Abel*, Alex thought.

The wrought iron gate around the property was locked, so Alex clambered over it. He rang the bell and waited. There were no lights on. If Will wasn't there, he had nowhere else to look. But he wasn't going to give up.

Alex walked around the perimeter of the house until he got to the back, where the kitchen was. Mrs. Sipher used to hide a key inside a fake rock next to the door, but it wasn't there anymore. Of course, Will would never do that. But Alex didn't need the help. He picked the lock in two minutes. As he opened the door, he thought he heard a scream but couldn't tell if it was human or animal. He stood still and listened, but whatever sound he'd caught inside the house had ceased. He moved inside as quietly as he could and locked the door behind him.

The kitchen hadn't changed at all in twenty years, except that in Mrs. Sipher's day it had been spotless and smelled of citrus; now, there were empty liquor bottles and greasy wrappers and a stench that suggested something had died underneath the rubble. The maple cabinets and cozy breakfast nook were still there, but there was grime on the floor, like an animal had tracked mud inside.

This wasn't like Will, he thought. He didn't understand what had happened to him, and at that moment, he was so angry that he didn't care. Before he could decide which way to go, he heard a woman cry out. That made up his mind for him. He raced through the kitchen and up the stairs.

The woman's screams got louder; it sounded as if she were being tortured.

"Emily?" Alex shouted. "Are you there?"

The scream died instantly; there was total silence instead. Upstairs, all of the doors were closed, but light spilled out underneath one. Alex rushed at it, shouldering it open.

Inside, Will was sprawled on a mattress on the floor. The walls were lined with photographs of his ex-wife, but the only piece of furniture in the room was a giant flat-screen TV; it was paused on a naked woman with giant breasts, her mouth open in a scream. The air smelled like burning plastic.

"What the hell are you doing here?" Will's deep voice was startlingly calm. He was holding a piece of aluminum foil and a lighter in one hand and a glass straw in the other. He wore an untucked white dress shirt and suit pants, as if he'd come home from the hedge-fund job he didn't have anymore. There was white tape over the bridge of his nose.

"What happened to you?" Alex asked, so astonished he set aside his anger for a moment.

"I had a little accident," Will said. "Or maybe a big accident. My nose may be broken. But I'm fine, fine, fine. Come on—sit down. Don't stand on ceremony. My mother isn't around to judge you."

Will had never really gotten along with his own mother. After Alex had moved in, Will had told him that Alex was the son his mother had always wanted. But Alex had no time to deal with Will's demons; he had enough of his own. He strained his ears, listening for any noise. Had the screams all come from that porno?

"Where's Emily?"

"How would I know?"

"If she's in the house, I'll find her," Alex said, turning and heading out of the room. The dark rooms on the second story didn't seem like likely prospects, but he checked each one out, stopping momentarily at the one with blue-striped wallpaper that had been his for a year. All of the rooms were devoid of furniture, though they had window shades that were pulled down. It was as if the house itself were in mourning.

"What are you looking for?" Will had gotten up and was standing in the doorway.

Alex didn't answer. He headed down the stairs. The grand rooms on either side of the front door were empty as well.

"Where is everything?" Alex asked.

"What?" Will looked around. "Oh, that. Mother's musty old stuff? Gone."

"You sold it for drugs?"

"It's not like I wanted all of that old lace and velvet," Will said. "I don't understand what you expect to find here."

"What's in the cellar?"

"Rats, probably."

In the low light, Alex couldn't see what, exactly, was on the parquet floor of the hallway, but it crunched underfoot. There was something feral about Will, now that he was in his den. It was as if he'd slipped out of a human disguise and taken a different form. "Why is it so dark?"

"Do you have any idea how much it costs to light this place?" Will asked. "Heat this place? It's a big old white elephant, and I can't unload it."

"I thought you were doing well for yourself," Alex said.

"The past few years haven't been easy," Will muttered.

Alex turned away from him and headed back to the kitchen. He opened the door to the cellar and headed down the rickety wooden steps.

CHAPTER 41

SHERYN

"So, I haven't come up with much on Stanton," Rafael said, squinting in the bright fluorescent light of an unfamiliar hallway. "But I thought his home address was interesting. Kind of a secluded spot near Huntington on Long Island."

"Secluded enough to hide an adult woman?"

"I'm way ahead of you, partner. Called Huntington PD to make a home visit. Stanton's cleaning lady was there. They only got as far as the front door, but everything looked copacetic."

"I'd feel better if they'd gotten inside." Sheryn stopped suddenly. "Hold on; I think we took a wrong turn. I really hate hospitals."

They were back at the Weill Cornell Medical Center on the Upper East Side, slowly making their way to the Brain and Spine Center. When they found it, Sheryn asked for Yasmeen Khan. They didn't have to wait for long.

"We need to show you a couple photos," Sheryn said, holding up a picture of Kevin Stanton. "Have you ever seen this man?"

Yasmeen stared at the screen for several seconds. "I'm sorry—I don't think so. Should I know him?"

"Don't worry about it. What about this guy?" Sheryn had a new picture on her screen.

Yasmeen inhaled sharply. "That jerk. I've met him, unfortunately. His name is Will Sipher."

"When did you meet him?"

"At the housewarming party Emily and Alex had back in February. He was drunk, or possibly high, or both."

"Sounds like a charmer," Rafael said.

"Oh, yeah. Oozing charm, or something," Yasmeen said. "He kept saying to Emily, 'Do you miss me?' He was like her shadow that night. He used to live in her building."

"Was he coming on to her?"

"He was hitting on *all* the women there, including me," Yasmeen said. "But he was bugging Emily. I asked Emily about him later, and she told me not to even mention his name. She didn't like him."

Sheryn filed that piece of intelligence away. "That's helpful. We also need to take a look at Emily's office while we're here. I have a warrant this time."

"Alex and I were in there yesterday. I guess he told you about that?"

"He did," Sheryn said. "What can *you* tell us about his visit?"

"Alex came over in the morning. We talked for a while. He's so worried about Emily. We both are."

"And he unlocked her office?" Rafael asked. "He had a key?"

"Um, no. He just, uh . . ." Yasmeen's eyes were wide. "Am I getting him in trouble?"

"Just tell us the truth," Sheryn said evenly. "All we care about is finding Emily."

"He picked the lock. I have no idea how," Yasmeen said. "It happened so quickly."

"And when you got inside her office, what did you do?" Sheryn asked.

"First, I tried her computer. But it's password protected, and we couldn't figure out how to get in," Yasmeen said.

"I guess Alex Traynor doesn't have hacking skills," Sheryn remarked lightly.

"Definitely not. And Emily wouldn't use a pet name or anything obvious as her password. It would be a random string of numbers and letters."

"You know, it's funny to be talking about Dr. Teare's office in the abstract," Sheryn said. "Let's go see it for ourselves."

Even though the office was next door, it took a few minutes to get the administrator, review the warrant, and obtain a key. Finally, Yasmeen nudged it open. Nothing had been disturbed since the day before.

"Our people in TARU won't have any problem cracking that computer," Rafael said. "We'll bring them in. For all we know, there could be train-ticket information on here, or destinations Emily researched."

"Do you think that could be true?" Yasmeen asked. "That Emily just chose to go away somewhere?"

"Let's just say it's not out of the realm of possibility," Rafael said.

"But, if we're being honest, the longer Dr. Teare is gone, the more it suggests foul play," Sheryn said. "That's why we need your help, and why you need to be completely honest with us."

"I thought Alex was going to show you the letters," Yasmeen said. "That's why he took them."

"We haven't seen them yet," Sheryn said. "There was a . . . situation yesterday, and the letters seem to have gone missing. Why don't you tell us about them?"

"They were in here." Yasmeen walked around the desk and pulled open the bottom-right drawer. She rifled through it, finally pulling out a file. "There were six letters, and they weren't threats, exactly, but they were scary. They said Alex was a murderer and that he would kill Emily next. None of them were signed." She opened the folder. "Alex put the letters in one envelope to take with him. There's not much here, just the other envelopes. Maybe they have fingerprints on them."

"You never know," Sheryn said, taking the folder from the doctor. She stared at the envelope on top. "It's got her home address on it, not her office address."

Yasmeen nodded. "Yes. But look closely. They don't have post office markings on them."

"Huh," Sheryn said, her brain busy on another track. "She kept the letters *here*, at her office." Sheryn closed her eyes and gave her head a shake. *Reset that brain. Don't make assumptions.* "Rafael, when I interviewed Alex Traynor yesterday, he told me about the letters and that he found them at the office. I assumed they were *sent* to the office. But they weren't. They were delivered to her home." She held the folder out for him to take. "If they didn't go through the mail, somebody had to hand deliver them."

"Be a hell of a lot easier if they'd run through the post office," Rafael grumbled. "For all we know, the letters could be old."

"Not that old. Cori Stanton died less than a year ago, and the letters referenced her death." Sheryn turned to Yasmeen. "Did Emily ever mention anything about feeling threatened or feeling like someone was watching her?"

"I don't think so. But I probably wouldn't know if she did. Emily doesn't really talk about things like that," Yasmeen said.

"Has she had any trouble at work?"

"None. She's fantastic with her patients."

"Sure. But any trouble with the staff?"

"No. Nothing like that," Yasmeen said.

"What was her fight with Alex about?" Sheryn asked suddenly. "You told me about it when we first met. You must've talked to Alex about it yesterday."

"I really don't want to talk about that," Yasmeen said. "Honestly, you should ask him."

"I'm asking you." Sheryn stared at the doctor until she ducked her head.

"He was worried that she might be using drugs," Yasmeen said quietly. "He confronted her about it."

"Was she?"

"No. Absolutely not." There was no doubt in Yasmeen's voice. Her gold earrings chimed as she shook her head.

"Alex Traynor isn't a kook, and he's had his own problems with drugs," Sheryn said. "He wouldn't have come running in here for no reason. Why was he worried?"

Yasmeen chewed on her lip while she stared at the floor. "Emily wrote some prescriptions. They weren't for any of our patients here."

"What kind of drugs?"

"Sedatives. And opiates."

Sheryn tucked that away for reference. "How many prescriptions?"

"I'm not sure. Please don't get her in trouble."

"She's already in trouble," Sheryn said. "We're doing everything we can to help her."

When Yasmeen left, Rafael shut the door behind her. "And now the search begins. Remind me what we're looking for, exactly?"

"Evidence of a double life, because something's not right. Sandy, my old partner, thought Emily Teare was an angel, but I'm not so sure."

"If she was using drugs, that could explain a lot. She could be off on a bender."

"She's normally so controlled," Sheryn said. "But control freaks are funny that way. Pull on a thread, and the whole edifice can unravel."

Sheryn went through Emily's desk while Rafael tackled the file cabinets. They worked methodically and meticulously. "Aha!" Rafael announced, after an unusually long silence. "A clue!"

"Good, 'cause I've got nothing."

Rafael held up a metal object. It was a flat, square box. "It's magnetic," he said. "Found it hiding on the underside of the cabinet." He slid it open. Inside lay a silver necklace, a medallion on a chain. Sheryn picked it up and held it up to the light. She'd seen it in every photograph of Emily in the field. There was an image of a man in the center, and around the edge was inscribed **REGARDE ST. CHRISTOPHE ET VA-T-EN RASSURÉ.**

"Behold Saint Christopher, and go on in safety," Sheryn murmured, holding it in the palm of her hand. For a moment, she had the oddest impulse to put it on. She held it up and realized the chain was broken. Why not just buy a new chain, she thought, or have it repaired? What did it say about Emily that, when something broke, her impulse was to hide it from daylight?

"Damn," Rafael said. "I thought I was onto something."

"Not going to fault you for trying. When did TARU say they were coming in?"

"Should be in an hour."

"Good. Because there's somebody we really need to talk to."

"Who's that?"

"Bobby Costa."

Rafael smirked. "That guy? Are you kidding?"

"Don't you recall what he said when we met him?" Sheryn asked.

"I remember him petting Emily's robe," Rafael said. "Like he was Gollum and it was the Precious."

"He asked us, 'Is that one of the letters?'" Sheryn said. "Remember?"

Rafael whistled. "Damn, you're good. He said something about a letter upsetting her. She went to see him about it."

"I wonder what else he knows," Sheryn said. "Let's hunt him down."

CHAPTER 42

ALEX

The cellar wasn't quite as desolate as the rest of the house. There was broken-down patio furniture piled against the wall, plus a collection of wine bottles that was probably worth more than the furniture. Funny that Will hadn't gotten rid of that, Alex thought. Priorities.

"I hope you're satisfied," Will said, coming down the steps behind him. "What did you think, that I was holding Emily prisoner here?"

"It didn't seem like a stretch," Alex said. "Not anymore."

"It's as if you suddenly think I'm a monster." Will picked a wine bottle at random. "Come on, let's have some Château Pétrus."

"I'm not drinking with you."

"Well, you know I hate to drink alone," Will said, marching up the stairs.

Alex followed him. "I found the woman you hired to break into my apartment on Sunday."

"It wasn't a break-in," Will said. "She had a key."

"Is that supposed to be funny?"

"If I stop joking, you'll know I'm dead," Will said.

"There's nothing funny about what you did. Just tell me why."

"Why, what, exactly?"

"Why you would be such an asshole?" Alex asked. "Why you would betray me?"

Will slapped his forehead. "Stop being so dramatic, Alex. You're acting like the world has ended. Let me be the one to tell you that it goes on spinning no matter what."

"Just tell me what you did."

Will sighed. "There's nothing sinister about it. Emily and I had a little arrangement."

Alex barely resisted an urge to choke the man. "What kind of arrangement?"

"Don't look so shocked! It was just business."

Alex felt weak in the knees suddenly. "The prescriptions Emily wrote. Were those for you?"

Will nodded. "I have certain needs that most doctors don't understand. Emily was helping me out."

Alex slammed his fist on the counter. "Don't bullshit me. Those prescriptions weren't all for your personal use."

"In case you haven't noticed, I'm not gainfully employed anymore," Will said. "In fact, thanks to my conviction, I'm not even employable."

"Meaning what?"

"Meaning that I have worker bees who'll fill prescriptions in the Tri-State Area. They work for a small cut. Don't give me those horrified eyes, like you just saw a dead man. We've had conversations about what a waste of resources the war on drugs is. I'm not some kingpin who hurts people. I'm a man with issues, who knows people with the same issues."

"That's how you justify what you're doing?"

"I'm not hurting anyone," Will claimed. "It's just a business arrangement."

"There's no way Emily would ever go along with what you're doing."

"Don't be so sure," Will said. "Everyone's got their soft spot."

That caught Alex short. "Soft spot?"

"I convinced her to help me—that's all."

Alex couldn't let that go. "What did you mean by *soft spot?*"

"Some people value themselves over everything else," Will answered cryptically. "They might respond to threats, but they won't help others out. Emily's not like that. She wants to help people."

"How did you get her into this?"

"You don't want to know."

Alex didn't think about what to do next. On an instinct he didn't realize he possessed, he shot one arm out and grabbed Will by the throat.

"Tell me." Alex's voice was a rough rasp.

Will stared at him in open astonishment, but he didn't answer. Alex squeezed his throat, feeling flesh give way under the pressure of his fingers. They glared at each other, until Alex noticed Will's pulse. Rapid and frantic, it felt like it was reverberating through his own hand. He realized where he was and what he was doing, and he let go. Will fell back against the counter, coughing.

"Never thought you'd go full Neanderthal on me," Will choked out. "The things love makes you do."

"How did you get Emily to agree to this?"

Will coughed again. "She did it for you, of course."

Alex froze for a moment. He had never imagined that Emily would trade in her integrity, her honesty, and her career for him. "What are you talking about?"

"The night Cori died . . ." There was a small catch in Will's voice, and he coughed again. "Someone actually did witness her death. I was on the roof with you. I saw you do it."

Alex's knees buckled, and he caught himself on the countertop. It was his ultimate nightmare. *Jump*, whispered Cori's voice in his head, but that was a ghost he'd conjured out of thin air. *She wanted to die*, he reminded himself, but that was his fault. He'd been responsible for a young woman's death in Aleppo; he'd cost Maclean his life. He had always known that he was ultimately responsible for Cori's death, too, because he'd helped her along her self-destructive path. But he'd never imagined that he'd actually pushed her off the ledge.

"Tell me what happened."

"Cori was in a foul mood that night," Will said. "I'd ended things with her, and she was not happy about it. She'd had these delusions that I was going to put a ring on it. Can you imagine? Trading down from Hadley to her."

"I didn't know you two were involved." Alex's voice sounded hollow. He was so cold all of a sudden. His breath rattled in his chest.

"We weren't in a relationship, Alex. Just sleeping together on occasion. Though she built it up in her head to be *so much more*."

"What. Happened. On. The. Roof?"

"Cori was furious that you rejected her. It was as if you'd insulted the essence of her being. She'd come downstairs to try to make me jealous, and I told her to go away. She said she'd make me sorry, but she finally left. I opened my window and heard you two arguing on the roof, but I couldn't hear that clearly, so I went up. Cori was swearing she'd destroy your relationship with Emily. She was going to tell her you were sleeping together." He wiped his eyes. "She shoved you, and you shoved her back. That was it."

"I actually pushed her off the roof?"

"It was an accident, Alex. Cori was, what, a hundred and ten pounds? And you're one ninety. She went flying over the edge."

Alex slid down the wall until he hit the floor.

"Don't you remember any of this?" Will's tone was acid. "Doesn't any of it ring a bell?"

"Your foot was broken," Alex murmured. "You whined about it all the time. I don't believe you came up to the roof. It would've taken you an hour."

"I was motivated by the fear of Cori's insanity," Will said. "And I was on some painkillers, so it didn't really hurt. I saw the accident. I know you didn't mean to do it. You were both out of your minds."

Alex was quiet for a long time. Will rinsed a glass under the tap and poured himself a drink.

"That's how you forced Emily to break the law, to risk her own career," Alex said finally. It was hard to get air into his chest. It felt like it was collapsing, like someone had pulled the pin that held him together and he was deflating for good.

"Think of it this way, Alex. Emily loves you so much she was willing to risk all of that for you. You should be thrilled. I wish I could find a woman who would love me like that."

"Did she . . . did she see me push Cori?"

"I'm not sure how much Emily really saw," Will said. "She was too far away. Still, she was willing to say *anything* to protect you. If that's not love, I don't know what is."

"You were going to report me to the police if Emily didn't help you?"

"I might have let her think that." Will was playing it coy. "But she was just as afraid of the guilt you would feel."

"You made her write prescriptions. What else did you force her to do?"

"When I needed the occasional cash infusion, she helped out," Will said. "Was that so wrong? Helping a friend out in tough times? Haven't I given you cash over the years when you needed it?"

"There's more, isn't there?" Alex said, getting up. He loomed over Will. "What else did you demand of her?"

Will shrugged and took another drink. The casual dismissal enraged Alex. Will had gone through life with delusions of grandiosity and entitlement, and he looked down on everyone else. Nothing would snap him out of that but a sharp, violent shock. The obvious thing was to grab a knife from its wooden block, but Alex would never use one of

Mrs. Sipher's cleavers on her son, and Will knew that. Alex had once witnessed Maclean taking charge of an unruly group of rebels at a watering hole on the border between Iraq and Syria. Just as his friend had done there, Alex picked up a wine bottle by its neck and smashed the other end against the countertop. Red wine splashed over the cabinet and floor, and glass flew everywhere. Alex held the jagged edge of the bottle against Will's throat. "What else?"

Will made a small squeak. "I didn't try to sleep with her, in case that's what you're suggesting."

"You think that makes this better?"

"Maybe?" His eyes darted around. "I can't believe you just did that in my mother's kitchen."

Alex pulled the broken bottle away from Will's throat by a couple of inches, but he didn't set it down. It wasn't much of a weapon; it wasn't much of a stunt, either, compared with Maclean's slick move. Alex's hand was sticky from the wine. He knew that Will wasn't afraid of the impromptu blade. It was the shock of seeing Alex, who'd always treated everything in Mrs. Sipher's house with care, suddenly smashing things that would keep him talking. "This is why she tried to get CJ to overturn your conviction."

"That's true," Will said. "I'd almost forgotten about that. CJ's such a bastard. You'd think he'd help out when his ex-wife asked him for help, but he said no."

"Ex-wife?" Alex repeated blankly. "Who?"

"Didn't you know? How could you not know?" Will gave him the tightest of smiles. "Oh, no. Emily hid that from you too."

Alex recoiled. It made no sense, and yet . . . the idea made the earth under his feet suddenly feel unstable, as if it were about to give way and let him fall into an even deeper pit. "What the hell are you talking about?"

"Emily and CJ used to be husband and wife." Will's irises were like black holes, alien in their opiate-induced expansion. "Maybe you should ask *him* where she went."

CHAPTER 43

BOBBY

"Whoa, you guys are back again?" Bobby shrank back from the cops at his door. He rubbed his eyes. "Seriously, I'm going to have to start charging you rent."

The two detectives glanced at each other, clearly unamused.

"We need to ask you some more questions, Mr. Costa," the lady cop said.

There was a sound in his head like the scratch of a record. He'd had trouble sleeping. Thoughts about Emily flitted through his mind. She wasn't *really* in trouble, was she? Alex was such a weirdo, with his odd hours and panic attacks and creepy mutt and druggie friends. It was probably all a false alarm. Bobby had read the note Emily left in the apartment, after all, and he knew she'd kicked stupid Alex to the curb. Everything could be explained away; he had no reason to feel bad. So why did he keep thinking about her? Finally, he'd turned to legal and illegal pharmaceuticals for assistance. Then he'd passed out for a nice, hazy while. Only that sweet slumber had left him ill equipped to talk to the cops.

"Right," Bobby said. "What do you want to know?"

"We'll give you a minute to put on some pants, Mr. Costa."

Bobby looked down. He had yesterday's briefs on and not much else. "Oh, riiiight."

He shut the door and rambled around his apartment. This was not a solid start. He pulled on his jeans and found a T-shirt that he thought might pass the sniff test, even if it had Cheetos dust on it. He could hear the male detective in the hall. "Pretty sweet deal being a super. You think they all get to sleep in till four in the afternoon?"

He couldn't hear the lady cop's answer. His hands were shaking. He lit some incense just in case there were any lingering smells that might raise suspicion.

"Sorry 'bout that," he said, opening the door again. "I get up real early, so sometimes I need a nap."

"We have more questions for you about Alex Traynor and Emily Teare."

"That guy is weird." Bobby lowered his voice. "You should probably come in. I don't want the other tenants hearing this."

The cops followed him inside.

"Sit, sit," Bobby said, pointing the cops toward his saggy olive sofa. He used to get such great stuff when tenants moved out, but it had been a while since there'd been a worthwhile couch. Most of the tenants were too lazy to move a good one inside a walk-up building. "You want anything to drink?"

"This isn't a social call," the male cop said.

"So, I guess you're here because of the stuff I told Alex last night?"

The cops shot each other a conspiratorial look. "Yes, exactly," the lady cop said.

"So, I've been thinking about it more, and I'm sure Emily was wearing gloves when she came in."

"It was seventy-five degrees last Friday," the lady cop said. "Why would Emily be wearing gloves?"

"I dunno." Bobby shook his head. He wanted to be as honest as he could about this. It wasn't like he wanted to see something bad happen to Emily. He'd be sad if she left the building and her sweet silky stuff disappeared with her. "She also had her hoodie pulled up over her head. It was kind of like somebody in a spy movie, you know?"

"What are you saying?" the male cop asked. "That it wasn't really Emily you saw?"

"No, it had to be her."

This was why Bobby hadn't wanted to talk to the cops. Give them a little dose of truth, and who knew what kind of trip you'd end up on? Anything he gave them, they'd tear into like wolves with red meat. When he'd seen Emily, he'd been hiding in her closet, panicked that she was about to discover him. He hadn't paused for one second to ponder whether that was *really* Emily under the hoodie. Instead, he'd been relieved when she'd finished her circuit around the living room and left again, locking the door behind her. He'd waited for a time, counting to a hundred, before he crept out of his hiding place. He'd looked out the window and spotted Emily across the street, handing some guy the laptop. He'd watched as Emily headed east and the man moved west.

"You don't sound so certain, Mr. Costa."

"No, I'm sure," Bobby said. "Sometimes people do that when they don't want to be bothered."

"Did she speak to you?"

"Maybe?" Bobby was sweating now. "She gave me a little wave."

"We need to talk to you about something else, Mr. Costa. On Monday, you told us about Emily receiving letters that upset her."

"Oh, yeah." Bobby was happy to shift to this subject. "There were a few of them. First one I remember was back in March. Emily came to see me because she was freaked out. She wanted to know who left it for her, because it had been sitting on top of the mailboxes in the lobby."

"Did you see who left it?"

Bobby shook his head. "No. But there was a letter every few weeks, I think. Emily asked me a couple times if I'd seen anyone strange in the building. The truth is not a day goes by when there aren't a bunch of weirdos around here. This is Hell's Kitchen, after all. I keep an eye on them, but no one stood out."

"We need you to look at some photos," the lady cop said, pulling out her phone. She held it up. "Do you know this man?"

"Oh, sure." Bobby felt relief; this was a question he didn't mind answering. "That Asian guy. He's a friend of theirs. I forget his name. He hasn't been around lately."

"What about this man?" She pulled up a different photo.

"Okay, that's Will Sipher. He lived in the building for about a year. He was going through a rough patch."

"Did you get along with him?"

"Oh, yeah. Will's a good guy." There were two kinds of tenants Bobby liked: ladies who smelled nice and had pretty underthings, and men who were good tippers. Will fell into the latter category, unlike that cheapo Alex. That was why Bobby was willing to overlook details, like that time a girl overdosed in Will's apartment. Will had been very, very generous with Bobby after that incident.

"Have you seen him around the building over the past few weeks?"

Bobby nodded. "Some of his mail still comes here. You'd think those guys at the post office would be able to handle a change of address, but I guess not." He laughed nervously. His palms were still sweating, and he rubbed them on the front of his jeans.

"When was the last time Will came by?"

"Uh, maybe a couple weeks ago?"

"Did you ever see him with Emily?"

"Oh, yeah, but she hates . . ." Bobby bit his tongue. Aargh, why had he blurted that out?

"But what, Mr. Costa?"

"Well, she, uh, wasn't happy to see him. Actually, she said something about kicking him in the nuts if he showed up again." He didn't like where these questions were going. Was Will Sipher that guy on the street with Emily? He'd been five stories up, peering nervously through the window. It was impossible to say for sure. But if it was, it proved Will hadn't hurt Emily, because she'd walked away from him. So why make trouble for Will?

The cops gave each other a loaded look, and then the lady cop swiped on her screen again. "What about this man?" She held it up again.

"*That* pain in the ass."

"Excuse me?"

"He's an asshole, that guy. I found him loitering around here a few times." Bobby squinted at the phone. "I got into it with him this one time in July, and he shoved me against a wall."

"Have you seen him recently?"

"Not since that time he pushed me. I was going to call the cops if he came back. What's his name?"

"Kevin Stanton."

"Doesn't ring a bell," Bobby said.

"He's the father of the woman who fell off the roof," the lady cop said. "Cori Stanton."

Bobby stared at the screen. "Holy shit."

"Excuse me?"

"I . . . I think I might've seen Emily on the street with him." Bobby's mouth was dry. There was no good way to give the cops this bit of intelligence. He was going to screw himself over if he wasn't careful.

"When?"

"Like, a week ago, maybe?"

"You don't sound very certain, Mr. Costa."

"Well, I'm not," he said. "Emily wasn't missing then. It wasn't like I was trying to spy on her, okay? She talked to a guy on the street. It was, like, a minute at most. He could be that guy, but I didn't get a great look at him. He was bald, though."

"Was it an angry exchange?"

"No. I mean, I didn't hear it. But it seemed . . . I dunno, polite?" He took a deep breath and tried to steady his nerves. "You don't really think this has anything to do with Emily running off, do you?"

"We're still investigating."

"Yeah, I know, but . . . she's not really in danger, right? This is just something between her and her boyfriend. I mean, that's the most likely scenario."

The cops regarded him coldly. "It's been several days, and there's been no sign of Dr. Teare," the lady cop said. "No contact with friends, no financial activity, no sightings of her. You want the truth? We're worried about her safety. The longer someone's missing, the less likely they turn up alive."

CHAPTER 44

ALEX

When Alex got to CJ's building, he felt like he was coming apart at the seams. Just his luck, it was Jayson who opened the door.

"Sorry to crash in on you," Alex said, trying to keep his voice steady, "but I really need to talk to CJ."

"Sure. He's in his study," Jayson said, keeping his voice low. "The kids are already asleep. Have you had dinner? We ate already, but there's plenty of Thai curried chicken left. Want me to heat some up for you?"

Jayson Leeward was one of the kindest people Alex knew, but he could barely look the man in the eye. "No. Thanks." Alex didn't mean to sound terse, but his brain was reeling. Emily had been married before? That news wasn't earth shattering. But Emily had been married to her gay best friend? That, he couldn't get his mind around. Will had to be lying. Only the lie was so outlandish, so ridiculous, it seemed like it might be true.

"Is there any news about Emily?" Jayson asked.

"Nothing yet."

"I'm so sorry." Jayson sighed. "You know where his study is."

CJ and Jayson's apartment was beautiful, filled with plants and overflowing bookcases and pieces of tribal art they'd gathered around the world. Alex could feel Jayson's eyes on him as he walked back to CJ's alcove. He knocked on the door, then opened it slowly.

"Alex!" CJ sounded genuinely happy to see his face. "Come in. Is there any word—"

"About Emily? Nothing. I'm here about something else." He closed the door behind him. The study was really just a converted walk-in closet painted a soothing pale blue and outfitted with a compact ergonomic desk and chair. "Actually, it is about Emily. Were you and Emily ever . . . *married*?"

CJ's face didn't betray any emotion, but he blinked. "How did you find out?"

"From Will Sipher."

"I didn't think Emily had told anyone. I certainly wouldn't have expected *that* character to be her confidant," CJ said. "Knowing him, he probably did a background check."

"You're telling me it's true?"

"It was a long time ago, when we were in college," CJ said. "It feels like another lifetime."

"But you're gay."

CJ eyed him coolly. "I understand why you'd assume that. But it's not like you and I have ever talked about our sexuality. I'm bisexual. I always have been."

Alex was embarrassed that this fact startled him. "You date men *and* women?"

"I'm dating, as you put it, my husband. We're been together for a decade. Please don't ask something stupid like 'How can you be faithful to one man if you're also attracted to women?' You're attracted to women, right? Yet you've been faithful to Emily, I think."

Alex gulped. "But if you were in love, why'd you get divorced?"

CJ leaned forward, steepling his hands. "First, we were only married for a few months. It was just after Emily's parents died in that horrifying car crash. We were both in school. She just . . . crumbled. Emily is one of the strongest people I know, but she broke down. I didn't know how to help her. When I look back, it was a stupid thing to do, but I wanted her to know I'd be there for her no matter what."

Alex felt like everything around him was happening too quickly, and he couldn't process it all. "Why did it end?"

CJ sighed. "Have you ever tried to sacrifice yourself to save someone else?"

Alex thought about that girl who died, the one he could've saved. "No."

"Mother Teresa said that for a sacrifice to be real, it must cost, must hurt, and we must empty ourselves," CJ said. "I grew up believing that. I felt like I had a duty to take care of Emily. That's what I told myself I was doing. But I wasn't being honest. I was attracted to men and didn't want to face that side of myself. It wasn't something I thought I could ever tell my family. By marrying Emily, I was trying to fix myself too. In the end, Emily was the one person I could really be honest with." CJ smiled. "That was the irony. I told her how I really felt, and we split up."

"Are you still in love with her?"

"No. I love her, but as my friend," CJ said. "In case you're wondering, she's not in love with me either. She's genuinely in love with you. And I'm in love with Jayson."

"Why keep it a secret?" Alex demanded. "Why didn't one of you tell me?"

"How much of your romantic past do you want to unbury for the person you love?" CJ asked. "Maybe that sounds like a cop-out, but Emily and I agreed it might make our partners insecure if they knew about our past. We agreed to let it stay buried."

"Did Emily tell you what really happened on the roof the night Cori died?"

"She's never talked about it," CJ said. "I thought you blacked it all out."

"I did," Alex said. "But tonight, Will told me what happened. He said I was arguing with Cori. She shoved me, and I shoved her back, and she fell off the roof."

"Do you think that's true? I don't believe anything Will's forked tongue spits out."

"It's true," Alex said. "I found prescriptions Emily had written for him. He was using what I'd done to extort drugs and money out of her." He looked at his hands and saw that they were shaking hard; his whole body felt like it was falling apart. "For the past year, Emily's been sacrificing herself for me."

"When she said she saw that poor woman jump, she lied?"

"Yes. Will said she was too far away to see what happened."

"But if she *didn't* see it, how are you so sure Will is telling the truth?" CJ asked. "What was Will doing on the roof?"

"He'd been sleeping with Cori, but he'd broken up with her. He heard us arguing and came up. Just in time to see it happen."

"I don't believe that. Not coming from him," CJ said. "Have you considered the other possibility?"

"What's that?"

"That it was actually Will who pushed Cori off the roof? He never admitted to the police that he was there. Maybe he framed you for what *he* did."

Alex turned that over in his mind. His relationship with Will was irretrievably broken; there was nothing he'd put past him.

"I wish I could believe that," Alex said. "But even if Will's lying, there's one thing that's true. Emily thinks I'm guilty. She's been trying to protect me."

"She never told me you did it," CJ said softly. He closed his eyes for a moment and pressed his fingers to his temples. "And now that we're talking about this, I can't believe I've been so stupid."

"What are you talking about?"

"The police came here to question me about Emily. They were pressing me for details, and there was something that came to mind, but I couldn't tell them."

"What?"

"Emily told me she met a woman who was in trouble. She said the woman was an illegal immigrant, and a man was extorting money out of her by threatening to call ICE agents on her. She'd had to steal money to pay him. Emily wanted to report the man for the crime, but worried the woman would get deported. She wanted to know if she could report him after the woman somehow got a green card."

"What did you tell her?"

"That the extortionist would go to jail," CJ said. "But one of two things would happen to his victim: she would either be deported, or she would go to jail as well."

CHAPTER 45

SHERYN

"I've got to be honest." Rafael shook his head in disgust. "You could smell the flop sweat coming off the super when we asked him questions. What are the odds that he's mixed up in Emily Teare's disappearance?"

"He's more mouse than man," Sheryn said. "He's nervous about his drug issues and thinks we're going to bust him for that. Funny thing is, I believe he might actually care about her safety. But he's definitely lying to us about something."

They were back at the precinct, both of them so keyed up that each time one of them sat down, the other got up and started pacing. It was stressful, but at least Sheryn had someone to share that burden with.

"You think someone is paying the super off?" Rafael asked.

"That's a guy who's been bought and sold a hundred times over. I did get the sense he's in Will Sipher's pocket. He *loves* that guy."

"How many buildings does he have access to?"

"I remember from the Cori Stanton investigation that there are two, plus a couple of others on the side."

"We need access to all of them," Rafael said. "Did you ever look at him for Stanton's death?"

Sheryn shook her head. "Nope. Bobby Costa was in Philly for Thanksgiving."

"How'd he get down there?"

"He drove."

"You ever check into when he left for Philadelphia?" Rafael asked. "Because I'm wondering if he drove down there after Cori Stanton died, just so he wouldn't be on the premises."

"We didn't look at him that hard. We didn't look at *anyone* else that hard. We thought it was Alex Traynor, and we didn't dig deeper." She rested her head in her hands. "When I saw Sandy today, I asked him why we were so quick to jump to conclusions. He said it was because there was so much evidence. But you know what the truth was? Neither of us liked Alex Traynor. It was a gut instinct that went sideways."

"You had enough evidence to damn him in most people's eyes."

"Maybe, but some of that evidence . . ." She grimaced. "Like the smashed-up burner phone. That seemed like such a slam dunk. Only, why was there a smashed-up burner phone under the table next to the door? I mean, you take all the trouble to break it to pieces, but you don't finish the job by putting it down the chute?" She spread her hands wide. "His prints weren't even on it. Either someone brought it over because they didn't want to dispose of it in their own building, or someone was framing him."

"Twenty-twenty hindsight," Rafael said.

"No, it's worse than that," Sheryn said. "You remember when I told you about how I had no trouble believing Traynor has PTSD, that I'd seen it before, up close? That was because of my father. He served in the army, but it . . . it broke his mind. He had hallucinations. He self-medicated with booze and dope. And he got violent. Seriously violent. My mother got the brunt of it. She finally left him after he almost choked her to death."

"I'm so sorry."

"The worst thing is I don't look at it like my father tried to kill my mother. I look at it like my father was wrestling with his demons and my mother got in the way. I know he wasn't a bad man."

"Wasn't. He passed away?"

"When I was in college." Sheryn paused, swallowing hard. She liked her partner, and there was a fragile trust growing between them, but she wasn't ready to tell him everything about her father, especially about how he'd died. It wasn't an easy subject for her to think about, never mind speak of. "Look, all I know is this: you send a man into a war zone, and what comes home isn't the same person. Maybe he's better and stronger for it. But, more often than we ever admit, what comes back is a badly broken shell."

"You're blaming yourself for bringing baggage to this job," Rafael said. "As if every single one of us doesn't do that. As if every bit of our perspective isn't shaped by what we've been through."

"Yes, but it's my job to stand back from that," Sheryn said. "To keep an open mind."

"You ever hear about the philosopher who wrote that it's the same thing to jump from a window as it is to be pushed out a window?"

"That's ridiculous."

"Most people think I'm Latino because of my name, but my mother was French," Rafael said. "She made me read all kinds of literature and philosophy when I was growing up. There was this one writer who fascinated me. His argument was that there's no such thing as free will, that everything we do is determined by our natures and by what we've done before."

"Then how is anyone ever responsible for anything they do, if there's no choice?"

"He said that they weren't, because no free will was involved."

"But people still know the difference between right and wrong," Sheryn argued. "If they choose to do evil, they're making that decision consciously."

"It's something I keep in mind when I'm talking to people," Rafael said. "It's not easy to separate a person from their programming."

"I've been carrying this bundle of ugly feelings about Alex Traynor around for the better part of a year. What I hate are people who think there's one set of rules for them and another for everyone else. I've been putting him in that boat."

"Then let's look at this objectively. Set the Stanton case aside. What do you see on the Teare case?"

"Kevin Stanton scares me," Sheryn said. "He's full of rage. I think he'd be capable of hurting someone if it meant Traynor would suffer too. I still want someone to get a look inside his house."

"Plainclothes cops at the Seventh are quietly keeping track of him," Rafael said. "He left work with his gal pal, Magda. They went to her apartment."

"Okay." Sheryn kept circling their desks like a distracted shark. "That's good."

"You know what we never talked about?" Rafael asked. "Emily Teare writing prescriptions for painkillers. What are the odds she's got an addiction problem?"

"Low. I honestly don't think that would escape the hospital's notice."

"Maybe she's a weekend user," Rafael said. "Her habit might still be in check."

"I still don't buy it," Sheryn said. "She got Traynor through rehab and helps him fight his addictions. She's going to suddenly start using the same drugs?"

"Well, then, maybe she's selling those scripts."

"That thought crossed my mind," Sheryn admitted. "But I've been keeping it on a choke chain, because she's the victim we're trying to help. I can't start eyeing her like a perp. Not until we find her."

"Yeah, I'm on that same page. But what if someone made her disappear because of those scripts?"

275

"That's like killing the golden goose. She can't write scripts for any-body now. So, unless she *chose* to disappear . . ."

"It doesn't really track, does it?" Rafael said. "Whatever angle you look at, this case is screwy."

"Let's go back to basics," Sheryn said. "The blood evidence in Traynor's apartment and in Teare's car. We've checked and double-checked, and that car did not drive into, or out of, the city. It doesn't add up. The apartment and car weren't in the same borough, and yet there's all this blood? To me, it's starting to feel like a setup."

"As if someone knew we'd look hard at Traynor if his girlfriend disappeared and we found evidence suggesting a crime."

"Exactly," Sheryn agreed. "He's the perfect patsy."

"Here's one thing I'm wondering about," Rafael said. "We've got these men we're suspicious of: Traynor, Sipher, Stanton, Leeward, and Costa, right? But we have that eyewitness account of a female walking away from Emily Teare's car."

"I thought you didn't believe that woman."

"I'm not sure if I do," Rafael said. "But what Costa said about the hoodie and gloves was wild. I'm starting to wonder if Emily actually came back from that run she took, or if that was someone else. What if there's another woman mixed up in this?"

CHAPTER 46

BOBBY

It was weird, being haunted by Emily. Bobby had always liked her, but suddenly she was on his brain 24-7. He kept telling himself it was no big deal, those white lies he'd told; he was just making sure he stayed out of the cops' crosshairs. People like him, they didn't do so well with the police. But the stress was getting to him, gnawing away at his stomach like a rat. He was getting an ulcer over this—he was sure of it.

Even though it was late, and all he wanted to do was sniff at some pretty underwear, he trundled up the stairs, breathing more heavily with each flight, until he got to the fifth floor. Then he knocked on Alex's door and waited. No one answered, and when he pressed his ear against the door, the apartment was silent as a tomb.

Suddenly, there was a bark, and Bobby's head turned back so fast his neck made an unhealthy crack, like a twig snapping. He knew that sound: it meant that ugly mutt was over at Mrs. DiGregorio's and that Alex was out for the evening. Bobby was tempted to let himself into the apartment, but the thought immediately depressed him. Imagine pawing over Emily's lingerie while she was missing? That felt like all kinds of wrong. It had been five days since anyone had seen her, and that didn't seem right. She hadn't run away. Something had happened to her.

There was relief in Alex's not being home. Bobby had decided he needed to confess the truth to Alex—he was going to come clean about the fact he'd been inside the apartment when Emily stopped in—although he didn't relish the thought. But not finding Alex meant Bobby's sense of guilt didn't let up either. It wasn't like he could tell Alex the whole story, but maybe he could reveal that he saw Emily—or this chick with the hoodie up, who knows who that was?—taking the laptop out of the apartment. That would give the cops a lead, right? He wanted to be helpful.

He headed down the stairs, moving slowly. He was starting to hate his job. It was convenient, and it allowed him the access he craved, but it also mixed him up in people's lives, and Bobby wanted no part of that. While she was alive, his mother had harassed him about finding a nice girl and settling down. But that had never been for Bobby, for reasons he could never voice to anyone. He liked girls—really he did. But he didn't dream about them, only their underthings. He'd read once that, in Japan, there were vending machines filled with worn panties. It sounded like heaven to him. By the time he reached the landing on the first floor, he was mentally planning a trip to Tokyo.

That was when he saw a man letting himself into the building with a key that didn't belong to him. He was one of the characters the cops had asked him about earlier. He couldn't remember the name, but he knew that man didn't belong there.

"What do you think you're doing?" Bobby asked, blocking his way into the corridor.

"Going upstairs," the man said.

"You don't live in the building, and those aren't your keys," Bobby said.

"I'm visiting a friend."

"No, you're not. You're the fuckhead who shoved me against a wall."

"I don't know what you're talking about." He tried to push past Bobby.

"Yes, you do. You've been hanging here like a spider for months. What do you want?"

"I'm just visiting my friend," the man answered through clenched teeth.

"Were you the one leaving those letters for Emily?" Bobby demanded.

"Leave me alone."

"The police were here asking about you. You're the one who was harassing Emily. You left letters for her, letters that got her upset."

The man's jaw was tight, and there was a vein pulsing in his forehead. "She helped her boyfriend cover up my daughter's murder," he said. "She deserves everything that's come her way."

"Did you hurt her?" Bobby asked.

"Of course not."

"You're leaving the building, or I'm calling the cops."

The big man gave a mirthless laugh. "I'm not doing a thing you say, fat ass." Then he shoved Bobby to one side, just as he had back in July, the last time Bobby had confronted him.

It took Bobby a moment to get his breath. In that time, the man was most of the way up the first set of stairs. "That was you on the street outside the building on the night Emily disappeared," Bobby called after him. "I saw you."

That caught the man's attention. He stopped in his tracks and turned his baleful eyes back on Bobby. "What?"

"The woman who went into Emily's apartment gave you her laptop. That wasn't even Emily, was it?"

"I suggest you slide back into the hole you crawled out of," the man answered quietly.

Bobby pulled out his phone. "Get out, or I call the cops."

The man didn't move a muscle. In the dim light of the stairwell, he looked to Bobby like a malevolent spirit, his face as lined as the bark of an old tree. His cold eyes were sunken in his head.

"That's it. I'm dialing," Bobby said. He tapped out 911, leaving his thumb hovering above the call button, ready to hit it in a heartbeat.

It was enough of a threat to make the big man move down the stairs.

"Okay," Bobby said.

"Okay," the man repeated. Then he shoved a knife into Bobby's throat.

There was a split second where time seemed to freeze for Bobby. He didn't feel any pain; in fact, he didn't feel the blade at all. There was a car horn honking outside, but it receded into the distance, as if it were hurtling away in space. The sound of his own heartbeat filled his senses. There was only Bobby and this man, and it wasn't even so much a man as a pair of haunted blue eyes in a face defined by fury. It was like staring into the ice, as if Bobby were freezing to death instead of bleeding out. Then the moment passed, and Bobby felt the most horrific pain he'd ever known.

"What's your emergency?" asked the 911 operator.

He tried to cry out, but he had no voice. The man picked up Bobby's phone, and his words filled the air. "I'm so sorry. My kid was playing with my phone and pressed the wrong button. I apologize."

Bobby heard the operator say goodbye and hang up.

"You just ruined everything," the man said, the calm tone he'd used on the operator replaced by frothing hatred. "*Months* of planning. All of it wrecked by a stupid piece of shit who should never have been born."

Bobby made a tiny squawk as he slid down the wall.

"Rot in hell," the man said. "I came here to do something important, but now I have to deal with your stinking carcass. You're going to pay for that."

He kicked Bobby in the stomach. Bobby couldn't cry out, but whatever little bit of air that was left in his lungs evaporated. Just before he lost consciousness, he felt his head hit the linoleum. The man was dragging him by the heels, away from the lobby.

Bobby's last thought was that he was leaving a trail of blood. Someone else would have to clean it up.

CHAPTER 47

ALEX

When Alex got home that night, it was late; the lights on the first floor of his building were off, as if they'd burned out. CJ and Jayson had talked him into eating something, and their company kept some of his darker demons at bay. He was ashamed of himself for rushing over in a frenzy because Will had managed, yet again, to push his buttons. What did it matter if Emily and CJ had once been involved, back when they were barely of legal drinking age? It was understandable to be shocked that Emily had kept the secret from him, but it had been churlish of him to be jealous. The person he needed to focus on was Will, who lied with such aplomb, largely because he baited his barbs with fragments of the truth. But Alex was certain he hadn't heard the whole story. Will knew far more than he was telling.

He paused in front of Mrs. DiGregorio's apartment. He wanted to reclaim Sid, but that didn't seem fair to either his neighbor or the dog. She loved the pup and spoiled him, and Alex knew that Sid would have a better night there than he would at his own apartment. Sid intuitively knew when Alex was struggling, and he always wanted to help. *At least one of us should get a good night's sleep*, Alex thought. He walked back to the staircase and followed it up to the roof.

He used to go up there all the time, but he'd stopped after Cori died. There were a couple of rickety metal folding chairs that looked in danger of imminent collapse, though they'd been up there as long as Alex could remember. He went to the ledge. It was ridiculously low by safety standards, just a little ridge of bricks that came up to his ankle. It would be so easy to fall off the side and end it all. The temptation was there. It wasn't far removed from his desire for drugs; they were both a quest for oblivion when reality became too oppressive. Yet he knew he couldn't do it. Emily was missing, and he wouldn't abandon her.

He looked down at the street. At this distance, in the dark, it didn't look that far away. What if Cori had jumped? Talking to CJ and Jayson had helped him, because neither of them took Will's story at face value.

He could have lied to you and to Emily, CJ had insisted. *If the police actually investigated him, what would they find?*

That was true. Will had never even admitted that he was involved with Cori until Alex had confronted him—and threatened him. He was a skeletal, drugged-out spider, spinning a web of lies that fell apart when you looked at it in daylight. Was he that ashamed of being involved with Cori? And why hadn't Cori told him . . .

He heard the door creak open behind him and half turned to see who was there. As he did, a projectile shot past him and over the edge of the roof. Kevin Stanton stood in the doorway, holding what looked under the moonlight like a handgun. Only the long projectile that had whizzed past Alex hadn't been a bullet.

"Fuck," Stanton said. "Literally nothing is going right tonight."

He fired again, and Alex dodged to the side, catching sight of a long, slim cylinder streaming past and over the edge. When Stanton fired again, Alex felt something dig into his shoulder. He pulled the dart out immediately and threw it on the ground.

"You're trying to kill me with poison?" Alex said.

"That's just a tranquilizer. It'll render your body immobile but keep your brain alert. I want you to be awake for this."

Wavy lines were creeping into Alex's vision, as if he'd suddenly entered a psychedelic tunnel. There was a dark spot in the center that was clear, and he focused it on Kevin Stanton's furious face. "You've wanted to kill me since Cori died. What took you so long?"

"It wasn't enough for you to die. You had to suffer first. I wanted you to experience the agony I've lived through this past year."

Alex felt a strong urge to lie down and melt into the roof; he had to fight to stay upright. "I always told the truth," he said. "I don't remember everything that happened the night Cori died. I know I wanted to end my life. Cori wanted to kill herself too."

"Because of you. *You're* the one who convinced her to die."

"You always denied that Cori was suicidal."

"Because the police wouldn't understand," Stanton answered. "If I'd told them Cori called me to say goodbye, they never would've investigated her death."

"She called you?"

"Cori told me you two were going to kill yourselves. She didn't want to die alone. Yet she died while you lived."

"Did you ever think why Cori tried to kill herself so many times?" Alex asked. It was getting harder for him to speak. His jaw felt wooden, and his tongue seemed swollen and gooey.

"She was dramatic. She loved the attention."

As much as the drug messed with his senses, Alex's mind was clear. "You sexually abused Cori after your wife left you," he said. "She told me." Cori had never uttered the word *abuse*, but Alex had understood the hints she'd dropped. It was part of the darkness she'd always carried with her.

Stanton rushed at Alex with a bloody knife in his hand. Stanton thrust it at his neck, but Alex grabbed his arm and shoved it into the air. Stanton's momentum knocked them both off their feet. They hit the macadam and rolled toward the tiny ledge.

It shouldn't have been so hard for Alex to pin the older man down and wrest the knife away from him, but his arms were like wet noodles; he could move them, but he couldn't quite control them. With his tunnel vision, he could see himself flailing away.

"Lie still," Stanton said, slowly rising until he was sitting on the ledge, his craggy face looming over Alex's. "Because if you don't die tonight, Emily will."

"What?" Alex said. For the first time, he realized his mouth wasn't cooperating anymore either. His lips were frozen, and the sound came out as *Ut?*

"Maybe I should've led with this," Stanton said, sitting up and staring at the blade of the knife. "If you love Emily, wouldn't you be willing to die for her?"

"Yes." It was like being in a dentist's chair, mouth open, able to form only caveman sounds. *Esss.*

"It's just one small sacrifice, when you think about it, because your life is worthless," Stanton said. "I've set up everything perfectly. If I die, Emily dies. If the police arrest me, she dies. There's only one way to avoid a tragic, painful, horrifying death for your girlfriend, and that's for me to get exactly what I want. Do we have a deal?"

You'll never get what you want, Alex thought. *Because that would involve Cori magically returning to life and suddenly adoring her father.* He knew that both things were equally unlikely. Cori's hatred of the man had burned deep.

"You . . . won't . . . hurt . . . Emily?" Alex asked. Choking out each word was an ordeal.

"No. Only you." Stanton almost smiled. He started to lift Alex's right hand onto the parapet but dropped it suddenly, as if he'd had a change of heart. Alex realized it was only a fear of being too close to the edge of the roof when Stanton moved to the other side of his body. Then he jammed the knife into Alex's left hand.

The pain was electrifying. Alex's scream was loud enough for the entire street to hear, but it blended into the dark melody of car alarms and traffic noise, broken glass and human shrieks. No one would hear a cry for help. It could be just another angry drunk rolling out of a pub.

"Good luck using that hand again," Stanton said, withdrawing the knife. "Oh, wait, you're going to die at the end of this anyway, so it doesn't really matter. Nothing does. I've learned that lesson this past year. Nothing takes your grief away or makes it better. It consumes you." He leaned closer. "So many times, I wanted to kill myself. But I couldn't let that happen, because I needed justice for Cori."

"Not . . . justice," Alex whispered in a labored rasp. "Revenge."

"They're the same thing," Stanton said. "I'm out of time. My doctor says I have only months to live. I had to make my move now. Even if the police catch me—and I expect they will—it won't matter. I won't live long enough to serve a day in jail."

"What did you do to Emily?" Alex could barely get the sounds out, but he realized his symptoms weren't worsening. His body felt slack, but his mind was sharp. How much of the tranquilizer had gotten into his bloodstream in that nanosecond before he pulled it out?

"Does it matter? I guess it does, to you." Stanton loomed over him, holding the knife in front of Alex's eyes, as if deciding which one to pluck out first. "She's trapped in a cage, like an animal. It seems only fair. She's the reason you were never brought to justice for Cori's murder. Emily deserves to suffer."

As he spoke, Alex realized that the deal Stanton offered—the right to torture and kill Alex in exchange for Emily's life—was a lie. Stanton hated him, and that loathing extended to Emily. Alex's death wouldn't be enough for him; he would ultimately kill Emily too. That thought ran through his body like electricity, firing every synapse.

"What will it be?" Stanton's face was so close to Alex's he could smell garlic on the man's breath.

Am I condemning Emily to death by taking this maniac out? Alex wondered. That thought was horrifying, but so was the idea of Emily being alive at Stanton's mercy. *Not your turn today*, Maclean used to tell him. Not your turn today, until one day it was. This was his day, Alex realized. This was where it all ended.

That realization powered through him as Stanton crouched over him, raising the knife again. Alex knew he didn't have much strength, but all he needed was some momentum. He reached for Maclean's lighter in his pocket. Stanton turned his head, watching Alex fumble with it.

"What are you going to do, set me on fire?" Stanton mocked. "Your fine-motor skills are gone."

"Don't need 'em," Alex muttered, dropping the lighter, grabbing Stanton, and rolling over the ledge. The knife sliced into his arm, but the pain didn't register because both he and Stanton were spinning in midair, hurtling five stories down toward the pavement.

THURSDAY

CHAPTER 48

SHERYN

It was one in the morning when Sheryn and Rafael met up at the crime scene. The stretch of West Forty-Eighth Street between Tenth and Eleventh Avenues was blocked off by squad cars. There was yellow police tape around the walk-up where Traynor and Teare lived. On the sidewalk directly in front of the building was a human form covered by a heavy white tarp.

"What the hell happened here?" Rafael said.

"We've got two dead males," a uniformed cop from the Manhattan North Precinct answered. He was on the young side, but with a grave demeanor that made him seem like he'd already seen too much.

"How did it go down?" Sheryn asked.

"Far as we can put together, two men were up on the roof of the building," the uniform said. "Kevin Stanton and Alex Traynor. They had a physical confrontation. There are knife wounds on both their bodies. They went off the roof together."

Sheryn walked over to the tarp and pulled a corner back. Kevin Stanton lay on the sidewalk. His head was turned to the side, but there was a knife sticking out of one eye. His other stared ahead, unblinking.

His mouth was open. *He must've been screaming when he died*, she thought.

"Where's the other body?" Sheryn asked, covering Stanton up again. He wasn't a good man, she reminded herself. Now, at least, he had a chance at peace. That thought wasn't as comforting as it should've been.

"Over there." The cop pointed at a gurney with another tarp pulled over it. Sheryn stared at it while her partner stepped closer to take a look. Something about the body didn't seem . . .

"This is the building's superintendent." Rafael sounded stunned. "Bobby Costa. His throat's cut wide open. What the hell happened to him?"

"There's a trail of blood from beside the staircase back to his apartment," the cop said. "That's why we found him so quickly. Yeah, he was stabbed in the throat and bled out."

"Where's Alex Traynor?" Sheryn asked.

"Bus took him over to Bellevue."

"He's alive?" Rafael asked. "The guy fell off a five-story building, right?"

"Yeah, right onto a pile of garbage and recycling with a mattress and box spring on top," the uniform answered. "He's one lucky bastard. Stanton might've survived the fall, too, if that knife hadn't gone into his head."

An eye for an eye, Sheryn thought, and shuddered. "What shape is Traynor in?"

"Hard to say. He was unconscious."

Sheryn nodded. It was too much to hope for a miracle that Traynor would be able to tell them what had happened that night.

"Are you going inside?" the uniform asked. "Because it's a bloodbath in the super's apartment. There's a little blood up on the roof, too, but it's not bad. We found a couple of these." He held up a clear plastic bag with a needle-topped cylinder inside.

"That's a tranquilizer dart," Rafael said. "The kind you take down a tiger with."

"How do you know that?"

"Don't laugh. When I started on the force, it was in San Diego," Rafael answered. "You know who they call when a critter escapes the zoo? You can fire these out of a pistol or a rifle."

"Gotcha," Sheryn said. "Stanton was a vet, so it's not hard to figure how he got animal tranquilizers. You think he used this on Traynor?"

"Sure looks like it."

"We also found this," the uniform added, holding up another baggie. Inside was a silver lighter. ELIAS MACLEAN was engraved on one side, with a date and what she took for an army service number. She recognized it immediately, even though the last time she'd seen the lighter was the night Cori Stanton died.

"This belongs to Alex Traynor," she said. "Can I take it?"

"It needs to be logged into evidence," the uniform said, taking it back.

Of course it did. She knew that.

"The thing is, why would anyone kill the super?" Rafael asked.

They both turned to stare at the shrouded remains of Bobby Costa.

"That man had his hands folded over his chest postmortem. His phone was placed underneath them," the uniform said. "The last number dialed was 911. But he told the operator his kid dialed the number by mistake."

"Bobby Costa doesn't have any children," Sheryn said. "I'd like to hear the recording of that call."

It took only a couple of minutes to get it. Sheryn listened, then passed the phone to her partner. "That's Stanton's voice," she said quietly. She turned her eyes on the uniformed cop. "I guess it's too early for any forensics?"

"If you're wondering about the weapon used, there's only one we've recovered. That knife." He jutted his head in the direction of Stanton's body.

"It's possible Bobby Costa got in Stanton's way," Rafael suggested. "He'd kicked him out of the building before."

Sheryn felt her heart squeeze inside her chest. "We showed Mr. Costa a photo of Stanton this afternoon," she said. "Maybe he was just trying to do the right thing."

"You want to head inside?" the uniform asked. "We've got cops posted on every floor."

"I'm going to head to the hospital to see Alex," Sheryn said. "You coming, partner?"

CHAPTER 49

ALEX

Alex wasn't sure if he was alive or dead. When he'd flung himself and Stanton off the roof, he was certain he was going to die. Their trip to the ground lasted only a second, but in Alex's mind, it felt like a lifetime passed. He had held on to the thought of Emily, to his love for her. *Don't let her die*, his mind shouted; that was as close to a prayer as he'd gotten since his mother had passed away. If he could've traded his life for hers, he would have in a heartbeat.

But instead of dying, he'd landed on top of Stanton, and the knife they'd been wrestling with had gone right into Stanton's head. Alex wished he could claim credit, but it felt like he owed a debt to gravity. They'd rolled to one side, sliding down a pile of trash until they hit the pavement and Alex blacked out.

As he came to, he realized his entire body was in searing pain. *Is this supposed to be hell?* he wondered. There were voices all around him, crowding his head and his thoughts and making him want to scream.

"Alex." Through the bedlam, he heard a low, gentle voice and felt a cool palm resting against the side of his face. When he opened his eyes, he saw Detective Sterling peering down at him. "It's okay," she said. "Do you know where you are, Alex?"

"No."

"We're at Bellevue Hospital. They don't have a bed for you yet, which is why you're in a gurney in the hallway. The nurse told me they've given you a few drugs."

"Everything is on fire." Alex's eyelids fluttered.

"They told me that's a good sign. Means there's no spinal damage. Maybe that's not much of a consolation right now."

"Stanton took Emily." Alex's mouth was so dry that moving it to speak made it feel like his lips were cracking. He remembered something and tried to sit up.

"Whoa, there. Let's take this slow," cautioned a man, putting a gentle hand on his shoulder. Alex hadn't noticed him before. His name floated through Alex's head and vanished. Sterling's new partner, that was the only part he could grasp.

"He said she's still alive, but for her to live, I had to die," Alex said. "I was going to let him kill me. Then he said Emily deserved to suffer. He was going to kill her no matter what."

"Did he tell you where she is?" Sterling asked.

"In a cage. That's all he said." His breathing got rapid; his heart fluttered like a bird in his chest. "He said if anything happened to him, Emily would die."

"Was there anything else he told you?"

"He said he was sick," Alex murmured. "He was going to die. That's why he did this."

The detective's phone rang. She glanced at the screen and handed it to her partner. "Could you take it?"

The man did, moving down the hallway.

"We're doing our damnedest to find Emily," she said. "Now that we know who took her, we're going to put this together. I promise you we'll do everything we can."

"I know you will," Alex said. His eyes closed again and his breathing deepened. He was fighting to stay awake. In the distance, he heard the partner's voice. "Sheryn, you are never going to believe who just resurfaced."

"Try me."

"Emily Teare," the detective said. "She's turned up at a bed-and-breakfast near Greenwich, Connecticut. We've got to get out there now."

CHAPTER 50

SHERYN

"I don't like this," Sheryn said. "It doesn't feel right."

"What are you talking about?" Rafael shot her a curious look. He had been driving when they left the city, but they'd switched places near Mount Vernon, and now Sheryn was at the wheel of his black Mercedes. It was five in the morning, and neither one of them had had a moment's rest that night. "This is an amazing ride."

"I wasn't talking about your car. Duh."

"Good. Because if you were, my husband would be offended."

Sheryn glanced at him. "Ooh, this is the first time I've heard about a Mr. Mendoza at home." She blushed slightly, hoping her partner wouldn't notice. Another assumption crushed; it had never crossed her mind that he was gay.

Rafael laughed. "He didn't change his name when we got married. It's Cohen. The car is a bribe. He got a huge promotion, but it involved moving across the country. I'm still not sure how I feel about that."

"I followed my husband down to Virginia for a teaching job once," Sheryn said. "That didn't exactly work out. But if he bought me a nice car . . . nah. I might've run him over with it. Honestly, we both couldn't get back to New York fast enough."

"Maybe I'll get used to it," Rafael said. "But I miss my family. My parents, my sisters, my cousins, everybody's out west."

"That's hard. Family was what pulled us back to New York. Can't live with 'em, but it's impossible to live without them." Sheryn stared out the window. It was hard to make out anything in the dark. Maybe it would've been pretty during the day, but it was just a gloomy blur before sunrise. "I'm still trying to wrap my head around Kevin Stanton's game. He goes to Traynor's building and murders Bobby Costa. Why?"

"I don't think that was premeditated," Rafael said. "That was a case of a victim in the wrong place at the wrong time."

"That's my take too. Okay, then Stanton goes after Alex Traynor. He tells him it's a choice between his life and Emily's. He makes Alex think his girlfriend is going to die. Then . . . bam! Emily magically turns up. And not, like, running out of her prison onto the highway turning up, which I could believe. But she's been a guest at a bed-and-breakfast all this time? No."

"I know it sounds crazy, but it's the first good news we've had," Rafael said.

"I'm not buying it," Sheryn answered. "Where's she been for the last five days? Unless she's been hibernating, it's hard to believe that she never used a credit card in all this time. You look at her accounts, you see this woman pays at the grocery store and everywhere else with plastic."

"I'm going to start calling you Kierkegaard," Rafael said. "In honor of the philosopher who said his depression was the most faithful mistress he'd ever known."

"You do that, and I'll tell the squad that San Diego PD would only trust you with a tranquilizer gun." Sheryn shook her head. "I can't get over the feeling that we're headed this way because Stanton planned something. Whatever it is, it's going to be ugly."

When they pulled up in front of the Amberley Inn, Sheryn couldn't help but admire it. It was a triple-decker old house that might well have been made of gingerbread. Gas lamps marked either side of the front door. Thick woodlands surrounded it, giving it even more of a fairy-tale ambience.

The front door was locked, so they had to ring the bell. After several minutes, an elderly woman with long gray hair pulled back in a thick braid answered the door.

"Sorry to bother you at this early hour," Sheryn said, holding up her badge. "I'm Detective Sterling, NYPD. This is my partner, Detective Mendoza. We're on a missing persons case, and the missing woman—or someone using her credit card—took a room here last night. Her name is Emily Teare."

"Sure. A very nice lady."

"Is this her?" Sheryn held up her phone. The woman squinted at it.

"Maybe?" the woman said. "Is that an old photo?"

"Maybe a year or two?" Rafael answered.

"I thought she looked older than that. She's quite tall."

"About five foot ten."

"Well, that *could* be her." The woman rubbed her eyes. "Sorry, I was pretty soundly asleep."

"We need to talk to her," Sheryn said.

"Now?" The woman's pale-blue eyes bugged out. "Not at this hour."

"When you've been a missing person for days, time is an issue," Rafael said. "If it's the right person, great. If not, we could be losing precious time to save the victim."

The woman grudgingly allowed them inside. She double-checked the register. "She's in the Gershwin Room. Our rooms are all named for composers."

"Great." Rafael didn't sound enthusiastic.

"Give me the key," Sheryn said. "We'll go up and wait. Call the room. We'll only let ourselves in if she doesn't answer."

The woman gave her a dubious look and muttered under her breath, but she did as Sheryn asked. The detectives headed up the sweeping staircase, which split at the landing, with one branch heading east while the other went west.

"This is a classy joint," Rafael whispered. "I'm going to have to come back here with Brett. He's a sucker for this kind of architecture."

They stationed themselves in front of the Gershwin Room, which had the name spelled out on the door, above a photo of the Gershwin brothers. The phone was already ringing. They let it sound off eight times before Rafael put the key in the lock. When the door swung open, Sheryn flicked on the light. There was no one in the room; the bed hadn't even been slept in. Knowing it was futile, she still checked the bathroom and the closet but came up empty. There was no sign of the woman claiming to be Emily Teare.

When they went back to reception, Rafael asked, "What kind of car was she driving?"

"I have no idea."

"Dead end," Rafael said. "This is bad."

"Stanton has been playing us all this time," Sheryn said. "Now he's dead, and he's still messing with us. Hold on." She sent a text to another detective at the precinct. Within a couple of minutes, she received the photo she'd asked for. "Could this have been the woman you saw?"

The innkeeper stared at it closely and nodded. "Yes, that does look like her."

"Magda Zimmermann," Sheryn said.

"Stanton's receptionist? Seriously?" Rafael shook his head.

"Also his girlfriend," Sheryn said. "She's in this with him."

"What do you want to do now?" Rafael asked.

"What I would've done yesterday if I'd had the time," Sheryn answered. "We need to check out Stanton's house."

"You think he stashed Emily there?"

"Maybe, but not necessarily," Sheryn said. "He was diabolical, so I don't expect anything to be simple. But no matter how good he thinks he is at covering his tracks, there will be evidence."

They'd been speeding on the way out to Greenwich, but they drove even faster to get to Stanton's house. If Magda Zimmermann was leading them in the opposite direction, Sheryn figured that was where Emily had to be. What scared her was that the clock was ticking. Kevin Stanton had planned to kill Alex that night, so he knew he wasn't going home. What awaited them there was anyone's guess.

They found the house just before eight in the morning. Rafael turned into a long driveway, and the road behind them disappeared behind a thick hedge. A few yards ahead was a two-story mock-Tudor house, with what looked like stained-glass windows on the top level.

"It's so secluded no one would be able to hear any screams," Sheryn said, stepping out of the car.

"True, but this Stanton bastard was nothing if not cagey," Rafael answered. "You think he'd stash a girl in his own house?"

"It's not like he could ask a neighbor. How many other places could he have?"

They approached the massive front door. Its brass knocker wore the face of a snarling dog.

"It's a big door. I could shoot the lock, but I'd like to find another way in," Rafael said.

"Don't do that. Let's circle the house. Meet you at the back."

They parted ways. Sheryn crept around one side, peering into windows and finding that everything that wasn't stained glass was covered with heavy blinds. Either Stanton had been allergic to daylight, or he was obsessed with privacy. She wondered what kind of a man he really was; never having known him before his horrible grief struck, she had no idea. Violence and vengeance had twisted him past the point of being recognizably human.

At the back of the house, she spotted a small cottage at the far end of the lot. "I don't remember that being here," Sheryn said quietly.

Rafael was coming around the other side. "You've been here before?"

"Just after Cori Stanton died. But Sandy and I were only at the front of the house and the parlor inside." She stepped toward the cottage. "Do you think the Huntington cops checked that out yesterday?"

"I doubt it." He looked at the kitchen door. "This guy *really* worried about burglars. There's an electric security system too."

"You want to handle the breaking-and-entering part?" Sheryn asked.

"My specialty."

"Good. I want to take a closer look at that cottage."

She ran down the garden. The cottage was painted white with crisp blue trim. The windows were covered with white lace eyelet curtains. The front door was locked, but she rammed it open with one shoulder.

Inside, she found what looked like a teenage girl's bedroom, only there were posters of horses instead of boy bands. The bed had a canopy covered in flowing pink tulle. There was a vanity table with a three-part mirror; above it on the wall were gold letters that spelled out **PRINCESS CORINTHIA**.

There were barely three rooms in the place, just the bedroom and a bathroom and a kitchen that might've been the right size for a frog prince. The bedroom was the showpiece; it was filled with photos of Cori Stanton, some of them at riding competitions. A collection of faded ribbons and unpolished trophies lived inside a glass case. Somehow, that made Sheryn the saddest: How might Cori's life have turned out if she hadn't died so senselessly?

She was just about to leave when her eye fell on a postcard lying on the night table. Sheryn couldn't remember the artist's name, but she recognized the subject immediately: Ophelia, lying dead in the water, with colorful flowers floating around her. It felt out of place in this frilly, girlish place, and Sheryn inched closer to it. Ophelia's eyes were open, and her lips were parted, almost as if she were in the embrace of a lover and not death. She picked it up and turned it over. Sir John Everett Millais, Tate Museum, London, was printed in the top corner; under it, in blue ballpoint pen, were handwritten words in Cori's distinctive old-fashioned script.

When I die, I'm not going alone.

Sheryn set it down, feeling a little shiver down her neck. It didn't matter anymore, whatever Cori Stanton had written. It wasn't going to help them find Emily Teare. Frustrated to come up empty, she let herself out of the cottage and caught sight of Rafael opening the kitchen door. At that moment, the house exploded, knocking Sheryn down and sending Rafael flying through the air.

CHAPTER 51

SHERYN

"You need to sit still," the EMT told Sheryn.

She hadn't realized she was moving. Her brain was struggling to process what had happened. It had taken refuge in the Ninety-First Psalm, which was playing on repeat, a familiar touchstone that centered her. "You will not fear the terror of night, nor the arrow that flies by day," Sheryn whispered.

"What's that?" The EMT wasn't a tall woman, but she had a squat build and shoulders that would've fit a linebacker. Sheryn's instinct was that she wouldn't want to meet her in a dark alley.

"I'm good," Sheryn said. "I need to see my partner. He's in bad shape."

"He's got some bleeding, second- and third-degree burns, and a blown-out eardrum. There's nothing you can do for him right now." As if realizing her tone sounded harsh, she took a breath. "We're taking care of him. You can see him at the hospital. He's in good hands."

"I need to see something." Sheryn gazed at the burned-out husk of Stanton's house smoldering in the near distance. She tried to stand, but the EMT put both hands on her shoulders and made her stay.

"You're not going anywhere until I get all the glass out of you," she said. "Now stop fidgeting."

Sheryn didn't let anyone boss her like that except her mother. But the part of her that was annoyed was surprisingly small; she respected people who knew how to get a tough job done.

"Good thing you put up your hand when the house blew up," the EMT said. "Otherwise, this glass would be sticking out of your face. Out of your *eyes*, for all we know."

Sheryn's skin burned as the EMT extracted another piece.

"You saved his life. You know that, right?" the EMT added. "At least, if he lives out the day, he owes it to you. Being at the door when the house blew up, he should by rights be dead now."

Sheryn only remembered a fireball coming toward her, consuming her partner. She'd run to him, knocking him down and rolling him over until the flames were extinguished. "Do you know what caused the explosion?"

"I can tell you they got the bigwigs here looking at that," the EMT said. "I can also tell you the conclusion ain't gonna be any different than when me and Ed got here. We've seen a lot of shit in our time. It was a gas explosion."

"Gas," Sheryn repeated. She closed her eyes for a moment to center herself.

"Yeah. The powers that be are going to hem and haw about whether it was from a gas leak or arson. I can tell you someone left the gas on and rigged a device to the kitchen door. There was one at the front as well."

"The owner of the house died in Manhattan last night," Sheryn said. "We believe he may have killed another man, and attempted to kill a third man, before he died."

"Shit," the EMT said. "You see a lot of crazy, doing this job. But balls-to-the-wall diabolical evil is not something you encounter every day."

Sheryn was quiet. For the better part of the past year, she'd thought of Alex Traynor as a perp and Kevin Stanton as one of his victims. Now, with blood dripping out of the cuts in her arm and a fire blazing a few yards away, she saw everything more clearly. Stanton himself had been a time bomb waiting to explode.

"It's worse than that," Sheryn said. "He also kidnapped a woman last week. We still don't know where she is."

"If anyone was inside that house, she's dead," the EMT said. "It's like a bomb went off. They should have the fire under control by now. You could talk to the fire marshal."

Sheryn felt guilty about not being by Rafael's side in the hospital. That was what partners did for each other, after all. But she knew he was in good hands; Emily Teare was not.

When the fire was reduced to embers and the marshal finally had time to talk, Sheryn blurted out, "He may have had a kidnapped woman in the house."

The man's thin lips pursed into a line. "That explains the remains we found. It looks like someone was in the basement when the house blew up."

Sheryn bowed her head and murmured a prayer. "Her name was Emily Teare."

"We're gathering the bones right now. There will be plenty of DNA evidence."

"Bones?" Sheryn echoed.

He nodded solemnly. "Yes, unfortunately."

"This I need to see." Sheryn headed for the shambles of the house. Nothing that had happened since the explosion felt real; a part of her was hoping to wake up from this nightmare.

"You really shouldn't go too close," the fire marshal called after her. "It's still not safe."

She was long past caring about safety, she thought grimly. As she got nearer, Sheryn spotted a small pile of bones, charred black and matching the asphalt in places.

"You have got to be kidding me," she whispered, picking up a femur.

She turned and limped back to the fire marshal. "Have you ever seen what a fireball explosion does to a human body?" she asked.

"What do you mean?"

"It can tear a person apart, limb from limb. But there's charred flesh on the bone." She held out the femur. "Unless Emily Teare was already a skeleton picked bare, this isn't her." She tossed the bone down on the driveway in disgust. "That monster played us every step of the way. He planted a skeleton in the house and rigged it to blow. This was supposed to make us give up on finding her. I hope he's watching from his perch in hell, because we are going to find her."

CHAPTER 52

SHERYN

There was a second veterinary clinic owned by Kevin Stanton in Babylon. Sheryn drove there in a mad dash. On the way, she called her precinct. "I need to know every piece of property Kevin Stanton owned in the last ten years. No, make that twenty years."

The clinic had a sign that reminded her of the one on the Lower East Side, even if it was older and the paint was flaking off. The receptionist inside matched the sign, aged and weathered, so that her pale skin crinkled like parchment.

"Detective Sterling, NYPD." Sheryn held up her badge. "Has anyone called yet about Kevin Stanton?"

"No, but he's never late like this without phoning me," the receptionist said. "I've tried his house and his cell phone. I'm getting worried about him."

Sheryn stared into her eyes. How did she tell a nice woman like this that her boss was a homicidal maniac?

"Kevin died in Manhattan last night," she said finally.

"Oh, no. Was it the cancer?"

"I'm afraid not. He tried to kill another man."

The woman winced and clapped a hand over her mouth. Her shoulders shook. "I knew something like this would happen, after Cori's death. He was a completely different person."

"I'm going to need to look around," Sheryn said. "Part of the investigation, you understand."

The receptionist's eyes were wet as she nodded. "Of course. Anything you need. I'll try to help."

Sheryn knew Emily wasn't in the basement of that building. It was too public a place with employees and customers and pets trooping in and out the door all day. Still, she headed down the linoleum-covered steps and stopped to take stock of what was down there. There were shelves lined with plain plastic containers; the labels read *detomidine* and *thiopental* and other chemicals she didn't think she could pronounce. Her eyes started to glaze over as she read them, until one hit her hard. *Ketamine.*

She swallowed hard. She had known that Cori Stanton used plenty of drugs; more than that, she was a dealer. Her friends had talked about her taste for angel dust and coke. The last dose of heroin Cori sold to Alex had contained ketamine, and seeing the word spelled out made Sheryn think of every wrong turn she'd made in that investigation. Mixed in with the guilt was another realization. She hurried up the stairs. "Where did Cori ride?"

"She took lessons at the Suffolk Equestrian Club in the summer and year-round at the Babylon Riding Center."

"Those sound fancy."

"Oh, they are. Only the best was ever good enough for Cori. Not that she appreciated it." The receptionist dabbed her eyes.

"Ah." That crystallized an idea in Sheryn's brain: all of this was about Cori. The fact that Emily's car had been found at Woodlawn Cemetery was no accident. Everything fit a pattern once she started to see it clearly. But there was no way Stanton could quietly stash anyone at a ritzy riding club. The man had been willing to go to crazy extremes, but he wasn't a magician. "Were there ever any smaller places where she rode? Not a club, but maybe a farm?"

"There was the farm where she boarded her horse," the receptionist added. "But it doesn't have horses anymore. One of the owners died last year. His widow was going to sell the place off."

"Who did she sell it to?"

"I don't know. I only heard about it because Kevin was looking at buying the place."

"Did he?"

"I'm not sure. He stopped mentioning it a few months back."

"I'm going to need the address," Sheryn said. "Can you write it down for me?"

CHAPTER 53

EMILY

When she wasn't completely delirious, Emily knew she was closer to death than she was to life. But she wasn't ready to die. As she lay on the floor of her cage, she knew as a doctor what was happening to her body. The muscles she'd worked too hard to build were being consumed by her own system in cannibalistic desperation. Her mouth tasted like something had died inside. The strangest thing was that she wasn't even hungry anymore.

Her dreams had radically altered as well. As she slid in and out of consciousness, she occasionally found her parents hovering over her, concerned looks on their faces. It was as if she were a kid again, like the time her family had gone to Bolivia to build a school and she'd come down with typhoid. For some stretches of time, she actually believed that she was in South America. The basement wasn't that different from the dark hut she'd been in for the first couple of days of her illness, before it was clear how serious it was and she had been evacuated to a hospital in La Paz. She'd thought she was going to die that time; her fear had been the product of an overactive teenage imagination. It didn't seem dramatic anymore: she was going to die on that dirt floor.

Now that her parents seemed to be in the cell with her, she'd stopped dreaming about their accident. That had been replaced by an image of herself, hurrying along a street in Hell's Kitchen. She was going to save Alex; she had to keep him from killing himself. But as she rushed along, a body slammed into the sidewalk in front of her. That was Cori Stanton, her pretty yet malicious face giving Emily a knowing wink. *You wanted me dead*, Cori said. *It's your lucky day.*

It was enough to make Emily scream and jolt awake. That wasn't how it happened, she thought. Cori had landed on the street, and Emily had been almost sixty feet away from her body. She had run to her, given her chest compressions, and tried to keep her alive, but it had been no use.

Be honest, Cori's voice whispered to Emily in the dark. *You would have been horrified if I'd lived.*

That was true, Emily acknowledged. But she'd also been aghast at Cori's death. It wasn't as if the woman had been a romantic rival who could be vanquished; she was a parasite who encouraged Alex's worst impulses.

Thoughts of Alex haunted her too. It was awful, knowing he'd learn the truth about her from other people. She'd thought she was protecting him, but now she only saw herself as a coward. *I've never met anyone so intent on helping people as you. You're fearless*, Alex had told her when he'd proposed. But he'd been wrong about that; she was afraid of so many things. Emily felt guilty, replaying the moment in her mind.

There are so many reasons I love you, Alex had said. *And so many reasons I want to marry you.*

Marry me? She had been genuinely astonished at that moment.

Too traditional?

Can I wear jeans to the wedding?

I was thinking barefoot on a beach.

If she hadn't been so dehydrated, she might have cried at that. She wanted to tell him the truth, all of it, but she would never have the chance.

When she heard the door creak open, she knew it was over. She'd thought she might die of thirst, but he was back to finish the job. She didn't have the strength to even lift her head, let alone her hand. She was going to die here, cold and alone, and no one would ever know.

A bright light shone in her eyes. She'd gotten so used to the darkness, she couldn't stand it. She shut her eyes, and a scratchy noise escaped from her throat.

"She's down here!"

It was a woman's voice, resonant and powerful. Emily squinted at the light. Whoever was holding the light shifted it to the side so it was no longer directly in Emily's eyes. She stared at the woman on the other side of the cage as if she were a vision.

"I'm Detective Sheryn Sterling," the woman said, kneeling in front of the bars. "Take my hand. I promise you're safe now."

FRIDAY

CHAPTER 54

ALEX

When Alex was finally allowed to see Emily, it almost broke his heart. She was propped up in a hospital bed like a doll, with an IV in one arm and bandages on her other arm and head. "Emily," he said, but the word broke as it crossed his lips.

She gave him a small smile. Her lips were cracked and shiny with Vaseline. It looked like it hurt to move them.

Alex moved closer, gingerly leaning over to kiss her forehead. "How are you feeling?"

"Like death, but not warmed over," Emily croaked; her voice didn't sound like her at all. "How are you even standing?"

"Everyone keeps telling me how lucky I am," Alex said. "I fell off a building and broke a few ribs. What are the odds of that?"

Emily smiled at him, but it looked more like a grimace. She was obviously in pain.

"If you don't want to talk, I can be quiet," Alex offered.

"No," Emily said decisively. "It was a nightmare, being in a dark hole with no one to talk to. Now I don't want to stop. The detective and I were already talking."

"The detective?"

"Hey, Alex."

Alex turned and saw Detective Sterling standing in the corner. "Hi." He couldn't have felt more awkward. The last time he'd seen her, he was strapped to a gurney at Bellevue.

"I'm sorry to spoil your reunion, being here," she said. "But Emily's badly dehydrated, and the doctors don't want her talking too much, so I thought she could tell us her story one time, together."

"That's fine with me," Emily said.

"I'll be asking some questions," the detective said. "I know you'll have some, too, Alex. I've also been gathering some information to help us piece this together. I'll try to keep this as brief as possible. Dr. Teare, are you ready to begin?"

Emily nodded.

"I'm going to tell you what we know, or what we think we know, and you can set me straight," Sheryn said. "You went out jogging in Central Park last Friday night, as you always do. While you were in the park, you were attacked."

"Yes. When I was running through the Ramble, I heard a snap, and something hit me in the back. I don't know what it was, but it was like I'd been shot."

"Kevin Stanton shot you with a tranquilizer dart, maybe two," Sheryn said.

"It happened so quickly. One moment, I was running. Then I hit the ground. It knocked me out fast. I blacked out for hours."

"Stanton was used to transporting animals," Sheryn said. "We think he wheeled you over to his van. It's not impossible that he carried you. He was a big man. His accomplice, Magda Zimmermann, denies any part in this. When we questioned her, she maintained that all she did was wait in the van. However, she admits to letting herself into your apartment with a key given to her by Stanton. She left a fake note for Alex—written by Stanton—along with your engagement ring. She also took your laptop and your car keys. Tell us what you remember next, Dr. Teare."

"When I woke up, I was lying on a dirt floor," Emily said. "There was a bottle of water, and I drank the whole thing. I was so thirsty. Then I passed out. I think there was something in it to drug me."

"The doctors said there are several different tranquilizers in your system," Sheryn said. "Stanton had you on knockout drugs the whole time."

"It was very Alice in Wonderland," Emily said softly. "I was in pain, and I felt weak. It was hard to see clearly in that cell, but my arms were bruised. I could smell blood on me, and I knew I had a concussion."

"We found your brother's car parked outside Woodlawn Cemetery in the Bronx," Sheryn said. "The trunk had your blood in it. We believe Stanton set that up—possibly with Magda's help, though she's denying it. She admits that Stanton thought it would help frame Alex. That seems to have been his goal all along. He wanted the police to believe Alex was responsible for your disappearance."

"No wonder I was so light headed," Emily said. "He took blood from me while I was unconscious."

"Did he ever speak to you?"

"Never. I didn't see him come in. I would pass out, and there would be a protein bar and water when I woke up," Emily said. "I realized if I was ever going to get out of there that I couldn't drink the water. I poured it into the dirt. Then I pretended to pass out again. After a long, long time, he came in. I grabbed him when he came close to the bars, but I was too weak to hurt him. He was armed with a Taser."

"It was a cattle prod," Sheryn said. "Even worse. I'd say you did well."

"He never said a word?" Alex ventured. "When he attacked me on the roof, he wouldn't stop talking."

"Maybe he had a thought about releasing Emily at some point," Sheryn suggested. "That could be why he didn't want her to see or hear him. But we'll probably never know."

"He wanted to hurt her because of me," Alex said. "Was there anything he didn't blame me for?"

"I doubt it. He poisoned other people against you too. He had Magda, his receptionist girlfriend from the clinic downtown, pretend to be Emily. She used your credit cards in Connecticut, Massachusetts, and Vermont. She cracked when we caught her, though, especially when she found out Stanton was dead. He wanted her to draw us away from the city. I guess he thought that would keep us from finding you."

"From finding me alive," Emily whispered.

They were all quiet for a moment. "I should let the two of you have some time together," Sheryn said. "Alex, could we speak in private for a minute?"

Alex followed Sheryn into the hallway. "How's your partner doing?"

"Rafael's tough as old boots," she said. "They're releasing him from the hospital today, heaven help us all. I'm driving him into the city. He's cranky, but he's fine."

"I'm glad. Are you okay?" He gestured at her left hand, which had a white bandage wrapped around the palm.

"I'm fine. I manage to get into trouble even at my desk," she said. "I wanted to let you know that the investigation isn't quite wrapped up yet. It will be ongoing for a few more days, at least," Sheryn said.

"It sounded in there like you know exactly what happened."

"With Stanton dead, there are going to be some things we'll never be certain of," she answered. "And there are some other loose ends. I'll be in touch with you a fair bit as we piece it all together."

"Whatever you need."

"I also wanted to ask how you're doing," she said. "You've been through the wringer."

"This sounds crazy, but clearer on a lot of things." Alex paused. PTSD was such a private circle of hell, and he felt uncomfortable talking about it. "This will sound terrible, but it's a relief to know that there was a reason for my paranoia. Stanton was out to get me, and Emily. All those feelings I had . . . they weren't just from PTSD."

"That doesn't sound wrong to me."

"In the past week, I've been out among crowds more than I have in six months. It's still not easy, but I think it might be getting less awful."

"I guess your students will miss their workshop tonight."

"No." Alex shook his head vehemently. "It's not like the hospital will let me stay here with Emily. We're meeting in Kew Gardens. There might be a break-in involved."

Sheryn raised an eyebrow. "I'm going to pretend I didn't hear that part." He knew she was only teasing him, but his heart pounded in his chest when she reached into her pocket and pulled out a folded sheet of paper. She slid it through her fingers a couple of times before holding it out to Alex. He was afraid to take it, wary that their détente was suddenly over.

"I wanted to give you this," she said. "We never had occasion to talk about this, but my mother's a therapist. Not that I'm suggesting you see her—because, hoo boy, don't get me started—but I asked her for some information. About counselors and PTSD and treatment and, well, you know."

Alex had never known Sheryn to ramble. She was the strong, silent type; there was plenty she had in common with his friend Maclean. He took the page from her and unfolded it. There was a lot of information there, neatly typed out in black and white, but it blurred in front of his eyes. "I appreciate this, but I'm getting everything under control."

"No, you're not. When things get better, you can tell yourself that, but it's an illusion."

Alex shook his head. "I don't think I'm the type to go into therapy."

"Why not?" Sheryn asked.

He stared at her, unsettled by the question. "I hate talking about what happened," he admitted. "It brings it all back. It makes it worse."

"It doesn't go away because you ignore it."

"No, but it's dredging up memories I'd rather stay buried."

Sheryn tapped the toe of her shiny black boot against the wall a couple of times, as if there were a tiny pebble inside that she wanted to dislodge. "You know, you remind me of my father in some ways."

Something in her tone made Alex examine her more closely. Her expression was neutral, but her dark eyes were oddly glossy. Not teary, but not far off from being that way.

"He served in the army," Sheryn said. "It was a proud family tradition. But then he was discharged, and we were told it was a heart problem, but that really wasn't it at all. He was paranoid, just full of conspiracy theories. He went into attack mode at the tiniest provocation. He'd walk around the house at night like he was guarding it. He was always a heartbeat away from full panic."

"I'm so sorry," Alex said.

"It got really bad," she continued. "Bad enough that my mother made him leave. They didn't divorce, but she was scared. And with good reason. He ended up killing a fellow veteran, a man who'd given him a job. Then he turned his gun on himself."

Alex tried to speak, but he couldn't find any words.

"I was a teenager, so I didn't understand everything going on," she added. "But I knew something was wrong, and all I did was pretend I didn't."

He started to answer, but she put up her injured hand. "I'm not done yet," she said. "That's why I became a cop. I don't let things go. I'm not letting *you* go. You're getting the help you need this time."

The paper was still in his hand, and he blinked at it as it came into focus. It was a bad sign, he knew, that even thinking about therapy made him so anxious. That could be taken as a clue to how much he actually needed it. "You're impossible to argue with."

"My husband calls me *relentless*," Sheryn said. "I like to take that as a compliment."

"I don't even know how to thank you."

She took a breath. "I owe you an apology, Alex. I went into this assuming the worst about you, and I was wrong to do that."

"I understand why," Alex said. "I don't blame you. Plus, you found Emily. She's only alive because of you."

"She's alive because of what you did too," Sheryn answered. "I didn't know what Stanton was, until it was too late." She glanced at her watch. "I should get going. Take good care of your girl."

Alex smiled. "I guess there's a first time for everything. She's always been the one who took care of me."

Sheryn gave him a long, searching look. "You're tougher than you think," she said. "I have the feeling she's going to need you more than you realize." Before he could ask her what she meant, she turned away, hurrying down the corridor and vanishing around a corner.

WEDNESDAY

CHAPTER 55

SHERYN

Sheryn waited until Emily Teare was discharged from the hospital before she went to see her again. A small part of her felt guilty while she watched the building, waiting for Alex to come out with Sid bounding along on his red leash. They walked up a block, and when Sheryn was sure they were well on their way to DeWitt Clinton Park, she headed upstairs.

When Emily Teare answered the door, she was wearing a long green silk robe. "I'm sorry to bother you, but we need to talk," Sheryn said.

"Of course." Emily opened the door wide. "Come in. Would you like some tea?"

The apartment was different with Emily at home. There were flowers in vases scattered around the room and the smell of perfume in the air.

"No, thank you. I'm here unofficially, but still on business, Dr. Teare."

"How many times do I have to tell you to call me Emily?"

"I think you'd best sit down," Sheryn said.

A shadow crossed Emily's face, but she obeyed and perched on the sofa. "You look so serious. What's happened?"

"The case has really come together," Sheryn said, taking a seat across from her. "Magda Zimmermann has been singing like a canary since we arrested her. I think Kevin Stanton's death shook her hard. It's not like she has any real animus toward you or Alex. She's been released on bail, but we don't see her as a threat to you. Obviously, if you see her around your office or your neighborhood, let me know. She'll be back in jail so fast her head will spin. And just so you know, she cried the whole time she was in jail. I doubt she wants to go back."

"That's good to know."

"We haven't found any other accomplices who worked with Stanton," Sheryn added. "When there's been a conspiracy against a person, or a couple, I'm normally pretty cautious, but in this case, I think you should feel free to go out as you see fit."

"I can't tell you how happy I am to hear that."

"That brings me to the second case, which is not so cut and dried," Sheryn said. "I need to talk to you about Will Sipher."

"What about him?"

"What kind of relationship do you have with him?"

"I know Will through Alex." Emily shrugged. "Alex has known him since they were little kids. There's a bond between them because of that. Will's mother unofficially adopted Alex in high school. I guess they're like brothers who don't like each other much."

"But you and Mr. Sipher became rather close over the past few months, didn't you?"

"I've had to spend more time around him because of living with Alex," Emily said.

"We actually started wondering, during our investigation of your disappearance, whether you and Mr. Sipher had perhaps become romantically involved."

"That would never happen in a million years," Emily said firmly.

"I can see that now." Sheryn gave her a small smile. "But we're still wondering about your professional relationship with him."

"We don't have one."

Sheryn cocked her head to the side. "Didn't you ask your good friend CJ Leeward about the possibility of overturning Mr. Sipher's conviction?"

"Will was very upset about not being able to work," Emily said. "It came up literally every time I saw him. Part of me felt sorry for him, I guess. I'd like to think that a person isn't defined by one bad action."

"Redemption. I like to believe in that too," Sheryn said. "But here's the thing. We've been digging into Mr. Sipher's life, and we've found evidence that he's engaged in a scheme involving prescriptions for opiates and other narcotics."

"Really? I wouldn't be surprised to learn that Will uses those drugs," Emily said evenly. "But running an operation?"

"Opiates are a big business, and a massive problem, in this country. You don't need to be bright to sell them. Though I'd argue that finding doctors to write prescriptions for you is fairly clever."

"Will did that?"

Sheryn admired Emily's poker face. She'd heard this woman was solid under pressure, and suddenly she could imagine her in a war zone.

"Cards on the table," Sheryn said. "We know that you provided Mr. Sipher with prescriptions for narcotics. I'm sure you know that is a federal crime. If I arrest you for it, the FBI will be involved, and the least awful thing that will happen to you is that you will lose your medical license. You'll be sentenced under mandatory minimum rules. The last doctor we arrested for this got two hundred years. With good behavior, he'll be out in sixty-seven."

"I'm not sure what evidence you think you have," Emily said. "It's true that I've written plenty of prescriptions for narcotics. Many people who have spinal surgery are in such pain that it prevents them from living any kind of normal life. I've also seen patients at various clinics in New York and New Jersey."

"Your colleague Yasmeen Khan noticed that you were writing prescriptions for people who weren't patients."

"That's true," Emily said. "Some of those people didn't have insurance. Some weren't in the country legally. They didn't have the luxury of visiting Presbyterian."

Sheryn sat back in her chair. She'd suspected Emily Teare would be a tough nut to crack. While she'd found evidence of the prescriptions the doctor had written, it would be hard to prove that she was involved in a scheme. The doctor had done a good job of covering her tracks.

"It was very clever of you to use that nursing home in Garwood as cover," Sheryn observed. "That certainly gave you a lot of leeway." Before Emily could answer, she put up her hand. "You don't have to say it. I know you're worried that I could be recording this. I'm not, but of course, how can you trust that? The fact is that Will Sipher is a menace and needs to be brought down. He's got a whole network of people working for his operation. I need your help."

"I don't know what I could do," Emily said.

"I'll let you think about that," Sheryn answered. "Here's another thing we're looking at: You know that Cori Stanton's death was ruled a death by misadventure, and because you're a physician, you know what that means. There are people I work with who would be happy to consider her death a suicide, but I'm not done with it yet. There are too many inconsistencies about that night, too many factors that haven't been fully explained. Right now, I'm considering the possibility that Will Sipher may have been responsible for Cori Stanton's death."

Emily stared at her but didn't speak.

"Speaking for myself and the NYPD, we no longer consider Alex a suspect," Sheryn went on. "We know Mr. Sipher was in the building that night. We also know he'd had a romantic relationship with Ms. Stanton that ended badly."

"Yes," Emily said. "I believe that's true."

"We also suspect that Mr. Sipher tried to frame Alex by putting the smashed remains of a burner phone in a bag planted in this apartment. Our theory is that he tried to incriminate your fiancé."

"I want to say that I can't believe Will would do that," Emily answered. "But the truth is I can."

"I don't recommend revenge as a motivation, but I think you've got a great opportunity here," Sheryn said. "Because if you saw Mr. Sipher on that roof . . ."

"I didn't," Emily answered softly.

"We have motive and opportunity," Sheryn prompted.

Emily was silent for a moment. "I hate Will," she said. "But I can't pretend that he killed Cori. He didn't do it."

It was Sheryn's turn to be silent. She'd known Emily Teare would not come clean about the prescription racket, but she'd suspected she would leap at the chance to put Will away for Cori Stanton's death. It was a kind of test, and it left Sheryn convinced of her mettle but unsure what motivated her.

"There's one other thing," Sheryn said, pulling a large, shiny silver disk out of her pocket and holding it up. The medallion was like a small starburst, catching the sunlight pouring in through the window and reflecting it in every direction.

Emily moved one hand toward it, as if to take it, but pulled back.

"It's your Saint Christopher medal," Sheryn said. "We found it in your office."

"I haven't looked at it in a long time," Emily admitted.

"Funny story," Sheryn said. "I was going to bring it to you in the hospital last Friday. I had the idea it might give you some comfort. But I guess I held it too tight, because it cut into my palm. That was when I realized the mark it made looked familiar to me, so I sent it to the lab."

She waited for Emily to answer, but the woman's expression was calm. It was, Sheryn felt, a studied blankness, the kind of face a doctor needed to make awful news seem less harrowing and to hold others steady in a war zone when everything was grim.

"They examined it for DNA," Sheryn continued, "but they didn't find any traces. Of course, a doctor would know how to get rid of the tiniest shred of DNA."

Emily's eyes were damp. She stared at the necklace as if hypnotized by it.

"But we do know that this object, or one identical to it, cut Cori Stanton's palm," Sheryn added.

She waited for the doctor to answer that, but she didn't. Emily seemed frozen in place, barely blinking or breathing. When Sheryn realized no explanation was forthcoming, she prodded, "Can you tell me how that happened?"

"She grabbed it from my neck." Emily's voice was soft. "I can still picture her face."

Sheryn set the medallion on the coffee table. "I'd get that chain fixed if I were you. It's no good to anyone broken."

"Thank you," Emily said.

"Don't thank me yet," Sheryn said. "Because we're not done. You're smart, and you have an answer for everything, but that's not going to keep you out of harm's way. I think you should've learned that by now."

CHAPTER 56

EMILY

By the time Alex brought Sid back from his walk, Emily had stopped crying and washed her face.

"What's wrong?" Alex asked.

"We need to talk," Emily told him. "Could you take Sid over to Mrs. DiGregorio's for a bit?" As much as she would have loved to have the distraction of having Sid underfoot, it wouldn't help. Once she decided on a course of action, she thought like a battlefield surgeon. No point easing that bandage off; it only hurt more in the long run.

When Alex came back a couple of minutes later, Emily was standing in front of the window, looking outside. "I need you to listen to me," she said. "There are some things I've never told you, and I was wrong to hold them back."

"I know about CJ," Alex said. "He explained everything. I've been waiting to talk to you about that. I didn't want to until you felt better."

"You deserve an explanation for that," Emily said. "It honestly felt like another lifetime to me. We were married for three months, right after my parents . . ." She swallowed a hard lump that rose in her throat. "Right after they were killed." She took a breath. "What I need to tell you is a lot more painful than that."

Alex stared at her. "Why are you crying?"

Emily could feel tears rolling down her cheeks. She'd been kidnapped, trapped in a basement for days, and she hadn't wept. Now she was sobbing? She gulped. "Just listen to what I have to tell you. That's all I'm asking."

"Okay."

"When I was flying back to New York last Thanksgiving, you sent me a message. I didn't get it until I got home, because the battery died on my phone. I remember it word for word. I love you with every last piece of my heart. Goodbye. I knew it was your version of a suicide note."

"I was never much of a writer," Alex said softly. "I didn't know how else to put it. I wrote what was true."

"I came straight over to your building. I heard a woman's voice saying, 'Jump!' I looked up, and there you were, up on the roof with Cori. You were standing on the ledge, and she was holding your hand, telling you to jump. I lost my mind. I grabbed the edge of the fire escape and pulled myself to the second floor, and then I ran all the way up. I know I shouted, 'Don't do it.' Cori heard me, and she started chanting. 'Jump, jump, jump.' She was trying to get you to step off that ledge with her."

Alex didn't say anything, but his eyes stayed on her face.

"I shoved you back, off the ledge, when I got to the top," Emily said. "You collapsed on the roof, and I couldn't get you to come around. You were barely breathing anymore. I called 911 to get help, but Cori snatched the phone out of my hand and hung up. She said I didn't get to play hero and save you."

She gulped down air and continued.

"She grabbed my hair and told me I should go to hell. Then she put her hands around my throat and tried to choke me. I shoved her away, and . . . that was it."

She wiped her eyes. Alex didn't say a word.

"Her hand caught on my necklace. The chain snapped as she fell." Emily closed her eyes and took a shaky breath; in her mind, it was all unfolding again, exactly as it had happened. "I was in shock. All I wanted to do was get you help. And I wanted her gone. But not like that." Emily struggled to get enough air into her lungs; it felt as if there were a stone sitting on her chest, squeezing oxygen out. "She was still alive after she landed. She made a little squawk like a baby bird. I jumped down to the fire escape and ran to her. I called 911 again and gave her CPR. That's why the police found me in the street with her."

Alex was shaking his head slowly. "Cori died . . . because of you."

"I didn't mean to hurt her. I'm so sorry." She wiped her face; she couldn't control the tears. "I told the police she fell. It never occurred to me that you would be blamed for her death. I thought it would be considered an accident. But then the police started questioning you. That's when I told them I'd seen Cori jump off the building."

"Why did you lie?"

"At first, it was because I was horrified by what I'd done," Emily said. "But then, the day after she died, Will came to see me. He'd been listening to everything from his window. He'd seen me run up and down the fire escape. He also watched me pry my medallion out of Cori's fist. He knew exactly what had happened. He told me that unless I did as he said, he'd tell the police that you killed her."

"Me?"

"He said they were champing at the bit to arrest you, and all it would take would be his testimony to put you away."

"He was involved with Cori," Alex said softly. "And he used her death to his advantage. Remember that burner phone the police found? Will must've planted it here."

"I was afraid to say anything. He was like a spider. For a while, he didn't do anything else. Like an idiot, I thought maybe he'd changed his mind. But then it started, with him asking for small sums of money that got bigger and bigger. Then he started demanding prescriptions. At first it was just some sedatives. Then Vicodin. I told myself I could live with that, because that was for his personal use." She took a couple of breaths. "When he started asking for fentanyl, I wrote the prescriptions, but I realized I could never give them to him. That was a line I couldn't cross. Kids have died just from accidentally touching a fentanyl patch. I couldn't put anyone in harm's way like that. Instead, I told Will I was writing the prescriptions but couldn't hand them over until it was safe. They just sat in my dresser. I would take them out and think about how low I'd fallen." She gulped down air. "I thought Will put me in that basement cell to punish me. Part of me felt like I deserved it."

Alex looked her in the eye. "Why are you confessing to me now?"

"Because I need to be honest about this," Emily said. "For months, I've been lying to you and everyone else. I can't ever publicly admit the truth about Will and the prescriptions—no matter how much Detective Sterling wants me to—because I'd lose my medical license and never be able to help people again. But she just offered me the chance to frame Will for Cori's death . . ."

"Why would she do that?"

"Maybe it's a way to lock him up? I don't know. The only thing I'm sure of is that I can't lie about it anymore. I have to take responsibility for her death." There was a lump in her throat that wouldn't go away, no matter how hard she swallowed. "It was an accident. I never meant to hurt Cori, and I never meant to hurt you."

Alex was quiet for a long time. Emily wanted to ask him what he was thinking, but she knew how much she was asking him to process.

"Cori wanted to die that night," Alex said quietly. "She said that to me, but she also told her father."

"What are you talking about?"

"He told me, up on the roof," Alex said. "He blamed me for it. Kevin Stanton wanted to hold everyone but himself accountable."

"He wasn't on the roof," Emily said. "I was."

"But what you're describing . . ." Alex took a breath. "I know Cori could be violent. Of course you shoved her away. She knew you would do that when she grabbed your throat."

"I don't know if Detective Sterling will see it that way," Emily said. "But I still need to tell her."

"I understand that. Confession is good for the soul. I just don't think it will change anything about the case," Alex said. "Cori attacked you, and you had to defend yourself. But if you want to do something brave, you have to help Sterling take down Will. Not by lying about his involvement in Cori's death. You need to tell the truth about the prescriptions."

"I'll lose my medical license . . ."

"If he keeps on doing what he's doing, he'll get people killed," Alex said. "You were involved in his scheme, even if it was against your will. You know he's amoral. He has to be stopped."

Emily stared at her hands for a long moment. Growing up, she'd always wanted to be a doctor. She remembered the first time her mother told her, *You have the hands of a surgeon.* Her parents had been so proud of her wanting to study medicine. She couldn't imagine doing anything else, yet she knew Alex was right. "The police didn't find my phone, did they?"

"Your phone?" Alex looked astonished. "What does that have to do with anything?"

"I recorded Will," Emily said. "Three, maybe four times. I definitely taped our last conversation. He was always angry that I wouldn't give him the prescriptions he really wanted, and he lost it when I told him I wasn't doing this anymore."

"You have all this on tape?"

"I was afraid he was going to do something to ruin my life," Emily said. "He kept threatening to. I know what a liar and a snake he is. I thought he might go to you with a bunch of lies about me, but my worst-case scenario was that he'd go to the police and lie about you."

"How much did he say?"

"More than you'd expect," Emily answered. Mentally, she cringed; Will had called her all sorts of ugly names, and she'd held herself back from responding in kind. Anyone else listening might think it had been weakness that held her back; she had been afraid of setting him off. "He was always so cautious, but he'd freak out when things didn't go his way."

"You have to hand it over to the police," Alex said. "They need to hear this. You might already have made their case against Will."

Emily gazed at him. He didn't really understand, she realized. He worked in a profession that allowed him to make his own rules; he'd never had to face the scrutiny of a board or commission. The stakes were so much higher for her. "If I do, I won't be able to practice medicine in this country, or anywhere else, again."

"You don't know that."

"In New York, a doctor can lose her license if she's convicted of not paying taxes," Emily said. "Being part of a prescription scheme means jail time."

"It wasn't your scheme. The police want Will, not you."

"That won't matter. I'll be caught up in this too. I can't lose my license. I can't."

Alex was quiet for a minute. "I don't believe for a second that you're okay with letting Will keep on doing this to people. Tell me what's really going on."

The tide of fear welling up inside her fell back a little when she gazed at him. He wanted to understand. Explaining it to him would be painful; she hadn't even fully thought it out herself. She had been carrying a dark mass of guilt and regret knotted together with a string of thorns.

"When I was kidnapped, I was haunted by memories," Emily said. "By my parents' deaths, but also by every terrible thing I ever did. It was like being in a circle of Dante's hell. I've always told myself that

I do what I can to help people. In that dark little cell, it felt like a lie. How can I ever make up for all of the things I've done? If I can't practice medicine, what good am I to anyone?"

"I don't believe that," Alex said. "You want to help people, and you'll always find a way to do that. I can't tell you what's going to happen with your medical license. Maybe it's a sacrifice you have to make."

When he said *sacrifice*, she sat up a little straighter. It was like an arrow to her heart. She'd spent most of the past year trying to hold everything together, and that hadn't worked. Perhaps it was time for her to try letting go.

"Do you have Detective Sterling's number?" Emily asked.

"Sure."

"Call her now," Emily said. "I want to tell her everything before I lose my nerve."

EPILOGUE

ALEX

Alex owned one good suit, and New York City Criminal Court seemed like the right place to wear it. At nine fifteen on a Tuesday morning in January, he stood next to Emily in a hallway lined with carved wooden benches. Both of them were too nervous to sit.

"You know you don't have to be here, right?" Sheryn told Emily. "This is just the start of Mr. Sipher's trial. With all the smoke he's thrown at us, it'll probably go on for weeks."

"I know," Emily said. "But Will needs to see that I'm here. He needs to know I'm going to testify against him, and I'm not backing down."

Sheryn smiled at her. "He was slow to get that message. He's a man who's used to getting his way all the time. That's not good for anyone."

"Reality should be setting in around now," Alex said.

"Last I heard, he's still resisting it," Sheryn said. "The ADA offered him a plea bargain, but he wouldn't consider it. It would've been a decent deal for him. Nowhere near enough jail time. What I call the premium package. It's only offered to white men who wear expensive suits."

"Why would he turn it down?" Emily asked.

"He wants to roll the dice. It's a big gamble on his part. He's counting on witnesses ghosting us." Sheryn took a breath. "The recordings you made served him up to us on a platter, dead to rights. But, if you don't testify, his lawyers are going to claim that they were forged or dubbed, that it's not really Will's voice. That's why it's essential for you to testify."

At that moment, the elevator chimed, and the door opened. Will Sipher stepped out, flanked by his lawyers. He wore a bespoke black suit and looked healthier than he had in a long time. When he spotted Emily and Alex, he gave them a long, hard look, then turned his head and whispered. The lawyers whisked him down another corridor.

"I guess someone's not feeling very social today," Sheryn commented. When neither Emily nor Alex responded, she added, "You two are wound up way too tight. This case is going to drag on for a while. You need to pace yourself. And you should remember what you're doing is important. You know how many slippery eels like Will Sipher slip off the hook? Nothing about this case was easy." She nodded at Alex. "I was saying the same thing to the ADA first thing this morning. He agrees with me."

"I guess I'll be happier when the trial is over," Emily said. "Right now, I'm just at home, twiddling my thumbs."

"I was sorry to hear about your job," Sheryn said softly.

"Once they knew I would be testifying in Will's trial, they had to let me go," Emily answered. "It didn't matter that I had immunity from prosecution. The hospital can't afford that kind of publicity. I hate it, but I understand why they wanted to part ways. I'll still work, I hope. Just somewhere else."

"Another hospital?"

"No, a refugee camp," Emily said. "There are a million people in camps in Turkey and Jordan who need urgent care. When the trial is over, that's where I'll be headed."

The elevator chimed again, and Rafael stepped out. He'd healed from the injuries he'd suffered at Kevin Stanton's house and was wearing an Armani suit that was easily on a par with Will's.

"Look what the cat dragged in, late as usual," Sheryn mocked. "You missed the perp show. Will Sipher came up five minutes ago, spotted these two, and ran away with his barbed tail between his legs."

"Hey, the trial hasn't even started, so I'm early," Rafael shot back. "And Sipher's not running anywhere without his passport."

"I kind of expected him to try to flee anyway," Sheryn said. "Drive up to Canada and bolt. It's a little disappointing that he didn't try."

"Because you wanted to hog-tie him like a runaway calf?" Rafael asked.

"Hell, yeah. I know how to have a good time."

Sheryn was working hard to keep the mood light. Alex reached for Emily's hand and squeezed it. "When you do testify, you'll be great," he murmured.

"I'll be lucky if they still let me into the refugee camps," she whispered.

Alex took a deep breath and glanced at Sheryn. "Would you mind giving us a minute?"

"No problem. We'll be down the hall." She nudged her partner's elbow and steered Rafael away. They walked to the broad wooden doors of the next courtroom over, their heads bent forward in close conversation.

Alex started to speak, but Emily cut him off. "We've talked about this. Please don't do it. It's just not worth it."

"I think it is," Alex said.

"Nothing good can come of it. He's only going to lash out at you." She reached into her handbag and pulled out an envelope, hand-addressed with Alex's name. "Do you need to read this over again? He only wants to cause you pain, and he will lie and cheat and spin you around until you can't tell which way is up. He will hurt you. He's tried to enough times before."

"I know that."

"He wants you to suffer, Alex." Emily's voice was quiet, but there was urgency in her words. "You could get in trouble with the court. Please, the risk is not worth it."

"You tried to protect me before." Alex touched her face. "But that didn't work out."

"You're not going to convince Will to do the right thing by appealing to his virtue. He doesn't have any."

"You have to trust me," Alex said.

Emily gulped, but she nodded.

Alex turned down the hallway where Will and his lawyers had vanished. Sheryn had been prepping him for the trial along with Emily, and he was starting to get familiar with the court building. It only took a minute to find the conference room. When he opened the door, he immediately spotted Will, sitting stiffly and staring at his folded hands with a stony expression. His face eased into a smile when he caught sight of Alex at the door.

"You can't come in here," barked one of the lawyers.

"Of course he can," Will said slyly. "What's the harm in a visit from an old friend?"

The other lawyer bent at the waist and whispered into Will's ear, but he waved the man away. "Go outside. This won't be any fun with you listening in."

The lawyers muttered to each other, glaring at Alex as they passed him. He shut the door and took the seat across from Will's.

"You're looking well, Alex."

"You too. Rehab obviously agreed with you."

"It was incredibly boring," Will said. "But it was the only way the judge would let me out on bail. Also, it got me into tennis again, so that's nice. I haven't really played since college."

"Sounds more like a country club than rehab."

"A bit of both, I suppose." Will shrugged. "I was wondering if you received that letter I sent you. You never responded."

"I got it."

"These rehab programs always want you to go about making amends," Will went on. "It's quite tiresome. But I know that I owe it to you. I don't feel bad about coercing Emily into writing those prescriptions, but I do feel guilty for sleeping with her. That was why I wrote the letter. I *owed* it to you."

Alex stared at him silently.

"I was afraid to tell you before." Will watched him closely. "And I can't imagine that Emily confessed to that. It's certainly not something I'm proud of."

"I know you're lying, Will."

"No, you don't," Will shot back. "You know Emily's version of events. I'm sure it conflicts with mine. Hers is refined to make her look good, or at least less guilty."

"And yours is designed to make me feel bad. Just like when you told me I'd killed Cori. The problem is that you lie about everything, Will. You're good at it. But it won't always work out for you. This is one of those times."

"There will always be a shred of doubt in your mind," Will said. "If you're with Emily a year from now, or ten years from now, you'll still be wondering if it's true."

"No, I won't," Alex said. "Because it doesn't matter."

"I don't believe you. If you want to tell me how much you hate me, I'll understand."

"I don't hate you, Will. Part of me even feels sorry for you."

"How very . . . enlightened of you." Will leaned back in his chair, suddenly at a loss. "If you're not here to punch me, what *are* you here for?"

"I came by to tell you to take the deal," Alex said.

Will gave him a terse smile. "And go to jail?"

"It's going to be a lot worse if you go through with the trial. You'll spend the rest of your life in jail."

"Or I'll get off scot free," Will said. "There are many, many steps between where we are now and the end of the trial. Don't forget the appeals! As my lawyers have assured me, even if I lose the first time around, I can still win."

"By then, they'll have bled you dry," Alex said. "No matter how many appeals you launch, you're going to jail."

"Thank you for your concern," Will said, "but I know you only care about keeping Emily out of jail."

"I don't have to worry about that. She has immunity from prosecution."

"Perhaps, but that won't save her medical license," Will pointed out. "After she testifies, her name will be poison. Her career will be over. That will be sad, because I know how much it means to her."

"You're willing to destroy the rest of your life to do that? That's not much of a trade."

Will stared at him silently, chewing that over.

Alex leaned forward. "You remember me talking about Maclean?"

"Your war-hero friend?" Will yawned. "Yes, I've heard lots about him. Saved your life and all that."

"He used to have this expression. *Not your turn today.* Maclean was . . . I guess the word is fatalistic. Whether you lived or died, it wasn't about how good you were or how smart you were. It was about whether your number had come up."

Will leaned forward slightly, intrigued in spite of his languid pose.

"When I was on that rooftop with Kevin Stanton, I knew my number was up," Alex continued. "I was going to die, and I accepted that. All that mattered was taking him down before he hurt anyone else. Suddenly, it *was* my turn."

"You really thought that?"

"That's why I threw myself off the roof."

"But you lived."

"By accident. The truth is, if I'd been focused on saving myself that night, I would've died."

They were both silent for a moment. "Is this your way of telling me to surrender to . . . what, exactly? Fate? A higher power?"

"I'm telling you it's your turn today," Alex answered. "It's all on you. You can focus on dragging out your trial as much as possible, at throwing mud and losing whatever money you have left through years of appeals. Or you can let go and move on."

"I'm not going to jail." Will's voice was tight.

"Yes, you are. The question is for how long."

Will turned his face away so that Alex couldn't read his expression. He was silent for a long time. "You *must* hate me so much, after everything I've done. Why are you here, really? Is it just to mock me?"

"It's not for you. It's not even just for Emily. It's for your mom."

Will glanced at him, a sidelong look full of suspicion. "What's that supposed to mean?"

"I loved her, you know. After I lost my mom . . ." Alex's voice trailed off. "It was an awful time. I didn't have anyone else. Your mom saved my life."

"You were closer to her than I ever was."

"No. You know why she took me in, don't you? It wasn't because of any feelings she had for me. It was because she wanted you to have a brother."

Will gave him a curt, almost imperceptible nod, acknowledging the truth of that.

"She loved you more than anything in this world, but she always worried about you," Alex said. "She's not able to be here for you anymore, but I am."

"You're not exactly on my side."

"But I know what your mother would say. She was always practical. You know if she were here, she'd tell you to take the deal, Will. You *know* she would."

Will took a long, ragged breath. "Nothing ever turned out how I wanted it to," he said suddenly, his sharp attitude sinking under the weight of his sadness. "I don't know how I got here. I keep hoping it's a nightmare."

"I keep thinking I should be dead," Alex said. "But I'm not. That seems like a kind of miracle."

"You've always been the fortunate one," Will said. "No matter what, you always get away unscathed."

"You can have my luck, if you want it," Alex answered. "Somehow, I doubt you really do."

"If I had it, I wouldn't wind up in jail," Will said. "I have to try my own luck with this. You understand, don't you? I'm not going down without a fight."

"That's exactly what Hadley said you'd choose." Alex got to his feet.

Will's entire demeanor shifted, and his eyes narrowed. "When, exactly, were you chatting with my ex-wife?"

"You don't have a clue, do you?" Alex shook his head sadly. "It was supposed to be a surprise, but I guess that doesn't matter now."

"Hadley is in Europe, with designs on snagging a title or an oligarch. She would never expose herself to the circus of a trial."

Alex shrugged. "Detective Sterling told her that her name was going to come up plenty in your trial. From the earful I got last night, Hadley thinks you're ruining her life for a second time."

"She's in New York?"

"Got in yesterday."

"She wouldn't. She—"

"Tell your lawyers to check the witness list," Alex said. "Sterling told me the ADA added her this morning."

When Alex left the room, the lawyers rushed back in. Alex retraced his steps along the hall, stopping in front of a row of tall windows. Finally, he turned the corner and found Emily and Sheryn. Emily's expression made it clear she was desperate to know what had happened; Sheryn watched him with her game face on. He gave her the slightest of nods.

"When will they let us into the courtroom?" Emily asked.

"When the judge is good and ready," Sheryn said. "This is why I hate coming to court. Hurry up and wait."

"Do you have to do this often?" Emily asked her.

"I've had to testify a bunch of times. It's not my favorite thing," Sheryn confided. "My old partner, Sandy, was the opposite. He loved coming to court and gabbing around here. Big gossip, that guy. But it was fine by me because I didn't have to trot downtown all the time."

"What about Rafael?"

"I'm still breaking him in," Sheryn said. "I told him he's got the wardrobe to be a courtroom star. He'll give the defense lawyers a complex because he's better dressed." She patted Emily's hand. "Hey, where the hell did Rafael go? Did you hear me telling him he could leave? I need to find him." As she stood, she whispered a single word to Alex. "Bait?"

"Taken," he answered.

Sheryn patted his arm. "See you in a bit."

Emily was so lost in her own thoughts that this exchange didn't seem to register. When Alex joined her on the bench, she reached for his hand. "How did it go?" she whispered.

"You were right about appealing to his virtue."

Emily's shoulders sank, and her head fell forward. The loss of composure was momentary; she took an audible breath and squared her frame.

"Now you get to watch me take that bastard down," she said.

They were quiet, waiting for Sheryn to return. Only she didn't; her partner, Rafael, appeared in her place. "Sheryn said she had to talk to the ADA," he explained. "You guys want to go out and get some coffee?"

Alex liked Rafael Mendoza, and he appreciated that the detective was determined to keep them in a good frame of mind. But he couldn't help but wonder about what strings Sheryn was pulling. He'd lied to Will about his ex-wife being in New York. Hadley had flat-out refused to come back to New York, though it was true that she was deeply upset at the thought of Will dragging her name through the mud in a trial. Sheryn, relentless as ever, was refusing to take no for an answer. When she finally reappeared, almost two hours later, she was wearing her poker face.

"I've got two words for you," she announced. "Plea deal."

There was a thunderstruck silence, broken by Rafael's applause. "Damn, Sheryn. You never say never."

"You're serious?" Alex choked out. "Will took the deal?"

"I'm not at liberty to explain all of it right now, but I can promise you that an agreement has been reached. Will Sipher's not going to be locked up for anywhere near as long as he deserves, but he's going to wear out a few prison jumpsuits."

"I don't understand," Emily said. "What changed his mind?"

"There was a whole constellation of factors," Sheryn answered. She put her hand on Emily's arm. "I need to have a few words with Alex right now. Can you wait here with my partner?"

Emily nodded. Alex followed Sheryn down the hall, into an empty nook near an open courtroom door.

"We did it!" Sheryn whispered excitedly.

"I did nothing," Alex said, "except slip that little nugget to Will about his ex-wife testifying. She knows all about his drug problems, and she's still such a sore spot for him. He flipped out."

"Exactly as you said he would. All that advance planning we did paid off. After you dropped that bombshell on him, he spent the next hour calling the most expensive hotels in New York trying to find her." Sheryn smiled. "Of course, he found her registered under her real name at the trendiest one. It's details like those that do the selling job for you. But that wasn't the coup de grâce. Hadley actually came through in the end."

Alex jaw fell open at that. "You got her to agree to testify?"

"Hell, no." Sheryn pulled out her phone and opened up an app. "I got Hadley to post on social media as if she were in town."

She held up her screen. Just discovered the best coffee in New York is now brewed in Brooklyn, Hadley had tweeted, with a photo of a red-taloned hand—sporting a sapphire ring—that cradled a white porcelain cup.

"What is that supposed to be?" Alex asked.

"It's an outtake from her last trip to New York," Sheryn explained. "And vague enough to look like she's here right now."

"Genius." Alex shook his head in admiration while Sheryn put her phone away. "Do you think he'll ever figure out that Hadley wasn't actually in New York? That we made this shit up?"

"Maybe one day. But that won't negate the plea agreement he just signed." Sheryn leaned in a little closer. "I feel bad about keeping this from Emily, but we had no choice. We needed Will to see how down she was this morning. Otherwise, he would've smelled a trap. You can tell her later if you want to. I know you two have had enough secrets between you."

"Too many," Alex said. "On both sides."

"I wondered what would happen to you two when the truth about Cori came out," Sheryn said. "When Emily confessed it all to me, I thought it might break you two up."

"It was a shock, but at the same time, it wasn't," Alex answered. "I half remembered Cori trying to get me to jump off the roof with her.

She wanted to die, but she was too afraid to do it alone. Cori would've taken Emily with her if she could." He paused. "What happened on the roof didn't make me love Emily less. If anything, it was the opposite. Deep down, I had the feeling she would ditch me one day. I couldn't believe what she'd sacrificed for me."

"You two are a pair of incurable romantics."

"So are you, Detective."

"How's that?"

"Emily and I both thought you'd charge her with obstruction or something like it."

"She wasn't responsible for Cori's death," Sheryn said. "It was a death by misadventure, just like the medical examiner thought. I wish Emily had come forward at the time, but there were extenuating circumstances, thanks to Mr. Sipher. My job is catching bad guys. I like to focus on that." She raised an eyebrow. "What's next for you?"

"I'll be with Emily, working in a refugee camp," Alex said. "I'm done with war zones. The therapist you recommended has helped so much with my PTSD, and I know I'm not ready to put myself in danger like that. I might never be again. But there are millions of refugees. When you hear about them on the news or read about them online, you can't wrap your mind around what they're going through. It's too overwhelming. I want to make people see the reality of their situation. I can't save a life the way a doctor can, but I can be a witness. I can tell their stories."

"A picture's worth a thousand words," Sheryn said. "I'm glad to know you'll be doing the Lord's work. Will Sid go with you?"

"Our neighbor, Mrs. DiGregorio, is going to take care of him while we're away."

"That's good," Sheryn said. "But if she can't do it for any reason, you should know there's a family who'd happily take him in, if Sid doesn't mind relocating to Washington Heights. My kids are crazy about dogs."

"Thank you," Alex said. "For that, and for everything else."

"You're welcome. Congratulations on the reengagement. I'm thrilled for both of you."

"I haven't actually asked Emily yet," Alex admitted. "I've been carrying the ring around for days, waiting for the right moment."

"What?" Sheryn said. "Are you kidding, Alex? What are you doing here, talking to me? Go get your girl."

She gave him a playful shove, nudging him in Emily's direction. She leaned against the wall, folded her arms, and added, "I'll be watching."

Alex smiled at her, then headed along the hallway. "I think your partner wants to talk to you," he told Rafael.

"What now?" Rafael groused as he trudged away.

"I still can't believe it," Emily said. "This doesn't feel real. You did it, Alex—you changed his mind."

"It wasn't just me," Alex answered. "I'll tell you about it later."

Emily leaned forward and kissed him, holding him tight.

"Sorry," she murmured, resting her head on his shoulder. "My legs feel like jelly right now. You'll have to prop me up."

They stood like that in the busy hallway, acutely aware of the terrible storm that had been averted.

"Whether it's because of everything that's happened, or in spite of it, I love you more than ever," Alex said quietly.

"I love you too," Emily said. "This is probably the worst time to mention this, but do you know what I keep thinking about?"

Alex closed his eyes for a moment. It felt as if he and Emily had been to war and back together. They still had raw emotional wounds that were only just beginning to heal, but that was infinitely preferable to the wall of secrets and silence that had built up between them in the past. He had been afraid she would leave him if she ever really knew him; that fear seemed so foolish now. They were in deep together, and there was no one he'd trust to have his back like Emily.

"Does it involve being barefoot on a beach?" Alex asked her. "Because that's been on my mind too."

ACKNOWLEDGMENTS

Writing a novel is a solitary adventure, but without the help of a crew of wonderful people, it wouldn't be possible. I'm incredibly grateful to my agent, Mitch Hoffman, who was really more of a double agent since he also served as this book's earliest editor. He also provided wisdom, enthusiasm, and friendship. I appreciate the support of the entire team at the Aaron M. Priest Literary Agency too.

A heartfelt thank-you to everyone on the Thomas & Mercer team for making the publication of this book such a joy. That's especially true of my wonderful editor, Megha Parekh, and developmental editor, Charlotte Herscher, who both pushed me to see more possibilities in the story. I'm also grateful to editorial director Gracie Doyle and author relations manager Sarah Shaw for all of their support. Thank you to my copyeditor, Susan Stokes, for fixing my mistakes, and to Laura Sarasqueta and Stephanie Chou for reading and rereading the proofs. Thanks, too, to the exceptional marketing team, especially Gabrielle Guarnero, Kyla Pigoni, and Laura Costantino, for their dedication and help, and to publicity manager Dennelle Catlett for all of her work to promote this book. There are so many amazing people who worked behind the scenes to get this novel into your hands, including production manager Laura Barrett, cover designer Christopher Lin, and art director Oisin O'Malley. I know I'm missing a few names here, and

I apologize for that. The truth is that working with everyone on the Amazon Publishing team has been a privilege and a pleasure.

My entire extended crime-fiction family deserves thanks, but there are a few people who deserve special shout-outs (in alphabetical order): Joe Clifford, Reed Farrel Coleman, Kim Fay, Greg Herren, Chris Holm and Kat Niidas Holm, Janet Hutchings, Jon and Ruth Jordan, Susan Elia MacNeal, Dan and Kate Malmon, Erica Ruth Neubauer, Brad Parks, Thomas Pluck, Todd Robinson, Alex Segura, Robin Spano, Steve Weddle, Sarah Weinman, and Holly West. I couldn't imagine a greater group of shady characters, and I'm lucky to know each one of you.

There are so many friends I want to thank, especially Beth Russell Connelly, Stephanie Craig, Kathleen Dore, Leslie Elman, Ghen Laraya Long, Helen Lovekin, Ilana Rubel, and Trish Snyder. You guys know where the bodies are buried.

I've had so much support from librarians and booksellers, from book clubs and festival organizers, and from the dedicated readers who show up at conferences such as Bouchercon and Left Coast Crime. I'm so grateful for all of you.

Last, but certainly not least, I owe many thanks to my family, especially my parents, John and Sheila Davidson (that's doubly true for my mom, who reads all of my books early and gives me feedback; my dad is forced to wait, since he can't keep a secret). My aunts—Amy, Evelyn, and Irene—are the world's best cheering squad. Most of all, thank you to my amazing husband, Daniel, for his eagerness to read my work, his endless encouragement, and his reluctant willingness to serve as a stunt double; I couldn't do this without you!

ABOUT THE AUTHOR

Photo © 2018 Anna Ty Bergman

Hilary Davidson is the author of the Anthony Award–winning Lily Moore series—which includes *The Damage Done*, *The Next One to Fall*, and *Evil in All Its Disguises*—and the hard-boiled thriller *Blood Always Tells*. Her widely acclaimed short stories have won numerous awards and have been featured in *Ellery Queen*, *Thuglit*, and other dark places, as well as in her collection *The Black Widow Club*. A Toronto-born travel journalist who has lived in New York City since October 2001, Davidson is also the author of eighteen nonfiction books. Visit her online at www.HilaryDavidson.com.